IMMORAL

MAFIA WARS NEW YORK - BOOK TWO

MAGGIE COLE

PULSE PRESS INC

PROLOGUE

Cara Serrano

HAMMERS POUND INTO MY SKULL. MY THROAT FEELS RAW, almost as if it has cracks in it from a lack of water. I attempt to open my eyes, but my head spins.

I squeeze my lids, trying to make it stop.

What happened?

Where am I?

Slowly, the last thing I remember flashes in pieces.

Uberto was screaming at me about Gianni. I insisted nothing was going on between us, but Uberto wouldn't believe me. I couldn't blame him. Gianni wouldn't stay away and not only warned me to break up with Uberto but threatened him too.

Gianni's face pops into my thoughts. My pulse increases, and I curse myself for the millionth time. No matter how much I try to convince myself I'm no longer attracted to him, I fail. Time

MAGGIE COLE

has only made him sexier, which I never thought would be possible. He's taken excellent care of himself, maintaining his ripped physique any male on Earth would envy. It complements the gray streaks in his hair and tiny lines around his eyes that only serve to enhance his dominant aura.

Stop thinking of him. Focus!

I lick my lips, wondering why my mouth is so dry and my head hurts so badly. I reprimand myself again and concentrate on my foggy memories, but all I remember is Uberto and how scared he made me. I'd never seen him so angry. I tried to leave, but he wouldn't let me. And then I remember him forcing me to the kitchen and jabbing something sharp into my leg. After that, everything turned black.

Rage fills me as I realize he must have drugged me. Then hurt replaces it followed by horror. I squeeze my eyes tighter, holding in tears. Was Gianni right all this time? Is it possible he wasn't just jealous and trying to ruin my love life?

That would be a first.

Several moments pass before I can push my emotions away. I need to figure out where I am and get out of here. Slowly, I open my eyes. Grey darkness surrounds me. As my vision adjusts, sounds hit my ears. I shudder as other women, all naked and lying on the concrete floor, become visible. I look down at my unclothed body, and a new fear shoots through me.

A shrill sound pierces through the air. The faint outline of three men appears as they step through a metal door. I sit up and hug my knees, trying to cover and protect myself.

One of the men stomps toward me. I recoil, looking at the ground, praying he isn't coming for me, shaking from the sudden cold air and fear. But then I see his shoes—shinny,

2

designer Italian loafers. I smell his musk cologne, and I know who it is.

Uberto.

How could I not have seen he was evil?

Why did I not listen to Gianni's warnings?

What is he going to do to me?

He crouches in front of me and grabs my chin, yanking it, so I'm facing him. My lips tremble, and tears escape my orbs, sliding quickly down my cheeks. He digs his fingers into my skin. His stale breath reminds me of someone who's been drinking for hours. The red in his eyes confirms my theory. His voice is an angry calm. "You were doing so well, Cara."

I stare at him, unsure what he means.

He leans closer. I attempt to retreat, but he holds me firm. His lips hit my ears, and I tremble harder as he states, "Since you're a whore, you get to live the rest of your days as one."

Words get stuck in my throat. I don't know all the details of what he means. Something tells me I don't want to find out.

He lodges his fingers deeper into my chin. I wince, and he grunts. "You should have thought twice before betraying me with a Marino." He releases me and stands.

I grab his leg. "Uberto! Please! I never—"

"Shut up!" He screams, tugs his leg back, and leaves.

"Uberto!" I call after him, but my voice is weak from whatever drug he gave me.

Another man comes over and yanks me off the ground. My mind says to fight, but my body still lacks the strength. He leads me to a wall. Other women are there. Before I can figure out what is happening, cold water forcefully gushes over me.

I shriek, along with the other women.

Everything becomes a blur. I'm ordered to shampoo and condition my hair, wash my body, and dry off. The men lead us to a changing room where a group of women are waiting.

These women aren't naked. I beg them to help me, but they avoid looking at my eyes. One of them blow dries and styles my hair. She puts more makeup on me than I'm used to wearing. One of the men orders me to put on a pair of stilettos. He fastens a collar with a leash around my neck and shoves me out of the room.

I go through the same door Uberto went through. The man forces me up the stairs and down a long hallway. The sound of men talking and laughing fills my ears. Cigar smoke wafts in my nostrils. We stop in front of a curtain. He fists my hair and tugs it so harshly, a pain jumps through my neck.

"Ow!" I blurt out.

He points a gun at my head and snarls, "Go on stage. When you're ordered to turn, you obey. Whatever you're told to do, you do. Understand?"

My pulse races so fast I get dizzy. I don't reply.

"Answer me," he barks.

I jump. "Y-yes."

He separates the curtain and pushes me forward.

The lights are bright. I stop, blinking to focus.

He growls, "Move to the X!"

I take a few steps and stand on the taped X. When I look up, I'm horrified. The room is full of men sitting at tables, drinking alcohol, and smoking. Some of the men have naked women on their laps. Scared expressions stare at me. The same type of collar I have on wraps around their necks.

I cover my breasts and lower body, but there's no hiding. A man in an expensive-looking suit stands several feet from me. He holds a microphone and orders, "Raise your arms to the side."

I freeze.

He steps closer and reiterates the same thing, only this time, there's a warning in his voice. "Raise your arms to the side."

His demeanor scares me. I do what he says. Tears fall fast and drip on the floor.

"Cara Serrano. Forty-one. Educated in New York. Spent quite a while in Europe. Speaks several languages," he rattles off.

My heart beats harder against my chest cavity. My knees wobble, but my situation only gets worse.

"Starting bid, $100,000," he proclaims, then demands, "Spin."

Unsure what to do, still foggy from whatever Uberto drugged me with, and not wanting to get killed, I turn around.

Men start shouting out numbers. I squeeze my eyes shut, wanting all of this to be over, wishing I had listened to Gianni and stayed away from Uberto when I had the chance.

The announcer slaps my ass, and I jump. He orders, "Bend over and grab your ankles."

Humiliated, I obey.

More numbers get shouted into the air until someone yells, "Ten million."

The room turns silent. Blood pounds so hard against my ears I wonder if they can all hear it.

"Going once. Going twice. Sold."

The room erupts in applause. A dark-haired man with a scar across his cheek comes on stage, grabs me by the shoulder, and steers me through the curtain. I'm still weak from the drugs, but I try to push away from him.

"Stop fighting me, or you'll make it worse for yourself," he warns.

"Please," I plead, but he doesn't even acknowledge it.

He takes off his suit coat, puts it around me, then opens a door.

Cold air rushes inside, slapping my nearly naked self. Everything is dark, minus the outline of an SUV. I try to fight again, but the man pushes me toward it then opens the back door. Before I can process anything, another man inside tugs me in and over his lap.

I scream, but it's on deaf ears. The slamming of doors ricochets through the air before the car starts moving. I try to sit up, but whoever has me over his lap won't release me.

Then I hear his voice and freeze. The fight in me changes into a new one.

I'm no longer fighting for my life.

This is a fight for my heart.

1

Gianni Marino

"STOP FIGHTING ME!" I DEMAND, PISSED CARA WAS IN THIS situation. I'm angry she wouldn't listen to me about Uberto. He's an Abruzzo snake. No matter how much I warned her, she kept denying it to spite me. And while I won't pretend I don't deserve every bit of her wrath for what I've put her through over the years, it doesn't make swallowing her pill any easier.

She freezes.

I slide my hand under the coat and over her bare ass, trying to calm my heart that's still racing. For three hours, I sat on pins and needles, waiting for my undercover guy, Luca, to outbid the room. Every second that passed tested my willpower. I fought not to bust down the door and shoot every thug in the room. But as hot as I was, I knew doing that would only result in Cara getting hurt.

I didn't have the backup to take out enough men. At least three hundred were in that warehouse, all placing money on women they wanted to own.

For months, Cara hasn't done anything without me knowing. I had her phone bugged and my most trusted guys trailing her. I had men on Uberto, too. I knew what he was capable of the first moment I laid eyes on him. Maybe if our past were different, Cara would have heeded my warning and dumped him. But there were too many times I told her to get rid of the guy she was seeing, only to be with her and let her go again.

I don't know why I always did it. Every time I would get too close, something made me run.

It was never long before I'd regretted it. Every single time, I'd kick myself. But then the next time, I'd do it all over again.

This time, no matter how much I told Cara I wouldn't run, she wouldn't budge. It's like she wrote me off, and no one has ever made me feel so desperate to have them.

Now, she's not going to have a choice about me in her life. There's only one way to protect her going forward. I'll make sure there's no way she can get out of it.

"Get your hand off my ass!" she orders, but her voice cracks.

I squeeze her cheek, then flip her, so she's on my lap. She tries to get off it, but she's too weak. I hold her firmly, knowing what the Abruzzos do to women. No doubt she's been drugged. Her ability to get out of my grasp is nonexistent. But that isn't what stops me from releasing her. Now that I have her again, I'll never be stupid enough to let her go.

I palm her head and study her. Anger reignites. Her blue eyes are bloodshot. She has makeup caked on her face, which is a sin as far as I'm concerned. Cara's mother is French, and her father is Latino. She has a natural beauty that doesn't need to be hidden by makeup. It's another reminder of how disillusioned the Abruzzos are, but what upsets me the most is how she's trying to hold it together. Her lips shake, and the hatred she has for me fills her eyes, mixing with the fear of what she just went through.

I press my forehead to hers, closing my eyes for a brief moment. I murmur, "You scared the shit out of me."

Her entire body shakes. A tear falls down her cheek. Her breath merges into mine.

All I want to do is kiss her, but I hold back. I ask the question I'm scared to find out the answer to but need to know. "Are you hurt, my Tesora?"

She whispers, "I'm not your Tesora."

A pain shoots through my heart. I tighten my arm around her, tugging her even closer to me. "You are. You've always been and will always be. Stop fighting me."

More tears slide down her face. "You gave up that right years ago."

I ignore the sharp ache, which grows more intense. I hold her head against my chest, wrapping my arms around her trembling frame. I repeat, "What did they do to you? Are you hurt?"

The gravity of the situation must finally be catching up to her. Her entire body erupts in convulsions, and she sobs hard.

More anxiety plague me. "Shh," I say, attempting to calm her, but she doesn't. I tilt her chin and lock my gaze into her emotional one, sternly demanding, "Tell me what they did to you."

She shakes her head, choking out, "Nothing besides the stage."

The war raging inside me, I try to control. Visions of her naked, on stage, wearing nothing but the collar and stilettos while men bid on her, burns every cell in my body. I'm not a man who sits back, allowing others to hurt those I love. It's no secret the Abruzzos are involved in human trafficking. It's a crime my family would never engage in, and the fact my Tesora almost was sold makes me ill. In a typical scenario, I'd act swiftly, brutally, and with precision. Not killing Uberto right now is testing all of my patience, yet taking care of Cara and putting the parameters in place to make sure no one touches her again needs to be my top priority.

I kiss the top of her head and hold her against my chest again. She's still trembling. Goosebumps are all over her skin. I grab the blanket next to me and wrap it around her, then murmur, "Drink some water, then try to sleep. We have a long drive."

She tilts her head. "Where are we?"

I lie, knowing she's going to flip out and fight me when she finds out what's about to happen. "Far from the city." I open a bottle of water and hold it to her lips. "Drink. He drugged you. The best way to get it out of your system is to stay hydrated and sleep."

She doesn't argue, drinking almost the entire bottle. She takes a deep breath, then leans into my pec, mumbling, "I still hate you."

"No, you don't," I reply, but I wonder if she really does.

"I do," she insists, then closes her eyes.

I kiss the top of her head again, then watch her fall asleep. My phone vibrates. I pull it out of my pocket and glance at the screen. Dante pops up, but I throw him into voicemail, not wanting to listen to him lecture me or try to talk me out of what I'm about to do.

A text appears.

Dante: *Where are you?*

I sigh, contemplate what to reply, then type my response.

Me: *She's safe. No one knew I was there.*

Dante: *I asked you where you are.*

Me: *On my way to the airport.*

Dante: *Why are you going to the airport? Where the fuck are you?*

Me: *All you need to know is I have the situation handled. Go back to your party.*

Dante: *Gianni, what are you about to do?*

I sniff hard, taking a few moments to respond. My twin brother knows me well. We have a connection that only the two of us can understand. It's his engagement party, and I feel guilty for not being there, but this is more important.

Me: *Doing what I should have done a long time ago.*

Dante: *Jesus. What the fuck does that mean?*

Me: *Making her mine.*

He tries calling me again, but I send him to voice mail.

Dante: *Goddammit! Answer the phone!*

Me: *There's nothing you can do, brother. Go back to your party. I'll let you know when I'm on my way home, but it's not going to be anytime soon.*

Dante: *You're making a mistake.*

I snort.

Me: *Is Bridget a mistake?*

Dante: *Don't even try to compare Bridget and me to what you're about to do.*

Me: *Seems like a similar situation to me.*

Dante: *No. It's not.*

Me: *Mind your own business. This conversation is over.*

Dante: *What about Uberto?*

I take several deep breaths to calm myself, opening and closing my fist. The things I want to inflict upon him flash before me.

Me: *After I do what I need to in order to protect Cara, I'll take care of him.*

Two minutes pass. I stare out the window, watching a thick blanket of snow surround the vehicle.

Dante: *We'll pick him up. He'll be waiting for you when you get back.*

Me: *No. I'll handle it.*

Dante: *Stop being stubborn.*

Me: *Don't cross me on this. I'm turning my phone off. Enjoy your party.*

I do as I state and slide my phone back in my pocket while staring at Cara. Mascara streaks her cheeks. Her pouty lips are bright red, slightly parted. I steal a quick kiss, then stroke her soft, dark hair, having an imaginary conversation in my mind about how I'm going to inform her what is about to happen.

She's going to want to kill me. Yet all I can think about is how she'll finally be mine. There won't be any way for her to continue to avoid me. She and I will be tied together until the day one of us dies because once we make our vows, there's no taking it back.

I shift in the seat, tightening my arms around her, letting my mind go to a place I shouldn't.

It's the spot that makes me a bigger bastard than I already am. All I can obsess over is how I'm not going to just let her say I do.

I'm going to make her repeat every promise I've ever wanted to hear her say. She'll be mine in every way, and anytime she wants to think otherwise, I'll remind her of her pledge to me—her husband—the one who would die to protect her. The one she's going to willingly give every part of herself to, over and over again.

All the ways we should have been together over these last few years will no longer be a should be. It'll be a reality, and my Tesora is going to love every minute of it.

Once she gets past it, I remind myself.

I glance down at her again, knowing every part of this scenario feeds into my warped self. I'm not ignorant about who I am. I know how deep my immorality is. Hell, Cara knows it too. She's the only woman who saw the true me. She never ran from it. It's how I should have known not to throw her away all those times. I was a fool, yet I no longer will allow myself to be one. There won't be a need to beg for any more chances. She's going to be mine, and no one besides me will ever have her again.

And I'm going to bestow the most painful death I can upon Uberto.

Then I'm going after the rest of the Abruzzos. Any man who was in that room tonight, I'll hunt down.

The SUV pulls into the private airport and next to the jet. I'm not taking our family one. I don't need my Papà or brothers coming after me.

Cara stirs, her eyes fluttering.

I stroke her cheek. "I'm putting the blanket over your head. It's going to be cold."

"Where—"

"Shh," I say, putting my fingers over her lips, lying again. "We need to get back to the city. Close your eyes."

She sighs but obeys.

I move the blanket over her, open the door, and step out. I barrel through the snow, up the stairs, and nod to the flight attendant. I go directly to the back bedroom, shut the door, then lie down on the bed with Cara, removing the blanket from her head.

Her tired blue eyes peek at me from under her long lashes. "My head hurts worse than before."

I grab a bottle of water from the nightstand, unscrew the lid, and hold it to her lips. "Here."

She drinks half the bottle.

I give her a moment, then ask, "More?"

She shakes her head and locks eyes with me.

I tuck a lock of her hair behind her ear. "Rest. We've got close to six hours."

She pins her eyebrows together. "Where exactly are we?"

"Far away from where we need to be." I slide down, so I'm lying flat on the bed, moving her with me. "Try to sleep some more. I'll wake you up when we get there."

She attempts to roll away from me, but I don't allow her.

"Just chill out. You're not well from the drugs. You can return to hating me later," I state, but my gut churns as I say it. I'd do anything not to have Cara loathe me and return to loving me. And I'm not naive. It's going to take time for her to hand her heart back to me.

She hesitates, her body stiffening against my frame.

I put my lips to her forehead and mumble, "No point arguing. You aren't strong enough to fight me right now."

She sighs, but her body relaxes. She rests her head against my chest, proclaiming, "You're still an asshole."

"Yep. I'm fully aware," I chirp.

She snorts. "You would think it's a compliment."

I glide my hand under the blanket, stroke her back, then palm her ass. "I don't take it as one coming from you."

"Stop talking. This conversation isn't helping my headache. And my ass no longer belongs to you."

I softly chuckle but don't move my hand. "We'll see about that."

She yawns and curls further into me. "I'm going to sleep now. Try not to take advantage of me."

"Based on my memory, you've always been more than willing," I tease.

"Shut up," she orders.

My grin widens. "Okay, Tesora."

"I'm not your Tesora," she quietly claims, but it sounds sad.

I don't respond. I let her fall asleep, curled into me, enjoying every minute of her back in my arms. She sleeps the entire way while I watch her.

When the plane lands, I gently wake her up, bracing myself for the fight I know is in front of me.

Her eyes flutter open. Her sleepy expression makes me want to keep her just like this, but there's no time. I have a small window to get this done, then get back into the air.

"Are we home?" she asks.

"Yeah. You're with me, so you're home."

She rolls her eyes and sits up. I scoot against the headboard and tug her back next to me. She turns to face me, opens her mouth, then shuts it, quickly looking away.

"What do you want to say, Cara?"

She glances at the ceiling, then pins her glistening orbs on me. "Thank you for rescuing me. I-I'm sorry I didn't listen to you about Uberto."

I lick my lips, counting to five so I don't say something I'll regret. Now isn't the time for an I told you so.

She continues, "He's going to come after me, isn't he?"

I reach for her hips and reposition her, so she's straddling me. I hold her cheeks. "Yes. And that's why we're here."

She furrows her brows. "Here?" She turns her head while not breaking my gaze, slowly asking, "You mean home?"

I clench my jaw, taking a moment to gather my thoughts. "No. We're in Vegas."

She jerks her head back then winces. She puts her hand on her skull, snapping, "Why are we in Vegas?"

I clasp my arms around her so she can't escape me. "To get married."

She gapes at me. "Are you crazy?"

"Nope."

"You've officially lost the plot!"

"No. I haven't."

She pushes against my chest. "Let me go, Gianni!"

I don't release her. "No. Listen to me. The only way to protect you is to marry you. No one, and I mean no one, will come after my wife."

Anger flares in her expression. "Did you plan this? Did you make sure I ended up on that stage?"

"What? Of course not. I'm going to kill that bastard as soon as I'm confident you're fully protected and safe. Then I'm going after any man that was in that room," I relay.

"Are you crazy? There were hundreds of them!"

I nod. "Yeah. And they all deserve to die."

Tense silence fills the air. She trembles, and her lip quivers. "I'm not marrying you."

"Yes, you are," I insist.

There's a knock on the door. The flight attendant calls out, "Mr. Marino. The officiant is here."

"Just a minute," I shout.

Cara shakes her head, grimacing, then yells, "Tell him we don't need him."

I smile, which I'm aware is another bastard move on my part. "Plan stays the same," I call out, then lower my voice so only

Cara can hear. "You don't think I prepared for your fight? Hmm?"

Her eyes turn to slits. She pushes to get out of my grasp. This time, I let her. She slides off the bed, and I follow her. She jabs my chest. "I'm not marrying you. Over my dead body will I ever be your wife!"

I make a point of letting my eyes trail her naked frame then sniff hard. "That's exactly what you'll be if you don't marry me. Dead."

"Bull shit!" She spins.

I stop her, circle my arm around her waist, and pull her into my body. I fist her hair so she can't avoid me. She gasps. I ignore my growing erection and bark, "You just got drugged, kidnapped, and put up for auction. What do you think any of those men in there would have done to you?"

She closes her eyes. Tears leak out of them and roll off her chin.

I soften my voice. "There's no other choice. Marry me, or you won't last a day before you're back in their possession."

She stays frozen, except for a sharp exhale through her nose.

I put my lips on hers, wrapping the leash connected to her collar around my fist, holding it outward so she can see it. She glares at me as I state, "I'm going outside. There's a dress in the closet for you. You have ten minutes. After that, you'll get married with the blanket around you and this. Take your pick, Cara."

More daggers fly at me. She whispers, "You don't own me."

I shouldn't say it. It's only going to make things worse between us. But I'm not a man who likes showing any weakness. If I can exert my power, I do. The sinister smile forming on my lips feels like an adrenaline high. With the hand holding the leash, I curl my finger on her chin. "Is that what you think?"

"Fuck you, Gianni."

There's no more control left in me. I grin wider and reply, "Looking forward to it."

"You're such a pig," she spouts.

My dick grows harder. Anytime Cara's pissed off at me, calling me names, it does something to me. I kiss her, forcing her lips apart with my tongue, not letting up until she kisses me back and her knees go weak.

"I hate you," she whispers again.

"That's your choice. And wash the makeup off your face. You're too beautiful for all that shit. Ten minutes. You choose how you want to marry me." I release her and walk out of the room with my stomach flipping. Everything I said was true about the Abruzzos coming after her. What I left out is that her predicament makes it so I'm finally getting everything I've ever wanted.

Her.

Now, she'll never be able to run from me.

My warped self is doing the happy dance, even though I know it's one of the most fucked up things I've ever done.

And I can't even count the low things I've done in my life to get what I want.

Yet, not a bone in my body is upset. She belongs to me. She always has. It's time she realizes what I've known for years.

She may not like it, but the tiny consciousness I have left doesn't nag me enough to stop me from moving forward.

The sooner Cara realizes the future, the better.

There will be no going back.

2

Cara

MY INSIDES QUIVER AS I STARE AT THE BACK OF THE DOOR. FOR more than half my life, all I wanted was to be Mrs. Gianni Marino. I fantasized about it, creating a happily ever after that isn't possible.

Not with Gianni.

I'm not that naive girl anymore. I know how foolish I was to think he could be anything other than the same boy he was in high school. At the end of the day, Gianni's a player. He used me too many times to stroke his ego, promising me the world and that he wouldn't hurt me, only to drop me like a hotcake again.

I won't fall prey to his charm like in the past.

"Eight minutes," Gianni bellows.

I squeeze my eyes shut. One thing he doesn't do is not follow through on threats. He's a cruel implementer. I always admired how he didn't back down. It made me feel like he'd always protect me, and we'd conquer the world together.

Now, I want to slap him.

I glance at the doorknob, but there's no lock. I contemplate staying naked, but the last thing I want is any other man seeing me bare. The flashback of all those men eyeing me over makes me shudder.

I was so close to being sold.

Sold. As if I'm a piece of property.

My heart races, and I hold my flipping stomach. Uberto's face and shoes fill my mind.

How could I have been so dumb?

Gianni warned me Uberto was an Abruzzo. I believed Uberto's lies when I asked him about it. I claimed his innocence, but Gianni kept insisting he was bad news. I said I didn't care if he was an Abruzzo. I wasn't part of their crime family world and wars.

How stupid could I have been?

"Seven," Gianni shouts.

I yank open the door. "Can you—"

A man, who I assume is the officiant, gapes at me.

Gianni threatens, "Don't look at my wife or I'll slice you to pieces!"

"I-I..." the officiant tears his eyes off me.

Gianni lurches toward me, and I back up until my knees hit the bed. He slams the door, steps in front of me, and holds my chin. My adrenaline ignites, and I don't fight back. I loathe how much my body responds to him. And Gianni knows it. Still, his dark eyes sear into mine. "Do you think I'm bluffing?"

Tears blur my vision.

"Do you want Uberto or the other Abruzzos to come after you?" he asks.

I shut my eyes, slowly shaking my head, wondering how my life has come to this. I have a successful career and have lived all over the world. I've always been free until now. At this moment, it seems like I am owned. The thought freaks me out. I can only envision Gianni taking full advantage of this situation.

"What other option do you have?" he questions.

I wrack my brain, but I can't think of any. I'm still foggy from the drugs, but I also know Gianni is right. No one would come after his wife. The Marinos are a crime family. They rule New York. I've known it since I was in high school. It's part of what attracted me to him. He's always been danger and sin wrapped in a perfect package of muscle. And no one messes with Gianni. If anyone tries, he's ruthless in revenge.

Somehow, I made the mistake that if Uberto were an Abruzzo, they would be the same as the Marinos.

Gianni firmly asks, "Do I need to dress you?"

I can't think, and my head won't stop pounding. I have no fight left. "No."

"Are you sure?" he challenges.

I push his chest, but he doesn't budge. "Go away."

"Five minutes. We have to get back in the air," he warns, then steps back and leaves once more.

Taking a deep breath, I go into the bathroom and wash my face. My brand of cleanser is on the counter, which adds to my irritation. How well did Gianni plan this? How long did it take him to make it all happen?

Probably seconds. That's the thing about him. He can make anything happen in a blink of an eye. He's the most determined person I know.

I used to admire that trait. Now it's annoying me.

I dry my face, go to the closet and freeze. Maybe it's the drugs or situation I'm in, but I start to laugh through tears. An expensive, delicate, white lace wedding dress is hanging up. It's form-fitting and barely has a train.

I know this dress. Every inch of the white fabric haunted me over the past few years. I first saw it when I was with Gianni.

We were in Italy several years ago. I had fled to Europe to get over him, and after a few months, right as I started getting serious about another man, he showed up on my doorstep. Like all the other times, he promised me the world, told me to dump my boyfriend, and vowed it would only be us going forward. It took longer than usual for him to convince me, but I finally did what he wanted, falling for his sweet talk.

One day, we were shopping. I saw the dress through the window. He stood behind me, wrapped his arm around my stomach, and pulled me close to him. He declared, "I'm buying that dress for when you marry me."

I froze. It was the first time he ever mentioned marriage. In the past, anytime I brought it up, he would run.

That night, he was an animal in bed. All night we made love like it was the last time we would ever be together. Little did I know, that was exactly what it was.

It was the final night of so many things.

Those hours were the last time I would ever allow myself to love him, feel his arms around me, or fall for his lies.

I finally fell asleep. It was almost noon when I woke up, and Gianni was nowhere. A note next to my bed read:

TESORA,

I NEED TO RETURN TO THE STATES. LOOK ME UP WHEN YOU'RE back in town.

GIANNI

ALL THE TIMES GIANNI LET ME DOWN, THIS WAS THE ONE THAT hurt the most. I beat myself up for months for letting him back in my life. Another year passed, and right as I was moving forward with my life, he showed up again.

This time, I wouldn't let him near me. And ever since then, I've held my stance.

Gianni Marino is nothing but a man with no conscience. If he had one, he'd never have played me all those years. He wouldn't have taken my love and tossed it aside as if it was worthless.

Now, the same wedding dress stares at me, mocking me further. I blink hard, wishing I wasn't getting emotional about this dress. It's a cruel reminder of the pain he's caused me and all the empty promises I believed in.

"Three minutes," Gianni's voice booms, pulling me out of my hop down memory lane.

With shaking hands, I pull the dress off the hanger and step into it. I slide my feet into the designer heels and zip the dress as far up as possible.

What am I doing?

There's no other choice. Uberto will kill or hurt me.

I put my hand on the wall to steady myself. Years ago, this would be my dream come true. Now, being Mrs. Gianni Marino only feels like a nightmare.

"Two!" he shouts.

I take a deep breath, then spin. I open the door. Gianni stares at me with a cocky expression on his face. I say nothing and turn for him to zip me up.

The bastard drags his finger over my spine. Zings burst in my nerves. I curse myself, shuddering, still unable to control my reaction to his touch.

His hot breath hits my neck, sending tingles down my back. He slowly pulls the zipper up. He says in a voice so low, only I can hear him, "I always imagined you in this dress."

I spin, glaring at him. "When did you buy this?"

Guilt, which isn't something I ever see on Gianni, floods his expression. His eyes dart down the front of my body, then back to my gaze. He answers, "The same day we saw it."

Anger slaps me in the face. I seethe, "Why?"

He straightens his shoulders and licks his lips. "You know why."

"No. I don't."

He arches an eyebrow as if I really do know why.

I cross my arms and tilt my head, pissed he's choosing to play another one of his games with me at this moment.

He studies me longer, then states, as if it's true, "You know you've always been mine, Cara. You were always meant to be my wife."

I huff, trying not to cry. The last thing I need is Gianni getting in my head again. After everything I just went through, I don't trust my emotions. I grit my teeth, managing to get out, "Do me a favor. Don't attempt to play me for the hundredth time. If you do, I assure you that I'll cut your balls off while you're sleeping."

He insists in the same voice he always has, "I'm not playing you."

I snort. "Sure." I turn to the officiant. "Can we get this over with?"

The man's face turns red. He shifts on his feet and nods. "Yes."

Gianni grabs my hands. I try to pull away, but he has a death grip on them. I avoid looking at him, focusing on the officiant.

He clears his throat. "Do you, Gianni Marino, take Cara Serrano, to be your lawful wife?"

I attempt to ignore Gianni, but he turns my chin toward him. "I do."

I scowl, not believing this is happening or I'm in this situation. Butterflies spread their wings in my stomach, making me feel nauseous.

Gianni steps closer. His Tom Ford, woody spice scent of leather, tonka bean, and sage wafts in my nostrils. It's a smell I used to love. Then it haunted me throughout the years. Anytime I'd smell it, my heart would ache all over again. At random times, I'd not be able to control the tears.

My insides quiver harder, and I chastise myself to pull it together. He holds my face firm while his long finger traces my lips.

Holding my breath, I don't move, resisting the urge to close my eyes and fall into everything that's Gianni. Instead, I study his dark, cold eyes, reminding myself they represent who he is and not to drop my guard with him.

In his confident tone, he states, "I vow to love, cherish, and protect you, in sickness and health, for better or for worse, for richer or poorer. Most of all, I promise to make up for all the bullshit I put you through over the years."

My heart almost stops. My lips shake against his finger. I clench my jaw and square my shoulders.

It's another one of his lies. Don't believe it. He's an expert at making empty, broken promises, I tell myself.

As if he knows what I'm thinking, he leans closer, stating, "It's true. I will make up for every sordid thing I ever did to you. I will honor you as my wife and the mother of my children."

A sarcastic laugh escapes my lips. Children? Every time I ever uttered anything about children, it made him run. And now we're in our forties. Does he honestly think we can erase the past and suddenly have a happy little family?

His face hardens. "Are my vows funny to you?"

Rage cyclones through me. All the years of waiting for him, taking him back, then upheaving my life for one I believed we could have take their toll on me. It's all a game to him, and this time is no different. As soon as I give him my heart, he'll stomp all over it again. I lift my chin out of his grasp. I spout, "As of matter of fact, they are funny."

Confusion fills his expression. "Why is that?"

"Save the lies." I turn to the officiant. "Is this the part where I say I do?"

Flustered, his face turns red again as his eyes dart between us.

"Well?" I ask, wanting to end this charade.

He swallows hard, then says, "Do you, Cara Serrano, take Gianni Marino to be your lawful husband?"

"Yep. Are we done now?"

His eyes widen.

"No. You need to say your vows," Gianni dryly interrupts.

I shoot him a dirty look.

The officiant instructs, repeat after me. "Do you—"

"I vow to never love, cherish, or honor you. I vow to always remember who you are and what you've put me through. I vow to accept your protection and be grateful for it, but nothing past that. I vow to stand by your side and always know the extent of your cruelness but never be fooled by it again." I take deep breaths, trying to settle my shaking insides.

Gianni's eyes turn to slits. His hands squeeze mine harder when I try to pull them away.

"Umm...ah...." The officiant mumbles.

I turn to him. "Are we married?"

He looks at Gianni for approval. I don't miss the fear laced in his expression. It's another thing I used to love about Gianni—how he can demand respect without saying it. And his ability to make grown men fearful of him I used to see as art.

Now I detest his abilities.

"Go on," Gianni orders.

The officiant twists his fingers together. "By the power invested in me, I now pronounce you man and wife. You may kiss your bride."

I lean back to avoid him, but Gianni already anticipates my move. He grabs the back of my head, palms my ass, and tugs me into his body. I push on his chest, but it's pointless. His tongue parts my lips and flicks in my mouth.

I wish I were immune to his kisses and body against mine. I hate that barely any time passes before my hands curl around his shirt, and I'm kissing him back.

He ravishes my mouth, just like every time he's kissed me. It doesn't matter if I was a teenage girl, in my twenties, thirties, or now. Something about Gianni Marino's mouth and tongue on mine is a one-way ticket to quivering insides and wet panties. It's impossible not to react. My butterflies go crazy, and I curse myself for the inability to show him he doesn't affect me.

When he pulls back, I'm breathless, weak-kneed, and unable to stand without the force of his arm around me. He turns to the officiant. "Thanks. Now get off my plane. We need to go."

I stare at Gianni's chest, trying to catch my breath, loathing myself for kissing him back.

"Umm. Yes, sir," the officiant replies, and I see him step away out of the corner of my eye.

I'm still clenching Gianni's shirt. He wraps his hand around the leash until he gets to the collar.

My face turns red. In my haste, I forgot to take it off.

Gianni's cocky expression lands on me. He fists my hair, so my face is directly under his. "You're mine now, Tesora. You need to let the past go. Let's focus on our future."

I scoff. "Do you think marrying me erases your sins?"

He sniffs hard. "No. I think it shows you how committed to you I am."

"Committed? You don't know how to be committed. But let me tell you something. When you get bored with this scenario, don't run to another woman. I'll slice you in your sleep," I threaten.

Amusement flickers on his expression. "Good to know. But since I won't be breaking our vows, I guess I'll stay in one piece."

"Yeah, right. I'm sure it'll happen in under a month."

He tightens his grip on my hair. In a firm voice, he states, "I'm not running from you this time, Cara. I meant what I said in my vows."

Of all the things I wish, it's that I could believe him.

I can't.

He's Gianni Marino. The man who broke my heart too many times to count. And I'll be damned before I let being Mrs. Gianni Marino ever forget our past.

Not flinching or avoiding his dark, cold eyes, I find strength in my voice. I declare, "Nothing has changed between us. Now let me go."

He stays frozen, and time seems to stand still.

"Now," I order.

He finally releases me and steps back.

"Where are we going?" I question.

"Kelowna."

"Kelowna?" I ask in confusion. I've never even heard of the town.

His lips twitch. "It's in Canada, northeast of Vancouver."

"Why are we going there?"

"It's in the middle of nowhere. No one will find us, and they have a proper spa. You love spas," he responds as if it's perfectly normal for us to be heading to the spa.

"Are we going to be on the run?" I ask.

He grunts. "No. I'll kill anyone who comes near you."

"You said no one will find us," I point out.

His grin widens, and I want to smack him before he says, "I meant no one will disturb us on our honeymoon."

My gut is a mix of dread and excitement. I once again detest myself for my body not getting on the same page as my brain. I square my shoulders. "We aren't going on a honeymoon."

He crosses his arms, and the flight attendant interrupts. "Mr. and Mrs. Marino, please get ready for take off."

My stomach flips. *Mrs. Marino.*

"We are," Gianni insists, then steers me into the bedroom, kicking the door shut with his foot. He reaches behind me and unzips my dress.

"What are you doing?" I cry out.

"Calm down, Cara." He shoves my dress to the floor then pulls the covers back. He points. "Get in."

"No! I'm not sleeping with you!"

His jaw clenches. He firmly repeats, "Get in."

I stay planted, placing my hand on my hip. "If you think I'm going to do whatever you say, you're wrong!"

"Fine. Keep your attitude for now." He picks me up.

I shriek, "Put me down."

He places me on the bed, tucks the covers around my body, then cages his forearms around me. My heart beats harder, and he states, "You need to sleep. I'll be in the other room if you need me. But make no doubt about it, you're *my* wife. You *will* sleep with me. So get that thought out of your head."

"No. I won't. I will never—and I mean never—sleep with you," I declare.

His eyes travel down my face, pausing on my lips then my breasts. My cheeks burn. He slowly meets my gaze again. His finger strokes my cheek. In his cocky voice, he proclaims, "One thing you seemed to have forgotten is I know you, Cara. I know how even when you hate me, your body craves mine."

I say nothing, breathing harder, wishing I could pull him into me and forget about the past.

But I can't. So I reply, "Keep telling yourself that. One day, you'll realize you don't know me anymore. I'm not the girl you can use and abuse anymore."

Something passes in his expression. I'd call it remorse, but Gianni Marino doesn't know guilt and regret. I remind myself not to fall for it. He studies me further, then lowers his voice. "I wasn't lying, Tesora. I'll right the wrong I've done to you."

I turn on my side and hug the pillow. "No, you won't. You can't. You have no heart. Now leave me alone."

Gianni

STALE AIR FILLS MY LUNGS. I KISS CARA'S FOREHEAD AND LEAVE the bedroom. Her reaction shouldn't surprise me, but my warped mind thought getting married would somehow change things between us. I thought she'd love the dress but I don't think she did. All I keep hearing is her voice.

I vow to never love, cherish, or honor you.

I vow to always remember who you are and what you've put me through.

I vow to accept your protection and be grateful for it, but nothing past that.

I vow to stand by your side and always know the extent of your cruelness but never be fooled by it again.

I scrub my hands over my face, plop down on the seat, then glance out the window staring at the gray sky. That wasn't what

I had played out in my mind while waiting for Luca to outbid the room. I assumed Cara'd give me some pushback, but I thought once she saw the dress and heard my vows, she would realize how bad I've always had it for her.

I'm an idiot.

"Mr. Marino, would you like something to drink?" the flight attendant asks, pinning her doe-eyes on me.

I almost groan out loud from boredom. Women are so predictable. If Cara weren't in the other room, if I hadn't just made her my wife, I'd bend this woman over and try to fuck the desperate need I feel for my Tesora out of me.

It never works, but I always try. I don't even know how many years have passed where I've done that. A dozen? Twenty? All the women I've screwed are one big blur. I wouldn't even know the names of most of them if I happened to run into them.

They weren't Cara, so I didn't bother to memorize their names. What was the point? They were just another avenue for me to try and extinguish the burning obsession I've always had for her.

Fucking those women was just another mistake. And since I learned my Tesora was back in town and dating that Abruzzo thug, I've kept my pants zipped. There's only one woman I'm ever touching again, and it isn't anyone but my wife.

"Sir?" The flight attendant asks again. Pink crawls into her cheeks, and she tilts her head. A tiny smile plays on her lips.

She's so predictable. She can't even play hard to get.

I know that expression too well. If I wanted her, I could have her, and there would be no objection.

I wonder how many rich dudes she's let have her?

Probably too many to count.

There's nothing I want from this woman other than a drink. I scowl. "Scotch. And keep your panties on, princess. I just got married, if you didn't notice."

She gapes at me, swallowing hard as her cheeks turn fire-engine-red. "S-sir. I...I..."

I fling my hand in the air, pointing to the front of the plane. "Drink."

"Y-yes, sir." She scurries away.

I tap my fingers on the armrest, still reeling from Cara's marriage vows. I knew I needed to win her back, but it'll be more challenging than I thought.

Now she's stuck with me. She'll have no choice but to change her attitude.

I huff at the thought. Cara might be just as stubborn as I am. It's one of the things I love about her. She doesn't easily back down. She used to but quickly learned in high school to make me beg for more chances. Part of my attraction toward her was the challenge of getting her back.

The first time she wised up, my dick turned so hard it hurt. No one ever denied me. And Cara saw my reaction. She knew the power she held over me.

For a while, I'd break up with her only to have to go through all of it again. Each time, she made me wait longer until she gave in to my wishes. For every occasion, I'd promise her I'd never do it again, and it would only be us going forward.

Then we'd have better sex than the previous times. I'd be happy for a short while then get spooked again.

I cringe, remembering how I treated her when we were teenagers. I took her virginity and stomped on it by screwing multiple girls. Back then, I told myself it didn't matter. She knew before she gave me her virginity what I was expected to do.

It all started with a game Dante and I played after his first girl-friend started flirting with me. He told me to screw her, so I did. After that, it became a challenge to see how many girls would participate in our sordid activities.

Each of us would do the same girl. The only ones we never swapped were Bridget and Cara. We had an unspoken rule—they were off limits.

But we had anyone we wanted. Sleeping with both of us was like a badge of honor. It shot the girl straight to the top of the popularity poll. That was how things played out in our school. And there might as well have been a billboard publicizing every encounter. Each one, Cara knew about within hours of it happening.

The flight attendant pulls me out of my trip down memory lane, clearing her throat. Annoyed, I glance at her. She holds the glass out, and her hand slightly shakes. "Your scotch, Sir."

I grab it, then drink a large mouthful. It burns my throat as it slides into my stomach. I turn toward the window, letting my twisted thoughts play out in my head, debating about going into the bedroom and showing Cara how much I've missed her.

Not yet.

Images swirl in my mind, and my pants get tighter. I've never been into collars, but something about seeing Cara, *my wife*, in one, with the leash wrapped around my hand, did something to me.

It's wrong.

They put that collar around her neck for a man to own her, but I've never been one to think moral thoughts. While I don't condone human trafficking, the notion of making my Tesora submit to me and wear a collar to show the world who she belongs to is stroking my unethical side.

Plus, it would drill into her that she's now mine. There's no more trying to escape me. I'm hers for life, and she's mine.

Grinning at our new reality, I take another large mouthful of scotch, swallowing it whole. My thoughts shift to the war in front of me. It's not a new battle. My family has always hated those Abruzzo pigs, even before one of them kidnapped my sister, Arianna. Now, they made it even more personal by going after my Tesora.

Rage flares inside me, growing hotter by the minute. I sniff hard and crack my neck. The monster in me wants to find Uberto now, tear him to shreds, then strap him to a flagpole outside Jacopo's compound. He's the head of their family and on my "kill through torture" list. Every command comes straight from him. Over the years, he's grown their human trafficking business tenfold. And I highly doubt Uberto put Cara in Jacopo's auction without him approving it.

Well, now he's going to know that I own Cara.

My chest tightens at the thought. Sick satisfaction mixes with guilt for what I'm about to do.

I pull out my phone, then turn it on. I connect to the plane's wi-fi then pull up my bank account. I wire twenty million dollars to Luca's personal account. I rationalize it by reminding myself I had to do it. There's no way I won't blow my guy's cover if I don't. It needs to be clear in all crime families' eyes who owns Cara.

The truth is I'd have paid Luca more than twenty million to save my Tesora from that situation. He's my cousin from Italy. No one in the States knows this except Papà, my brothers, Tully and his sons. He arrived here as a kid and only has an accent if he needs to use it.

Over the years, he's learned more secrets about the Abruzzos than I can count. When I learned what Uberto did to Cara, Luca was the only person I could think of who could get the job done and also be discreet. But I knew my window of time was small before my family figured out what was happening.

My gut churns faster, thinking about my Tesora, naked and on the stage for all those pigs to fantasize about her being theirs.

Now, they'll know who she belongs to, I think with a warped sense of satisfaction.

My family may stay out of the human trafficking business, but no matter what your family is involved in, there are rules all crime families ahere to.

Rule number one: Don't go after women and children.

I squeeze and release my fist, thinking about how the Abruzzos disobeyed that when they kidnapped my sister.

Rule number two: If a man buys a woman, she's his property. No one better lay a finger on her.

My anger doesn't dissolve as I think about how we shot up the underground sex club to rescue Brenna from Giulio Abruzzo. The only reason no one came after my family is because we didn't leave any witnesses. Also, Declan O'Malley hacked into the security footage and deleted it. Since Brenna reunited with

Finn O'Malley, there are rumors, but so far, no one has attempted to take us out.

My gut twists from the thought of me owning my Tesora. I don't condone any part of a human being owning another. It's always disgusted me. Yet, I can't deny the gratification filling my soul from sending the money over to pay for her.

I close my eyes and rest my head against the back of the seat, grasping my tumbler tighter. Ever since I was a child, I felt semi-crazy. I knew I wasn't like other kids in my class. Something about Cara always made the wickedness in me expand. I've often wondered if it's a big reason I'm obsessed with her. Women pretend to understand me, but it never takes long to see the fear in their expressions when they learn the devil is inside me.

It's not that my actions haven't ever shocked Cara, but not once did she look at me in fear. She grew up in a wealthy, non-crime family. She's not from my world, yet she slid right into it without any hesitation. There's never been any drama around what I do. And she's the only woman who can truly see through the persona I show most of the world.

Fuck. My current moment of truth isn't new. It swirled around me the last few years, only to turn into a hurricane over the last few months. I take another sip. It's probably the reason I ran from her all those times.

Cara would always say, "I see you, Gianni. The real you." Then she'd curl up to me and fall asleep as if it somehow gave her a sense of peace that she knew I was such a cruel bastard.

What drove me more insane was she wasn't slinging bullshit. Cara understood the depth of my sordidness almost as well as I did. She accepted every ounce of it. In fact, all she ever did was show me she'd stand by me and continue to love me, yet I had to push her away.

For the last few years, I've been paying for my mistakes. She cut off all contact with me when she was in Europe. I flew over there, begging her to give me another shot. No apology or promise would change her mind. When I finally went home, I tried to forget about her, but it was impossible.

She consumed all my thoughts. Every woman I met, I compared to her, then tried to pretend they were her. Yet no one could stop the bad feeling in my chest from expanding. The more I tried to erase it, the worse it became.

I didn't know she was dating Uberto until she got back to New York, nor did I even know she was in town. Seeing her again only made my endless infatuation inflate. And her determination to not allow me back into her life made every ounce of my insanity come to life.

The ability to hold my temper and analyze a situation before I acted flew out the window. I pissed my Papà off too many times to count. It's created a rift between us. The trust he once had in me has diminished.

Dante has also questioned my decisions. He's a few minutes older than me, which means he's next in line to take over the family. I've always had his full trust until now. We've always seen eye to eye, but lately, I'm unhinged and unable to control myself. It's like the interest the Abruzzos had in Cara opened Pandora's box, which held all my self-control.

I glance at my phone. The flight time is estimated to be another four and a half hours. I pull up the internet and do a search. I type: *real diamond collars with leashes near Kelowna.*

It pains me to pay for jewels when my family has built an entire operation, but my itch is growing. I scroll through images and stop. A perfect platinum collar, with twelve diamonds, each several carats a piece, beams at me. I click on it, read the description, then scroll through all the photos. It only excites me more. The collar can be detached so it looks like an expensive choker. It's a statement piece that'll get the point across to Cara.

She's mine.

Forever.

It's so perfect, my cock strains against my zipper. I can imagine Cara in it, kneeling and then begging me.

I click to purchase it, but there aren't any same day shipping options. I call the jewelers.

An older sounding man answers, "Greetings. What can I do for you?"

"Yes. I saw on your website the twelve diamond collar. Do you still have it available?" I tap my fingers on my tumbler, feeling like I might explode if he doesn't.

"Well yes."

"Great. I'll take it, but you need to get it to the resort I'm staying at tonight. I'll pay extra to make it happen," I state.

He clears his throat. "Are you staying at the spa?"

"Yes."

"I'm afraid I'm the only one in the shop. The spa is a twenty minute drive. I couldn't deliver it until after I close down for the night."

"What time do you close?"

"Eight."

"Can you drop it off by 8:30?"

There's a pause.

I take a deep inhale, feeling like my skin is crawling. "I need it tonight. I'll add an extra $10,000 to the total for your special attention in this matter."

"Oh. That's not necessary. I don't want to take advantage of you. I can make sure it's there by 8:30."

Another thought occurs to me. "Perfect. I'll leave instructions at the front desk. Can you do me one last favor?"

"What's that?"

"Do you do engravings there?"

"Yes."

"I need you to add, *Tesora, Forever means forever. Love always, Your Husband, Gianni.*

"Can you spell that for me?"

I do as he asks and add, "I need it gift wrapped. I want a white paper, but it has to be quality, not something cheap. And add a white bow. Can you do that?"

"Sure, but the necklace box is silver with white satin inside. Is that okay? I don't believe I have anything else to fit it," he frets.

"Yes. That's fine." I give him my name, credit card information, and the name of the hotel just to make sure he was referring to the same spa resort.

Satisfied and hornier than ever, I finish my drink, then can't help myself. I rise and go into the bedroom, shutting the door as quietly as possible.

My heart skips a beat, watching my Tesora sleep. She's on her side. Her long, dark hair splayed across the pillow. Her flawless skin looks soft, and I'm too aware of how it feels.

I groan inside, debating my next move. I've never gone this long without sex. It's an inherent need within me, but I wasn't giving in to any temptation until I had her back. Now she's in front of me, Mrs. Gianni Marino, and my needs are only getting stronger.

She keeps her eyes shut and mumbles, "Go away. I was sleeping."

I chuckle, then move onto the bed. I kick off my shoes and slide under the covers, tugging her into me.

Her body stiffens. She demands, "What are you doing?"

I turn her, so she's facing me and lying on my chest. I drag my finger down her cheek. "How's your head?"

She slowly meets my gaze. "Fine. Can you leave now?"

"No."

"Jesus. Go away." Her eyes fire daggers but she doesn't push me away.

I take it as a sign I'm making progress. I tighten my arm around her and kiss her forehead. She yawns as I proclaim, "I'm tired. We have a long flight. Go back to sleep."

She stares at me for several minutes.

I repeat, "Go to sleep, Cara. The drugs need to work their way out of your system. You can hate me later."

She sighs. "Don't try anything."

As much as I want to, I know she's going to be more pissed if I do. "You're drugged. I prefer my women to be coherent, remember?"

She rolls her eyes. "Since when do you have morals?"

I rub my thumb over her hip, noting again how well she knows me. "I don't. Now go to sleep."

She doesn't move.

I lean closer, so my lips graze hers. "Do you want me to wear you out?"

She takes a deep breath then smirks. "I thought you liked your women to be coherent."

"I said prefer. And I remember several occasions where we were both pretty hammered but still had a good time."

She licks her lips, and I refrain from shoving my tongue in her mouth. She challenges, "So it doesn't matter if I'm drugged then?"

I push the anger over what the Abruzzos did to her to the back of my mind. I tug on her hair.

She gasps, making my dick twitch against her stomach.

I hold her head in place and reply, "I told you I don't have morals. Not that you don't already know this, but are you trying to test me? I can assure you, my Tesora, I haven't changed."

She closes her eyes briefly, then drills her blues into me. A deep detestation fills her voice. "Yeah. I know you haven't changed."

My heart sinks, but nothing she states is untrue. Every bite she gives me, I earned. I sniff hard and release her hair. "Then go to sleep." I reposition her body, so she's curled into me. It was always her favorite way to sleep. It was mine too, but I never told her. Anything that showed her how much she meant to me, I hid, too big of a coward to reveal.

I regret it all. Every moment that I didn't tell her how special she was or what I loved about her, I kick myself over.

She finally gives in, closing her eyes, and within minutes she's softly breathing.

It's music to my ears. I started to wonder if I'd ever hear it again or feel the tickle against my chest from her tiny exhales.

Not a second goes by that I sleep. I keep my embrace tight around her, my palm firm on her ass, and ignore my raging erection. I spend the rest of the trip wondering how I'm ever going to get back into her good graces. Besides all my past methods, which no longer seem to work, I'm no closer to winning her over than before we got on this plane.

Not a bone in my body is ready to stop trying.

I *will* make her love me again.

I'm just unsure how.

4

Cara

"Tesora, wake up." Gianni's deep voice is soft, which is rare. It's usually powerful and commanding, which is something I've always loved about him. But these moments where I'm asleep, and he's gentler get me too. I don't know if anyone else has ever heard him like this.

I snuggle against his muscular frame and toss my arm around him, keeping my eyes shut. I mumble, "Let's stay like this all day."

He chuckles, then tightens his embrace. He slides his warm hand between my thighs. His hot breath hits my neck. Zings fly down my body, right to my pussy. I roll my hips, and he cups my sex, dragging his middle finger through my slit.

I whimper, still not opening my eyes. Heat shoots through my veins. My insides clench his digit as his thumb rolls on my clit.

He nibbles on my lobe, gliding his finger in my wet heat, murmuring, "It's been too long, Tesora."

Too long? What's he talking about? Surely we made love last night if he's next to me.

Yawning, I smile and reply, "How many hours has it been?" I'm still tired and not ready to fully wake up. I move my face until my lips connect with his, lacing my fingers in his thick hair.

Upon contact, his tongue slides in my mouth, slowly rolling against mine, then speeding up with intensity. He taunts me until I'm on the verge of a full blown sweat.

"Don't tease me," I barely get out against his lips.

"I'll do what I want. I own your pussy. You know this," he states, then dips his head to my neck and bites it.

"Oh fuck!" I cry out, holding him tighter, circling my hips into his hand harder. It's something only he's done to me. I don't know why it turns him or me on, but it does. I open my eyes, but everything is dark.

His hand grasps the back of my neck, squeezing it firmly, while he bites me again, then rubs his thumb over the spot his mouth was on.

A moan escapes my lips. He pinches my clit, then rolls it quicker, and I beg, "Please."

He tugs on my hair until his eyes meet mine. They're darker than the room, and every ounce of his dominance shines through them. He demands, "Tell me who you belong to."

"You. Only you," I whisper. Adrenaline pools in my cells, waiting to erupt. I add, "Please, Gianni."

The corners of his lips turn up, and he arches his eyebrow. My heart races, and I dig my nails into his head. I know that look. He's going to make me wait longer.

"Please," I plead, but what Gianni wants, he gets. Edging me until I'm soaked and on fire gets both of us off.

His fingers continue to perfectly manipulate me. The cocky, focused expression on him never falters.

My begging gets louder until sweat pops out on my skin.

"Who do you belong to?" he barks again.

"You! Please!" I answer.

He bites my neck, and I arch into him. His hard erection pushes into my thigh. He swirls my clit faster, and all hell breaks loose in my body.

"Holy shit!" I moan as white stars burst into my vision.

He bites me again as I'm orgasming, intensifying the high. Then he mumbles, "My mouth missed your pussy. Tell me I can have it."

Confused about why he's asking me, I slide my hand down his back to pull the covers away, but my fingers slide over his belt.

Why is he wearing clothes?

His hot mouth slides over my breast, and his tongue flicks on my nipple.

Caressing the side of his head, I blink a few times. His face moves to my torso, and everything comes flying back to me.

The dress.

The wedding.

Our vows.

I try to sit up, but his hand is still holding the back of my neck. He drags his tongue to the tip of my slit, and I almost allow myself to let him have me this one time.

No, no, no!

"Get off me!" I burst out.

He freezes, then pins his gaze on mine.

"I said get off," I repeat, but my voice cracks.

He licks his lips, drags it over my clit, and I whimper. Arrogantly, he asks, "You sure you want me to stop?"

No.

Yes.

Crap!

I find my strength and push the butt of my palm on his forehead. "You heard me."

He sniffs hard, deeply inhaling, not taking his orbs off mine. "Seems like you were enjoying yourself."

Another wave of heat flushes my cheeks. The last thing I wanted was Gianni to know he still turns me on. I angrily claim, "I wasn't."

He stays planted over my frame, challenging, "Is that why you were begging me?"

"Shut up," I order.

"You know you're my wife now. This game you're playing isn't going to last long."

Panic flashes in me. I push his forehead again. "Off!"

He groans and rolls off me, shaking his head. "It's time to get over your issues with me and forgive me."

I huff. "I'm never forgiving you! And I won't fall prey to you ever again!"

He scrubs his face, then lunges at me. He grabs my wrists and pins them to the headboard.

I gasp and hate myself when my legs widen. His hard erection presses against my sex. I detest myself further because I immediately think, *why can't he be naked right now?*

"You think you're my prey?" he asks.

I stay quiet, fighting my body's desire to arch into him further. My hitched breath merges into his. Power, control, and assuredness swirl in his dark eyes, and everything about it makes me cringe inside.

There's no denying I'm attracted to him. One look is all it ever took. Who he is and how he handles himself is a match lighting every part of my soul. Fighting him all these months didn't get easier. It became more challenging, but I held my ground. Now, I'm unsure how I'm going to survive him—survive us.

When I'm Gianni's, everything feels right in my life. We fit together in all ways. It's not just physical. It's an emotional and mental level that I've never experienced with anyone except him.

Every time he returns and makes his promises, it's like diving deeper into the abyss. Then he bails. Each instance, it gets harder to pull myself out. And I'm not naive enough to know this time won't be an exception.

He presses his lips in butterfly kisses over my forehead, nose, and cheeks, then studies me as I hold my breath. He finally states, "If you want to experience what it's like to be my prey, I'll show you, my Tesora. But I'm afraid you'll love it too much. Then what would we be? Hmm? A husband hunting then caging up his wife, playing into the game that she craves? Because you know I'd never kill you, but I'd have to figure out how to tame you."

My stomach quivers. Something about his statement excites and scares me. It's a true sign I'm officially as fucked up as Gianni. A vision of him hunting then caging me up in his suite, turning me into his prisoner as I anxiously await his return, gives me tingling goosebumps. A drop of my juice slides down my skin.

He strokes my cheek with his finger. His lips hover on mine, and eyes light up. "Ah. There's the truth. Maybe that's what we'll do then. I'll treat you like my property since technically you are and would like every moment of it."

"I am *not* your property," I declare through gritted teeth.

A sinister expression I've seen too many times in my life appears on him. "You don't know the depths of what I've done to have you right here, underneath me."

"What are you talking about?"

He wraps the leash around his hand and tugs it in front of my face. My heart beats harder. I didn't realize I still had it on. Something about seeing it around Gianni's large fist, feeling the pressure of the tension on the collar, makes my insides pulse.

His lips curl. "It's not your concern. But make no mistake, Cara, you are my property. And I'm a man with needs. This attitude of yours I'm only going to tolerate for so long, so know this. What-ever I've done up until now, it's a mere fraction of what I'll do going forward to keep you safe and as mine."

My blood charges through my veins. I seethe, "You don't own me, Gianni."

Satisfaction surges into his expression, making my gut dive. He opens his mouth, then snaps it shut. In a quick move, he releases the leash and collar from my neck. He rolls off me and jumps off the bed. "We've landed. It's cold outside so make sure you wear all the layers." He motions to the end of the bed.

I sit up and glance at the pile of clothes before aiming my daggers at him. Everything about the wedding dress and designer attire pisses me off. I fire, "How long were you planning this? Did you know what Uberto was going to do to me?"

He crosses his arms over his chest. "I told you he was an Abruzzo. I warned you to cut it off with him. Did I have any previous knowledge that he would drug and auction you off? Not anything specific. But it doesn't even matter. In the future, when I tell you to stay away from someone, you listen. You obey me. Are we clear?"

Sharp rage intensifies, digging into my bones. I lift my chin. "I'm not your child, nor will I ever obey you. The days of me trusting you are over."

His nostrils flare. "Do you wish I didn't rescue you, then?"

I look at the blanket, then close my eyes. My stomach pitches. If Gianni hadn't saved me, where would I be right now?

Not married to him.

It's better than the opposite.

Is it?

Jesus, how can I even ask that.

It's Gianni Marino. King of breaking my heart too many times to count.

"That's what I thought. Get dressed. You're Mrs. Gianni Marino now. It's how it always should have been and isn't going to change," he orders.

Sure. Until you're bored with me again, I think but don't voice it out loud.

When the sound of the door shutting hits my ears, I open my eyes, taking several deep breaths. I reach up and hold the spot on my neck Gianni bit, wondering how he can still physically affect me after he's hurt me so much.

I slowly pick up all the clothes stacked on the bed, debating whether I should wear the sexy gold and black bra and panties. Normally, I'd love them, but it's Gianni's taste. I'm sure he has lots of visions about what he wants to do to me in them.

It again makes me wonder how long he knew about my kidnapping. Was this planned? Did he allow me to be drugged and sold so he could get his way?

I swallow hard, not putting it past him. He'll do anything without hesitation if it's a means for taking what he wants. So I can't trust anything he says about that situation or anything else.

I stare at the lingerie, still contemplating whether to wear it or not. I finally decide I'm going to use it to my advantage. I'll wear it, then prance around him later tonight, only to torture him.

If he wants me to be Mrs. Gianni Marino, I'll show him what that means. Only I'm not going to be the dutiful wife who dotes on him. He'll see what he gets for tricking me into marrying him.

I get dressed, then go into the bathroom. I splash cold water on my face, then study myself in the mirror.

I can do this.

I just need to keep my pants on where Gianni Marino is concerned.

I give myself a pep talk, then leave the bedroom. Gianni is waiting right outside the door. He gives me a look of approval, then tosses the collar and leash on the chair. His arm slides around my waist. He dips down, so his breath hits my ear. "Don't worry, Tesora. I'm getting you a new one."

I turn into him, hold my breath and reprimand myself for the adrenaline rushing through my body. I shouldn't want anything from him—especially not a collar.

His cocky expression grows. He slides his hand over my ass, palming my cheek.

My knees weaken. I lean into his support, cursing myself again.

He sniffs hard. "It took me by surprise too. But hey, maybe it's what's been missing between us all these years."

"What's that?" I ask, but shouldn't.

His lips curl. He drags his finger over the spot on my neck he bit, making me squirm. "You in the risque outfits I choose, wearing a collar representing that you belong to me, kneeling and waiting for my command."

I glare at him, hating how much that statement makes my pussy pulse. I fume, "Never. I will never kneel for you."

His expression tells me that he doesn't believe me. He traces my lips with his thumb. As if he has zero doubt, he declares, "You will. In fact, you're already craving it. I see it in your eyes, my

Tesora. And no matter how pissed at me you are, you're never going to stop wanting or needing what I give you."

"Fuck you," I whisper.

His grin widens. He says nothing else and leads me off the plane and into the car that's waiting on the runway. As soon as the door shuts, his phone rings.

I ignore him during the drive, staring out the window and trying to drown out his voice. He barks orders in Italian at whoever called. More irony hits me. I used to love listening to him exert his authority over others. Something about it made me fall deeper for him. Now, it reminds me how much more power he has than me.

When his hand slides over my thigh, I don't even attempt to move it. Deep down, I know everything he said is correct. I've always craved what only Gianni can give me. All I ever wanted was to be his. And damn the truth because I always needed it like a drug addict needs a fix. But now, I can't give into my desires. Whatever I do, I need to remember that Gianni Marino, my husband, is nothing but a snake—a cold, venomous snake who will stop at nothing to destroy me when he gets bored again.

5

Gianni

"YOUR PAPÀ CALLED A FAMILY MEETING AND BROUGHT ME INTO it," Luca states as if he's slightly bored.

I study Cara. She's been staring out the window the entire trip. I slide my hand on her thigh, watching a blush creep up her cheek. Satisfied I wasn't wrong and she still responds to my touch, I hold myself back from tossing my phone on the other seat and taking her in the car. Instead, I tell myself to be patient. I speak in Italian and ask, "What did he order?"

Luca grunts. "He wanted me to tell him where you're going."

My cousin is a few years older than me. While he respects my father, he's not scared of him. It drives my father nuts, even though he's never admitted it. But I also know he's loyal to Papà. And I am aware of how skilled my father is at getting the information he wants from men. So I didn't trust Luca with any information on where I was taking Cara. I state, "Good thing you don't know."

Luca doesn't respond to my comment. He informs me, "Dante argued with your Papà for quite a while. He's ordered a hunt for Uberto."

I squeeze my fist, taking a deep breath. I told my brother not to go after him. I want every bit of satisfaction when I capture him, and he begs for mercy. However, I should have realized my Papà would get involved. I ask, "How mad was Papà?"

Luca yawns. "Oh, the usual. You didn't miss much. I got assigned to Tristano's team."

I run my hand through my hair, tugging at the back, and slide my other palm to the inner part of Cara's thigh. She takes a deep inhale but still doesn't look at me. I tell Luca, "Make sure it's clear no one, and I mean *no one*, lays a finger on him until I get home."

He replies, "Already done."

I hang up and dial Dante.

He answers after one ring. "Where the fuck are you?"

I count to five in my head. For some reason, numbers have always calmed me. I keep my voice at a level I feel is in control, so I don't freak Cara out. She's fluent in Italian, so she can understand everything I'm saying, but I've never worried about her listening in on my business calls. There's always been an inherent trust between us, even though we've never discussed my dealings. I continue speaking in Italian and reply, "None of your business. And I told you to wait until I go home."

Dante hurls, "Fuck off, Gianni. You knew Papà would decide what to do about this. And he wants you to call him and get your ass home."

I'm not doing either of those. My Papà already left a voice message that I've not listened to and several nasty text messages. I question, "What did you tell him?"

Tension fills the air. I count to fifteen before Dante replies, "Nothing. He knows I'm lying to cover your ass again."

I cringe inside. I hate that Dante is constantly going to bat for me lately. Yet, I can't seem to stop getting into these predicaments. But now that I have Cara as mine, hopefully, I'll be able to get back on the same page as my Papà.

Dante sniffs hard. "Did you force her to do it?"

I don't have to ask how he knew I married her. We've always had a sixth sense. I rub my thumb over Cara's thigh, an inch from her slit, and more heat flushes her cheeks. I'm tired of this conversation and reply, "Why are you asking me things you already know the answer to?"

"Jesus. You didn't have to do that. You know we could have protected her without forcing her to marry you," he states.

I count to ten, then respond, "Nothing makes a statement to other crime families than paying for a woman and then marrying her. You know this."

Cara's head snaps up. She gapes at me, then her eyes turn to slits.

Dante barks, "Goddammit, Gianni! We don't do that in our family! What you just did is wrong."

"There was no other option after she was on stage, and you know it," I growl, not taking my eyes off Cara's.

The sound of Dante deeply inhaling fills the line. He finally says, "What am I going to tell Bridget?"

I snort. "I don't give a fuck. You deal with your woman, and I'll deal with mine."

"You know Cara will talk to Bridget when she's back."

"So? Since when are you scared about what your woman thinks?" I ask, brushing my pinky against Cara's pussy. Heat radiates off her black leggings. Her lush lips part. All I can suddenly think about is eating my way through the delicate, gold and black lace lingerie I chose for her.

"You mean my soon to be *wife*. The one who *agreed* to marry me and will be the head of the family with me," Dante points out, which only pisses me off. He's the future leader only because of a few measly minutes.

Normally, I'd get into it with him. He doesn't throw his weight around often unless he's super angry with me, but I'd still put him in his place. Right now, I don't take my gaze off my Tesora, getting harder at the thought of her writhing under my face. I ignore Dante's statement and claim, "When I'm back, we're going after all of them."

A moment of silence fills the line except for his tense breathing. I slide my pinky back and forth faster over the material of Cara's pants.

Her glare softens. Blue flames filled with a needy desire. It's an expression that's always driven me insane. It haunts my thoughts when she's not with me. All kinds of women have looked at me for sex, but the way my Tesora's always gazed at me instantly fires up my blood. At this moment, it only serves to make my blood boil hotter.

I reply, "No one touches him until I return. Then the war is on. Every Abruzzo who was in that room is going to die." I hang up and toss my phone in the cupholder. I tuck a lock of her hair behind her ear.

She slowly licks her lips as if deep in thought, driving me crazier. No one on Earth is a bigger tease than Cara. I swear she knows she's doing it. She'll appear clueless, but surely she knows? So moments like these, I'm unsure if she's intentionally trying to make my balls bluer or if she's naive to what she's doing.

"What's going on in that head of yours?" I ask, dragging the back of my three fingers down her neck and over the tiny bite mark I left on her.

She swallows, then surprises me by crawling on top of my thighs and straddling me.

Happy she's coming around and remembering that it's been way too long since she sat on me like this, I circle my arm around her and fist her hair. I tug it gently and hover my face over hers. My dick pulses against her stomach. Her lips twitch, and I hold back my grin. "Are you enjoying what you're doing to me?"

Her eyes widen, feigning innocence. She bats her long eyelashes. "Isn't that what you wanted? Your wife, submitting to you?"

My pulse beats faster. I study her face, my body aching for her to give me some sort of release. I don't even care what kind. A blow job. Sex. Anything. She could give me a hand job like a high schooler right now, and I'd be happier than I've been in years. Because that's the last time she touched me.

Nothing's been right since she's been out of my life. But I'm not about to give in to her without making it clear what the future holds. My new obsession that started forming on the plane isn't about us returning to our old ways. It's about something new in our relationship. It'll make it clear to her who she belongs to and remind her what only I'm able to give her. And it's going to make her thank her lucky stars she's Mrs. Gianni Marino. So I ignore my raging hard-on and reply, "This is better, but it's not fully submitting, now is it?"

A mixture of emotions flickers in her expression. She's confused because she wants it too. I know her too well, and there isn't anything she can hide from me. She's always enjoyed me domi- nating her, but when I wrapped my fist around the leash, her eyes lit up. I couldn't have ignored it if I tried. So this is going to take my possessive tendencies to an entirely new level. And because I know her so well, I can see she's trying to understand why this new notion of submitting to me turns her on when she wants to keep hating me.

I tug her hair a bit further back and clasp my other hand around her neck. "This will be a lot easier and more fun if you think about how I saved you instead of all the stupid shit I did to you in the past."

Her hands reach for my belt. Like always, she takes hardly any time to free my stiff erection and wraps her palm around it. She strokes her thumb over the head and asks, "If I'm submitting, I can't do this."

"Sure you can. I give you permission," I arrogantly add, then steal a quick kiss. Her hand on me is pleasant torture. I release my grasp on her hair so she's sitting straight up, then slide my hand in her pants and cup her ass cheek. "This is better, don't you think? Like it should have always been."

She slides her knees until they hit the back of the seat, and there's no room between us. I tighten my embrace around her, and she runs one of her hands through my hair. Her lips stop an inch from mine. She asks, "How should it have been?"

I don't hesitate. "You. Me. No one else."

A tiny laugh escapes her lips. She strokes my cock and states, "Gianni Marino and no one else. There's an unrealistic statement. What would all of your whores done?"

I cringe inside. I've made my own bed, but it sucks to hear her speak of my past. I know I hurt her. I used to justify it by saying I never cheated on her, but in some ways, maybe that would have been easier for her if I had. Anytime I slept with someone, I made it clear Cara and I were over before I touched them.

Well, after high school. That was just a sick game, and all the kids in our school understood it, including Cara. But once we got out of high school and I stopped that shit, Cara and I got serious. I promised her the world over and over again. Then everything between us would get more intense.

Something about how she could read my mind and loved me even though I'm flawed and twisted scared the shit out of me. Perhaps, if I had cheated, she could have moved past me. There's no way to be sure, but no matter how much she wanted to reject me over the last few years, I still felt it between us.

If only I hadn't run like a coward.

I put more pressure on her ass and caress her collarbone. She shudders, which makes my erection twitch. I declare, "There won't be any more breakups or anyone else ever again. I promise you."

She tilts her head and strokes the hair above my ear. She replies, "No. There won't. If I find out about any women, I'll cut off your balls while you sleep. Do you understand?"

"Do you realize you've threatened my balls two times in a matter of hours?" I tease, trying to lighten the mood.

"Have I?" she innocently questions.

"I have better ideas of what you can do with my balls, Tesora."

Her lips graze mine then she whispers in my ear, "You know what I remember?"

"What?"

She flicks her tongue on my lobe, and I about lose all control. I'm ready to flip her on her back and show her what her husband can do for her, but I fight the urge. She taunts, "I remember how much my tongue loved your cock. Do you?"

I grin. "Why don't you be a good girl and refresh my memory."

She laughs again and kisses my neck. "Do you want me to do that thing with my hand when I take all of you in my mouth?"

I groan. My blood rushes through my veins, going straight to my brain. I tug her hair, so her face is in front of mine. "I'd rather you do it while I eat your pussy."

The corner of her lips curves up. She slides her hand over my cheek. Her other one strokes my cock faster. She murmurs, "Or, I could have you cut off my pants and sit on you. Remember the time you did that?"

Pre-cum drips out of my dick. She swirls her thumb around it. I groan again, then declare, "I can get my knife out."

"Tsk, tsk," she states in a teasing tone. "Then I won't have any pants to wear into wherever we're going."

"You can wear my coat."

MAGGIE COLE

"Yeah?"

I take her question as permission and grab my pocket knife. In a few seconds, I slice the sides of her pants, then pull them off her. Then I split the front of her shirt.

Her chest rises and falls faster. The goldish-black bra hugs her breast in perfection, displaying a peek of her nipples. The matching thong has a small triangle covering her pussy.

"You look hotter than I imagined," I state, taking her in one more time, then firmly palming her head and kissing her.

She moves her panties to the side and slides on me, sheathing me in her wet heat.

"Fuuuuck," I growl. It's been too long since I've had her. The memories of what it felt like to be inside her, with my body wrapped around hers, weren't anything compared to reality.

She digs her nails into my skull, circles her hips on my cock, and kisses me back.

Everything is finally as it should be.

Her.

Me.

Together.

Joined for life.

I slide my hand over the back of her neck. I lower my head and bite her neck while squeezing it.

Her body fully submits to me. Her walls spasm on my shaft, and her whimpers fill the air.

"Good girl," I praise, then bite the same spot on her neck again, this time slightly harder.

"Oh God!" she cries out, riding me faster.

"Jesus, you feel good," I mutter against her lips, then swirl my tongue in her mouth. Adrenaline fills my veins, growing hotter every second. I resist the urge to come inside her. One thing I won't do is make this about me. I'm making her come several times before that happens.

Her body begins to tremble. Sweat pops out on her skin, and I'm in goddam heaven. It's something I know well and missed feeling.

I grab her hip and slow her down. "Say please, and I'll let you come," I order, wanting her to remember who's in charge and what I'm able to give her. It's not the first time I've withheld her orgasm. I used to spend hours making her beg, getting her off, then doing it all over again until she was a ragdoll, and I couldn't hold out any longer.

Right now, I just want to hear her plead with me for her high and remember the good times we had.

"Please," she whispers.

"Louder," I demand since I'm an asshole that gets off on listening to her beg.

"Please," she says louder, but her voice cracks, making me harder.

"You love me inside you?" I taunt, allowing her to move her hips slightly faster, but not how she wants.

She shuts her eyes. "Please."

"Open your eyes and answer me. Do you love me inside you?" I repeat.

She obeys, drilling her heady blues into mine. "Yes."

"Good girl." I kiss her, allow her to ride my cock how she wants, and do everything in my power not to release inside her.

Within seconds, her body's convulsing on mine. The sounds that fly out of her mouth are another thing I longed to hear again. I study her face, loving every change in her expression and the way her eyes roll.

She comes hard, riding my cock and torturing it with her intense spasms. When she's coming down, I squeeze her hip and keep her moving. I put my mouth on her ear. "God, I've missed you. So much." I suck on her lobe, then move her face in front of mine. "Ready for round two, Tesora?"

Her eyes turn to stone. "No."

Grinning, I arch an eyebrow. "No?"

"Stop."

"Stop?"

She shoves her hands against my chest. Her voice turns cold. She yells, "I said stop!"

I freeze. "What's wrong?"

She pushes my pecs again. "Stop! I know you know what that means."

I put my hands in the air. "What's wrong?"

She rolls off me and sits in the seat. Without looking at me, she holds out her hand. "Give me your coat."

"Cara, what the fuck is going on?" I bellow.

"I said to give me your coat," she declares.

Not understanding what's going on, I grab the coat from the seat across from us and hand it to her.

She puts it on and turns toward me.

"Want to tell me what just happened?" I question.

Her eyes dart over my face, down my body, then stay on my dick. "Zip your pants."

"Zip my pants?"

"You're starting to sound like a broken record," she comments.

I tilt her chin and force her to look at me. "Cara, what in God's name is going on right now?"

She pins her gaze on me, and I want to crawl into a hole. They're full of more hatred and anger than I've ever seen before. She takes a few moments to compose herself, then seethes, "I hope you enjoyed our trip down memory lane. That's all you're getting for the rest of your life from me."

"Is this a joke?" I blurt out.

She shakes her head. "Nope. Now you know how you make me feel. And I may have married you, but know this, Gianni Marino. You had your chances. All you did was throw them away. If you think a shotgun wedding on an airplane will make me ever trust or want you again, you're sadly mistaken."

My heart comes to a halt. I knew she didn't trust me, but she's always wanted me. I fire, "Seems like you didn't have any issues wanting me a few minutes ago."

A twisted smile forms on her face. I've not seen it before. I'm the one who's warped, not her. Yet everything about her expression tells me I've underestimated her in many ways. "It's easy to make someone pretend you want them, isn't it?"

I open my mouth then shut it. Is that what she thinks I've done?

She scoffs. "Yeah. That's what I thought. I hope you enjoyed it because that's all you're getting. And my threat still stands. If you touch another woman, I *will* cut your balls off. The last thing I'm going to be is a wife who turns the other eye."

6

Cara

GIANNI'S COAT IS ENORMOUS ON ME. I TUG IT TIGHTER AND SIT on the chair in the lobby, overlooking the lake. We seem to be in the middle of nowhere. Snow-covered mountains, or maybe they're just really big hills, surround the resort. The check-in area boasts a peaceful, zen atmosphere, complete with a fresh and invigorating eucalyptus scent, but it does nothing to calm my raging nerves.

My head no longer hurts, which leads me to believe the drugs wore off. The bellhop handed me a bottle of water when I walked inside, and I drink a mouthful. My resentment toward Gianni only grew the more he kept his hand on my thigh in the car. He would think he could marry me, and every issue we have would disappear as if his sins didn't take place.

Well, I'm not falling for his lies this time. The revolving scenario of him making me fall back in love with him, using me, then moving on is ending now. I'll be damned if I'll become his doormat again.

As I sat in the car, all I kept thinking was that Gianni thinks with his cock. Well, hopefully now, he realizes what he's done to me all these years.

The beautiful, serene landscape is the polar opposite of our toxic relationship and current situation. Flashbacks of him stating his vows mock me.

What the hell did I do?

He planned this.

What Gianni wants, Gianni gets.

He's not having me ever again.

He comes behind me. I don't see him, but I can smell his luxury scent. I close my eyes, wishing my loins didn't burn whenever I inhaled the woody spice scent. His voice is semi-harsh which tells me he's pissed off about the little lesson I gave him in the car. That gives me a bit of gratification. He informs me, "Cara, the room's ready."

I rise and ignore him. He doesn't put his hand on my back or touch me, which feels odd. As much as I need to stay away from anything physical with him, we've always fit together. Wherever we went, I felt protected and powerful. Gianni made it clear I was his when he led me through a sea of people or just through a door and onto the street. This new version of us, where I'm next to him, but he's not touching me, feels uncomfortable.

It's better this way, I try to convince myself. I step into the elevator and continue not to focus on him, praying there are two beds in the suite so I don't have to lay next to him all night.

He hits the button for the top floor. The doors shut, and his signature scent flares in my nostrils. Tense silence is so thick it could suffocate me. The elevator stops on our floor, but Gianni presses the closed-door button as soon as they start to open.

I snap my head toward him. "What are you doing?"

His eyes turn to dark slits. "That wasn't cool what you did in the car, Cara."

I put my hand on my hip and huff. "Don't lecture me after all you've done."

"I apologized dozens of times. Or have you not heard a word I've said since you got back to New York. Hell, *before* you returned to New York!" he roars.

"It's not been dozens of times. It's been hundreds. Did you forget about the last twenty-some years?" I fire back.

He scrubs his face, shaking his head. "What do I need to do so you get past this?"

"Nothing. There's nothing you can do."

"I don't believe that."

Hot blood burns in my veins. I jab him in the chest. "Yeah, you would think you can roll back into my life, and I'd be stupid enough to forget the past. Well, guess what, Gianni? I'm not the same dumb woman I was all those years."

He grabs my hand, closing his fingers around it. He lowers his voice. "I know you aren't stupid. You've never been a dumb woman. I was an idiot, and I promise you, I won't ever be again."

Tears hit me fast. I blink hard, willing not to show him any emotion regarding him, but they slip down my cheeks. "How many times have you said that same statement to me? Your word means nothing to me. *Nothing!*"

Pain leaps into his expression. Then his face hardens. He grasps my hand tighter and holds my chin with his other hand. "I'll prove you wrong, my Tesora."

I scoff, and tears run over his fingers. "I've heard that before as well. And I'm not your Tesora!"

More agony flickers in his dark orbs. He moves closer, and I step back until I'm against the wall. His body presses into mine. He firmly demands, "Listen to me. This isn't like the past. I married you, for God's sake. You know that's not something anyone in my family does on a whim."

My insides quiver and dive like I'm on a big hill of a roller-coaster ride. "You had me marry you when I was still drugged. You had everything planned, didn't you?"

He pauses, probably counting numbers in his head. He admitted to me once that's what he does to calm himself. After his admission, I could always tell when he was doing it. About ten seconds pass before he replies, "You don't understand what the Abruzzos are capable of, even after being in their auction, do you?"

Fear annihilates me. Flashbacks of waking up wherever I was and the cold water blasting my body torpedo me. I'm not ignorant. Anyone who would kidnap and auction women off is someone who would do things I can't even fathom. I was super close to being a sex slave, yet I haven't even had time to process all of it. My lips shake, but I manage to admit, "No. And I don't think I want to know."

Gianni inhales a deep breath, sliding his hand over my cheek. "I won't lie to you. The sick part of me loves the fact you're at my mercy. No one on Earth will protect you as I will, and deep down, you know this is true."

His statement solidifies everything I already knew about him but also brings out a warped part of myself. I should hate him more for confessing his love of my reliance on him. I can't deny that the notion of him keeping watch over me makes me feel safe, nor can I ignore the flutter in my belly when he stated I'm at his mercy.

It makes me wonder if I'm as sick as Gianni.

"Admit it, Tesora. Being my wife is in your best interest," he insists, peering down at me.

I bite on my lip, fighting my urge to hate him and love him. I finally acknowledge the truth. "Yes. I know you'll protect me better than anyone else."

His eyes grow darker. "That's right. And what will I do to anyone who attempts to harm you?"

Goosebumps pop out all over my skin. I don't hesitate. "Kill them."

He slowly shakes his head. "You're only half correct, Tesora. I won't just kill them. I will torture them and make them beg for their lives as long as I can. Their life will only end when they can no longer feel my wrath."

My mouth turns dry. I've always known what Gianni is capable of, and not once have I run from him. Yet it's different hearing him speak the words out loud.

The elevator doors open again. He pecks me on the lips then steps back. I start to reach for him, then remember this doesn't change our past. I pull my arm back and wait for him to lead me out of the elevator. This time, his hand is on my back. I lean into him, unable to stop myself.

We get in front of our room. He waves the keycard over the lock and opens the door, then motions for me to go inside.

I walk inside the suite, noting the one King size bed. A few minutes ago, I wanted separate ones. Now, I'm confused again by my lack of ability to segregate my gratitude for him protecting me over my need to protect my heart. His commitment to go to extremes to keep me safe toys with my rationale that won't let me forget all the years of pain he's put me through.

His phone rings, pulling me out of my trance. I glance at him. He holds up his finger and answers it in Italian.

I spin away, stroll to the window, and once again take in the white-covered caps and frozen lake. Daylight is turning into nighttime darkness. If we weren't in the situation we're in, I would love everything about this place.

The suite is modern with light wood cabinetry. The entire wall is a window overlooking the breathtaking scenery. A two-person, white jacuzzi tub is in front of the window. Indie music plays through the surround sound, and soft lights outline the ceiling. Everything about it screams romantic getaway, which only makes me sad.

Gianni continues to speak in Italian. I unbuckle his coat since the room is warm. I don't take my eyes off the view in front of me until I hear a pop.

I spin and see him pouring a glass of champagne. He fills two flutes, then hands one to me. I take it. He clinks my glass, winks, then continues speaking in Italian while letting his eyes roam over my body.

Everything about his look makes me want to squirm. It's his signature leer, undoubtedly full of naughty, indecent thoughts. Heat grows in my cheeks as he fixates on my lower body.

The moment his intense gaze meets mine again, I realize I'm half-naked . I freeze until he nods at my champagne.

Happy to do something, I take a sip, fully aware he's still studying me. Then I sit in the armchair facing the window, cross my legs, and try to slow my racing heart.

Several moments pass. Gianni's tone gets rougher, but I'm used to it. He never speaks English when he has work conversations. I've never pried into his business. In some ways, I'm happy to pretend to stay ignorant, but the pieces of his conversations usually give me a good idea about what's going on.

I take another sip of champagne. He hands me a white, luxurious robe then barks out something that could be an order.

I put my flute on the table, rise, then take off his coat. My back is toward him, yet I feel him watching me. I quickly slide the robe on. He takes his jacket and hangs it up. I return to my seated position, noting how quickly the darkness is rolling in.

Several more moments pass. I'm halfway done with my champagne when he sets a plate of chocolate-covered strawberries on the table and refills my glass.

My heart stammers. This is the Gianni I know and love. The one who makes sure to take care of me no matter what else is happening. He can dote on me while multitasking like a boss. Not once have I ever felt as if his attention wasn't on me even a little.

When I don't pick up the strawberry, he does. He holds it to my lips, rattles something else off, and moves the phone away from his mouth. "Eat, Tesora."

I don't argue, suddenly hungry and wondering how long it's been since I ate last. I take a bite of the hard chocolate shell, and the juice of the strawberry rolls over my lip and down my chin. Before I can wipe it, Gianni puts his phone to his ear and swipes at it. Then he shoves his finger in his mouth, sucking on it and staring at me while unbuttoning his shirt.

My butterflies spread their wings. It's another problem I have. Everything about Gianni Marino reeks of sexual tension. His ripped pecs and torso, sculpted from years of boxing workouts, peek out under his blue shirt. I lift my eyes and realize he's caught me gawking at him.

His lips twitch before he barks more Italian. He takes my hand and pulls me off the chair. He leads me to a closet and opens the door. He holds the phone away from his ear again and says, "Get dressed for dinner."

I peer in the closet, gaping at the handful of designer dresses, shoes, shirts, and pants.

"Cara," he calls out.

I spin, and he taps the dresser, then opens the drawer. The inside is full of delicate bras and panties. I glance over at Gianni. His back is to me, and he's tugging on his hair. I wonder again how long he knew Uberto's plans. It's hard to know for sure. Gianni knows how to make things happen, so a closet and drawer full of clothes isn't out of his abilities to make happen.

Still...

He spins, arches his eyebrows, then covers the phone. "Is something missing?"

I slowly shake my head. "No."

He points to the clothes. "Then get dressed. You need to eat." He returns to his call, belting out orders.

I glance at the drawer. Delicate lace and intricate patterns weave through each piece. Most of them are solid black. Some have other colors in it, like the gold and black set I'm wearing right now.

I pick an all black set, then study the clothes in the closet. I choose another black piece. It's an off-the-shoulder, long sleeve mini dress. I take everything into the bathroom and freeze.

My hair products are in the shower. My brand of makeup sits on the counter. Part of me likes how Gianni paid attention over the years to know what I use, but the question still lingers. *Did he know about my kidnapping and the auction longer than he claims?*

There are no definitive answers. I would never have questioned Gianni's role in this situation years ago. But the last few months, he was unhinged. He had me followed. I think he even had a tracker on my phone. I confronted him numerous times. He never admitted or denied it, but that's the thing about Gianni— he rarely shows his cards. He has a poker face the best player in Vegas wouldn't stand a chance against.

Gianni kept showing up places Uberto and I went. He threatened Uberto several times to stay away from me. It's what made Uberto crack—not that I'm giving him an out for kidnapping and auctioning me off.

I shudder, still trying to comprehend what happened.

Thank God Gianni did save me.

But did he know longer? Was this just a trick of his to get me to marry him?

I pull out the vanity seat and sit. If only it were a few years ago, and he hadn't left me with that note in Italy. I wouldn't be questioning any of this.

I sigh, then pick up the hairbrush. I twist my hair into a messy bun, securing it with the bobby pin someone left for me. I don't usually wear a ton of makeup, so it doesn't take me long to finish. I slide out of my current undergarments, then put on the fresh ones and the dress.

When I leave the bathroom, I go back to the closet and select a pair of red stilettos. They're strappy, but there is a zipper on the back, allowing me to easily put them on. I spin into Gianni.

His scent annihilates me, making me once again crave everything about him. He wraps his strong arms around me, placing one hand on my ass and the other on my back. In a quick move, he tugs me even closer to him. "You look great, Tesora."

My heart beats faster. I tilt my head up, taking in everything I've always loved about him. His hard body. The way his lips curve when he's being his cocky self. And the streaks of gray running through his hair along with the tiny wrinkles around his eyes. They only recently popped out, but it makes him even sexier.

His dark eyes twinkle. Mischief fills his expression, making flutters erupt in my gut. "Are you ready?"

I manage to mutter, "Yeah."

In the same way he always takes charge, he sweeps me through the room, into the hallway, and through the building.

"Where are we going?" I question when we're in the lobby.

"The restaurant."

"Oh."

He adds, "There's not a lot around here."

"No?" I ask.

He eyes me over, then his lips twitch. "Nope. Designed to keep people relaxed at the spa and fucking in their rooms."

I laugh. I can't help it. All Gianni thinks about is sex. I've never complained in the past. He's an animal that's never satiated. And I wasn't unhappy to be his prey.

Maybe that's why he always got bored with me. I never was enough. He'll always need multiple people to keep him interested.

The thought stops me laughing right as we approach the restaurant. The hostess glances at me, then Gianni. Her smile widens, and she bats her eyes. "You must be Mr. Marino?"

He nods. "That's correct."

She tosses her hair over her shoulder. "Have you traveled a long way?"

Here we go, I think, shifting on my feet. It's not new for women to flirt with Gianni even when I'm standing in front of them.

"Far enough. Is our table ready?" Gianni questions in his annoyed voice. Most people would recognize it as rude, but it never bothered me.

The hostess seems oblivious to it. She leans across the stand and lowers her voice. "Is that an East Coast accent I detect?"

Gianni tugs me close to his side. "Yes. So our table? Is it available?"

She steps to the side of the wooden platform and tilts her head. She puts her hand on his arm. "What part of the East Coast?"

Every jealous bone in my body flares. Gianni may not be encouraging her, but it's another reminder of our issues. I snap, "Is the manager around?"

She furrows her brows and pins her gaze on me as if noticing for the first time I'm here. "Yes. Of course. Why do you need a manager?"

I seethe, "To tell them how their employee won't keep her hands or eyes off my husband."

7

Gianni

IT'S GETTING HARDER TO STOP MY GRIN FROM FORMING. FOR THE last five minutes, Cara's been talking to the manager. The hostess is trying to claim innocence, but my Tesora isn't letting her off the hook.

I'm used to women flirting with me. The last thing I needed was this one giving Cara another reminder about why she doesn't trust me. At first, I was annoyed by the hostess's attention, but now I'm kind of grateful for it. Someone should pop some popcorn for me. Every time I hear Cara enunciate *my husband* and give the hostess more daggers, pride sweeps through me. Plus, my dick's so hard right now that if I weren't aware that it's been days since she's eaten, I wouldn't even make it back to the room with her. I'd find a dark corner to remind her of the bene-fits *her husband* offers.

"Ma'am, I can assure you this was a mistake that won't happen again," the manager tries to reason with my wife for the tenth time.

My wife.

Elation flows through me. I finally got what I wanted. The ironic part is the Abruzzo's gave me my window of opportunity.

I'm still taking all of them out.

My Tesora glares at the hostess again and seethes, "Don't you even think about touching my husband again. Do you understand?"

The manager steps between the two women and holds his hands in the air. "I promise you I will take care of this. Can I show you to your table?"

Cara doesn't move. I put my hand on her back, deciding the shows over. "That would be great." I tilt her chin, then slide my tongue in her mouth so fast she gasps. I kiss her until her knees buckle, making it loud and clear for anyone to see, including her, that she's mine.

I retreat an inch from her lips. Her blue flames meet mine, and the thought of not going to dinner enters my mind again. I push it away and slide my thumb on her cheek. I speak what's on my mind, but it's not about food, and Cara knows it. "I'm hungry. Are you hungry?"

Her lips twitch, and the temptation to find a dark corner over-powers me. Then her stomach growls. I chuckle. "Time to eat." I tug her into me, then turn to the manager, avoiding the hostess at all costs. "Can you show us to our table?"

Relief fills his expression. He nods. "Right this way."

I guide Cara through the restaurant, puffing out my chest and standing a bit taller, happy she's my wife and thinking indecent thoughts.

Fuck I want to eat her pussy.

How long has it been?

Too damn long.

I hope they put us in a booth. In a booth, I can at least slide my hands under her dress and edge her until she's begging me and hardly able to keep quiet.

Jesus, I've missed everything we had together.

I kick myself again for being a stupid moron years ago. The night before I left her in Italy, we fucked until early morning. After she fell asleep, I did too, for a short time. I dreamed we were getting married. She was in the same dress she wore on the plane earlier today.

It freaked me out. The ironic part is I was the happiest I'd ever been in my dream. I felt a similar high that day in the street when we saw the dress in the window. I knew it was perfect for her. Since then, that wedding gown haunted me. Dreams of her wearing it plagued me all these years. I'd be elated in my dream then wake up to reality. It was a hard crash every time. I never felt so alone, and nothing I did to win her back worked.

We get to the table, and I groan inside. It's a small two-top, with seats across from one another. I glance around the room until I spot an empty booth. It's a half-circle meant for at least six people. A gold metal reserved plague is on it. I point to it. "I want that table, please."

The manager glances at it. He meets my gaze. "That's reserved for a party of six."

I squeeze Cara's hip and count to ten while scowling. One thing I'm used to is getting my way. And when I want something, I don't back down. In a calm but intimidating voice, I assert, "Your hostess upset my wife. It's our honeymoon. I want that table."

He clenches his jaw, but red creeps into his face.

I arch my eyebrows, making it clear if he doesn't give me my way, he's going to have another battle on his hands.

He forces a smile. "Right this way." He turns to lead us to the booth.

Satisfaction races through me. It happens whenever I get what I want. "Thank you," I say when we get to the table. I motion for Cara to sit, and I slide next to her.

"Carl will be with you shortly," the manager states, then motions to a server who is carrying an empty tray to join us. When she gets to the table, he stacks the extra water, wine glasses, and silverware on her tray.

"Please bring bread right away. My wife hasn't eaten in a while," I order.

The manager nods.

They leave, and I slide my arm around Cara. I lean into her ear. "I like this new possessive side of you."

She turns to face me. "I wasn't just throwing words out, Gianni. If I'm your wife, I'm not going to turn a blind eye to your whores."

My stomach dives. "I don't have any whores, and I'm not going to."

Her expression hardens as if she doesn't believe me.

I sternly declare, "I don't cheat, Cara."

She closes her eyes, moves her head away, and blows out a big breath.

I cup her chin and force her to look at me. I repeat, "Not once have I cheated on you."

Anger flares in her cheeks. "You spent high school letting whoever wanted to do anything with you do it."

I count to twenty-five, kicking myself again for all the dumbass things I did in my life. I try to rationalize it to Cara, stating, "We were in high school. Not once did we discuss exclusivity. And you know I stopped that shit when I graduated."

She pins her eyebrows together. "Did you?"

I open my mouth to assure her I did, but a server sets down a loaf of bread. He proclaims, "I'm Carl, and I'll be your server this evening. Have you had a chance to look at the wine menu?"

I tear my gaze off Cara. He's got long blond hair pulled into a slick ponytail. His teeth are slightly crooked, whiteheads need popping in several places, and he's pencil skinny. He appears barely sixteen. I address him. "No. Hold on." I glance at the menu in front of me and order, "A bottle of the Giacomo Conterno Monfortino, please."

His eyes light up, which doesn't surprise me. It's a $1200 bottle that will cost even more tonight because of the hefty restaurant markup on it. He beams, "Our finest Barolo."

I resist a snide remark about how he probably doesn't know the first thing about wine. I doubt he's ever even experienced a cheap glass, much less one that bursts into flavors the minute it hits your tongue.

In my family, we drink Barolo every night at dinner. Anytime I dated a woman who didn't appreciate it, I got rid of them fast. I never had that problem with Cara. She's always loved a good bottle as much as I have.

"Are you ready to hear the specials?" Carl asks.

"No. Wine first," I dryly state.

Surprise fills his face. "O-Okay. I'll bring it right away." He hurries away.

I pick up a piece of bread. It's fluffy and warm. The scent of herbs flares in my nostrils. I realize I haven't eaten since I found out Uberto kidnapped Cara. I stab my fork in the butter, sniff it, then shake my head. I turn to my Tesora. "I'll be back."

"Where are you going?"

"This has honey in it. I'll be back."

"I can wait."

I peck her on the lips. "No." I grab the pot of butter, rise, and scour the room.

The manager sees me. His eyes widen, and he rushes toward me. "Mr. Marino. Do you need something?"

I hold out the dish. "This has honey in it."

"Yes. People come all over for it. They love it," he states as if there aren't any issues.

It angers me. I count to five, then seethe, "My wife is allergic to honey. If she put that in her mouth, she could die. Don't you ask guests if they have allergies?"

His face turns beet red. "Umm..." He swallows hard. "I'm sorry. Let me get you plain butter."

"Does the bread have honey in it?"

Uncertainty fills his expression.

"Check," I bark.

"Yes, sir."

I count to three. "Thank you." I sit back down and take a sip of my water to cool off.

"You didn't have to bite his head off," Cara declares.

I sniff hard and turn to her. "You could have died."

"They didn't know."

"They didn't ask."

She shrugs. "You always check anyways."

I turn into her further. "That's right. And what if I put that in my mouth before I found out?"

A line forms on her forehead. "Did you suddenly develop an allergy I'm not aware of?"

I confidently boast, "No. But if I put that in my mouth, I wouldn't be able to do all the things I'm going to do to you later tonight."

"Fat chance." She picks up her water glass and takes a long sip.

Not willing to admit defeat, I slide my hand between her bare thighs and murmur in her ear. "Let's make a wager."

She slowly looks at me. "Don't you have enough money?"

"Which is now all yours," I add.

She rolls her eyes. "I don't want your money. I never have."

I slide my arm around her. It's another reason I love her. Tons of women wanted me because of my wealth. Cara never cared. And she's made her own way in life even though her parents are well off. I reply, "Yes. I know. And this wager isn't for money."

She tilts her head. "Then what's it for?"

An uncontrollable grin forms on my lips. The thought alone makes my cock strain against my zipper. I choose my words carefully, knowing I only have one chance to get her to agree to what I want. I drag my eyes over her face, down her body, and then back up. Knowing she isn't one to back down from a challenge, I play my cards. "Nevermind. You can't handle it."

She scoffs. "Doubt it."

"Oh, I know you can't," I claim just as Carl appears with the butter, another breadbasket, and Barolo.

He opens the bottle, pours a small amount in a glass, then hands it to me.

I slide it toward Cara, trusting she's more than capable of accepting or denying it.

She circles the glass on the table, swirling the wine. Then she picks it up and holds it near her nose. She takes a deep inhale, waits a moment, then takes a sip. I watch her with pride as she nods to the waiter.

"Splendid. Are you ready to hear the specials?" he asks while pouring a full glass.

"No," I reply.

Surprised, he glances at me.

"I'm going to enjoy a glass of wine with my wife first," I inform him.

"Very well. The bread doesn't have honey in it, but I thought you might want this basket. It just came out of the oven," he states.

Pleased he took the initiative, I smile. "Good man. Thank you."

He raises his chin. "You're welcome. I'll be back to check on you later."

I nod, and he leaves. I hold up my glass and turn toward my Tesora. "To you. My wife. May you soon realize I'm not the dumbass I used to be in my younger years."

She rolls her eyes, but a smile plays on her lips. "That's a big wish, Mr. Marino."

"One I'll prove to you."

"How? You can't take back the past," she states.

I set my glass down and sigh. I lower my voice. "No. We can only move forward. Do you want to move forward?" As soon as the question comes out, my stomach pitches.

She bites on her lip, redirecting her blue orbs to her wine glass. She circles it on the table again.

"Tesora—"

"Of course, I wish we could move forward," she declares, snapping her face toward me. "But it's not that simple, Gianni."

Her admission that she wishes we could move forward gives me a spark of hope. I admit, "I understand."

Rage floods her expression. "Do you? See, I don't think you have any clue what it's been like for me."

The pit in my stomach grows. "I know I hurt you. What I did was stupid. I promise you that I'll never do anything like that again."

Her eyes fill with tears. She blinks hard, sarcastically laughs, then takes a sip of wine while avoiding me.

I scoot closer. "I kick myself every minute of the day for leaving you that letter."

She fires, "Why did you leave me that pathetic, cowardly note?"

My pulse beats so hard in my neck I'm sure she can see it. She's right. I was a coward. I confess, "There aren't many things in my life I'm ashamed I did. How I've treated you is one of them."

"Why? Tell me why you left me."

I count to thirty, trying to string my words into something coherent that doesn't sound weak. Nothing does. I finally admit, "I had a dream before I left. You were in the wedding dress, and it was our wedding day. I'd never felt so happy."

More tears emerge. Her lips shake. She enunciates, "You left me because you were happy?"

I place my palm on her cheek. "I know it doesn't make sense. And you're right. I was a coward. It freaked me out, and I made a horrible choice."

She glares so intensely it feels as if she's throwing fire at me. "It freaked you out? You broke my heart because feeling happy freaked you out?"

A fist could be squeezing my heart right now. I hate how I've hurt her. "If I could take it all back, I would. You don't know how many times I wished I could redo that day."

She shakes her head in tiny movements, which only makes my chest tighten further.

I wipe the tears off her hot cheeks. "I've always been a bit screwed up. A lot of shit I've done doesn't make sense. You're the only person who knows me—who really gets me."

"Which is exactly why I'll never be able to trust you. I gave you the benefit of the doubt too many times. Yet you always throw it in my face at the first chance you get, don't you?"

I count to fifteen. I'm not angry with her. I'm pissed at myself. If I were her, I wouldn't trust me either. I slide my hand so my fingers are on her hair. My heart thumps into my chest cavity. "I vow to you, I'll never let you go again."

"I don't believe you," she mutters, then shrugs out of my hold. She refocuses on her wine and takes another sip.

I debate whether to keep pushing this conversation or not. Her stomach growls, and I hold off. I pick up a piece of bread, butter it, then hold it near her mouth. "Eat, Tesora."

"I'm not hungry." She takes another drink of her wine.

I keep my voice calm but warn, "You haven't eaten in days. Don't fight me on this."

She scowls. "Or what, Gianni? What are you going to do if I don't eat?"

I count to twenty-three, feeling the burn of her laser glare, before I sternly order, "Eat, so I don't make a scene."

She caves, releasing a breath, then grabs the bread from my hand. She takes a bite.

Satisfied she's eating, I butter another piece and put it on her bread dish.

She glances at it, swallows then pushes the plate toward me. "Don't make me eat on my own."

My hunger pains intensify. I pick up the bread and take a large bite, groaning. "This is so good!" I shove more into my mouth.

Her lips twitch. She takes another bite, and we eat in silence until the bread is gone. She tilts her head. "So what's the wager?"

My ego wakes back up. I nonchalantly shrug. "Don't worry about it. It's not really fair to you."

Her eyes narrow. "Oh? Why is that?"

I put my arm around her shoulders and lean closer. "You'll lose."

She scoffs. "Always so sure of yourself."

I feign innocence. "Hey, I just don't want my wife pissed at me or thinking I tricked her."

She smirks. "But you trick everyone. Why would I be any exception?"

I can't argue it. And I am trying to trick her, so I don't want to lie and say otherwise. I move my mouth inches from hers. "You seem confident you wouldn't lose."

She glances at my lips then pins her steel gaze on mine. "I've been around you a long time. Whatever you have up your sleeve, I can outsmart you."

I chuckle. "Is that so?"

"Yep."

"So I've worn off on you?"

She shrugs. "Maybe."

I slide my hand between her thighs. She shifts in her seat, squeezing her legs tighter. I ask, "Are you sure you want to place a wager?"

"What are we betting?"

"If I win, I get you all night. *However* I want you." My pulse races at the thought.

Pink crawls into her face. She asks, "And when you lose?"

I sniff hard, staring at her cleavage, then lips. I meet her blue gaze. "What do you want, my Tesora?"

"I—" She halts, pinning her eyebrows together.

"What is it?"

She takes a deep breath, then raises her chin. "I want a wild card for playing. If I win, I get two."

"A wild card?"

She nods. "Yes. A wild card. I get to tell you what I want whenever I decide what that is. And you have to agree to do it no matter what."

My gut flips. I don't like taking any risk of not knowing what the future holds. But I want to get back to who we used to be together. And that involves making sure my wife remembers every pleasure-filled thing I can do to her.

She bats her eyes. "What's wrong? Scared I'll win, and you'll owe me two things?"

I sit back, take a large mouthful of wine, then swallow. "Okay, Tesora. You get a wild card just for playing." I palm her head and hold it in front of my face. "But I get to create all the rules. And you can't use the wild card tonight."

She opens her mouth, then shuts it.

"Are you in or out?" I eye her lips again.

Her voice cracks. "In."

I move my finger until it touches her panties, stroking her slit. She sharply inhales. I murmur in her ear. "Here's the only rule. Don't come at the dinner table."

Cara

HEAT FIRES IN EVERY CELL OF MY BODY. GIANNI'S ARM IS AROUND my waist. His hand is discreetly cupping my pussy. His dextrous middle finger is inside me, and his thumb hasn't stopped rolling on my clit since dinner came out.

He's not even using his predominant hand.

I'm screwed.

I'm doing everything I can to not give in to the high my body wants. Yet I know this is a game I probably won't win.

What Gianni wants, Gianni gets.

How did I agree to this?

It's not the sexual acts in the restaurant that I'm opposed to. Hell, Gianni's done all sorts of indecent things to me in public before. It's part of the thrill of being with him. But this bet...

Gianni's voice keeps echoing in my mind. *If I win, I get you all night. However I want you.*

Since I got back into the states, he's pursued me relentlessly. I tried for months to stay away from him. The thought of sex with him never made me feel ill or disgusted like you usually feel with an ex. It's always been the opposite. The temptation was always there to give in. Sex with Gianni isn't something you can forget or not crave. It's like lighting up a firework and not wanting to watch it explode.

It's impossible.

The problem's all about Gianni's dominance. It's part of who he is in life, but it's an entirely different experience to have him exude power over you in the bedroom. He requires complete submission. He's never stated it until today on the plane, but it's always been there. And now, who knows what he has up his sleeve.

Allowing him to have me however he wants isn't going to allow me to keep a level playing field with him, which is the only way I'm surviving in this marriage. Yet I'm unsure how to get out of this bet—not that I can think straight.

With his free hand, he feeds me a bite of chocolate cake, just like he fed me the rest of my dinner. Others around us probably think we're having a typical romantic dinner. Every bite of lobster thermidor, or whatever the potato casserole was next to it, involved him whispering dirty words in my ear. Throughout the meal, he played my pussy like a professional violinist.

Several times, he studied me. I looked him straight in the eye and please actually flew out of my mouth. It was barely audible, but he heard it. I heard it. It was everything his ego needed.

He hasn't let me come. Instead, he's edged me the entire dinner, keeping me on the verge of exploding. Right now, I'm not in a full-blown sweat, but my skin's glistening.

The chocolate cake hits my tongue, and he increases his pressure. I whimper. It's my favorite dessert which is why Gianni ordered it. I chew it and swallow. He brings his lips to mine. "You have chocolate on your mouth."

I lick my lips, and he slides his tongue against mine, kissing me like he's trying to wipe all the remaining chocolate out of my mouth.

His thumb circles faster, and I suddenly can't hold back anymore. Gianni tastes more delicious than usual, and that's a hard thing to do.

I wrap my arms around his shoulders, digging my fingers into his neck. Tiny sounds lodge in my throat.

He doesn't stop this time. Adrenaline hits me so hard, the room disappears around me. It's only Gianni's delicious tongue dancing in my mouth, his hot breath merging with mine, and his kisses muffling my whimpers.

It feels like my high goes on forever. Gianni kisses me through it, working my body as he always does, making his presence and power over me known.

It's part of why I could never get over him. Sex with others was always second best. He's the stallion in the field. Once you have him, there's no way the quarter horse will satiate you.

When my quivering isn't as violent, he mumbles between kisses, "I get you all night. *However,* I want you."

"I still have my wild card," I blurt out.

His lips curl. "Yes, you do. You can use it anytime after tonight." He resumes owning my mouth.

The butterflies in my stomach furiously spread their wings. The tug of war between wanting what only Gianni gives me and not letting him back into my heart reignites. I retreat and manage to warn, "Don't think this goes any further than tonight."

Hurt flashes in his eyes. Guilt shoots through me, but I remind myself I can't allow him to hurt me again. And he will. I know his game too well.

He recovers quickly. "Don't write me off so fast."

I scoff. "Fast? It's been over twenty years of coming to my conclusion."

He pulls back, sniffs hard, then reaches into his pocket. He tosses cash on the table and slides out of the booth, holding his hand out. His dark eyes, the ones that feel like they're undressing me, get more intense. "Let's go."

Knowing there's no way to get out of this and trying to convince myself it's just sex and doesn't mean anything, I take his hand. My butterflies flutter faster.

He guides me quickly through the hotel, ignoring the waiter as Carl calls out. "Have a good night, Mr. and Mrs. Marino."

I blink several times. It's the first time anyone has called me Mrs. Marino besides Gianni.

It doesn't mean anything.

I'm finally his.

No, I'm not.

This is not the time to forget everything you've learned over the last few years.

He palms my ass, and I sink into him, unable not to. It hits me that I'm already submitting to him. Part of me loves how it feels right. The other side wants to strangle and slap myself until I return to hating him.

We get to the room. He unlocks the door, then leads me through the suite. There's a white box with a matching bow on the desk. He picks it up, then turns into me. His eyes are dark flames, burning hotter. It's how he looks when he's unhinged, losing his mind. I've only seen him look that way a handful of times when he's had some issue going on with work. Something about that expression and the fact it has to do with me makes me more nervous.

He holds the box in front of me. "Open it, Tesora."

I hesitate, then ask, "What is it?"

He shakes the box. "Open it."

I take a deep breath, then pull the bow and open the lid. My heart pounds harder, and butterflies go crazy again.

A diamond platinum choker with a matching leash is inside. I gape at it, then slowly look up at Gianni, feeling more confused than ever.

Why am I excited about this?

This is wrong. He cannot exert this much power over me.

Oh, God. What would it feel like to submit to him in this?

Gianni reaches around me and unzips my dress. It falls to the floor. My pulse races and my chest rises and falls faster. He removes the collar, unhooks the leash then steps behind me.

I lock eyes with him in the mirror.

His hand slides around my throat, squeezing gently. My lips shake, and I reach behind me to grasp his thighs.

His hot breath hits my ear. "The leash is only for me. But you'll wear this choker for the entire world to see who you belong to."

I stay quiet, unsure what to say or even my true feelings on this matter.

He unclasps it and holds it in front of my eyes. "Read it."

I drag my gaze off him and study the metal. My insides quiver, and I dig my nails deeper into his thighs. Tears form, but I blink hard, not sure why this makes me emotional and not wanting to show Gianni any weakness.

"Read it," he orders again.

My voice shakes. I open my mouth, but nothing comes out. He presses closer to me, and his erection hits my spine. I clear my throat and whisper, "Tesora, Forever means forever. Love always, Your Husband, Gianni." I swallow hard, meeting his gaze.

He nods. "You, Tesora, are my heart. There is no escaping me. I'm not perfect, but I won't be a foolish man any longer. You are mine. Forever. The sooner you get it into your head and forgive me, the quicker we can move forward and be happy again."

Happy again. How many times have I been happy "again" with Gianni?

But it always feels so good when we're happy. Like we can conquer the world together.

All I ever wanted to do was move forward with Gianni. I almost tell him I forgive him, but I don't. I can't. I've done it too many times, and each one had worse repercussions than the last. And this will be the cruelest joke of all if I fall for his promises again.

Several moments pass before he moves the collar and secures it around my neck. His gaze never leaves mine. The platinum choker fits perfectly, not too tight nor too loose. It's the most stunning piece of jewelry I've ever worn. Surprisingly, the weight of it makes me feel as if it's a security blanket.

He traces my skin around the metal, and I shudder. His lips twitch, and he grabs the small ring at the front. He leans forward and turns my chin, so I'm facing him. "You will submit to me. Not just tonight—all nights. I'm your husband. There's no other person in the world who knows what you need. And I'll give it to you. Every ounce of what you need will come from me. In return, you *will* give me what I need." He clasps the leash on the collar.

I blurt out a confession that makes me cringe as soon as it leaves my lips, "I'm not forgiving you. I-I want to. God, I want to. But I don't know how." My cheeks grow hot. I attempt to turn away from him, but he holds me firmly in place.

His expression rotates between hard and soft as if he's struggling to know how to respond. He slowly inhales a big breath of air, then states, "You will find a way. Your submission will help you."

"I'm only submitting tonight. I know how I'm using my wild card," I declare, before I can even analyze the thought that just popped up in my head.

He freezes. "There's no wild card tonight, Cara. I made that clear."

"Tomorrow then. I'll use it tomorrow. It's going to be no more submission," I warn, too far into this now to not move forward, but my gut dives as I say it.

A tornado of so many emotions swirls in his eyes, including agony. For a brief moment, I wish I could take it back, but I can't let Gianni have the upper hand in whatever this relationship now represents. He'll destroy whatever's left of me.

He stands taller and spins me into him. In a confident voice, he states, "No, Tesora. After tonight, you won't be able to deny yourself all I offer. You already crave me—you've always craved me. But now, I see it in your eyes."

"See what?" I question.

His lips curl, and all the evil I know he's capable of bursts into his expression. He stares at me for several minutes, then turns me back, so I'm facing the mirror. He moves my head inches from the glass and holds my chin. "Look at your eyes. You see how bright they are?"

He's right. My blue orbs seem to have taken on a brilliant, sparkling hue. Yet, I don't answer, afraid of what my agreement would mean.

He flicks his tongue behind my ear, then murmurs in it, "That light showed up the minute you saw the collar. It intensified when I put it around your neck. I own you, Tesora. Your body. Your mind. Your heart. There will be no wild card revoking your submission. You won't be able to resist."

I tear my gaze off my reflection and pin it on him. I attempt to sound strong, but it comes out weak and we both know it. "I'll prove you wrong."

He scoffs. "No, you won't. Deep down, you know I'm right. I may be an asshole, but I know you better than you know yourself. Now wash the makeup off your face. You're too beautiful for anything to cover you up." He slides his hand over my stomach, then drops it and cups my pussy. "And when I come inside you, Tesora, you're going to already be burning for me to do it again." He steps back and releases me.

I spin and fold my arms over my chest.

He walks to the bar and pours a Scotch. He goes to the window and drinks half of it. Without looking at me, he challenges, "Are you going to back out of our agreement? I've never known you to not keep your word."

I straighten my shoulders and push my chin in the air. One thing I never do is go back on a deal. "No. Of course not."

"Then your job is to fully submit. Wash your face. When you finish, strip and kneel in front of the window looking toward the glass."

My butterflies take off, and I hate myself once again. Without saying a word, I go into the bathroom, wash my face, then remove the bobby pins from my messy bun. My dark hair falls in long waves. I clutch the corner of the counter and close my eyes, taking deep breaths.

I just need to get through this night.

Tomorrow, I'll use the wild card. I'll make it clear Gianni is never again allowed to order me to submit.

My chest tightens at the thought. I silently reprimand myself for wanting any part of this. I give myself a pep talk, then strip.

When I'm naked, wearing only the collar, I wrap the leash around my fist, staring at myself in the mirror.

I trace the large diamonds, falling more in love with it every second it's on me. Whoever designed it made sure it could be worn anywhere and look like a high end choker. The ring attached to the leash is small and integrated into the design. If you don't know a leash can attach to it, you'd be oblivious to it. I scold myself again for not only loving the brilliance of it, but how it looks and feels on my neck.

Several more minutes pass, and I finally work up the courage to walk out of the bathroom. Candles flicker against the wall. Soft music plays. Gianni sits on the armchair, facing the window. There's a blanket on the floor in front of him. He doesn't acknowledge me, only points to it.

Flutters intensify. I take a deep breath and walk to the window. I glance at him, and he doesn't have to say anything. I know he's daring me to go against my word.

I step in front of him, then lower myself to the ground, facing the window. I bow my head, trying to regulate my heartbeat.

He does nothing for a while. Every minute that passes is torture. I do everything I can not to move, keeping my focus on the tan blanket.

Anticipation crackles around me, intensifying until my chest is rising and falling faster and a drop of my arousal drips down my thigh.

He finally moves. I hear him but stay still, not daring to move. He drags his finger over my ass crack, then up my spine.

My pussy pulses, and I shudder. A whimper flies out of my mouth.

He traces the collar. Tingles race everywhere. He sniffs hard, sits back in the chair, then commands, "Turn and look at me."

I stay on my knees and face him.

He widens his legs, then curls his finger.

I move closer until I'm between his legs. He grabs the leash, winds it around his fist until there is no tension left, then he tugs it so my face is hovering over his pants-covered cock. He demands, "How much have you missed my body, Cara? And no more lies. I want the truth. How much?"

Something about being under his control doesn't allow me to keep my walls up. I confess, "Too much to put into words."

He tilts my chin. A tornado spins in his dark orbs like a storm out of control. I gasp, knowing he's in a spot I've not seen him before and aware our situation has done this to him.

"And me? You've missed me, admit it."

"You know I have," I say without being able to stop myself.

He licks his lips and orders, "Stand."

My knees shake, but I obey. He slides forward in the chair, tugs me until my lower body is near his face, and takes a dozen long inhales.

Something about it makes me lock my hands in his hair. My entire body quivers and pulses. He continues to breathe me in, and I whisper, "Oh, God."

He tilts his head up. A cocky smile plays on his lips. While staring at me, he shoves his tongue through my slit.

"Gianni!" I cry out, my knees buckling.

His palms grab my ass cheeks before I fall. They push me closer to his face, and his tongue becomes a snake flicking through me. Fast, then slow, then fast again.

Tremors fill my body. He slides off the chair and repositions me, so my knees are on the seat.

"Grab the back and ride my face and show me how much you've missed me," he barks.

The power he always has over me bursts into flames. I fall forward, obeying his orders, submitting to everything Gianni.

In an instant, all the years of pain get tossed aside and pushed out of my thoughts. The cravings we've both had gets acted upon. I ride his face as his grunts fill the air. He slaps my ass, and I come so hard I arch in the air.

He continues eating me out, and it's everything I remember from before and nothing like I recall. He's relentless, showing me no mercy, making me come so many times my head is spinning. Sweat rolls off me, and I dig my nails deep into the back of the chair.

Unlike dinner, I'm not trying to muffle my sounds. I'm on a constant cycle of pleading with him to keep me full of adrenaline and begging him to back off. My voice goes hoarse from my cries. My pussy's so sensitive every move he makes is pure pleasure. He keeps me so high I can't seem to get past the dizziness.

When he finally comes up for air, he re-wraps the leash around his fist, slides that hand in my hair, and tugs my head back. He breathes hard, wipes his face on his bicep, then leans down and bites my neck.

"Oh, God! Yes!" I scream, not realizing how much I missed all the ways he knows how to dominate my body.

He holds his head over mine, pinning his cold gaze on my eyes. "You still want to use your wildcard how you intended to use it?"

I open my mouth to say no, then snap it shut. I swallow hard, not sure how to answer.

But instead of getting upset, he smiles. The longer I don't answer, the wider his grin becomes. He finally states, "Glad you want to play, Tesora." He gives me a chaste kiss on the lips, then releases my head. He brings his lips to my ears and murmurs, "Game fucking on, gorgeous. I'll fuck you until you can't walk if you want to play hardball. But at some point, you will give me a no. Now give your pussy a break, sit in the chair like the good wife you are, and suck my dick like only you know how."

9

Gianni

A SOFT GLOW ILLUMINATES THE ROOM. AS THE CANDLES FLICKER, the diamonds on Cara's collar sparkle. My Tesora is on her knees, naked except for the jewels which mark her as mine. Her lush mouth is working my cock better than I ever fantasized about all these years.

My chest heaves. I fist her hair harder, controlling the speed. She takes every part of my shaft as if her throat was meant for only me. It's not an easy thing to do. Most women can't get more than half of me in their mouths. But my Tesora learned in high school how to open the back of her throat.

Pride mixes with my arousal. She's more beautiful than ever, and time hasn't ruined us. We still fit together. It's not something you find with just anyone. The last few years without her made it clear how bad I had screwed up.

She twists her hand over my shaft as her mouth travels up my erection. I grit my teeth and bellow, "Fuuuck."

Her blue eyes dart up, pinning into mine. She doesn't miss a beat and continues working my cock.

Between the sensations she's giving me and the naughty look in her eyes, I'm about to erupt. But I can't have that, so I tug her hair until her mouth is off me.

She smirks, which only makes my heart soar. I love everything about her, but this sassy expression is one I've especially missed. It's challenging and laced with dirty desires. It makes me believe we've gotten past our issues, and we can have the life we should have had all these years.

Breathing hard, I take my thumb, wipe the saliva off her lips, and then push it into her mouth. She sucks, dragging her tongue over it at the same time.

Christ, I love this woman.

I let her have her fun for a moment before I remove my thumb. I rise and tug on the leash, so her head tilts toward the ceiling. Something about standing over her while she's kneeling, bare except for the collar, riles me further. Her soft, dark hair hits the middle of her back. Her blue eyes widen, and her hard nipples rise toward the ceiling. She's at my mercy in an entirely new way. And the devil within me is celebrating. Whatever I want her to do, I know she will. However I want to take her, I know I can. Everything about those two things invigorates every dominating urge existing within me.

And now she's my possession. No one else will touch her.

For life.

I count to fifty while studying her. Part of me wonders if this is a dream. Will I wake up, and she'll be gone? The other side is a hurricane spinning with all the thoughts about how I want to have her.

Pink fills her cheeks. The longer her blues are fixed on me, the more shallow her breaths become. She's a vision of perfection I don't want to ever forget, so I reach for my phone on the table, quickly snapping a photo of her.

She pins her eyebrows together. "What—"

"Shh," I order, cutting her off before she can object. It's not the first time I've taken shots of her naked or in compromising positions. I take a few more pictures then toss my phone on the chair. I slide my hands under her armpits and tug her onto her feet. When she's stable, I put my hand on her cheek. "I want to pull those images up whenever I get the urge. And I'm your husband. Even before I was, you know I'd never show them to anyone. Hell, I'd kill any man who ever tried to look at them. You already know this. Or have you forgotten?"

Her face relaxes, then she shakes her head. "No. I haven't forgotten."

My lips curl in satisfaction. I lean down and kiss her. When her tongue hits mine, I retreat, commanding, "Go lie on the bed. Face toward the ceiling."

She bites her lip then takes a step.

I reach for her arm. She turns, her eyebrows arched.

"Crawl. Get your ass in the air."

Her pink cheeks turn into red flames. More light bursts in her orbs. I've never told her to crawl before, nor did I have the desire to see it. Now, I'm obsessed with making her do it.

"Move your hair over one shoulder so I can see your collar. Then show your husband how sexy you can crawl," I restate, releasing my hold on her.

She takes a deep breath then lowers her body to the floor. As ordered, she moves her locks over one shoulder. The diamonds seem to sparkle brighter. She lifts her ass high in the air. I fist my cock, rubbing my pre-cum over the tip.

She slowly crawls, pushing her ass toward the ceiling as if she's done it a thousand times.

It's like studying fine art. I praise her, "Absolute perfection, Mrs. Marino."

She pauses near the bed, turns her head, and slowly licks her lips.

"Fucking naughty tease," I compliment, stroking myself slower, so I don't ruin the rest of our night. "Now, get on the bed."

Her lips twitch. She climbs on the mattress, keeping her ass toward me, then flips. She widens her knees then slides her hands up and down her thighs. She bats her eyes. "What are you planning on doing to me, Mr. Marino?"

My adrenaline rushes at me fast. I release my cock, counting to thirty. I go to the closet, find a black tie, and make my way toward the bed.

Time to make her really submit.

I've blindfolded Cara before. It's not something I do a lot because I want to see her eyes when she's begging me and coming. But there's no better way to make her fully trust me.

Awareness flashes in her blues. A mix of desire and nerves fill them. I don't have to tell her my thoughts. She knows me well.

"That's right, Tesora. I'm in total control. Not you. And I'll do whatever I want with you," I boast. I slide the tie around her head, then secure it. I lean into her ear and flick my tongue on her lobe, breathing in the scent of her skin.

She shudders, gasping in tiny breaths.

I drag my finger around her collar. I move her hands above her head, then position them on the headboard, commenting, "So many ways to make you submit with this. Hold the bars."

She grips the metal rods. Her lower body squirms which makes me grin.

I wrap the leash through the headboard, then secure her wrists so there's no tension and her head is slightly tilted back. I dip down and run my tongue through her wet heat.

"Oh God!" she cries out.

I kiss her clit then shove her thighs to her chest. She swallows hard, and her breath hitches. It's always been one of our favorite positions. I have complete dominance over her this way, and she loves it.

I cage my body over hers, glide my arms under her shoulders, and shimmy my cock over her clit.

"Oh, Jesus."

"You missed it, Tesora, didn't you?" I mumble, then possessively palm her head.

"Yes," she breathes.

I keep moving my shaft over her, then rotate between sucking and biting her neck.

Her legs quiver, and her back arches into me. She whimpers, "Oh, God!"

I move faster, bite harder, then push hard, rubbing my thumb over her bite mark until she comes completely unglued, screaming my name.

When her orgasm subsides, I sink into her, pressing my lips to hers. We both groan into the other's mouth. Her walls clench my shaft, spasming so hard I start counting so I don't release in her.

It's a sweet relief. It's been too long since I've had sex, but it was boring even before I went on my hiatus. No one excited me. No one felt right. She was all I thought about and wanted. Yet, I couldn't have her.

Now, I can have her whenever I want.

After tonight, she'll return to showing me how much she wants me like she used to.

Slowly, I take several thrusts, wanting to savor every moment, devouring her mouth like I haven't been kissing her all night.

She mumbles, "Gianni, wait!"

My stomach flips. I pause and ask, "What's wrong?"

"How-how long has it been since Uberto kidnapped me?"

My gut dives. Anger seers through me about what that bastard did to her. Hearing her speak his name while I'm inside her turns my jealousy into flare guns. I seethe, "Three days. Why?"

Her forehead creases with lines. She frets, "I haven't taken my pills. They're at my house."

"Yeah? What's your point?" I state, then resume flicking my tongue in her mouth and thrust my cock deeper in her.

She gets out between kisses, "I won't have any protection. I could get pregnant."

I move my mouth to her neck, sucking on her bite mark.

She shakes harder, sharply exhaling.

"Yeah. We aren't getting any younger. I'm ready to knock you up," I reply, then bite her again.

"Fuck! Gianni!" she calls out.

I circle my hips in her, pull out to rub her clit some more, then slide back into her.

She whimpers the entire time. I thrust with increased speed.

"We can't," she whispers.

"We can't do what?" I ask, sliding my tongue under the collar. I glide my hand up her arm and wrap my fingers over her bound wrists.

"Have a baby."

I grunt. "Why not? You always wanted kids. I'm ready to give you as many as you want." I pound into her like a jackhammer that just got a new battery.

"We're...oh...oh God!" she screams, and convulsions ripple through her frame.

I don't let up, kissing her, biting her, sucking her skin until I know it's bruised.

She doesn't stop shaking or moaning.

I assert in her ear, "You're *my* wife. I *will* give you everything. And you *will* bear my children."

I remove her blindfold then squeeze her neck close to the point I shouldn't go past. It's halfway cutting off her air supply.

Her blue flames widen. Her chest heaves harder.

"Tell me you understand, my Tesora," I order, adding a little more pressure, then burying my cock deeper than before.

Her body writhes under mine. Her eyes roll, and her walls collapse harder on my shaft.

"Fuuuck!" I growl, coming in her like a freight train sliding off the tracks. Adrenaline makes my vision turn blurry. I kiss her, keeping my hold on her neck, shoving my tongue as far into her mouth as possible.

Her back arches into mine, and incoherent noises fill the room. I ride my high as long as I can, trembling into her spasms.

When it's over, our sweat and breath continues to merge. I stroke her hair and kiss her again, rubbing my thumb over her bite mark and applying pressure.

She whimpers in my mouth. It's a pleasant pain. I know all about bruising from my years of boxing. And it's not the first time I've done this same thing to her. She admitted to me once that she doesn't just enjoy it.

She craves it.

The emotional, mental, and physical part of the last few days has my senses overstimulated. I usually take longer to get hard again, but within minutes my erection is back.

"Gianni, we shouldn't have kids," she mumbles in my mouth.

I freeze and lock eyes with her. "Why wouldn't we have kids?"

Her lips shake. She hesitates. "Are you going to untie me?"

"No. Answer my question," I order. My heart beats so hard it feels like it'll tear through my chest.

She swallows hard. "When you get bored with me, it won't be fair to our kids."

Sharp pains cut through my torso. I firmly state, "You haven't been listening to me very well, have you?"

She shuts her eyes, exhales sharply, then keeps them shut.

"What do I need to do so we can get past this?" I ask for what feels like the billionth time.

She opens her blues. "Release me."

My sadistic, controlling, have-to-prove-a-point-self answers, "No. We made a deal. You're to submit to me all night. I get you *however* I want you. Or did you forget?"

Her eyes harden.

I challenge, knowing she won't go back on her word, "Are you not going to comply?"

She stays quiet.

"Let go of the bars," I demand.

She obeys. I move her hands away from the headboard, then flip her over so she's on her knees. I order, "Grab them again."

She tightens her fingers around the metal. I wrapped my body around her, weaving my hand in her hair, then grasping all her locks. I apply pressure to her bruises again, savoring her tiny moans. Slowly, I shimmy my erection between her legs, making sure I hit her clit. She arches her back into me, quivering. I lean into her ear. "You think I'm going to get bored with you when all I did was obsess about how to get you back for years?"

She stays quiet, lifting her hips to shimmy on my cock faster.

"Answer me," I bark.

Her voice cracks. "You always do."

I turn her head so she can't avoid me. "The past is not our future. Do you understand?"

Her eyes glisten. She shuts her eyelids.

"Look at me!"

She opens her eyes, and tears fall.

I ask again, "Tell me what I have to do!"

A river of tears drip onto the pillow. Agony crumples her face. "There's nothing you can do. It'll always be this way."

I might as well have just gotten stabbed. "That can't be true."

"It is," she chokes out.

"No, it's not," I insist, but for the first time ever, I'm scared she might be right. Did I hurt her so badly there's no way to earn her trust again?

She squeezes her eyes shut. "Please. Stop talking about this tonight. Just fuck me."

It's a rare occasion where I don't know what to do. Right now is one of them. I start counting in my head. When I get to twenty, my heart hurts more because only she knows what goes on in my head.

She whispers, "Twenty-one. Twenty-two."

I freeze.

Her raspy voice begs, "Please. Stop counting and fuck me. I don't want to think anymore."

"Let go of the headboard," I demand.

She does it, and I roll over on my back, bringing her with me. I unhook her leash and unwrap it from her wrists. I tug the covers over her back and tighten my arms around her.

Her fingers lace through my hair. Our mouths meet in an inferno of too many emotions—her pain, my newfound fear, the burning desire we both have to fix this problem between us, yet we can't seem to figure it out.

I palm her head, declaring, "I love you. I always have. Not once have I ever thought about loving anyone else."

She sniffles and doesn't respond. Her warm tongue slides against mine and she sinks on my cock.

I tug her head back, pinning my gaze on hers. In desperation, I order, "Tell me you believe me."

She doesn't speak, but the truth is all over her expression.

And I finally fully comprehend how much damage I've truly done. My Tesora doesn't just not trust me. She doesn't even trust the love I've always had for her.

There's not been any way to stop the flood of regret I've felt in the last few years, but now, it's like a dam breaks. It seizes my chest until I feel like I've taken a punch to the gut and can't breathe.

"Stop talking about the past tonight. Go back to being you. Please," she whispers.

So I do the only thing I can. I respect her wishes and don't say another word about it. Morning is breaking through the darkness when we finally stop fucking. She falls asleep in my arms, and everything I've tried to push out of my mind over the last several hours annihilates me.

Exhaustion sets in, yet I don't sleep. I can't. I always believed I could regain her trust. Now, I don't know how I ever will. The confidence I had that we would be fine is long gone. All that remains are ashes, and once something's burned so badly it hits that stage, there's no way to restore it.

I tighten my arms around her, kissing her hair. I make a new vow. No matter what, I'll prove to her we can have the future she's always wanted.

Then I try to shut up the voice in my head, but it's impossible. All I keep thinking is, does she even still want it with me?

10

Cara

THE TENDERNESS THROUGHOUT MY BODY IS A REMINDER OF ALL the hours of sex we had. Gianni's fading Tom Ford scent lingers in my nostrils. His warm arms cocoon my upper body, his leg is pretzeled around my thigh, and my cheek is on his chest. My heart races faster. I keep my eyes shut, resisting the urge to open them and replaying every moment of last night.

What did I do?

I lost a bet.

I should have backed out.

I should have known not to let Gianni lure me into any deal.

More flashbacks occur, and I squeeze my eyes tighter.

I wish I could say it was horrible, or we no longer had any chemistry. It would help my predicament if he somehow had become a lousy lover, or it was even an inkling not quite as good as it was in the past. Instead, to torture me further, I'd have to rate it as the best sex we ever had.

At least on my end.

Who knows where Gianni rates it. For all I know, he could be comparing me to all the other women he's slept with over his lifetime.

He drags his fingers up my spine, making me shiver and curl closer into him. They approach my neck, and I hold my breath as he traces the collar.

It's like lighting a match and tossing it in hot cinders. Heat floods my veins. Sweat sits on the verge of popping out on my skin. My insides throb, and my breaths become shorter.

His lips hit my forehead, right next to my hairline. He mumbles so quietly, I wonder if I imagine it. "I'll find a way for you to believe in us again, my Tesora. I promise."

I fight the tears swelling so fast I can't control them. They leak through my closed lids.

He slips his fingers through the collar, so he's fisting it, and there's no more tension. Then he takes his thumb and slides it back and forth over where he bit me last night.

A delicious sensation aches. The mix of pleasure with border-line pain is addictive. All I want is more. My emotions lodge in my throat. I whimper, then reprimand myself when I open my eyes and tilt my head up.

His other hand fists my hair, holding me in front of his face. His lips and tongue devour my mouth, lighting up every last ounce of desire I have for him until it's impossible not to return his level of affection.

He keeps his dark flames pinned on mine. When his hands grab my ass and pull me on top of him, I don't fight it. My knees sink into the mattress next to his legs. He slides his palms to my thighs and tugs them to his hips.

The voice in my head telling me it's no longer last night and to stop this before it goes any further gets shut down. My insatiable desire for him wins, and my body submits to him again. I lock my hands behind his head and sink on him, gasping as his erection slides against my already overstimulated walls.

He keeps one palm on my ass cheek, then returns to fisting my hair. His mouth moves across my chin, over my lobe, then to the spot on my neck he always marks as his. The moment his teeth dig into my swollen skin, sweet chaos shoots right to my pussy.

"Oh, God," I whisper, arching into him.

He flicks his tongue on the spot, sucks it, then bites harder.

"Gianni," I cry out, my voice cracking, yet everything about it sends me into a deeper tunnel of beautiful oblivion.

In a quick move, he flips me over, bringing my thighs to my chest. Then his hands are on my cheeks, his thumbs stroking my chin, and his dominant gaze locked into mine. His cock slides over my clit, working me like a dog in heat until an earthquake rips through me, destroying my ability to control anything in my body.

Like everything Gianni does, he sees my high through, taunting it, extending it, repeating it until I'm sweating and writhing underneath him.

Then he reenters me. His thrusts are slow at first, plunging deeper and deeper until I'm so full of him I can't tell where either one of us starts or ends.

The room disappears. I can't see straight. He uses every part of his body, controlling me with perfection as if he knows how every move, every touch, every thrust into my body makes me feel.

I never stop quivering, at times shaking so hard, I can barely breathe. When he detonates inside me, he growls into my ear, "My wife."

His words create a vicious pool of panic swirling with happiness in my aftermath. I don't release him, keeping my arms tight around his shoulders, attempting to take deeper breaths but unable to.

I'm unsure how much time passes until he tries to pull his head away from my neck, but I only squeeze tighter. The ceiling seems to move closer. No matter how hard I try, air continues to feel stale in my lungs.

He breaks from my grip, sitting up and pulling me with him. His palms hold my cheeks. His voice is full of worry, but everything is dizzy. "Tesora, what's going on?"

I can't answer. I've never experienced anything like this before. Pain shoots through my heart.

Why can't I breathe?

I'm Mrs. Gianni Marino.

What have I done?

"Breathe, Cara," he belts out.

His harsh tone snaps me back to reality. His dark eyes come into focus. He models how I should take in oxygen, and I begin to follow his lead.

A long time passes before the pain leaves my chest, and the air feels fresh. When everything is normal again, Gianni strokes my cheek, questioning, "Has that happened before?"

I admit, "No."

Something passes in his expression. I'm unsure what it is, but the urge to get away from him overpowers me. I slip out of his grasp and jump off the bed. "I'm going to shower."

His expression intensifies. "Cara—"

"I don't want to talk about this," I blurt out and high-tail it to the bathroom. I shut and lock the door, not trusting for one moment he won't barge through the door and step into the shower with me.

I turn the water on, then put my hands on the counter and study my reflection in the mirror, wondering what just happened. When steam begins to fog up the glass, I step under the warm water.

All the brands of shower supplies I use are in front of me. Once again, I wonder how much of my current predicament Gianni planned.

What Gianni wants, Gianni gets.

But now he's mine, so maybe it doesn't matter how this happened?

He's only mine until he gets bored, then what happens?

Visions of my future don't ease any of my worries. Gianni isn't a man who believes in divorce. He would fight me and do what-ever he could to stop me from leaving him. I'd become the woman I never want to be, the one who has to stay in a marriage knowing her husband is cheating on her but can't leave—especially if we had a baby.

Oh, God! What am I doing?

I cannot have his baby.

I'm already forty-one. It's now or never.

Not with him. He'll probably cheat on me while I'm pregnant.

He's never technically cheated.

So he says. What's the truth?

He doesn't lie.

He's lied all those times I took him back, saying he wants to be with me forever.

He'd be an amazing father.

It doesn't matter! We shouldn't be bringing a baby into our mess.

I press my hand on the tile to steady myself. Tears mix with the water, and my body begins to heave in sobs until my knees buckle. I crouch on the floor, hugging my thighs to my chest, wishing I was clueless to my fate.

How many times can a man crush your soul? I could barely thread my heart back into one piece after the last time he left me. This new us feeds into all the fantasies I always had of our life together—husband, wife, babies.

All his promises to never hurt me again, I want to believe. It makes it all that much more dangerous. I won't survive when he breaks me again. At least last time, I didn't have to see him with other women. If he cheats on me, I'll have to see it.

Well, I never saw it except the first night I went to the sex club in New York.

Visions of it make me cry harder. Uberto texted me to meet him at the sex club. I had been to it before with Gianni. It was years ago before I moved to Italy.

That first night back at the club, I convinced Bridget to go with me. She picked me up, and when her driver pulled up to the building, my heart almost stopped.

Somehow, I managed to go through the motions, faking excitement and telling myself again that I needed to get over Gianni. It had been years since I saw him. Up to that point, I avoided going anywhere I might have run into him. Once inside, I led Bridget to the suite Uberto was in and convinced myself to focus all my attention on him.

Halfway through the night, I needed to go to the restroom. Bridget was nowhere in sight. Uberto told me his friend Michelotto and she left.

Sure enough, I saw Gianni and his brothers in their suite. I froze outside the glass, watching some woman who was way younger than me sit on Gianni's lap while unbuttoning his shirt. All the pain I thought I got past over the previous years attacked me like I was in the ring and getting punched while pinned to the ground. I didn't stay to see the rest. I practically ran to the bathroom, spending a good fifteen minutes trying to pull myself together.

Later that night, I learned Michelotto tried to assault Bridget. Dante and Gianni stepped in. I wasn't in the room but learned about it when Gianni returned to the club to find Michellotto. Uberto had learned about the scuffle. He was in a deep conversation with some other men. I stepped out of the room and went to a dark corner. I called Bridget, but she didn't answer. Before I turned away from the wall, goosebumps broke out on my skin. I could smell and feel Gianni without even looking at him.

Since then, he's done everything possible to be a thorn in my side. And now, there's no way to keep my heart protected. He'll destroy me again, only this time, I won't be able to escape him.

The hot water continues to fall all around me. I find the strength to rise, then shampoo and condition my hair. I wash my face, shave, then take the loofa and pour my body wash on it. By the time I finish washing, I have a better hold on my emotions.

I step out of the shower and dry off, wincing at my bloodshot eyes. I glance at the counter and shake my head. Gianni even remembered my brand of eyedrops.

I spend another hour on my hair, put on a thin layer of makeup, and finally feel human again.

I can handle this, I tell myself and nod in the mirror.

The white spa robe is on the hook behind the door. I put it on, tightening the belt around me as if it'll protect me from Gianni's wandering hands.

When I step outside the bathroom, he's on the phone, deep in conversation. He stares out the window, speaks in Italian, and wears nothing.

I shouldn't fixate on him, but it's impossible not to. He's the epitome of a perfect male physique. Olive skin stretches across his sculpted flesh. Every inch of his backside, whether it's his shoulders, his waist that v's flawlessly, or his hard ass and thighs, makes my mouth water.

As if he can sense me, he spins.

My face heats. I state, "I'm out of the bathroom," then pull open the dresser drawer.

He barks more orders in Italian, then says, "Ciao."

I concentrate on what undergarments to wear, wishing I had some granny panties and a sports bra to hide in, but there's no such luck. Gianni made sure everything was sexy and risque, pretty much guaranteeing that he'll be imagining me in them all day.

He's so predictable.

I used to love it when he bought me lingerie.

Look where that got me.

He stands behind me and circles his arm around my waist, tugging me against his hard frame. The delicious aroma of his skin flares in my nostrils, creating warmth in my blood. His mouth hits my ear, and I stiffen. "I made us a reservation for breakfast then booked us a full afternoon at the spa. Nothing but the best for my wife."

My flutters take off. I tilt my head up, questioning, "You're going, too?" In the past, Gianni wouldn't spend a lot of time at the spa when I had treatments because he said anything more than a massage required too much of his time. He had a business to run, claiming going off the grid for an entire afternoon was impossible.

"Sure am."

I turn into him. "What about your business?"

He tugs me closer, smiling. "Don't worry about it. Everything is fine."

"In the past, you said—"

"I know what I said. From now on, I'm making different decisions."

My pulse races. "Like what?"

He tucks a lock of my hair behind my ear then palms my cheek. "Enjoying life with my wife."

Tense silence erupts all around us. I swallow hard, fighting the urge to believe him and order him to stop making promises I know he won't keep. It's not that his business ventures ever bothered me. If anything, I respect him because of how he conducts himself and the dedication he has to making things happen. But more time with him where we're focused on each other isn't something I would have ever passed over. Now, I shouldn't want it because it'll just confuse things further.

"I'm serious, Tesora," he firmly declares.

I still don't reply. More than anything, I want to believe him and that this can be our new reality forever.

If only I could forget our history.

He inhales slowly. "I'll prove it to you. I need to get ready, so we aren't late for our reservations. Your suit is in your new bag."

"Suit?"

"For the pools."

"Oh," I reply, still unsure what this resort offers.

He releases me and gives me a chaste kiss.

I watch him go into the bathroom, then glance around the room. There's a rose gold, oversized Gucci bag. I open it and pull out a matching, skimpy bikini.

"Have to hand it to him. He's got excellent taste," I mutter. I toss it back inside, select a matching panty and bra. The material is black with a bit of red running through it. I slide them on, then go to the closet and assess the outfits.

Everything looks way too fancy for a day at the spa. I open the bathroom door and call out, "By any chance did you get me anything casual?"

He sticks his head out of the shower and grins. "Yep. Yoga pants, tops, and a wrap are in the second drawer."

I can't help but smile. "Thanks."

He winks, then returns to his shower.

If only he weren't so charmingly sexy.

I tear my eyes off the water dripping over his hard body, find the clothes, and get dressed. Within a few minutes, Gianni steps out of the bathroom with a towel wrapped around his waist.

I fold my arms and lean against the back of the chair. "What are you wearing?"

"Joggers."

"Of course you are! Let me guess. They're gray?" I tease, but I've always loved him in them, and he knows it. When the trend for gray sweatpants started, I bought him several pairs.

He chuckles. "Did you ever state your adoration for me in anything but gray?"

I claim. "Gray was a fashion statement, that's all."

"Sure." He opens another drawer and pulls out the joggers and a form-fitting white T-shirt. He puts them on and slides his feet into his shoes, asking, "Are you hungry? I'm starving."

Hunger gnaws at my gut. "Yeah."

He slings his arm around my waist, guides me out the door, and down the hallway. His phone rings, and he pulls it out of his pocket. "I have to take this, Tesora."

"Okay."

He answers in Italian and starts speaking fast. We step in front of the elevator, and he barks out a phrase I don't understand. The doors open, and we get into the lift. His voice becomes more aggressive. He barks out more orders, then hangs up. His face turns red with anger. He pounds the button then focuses on the ceiling.

I count in my head, waiting for him to speak. The elevator stops, and the doors open.

He whisks me out and toward the restaurant.

"Everything okay?" I cautiously ask.

He sniffs hard, avoiding me. His voice turns so cold I get chills. "Will be."

I stop, forcing him to look at me.

He meets my gaze, questioning, "What's wrong?"

"Is this about Uberto?"

His face hardens. Twenty seconds pass before he orders, "Don't ever mention him again."

I tilt my head. "What do you want me to call him?"

Fire blazes in Gianni's eyes. "Nothing. Don't even think about him again."

My chest tightens. "After what he did to me, don't you think I deserve to know what you're going to do to him?"

Gianni shakes his head. "No. His fate is in my hands, and that's all you need to know."

Everything about his statement angers me. It feels like the precursor to our future life and what I know will eventually happen. "So I just get to be ignorant and stay in the dark?"

"You aren't in the dark."

"What would you call it?" I hurl.

"Trusting that your husband isn't going to let anyone who hurts you—scratch that. I won't let anyone who even attempts to think about harming you, continue to breathe on this Earth," he replies.

I should drop this, but it's not about Gianni taking care of Uberto. I know he'll take care of him. I'm fighting him about not being a naive wife who lets her husband get away with infidelity and I'm using this to hide behind. And I hate how insecure he's made me when I'm usually nothing but confident. "So I'm supposed to blindly trust you?"

Gianni's eyes turn to slits. He firmly states, "Don't you dare compare our other issues to me taking care of someone who's harmed you."

My face heats with embarrassment that he knows what the underlying issue is. I sarcastically laugh.

"What's so funny, Cara?"

"How convenient for you. What's next?"

He shifts on his feet and scrubs his face. "Stop making this into something it's not."

I scoff, not breaking from his intense scowl. "Glad to see nothing has changed," I state, spin, and approach the hostess stand.

When the hostess turns, I cringe inside. It's the same woman as last night.

Her eyes widen. She clears her throat. "Mrs—"

"Do whatever you want with him. I don't care. Can I have that table?" I point.

She opens her mouth, shuts it, then looks in the direction I'm pointing. "Sure."

"Great. Thanks." I stomp past her and plop down on the seat, fighting myself not to look back. I might have told her to do what she wants with him, but the last thing I want to see is either of them flirting.

And I wish I could believe it would only be her.

11

Gianni

"Mr. Marino! It's so nice to see you this morning," the hostess from last night chirps.

I groan inside and scowl, pinning my eyes on hers to make it clear. "Not interested." I grab the menus from her hands, slide past her, and go to the table Cara chose. I place the menu in front of her and lean down until my lips hit her ear, warning, "The next time you want to have a temper tantrum in public, I'll make such a big scene you'll never do it again."

She tilts her head, glaring at me. "Don't threaten me."

"Stop insinuating I want anything to do with that woman," I seethe.

"Why? You're not bored with me yet?"

I slide my hand on her neck, brushing my thumb over her small bruise. She inhales sharply, making my dick twitch, but I'm

IMMORAL

already tired of having to reiterate that I've changed. I know I haven't earned her trust yet, but I'm not a patient man. The last few years, I suffered without her. Since she got back to New York, I've done everything I can think of to win her back. So our timelines may not be jiving, and I understand why she can't trust me, but I'm getting close to the end of my rope. I put my mouth an inch from hers, stating, "We've been over this. I'm not addressing it for the rest of my life. Decide if you want to live in the past or the future. I can assure you the future is a better scenario for both of us."

She throws me another defiant, dirty look.

All it does is make my lips curl. I release her and sit down in the chair next to her, instead of across the table. I pick up her menu and hand it to her, stating, "They have skillets here." I arrogantly smile. It's her favorite breakfast food. I looked at the menu online when I booked this place.

She takes the menu, and I pick up mine. I already know what I'm getting, but I count to one hundred in my head, pretending to read it, trying to calm down.

My phone call didn't help matters. Massimo informed me that Uberto is missing. All our guys are out hunting him, yet he seems to have vanished. It only angers me. He's not smart enough to disappear into thin air. Jacopo Abruzzo has to be involved in this, which makes my hatred for him and desire to destroy his family more potent.

"Good morning, Mr. and Mrs. Marino! I'm Kelsey and going to be your server this morning. Can I start you off with coffee?" an older woman with lots of wrinkles and gray hair beams, holding a coffee pot.

Relieved she's not someone Cara will think I want to bang, I smile and turn both our mugs over. "Yes, please."

Cara looks up and nods.

Kelsey's face lights up. "Well, aren't you beautiful!"

"Yes. She is," I agree, filling with pride.

A pink blush fills Cara's cheeks. "Thank you."

Kelsey fills our cups and states, "Our chef has a salmon eggs benedict that's to die for! Do you have any questions on the menu?"

I arch my eyebrows at my Tesora.

She shakes her head, stating, "No. I'll have the Mediterranean skillet, eggs over easy, please."

"Great choice. That comes with our signature toast. It's freshly baked and has no honey. I heard you had an allergy, dear?"

"Yes. I'll swell up like a blowfish," Cara informs.

"Well, we don't want that. I'll make sure the chef is informed. And what will you have, sir?" Kelsey questions, refocusing on me.

"Denver omelet, with a side of bacon, please."

"Another great choice. Can I get you orange juice?"

Cara and I both decline, and Kelsey leaves.

I take a sip of my drink, counting while the hot liquid travels to my stomach, studying the way my Tesora drinks her coffee. I've done it before, but something about it always mesmerizes me. Maybe it's the mark of my mouth on her neck that's part of my fascination. Watching her swallow and the bruise flex sends a rush of testosterone straight to my cock.

"Why are you staring at me?" She asks, arching her eyebrows.

I ignore her question. "Tell me, what's going on with your clientele?"

She smirks, "You don't already know since you stalked me?"

My lips curl. "Humor me. Plus, I only know outside details."

She's always had a thriving career. In her twenties, she learned everything about the modeling business and created an agency. Europe proved to be a good move for her. She's now known worldwide. From what my intel gathered, the major models in New York, L.A., Milan, and Paris are all signing with her. As she speaks, her eyes light up, but she stays humble, which isn't a new thing. She admits, "Last week, I found out they chose my agency for Fashion Week."

Adrenaline rushes through my veins. I put my hand over hers. Fashion Week has been on her bucket list since she started her agency. It's a huge accomplishment. "Tesora! That's amazing! Congratulations!"

"Thanks. I actually called your sister."

"Arianna? Why?"

"I have models flying in from all over Europe. I want to make sure they're taken care of and aren't leaving New York exhausted. My assistant said Arianna started an event company in Chicago but still has her hands in the fire in New York. I thought she could help me figure out more of a rest and relax type of scenario for my models."

More pride sweeps through me. It's going to cost her a pretty penny to do that, but making sure her models are taken care of has always been Cara's first priority. Still, I whistle. "How much is that going to set you back?"

She shrugs. "Doesn't matter. They perform better when they're rested and not stressed out. The photographs and video footage alone will get them more bookings. And a few of them are skyrocketing quickly, but they're newbies. They haven't done New York Fashion Week yet. It'll help alleviate their nerves. Plus, hopefully, they can all make some connections and reduce some of the cutthroat attitudes."

I grunt. My experience dating models leads me to believe that's a hard goal to accomplish. I haven't come across one who isn't insecure. Cutthroat is part of their language. It's a common reaction to trample anyone they think might get in their way.

It's actually the reason I always dumped them. Their lack of confidence in their skills always drove me nuts. Every time I got rid of one of them, I told myself no more models. Then I'd get tired of thinking about Cara and how I needed to find someone to get past her. I'd see another woman who caught my eye and start the process all over again. I add, "Good luck with that."

Confidence appears on Cara's face. She straightens her shoulders, takes another sip, then smiles. "It does happen, you know. Not every model is incapable of developing friendships with other models."

"But are they real relationships or only surface level until they feel threatened?" I ask.

She shrugs. "Depends on the model. Anyways, Arianna said she'd love to work with me on it."

More pride fills me. My sister has always loved fashion. I bet she was jumping out of her skin when Cara called her. I reply, "I'm sure she's counting down the days."

Cara nods, her eyes brightening further. "She practically squealed in excitement."

"You know how she loves your world."

"I was always surprised she didn't model, especially with your mother's genes."

My mamma had a thriving career before she met Papà. Once they got engaged, she retired from the industry. I shift in my seat and sniff hard, declaring, "There was no way either of my parents wanted her exposed to that life. Who knows what she would have gotten involved in."

Cara tilts her head, smirking, "Like you and your brothers would have let anything happen to her."

I pick up Cara's hand and kiss it. "Good point. I still don't want her plastered everywhere with men drooling all over her. Her social media accounts are bad enough."

Cara snickers. "She's done well growing those. I bet it's been huge for her business."

"Have you ever read the comments from all the losers?"

"How do you know they're losers?"

"Read the comments. I'm surprised Killian doesn't shut that down," I respond, tapping my fingers on the black ceramic mug.

Cara arches her eyebrows.

"What?" I ask.

Her voice turns sharp. "His account is just as bad. And should I point out that he would have no right?"

"Sure he does. He's her husband."

Her eyes turn to slits. "I can see you're existing in a cloud of false reality."

My chest tightens. I lean closer, preparing to battle. I've always known Cara's independent, but now that she's mine, it's time she realizes that I do have a say in her life and choices. I innocently question, "How's that?"

"Don't play dumb with me, Gianni."

Locking my eyes with hers, I brush my fingers up her arm until I get the bruise on her neck. I lightly press on it.

Cara holds her breath, but the combative look in her blues never falters.

I smile, stating, "Maybe we should clarify our roles."

She crosses her arms, angrily repeating, "Clarify our roles?"

"Mmhmm," I calmly mutter while sliding my fingers over her bruise with increased pressure.

She uncrosses and recrosses her legs, so I slip my hand under the table, sliding it between her thighs. She takes a deep breath, giving me a death stare.

I continue, "I'm your husband. You're my wife. If something is dangerous or inappropriate, it'll cease."

She huffs. "If you think you'll be telling me what to do—"

"If it's dangerous or inappropriate, I'll stop whatever it is, Cara. There won't be a warning, and you can remove all the *I am woman hear me roar* comments in your head. My wife won't be in any compromising positions."

Anger lights up her cheeks. She moves her head, so my fingers leave her neck. "I'm not your little Stepford wife. I will make my own decisions. You don't get a say in any of them. And I'll be damned if I let you destroy my career that I've sacrificed my life to build."

I reach for her chin and hold it firm, leaning closer. "I have no desire to ruin your business. I've never tried to stop you, and you know how proud of you I am. But if I say something isn't safe or you're not to do something, then you're going to listen."

"Jesus. You should listen to yourself. You sound like it's 1950," she fumes.

I count to ten, trying to reduce my irritation, so we don't end up in a fight all day. I firmly remind her, "I already saved you once. You didn't listen to me. We will *not* have any repeats."

She closes her eye for a moment. "That's different, and you know it."

"How?"

"I won't be in that situation ever again."

I nod. "That's right. I'll go to my grave, making sure you aren't. And this rule, it's not a choice, nor is it breakable. Let's get crystal clear on this topic."

"Rule?" she seethes.

Satisfaction and excitement explode in my gut. Having a bit of control over Cara and her pissed-off about it only serves to stoke my twisted moral compass. Visions of taking her on top of this table while she shoots her daggers at me until her eyes roll appear. My pants grow tighter, and I arrogantly reply, "Yes, rule. It's my first one. I'll let you know when you're ready for the second one."

"You're delusional. If you think—"

"One skillet and one Denver omelet. Is there anything else I can get for you besides a refill on coffee?" Kelsey chirps, setting plates of food in front of us.

My Tesora forces a smile. "No, thank you."

"That will be all," I reiterate.

"Very well. Enjoy your breakfast," Kelsey states, then motions for a server with coffee to refill our mugs.

We wait for the man to finish, then thank him. Once everyone is out of earshot, I point to Cara's plate. "Eat before it gets cold."

"I'm suddenly no longer hungry," she claims, pushing her plate away.

I move it back in front of her. "You need to eat. Let's not argue over this."

"Gee, is this rule number two?" she glowers.

I tuck a lock of her hair behind her ear. "No, gorgeous. But I can make it rule eleven if you want."

She opens her mouth to fire something off, but I stop her.

I put my fingers over her lips. "I'm joking. Chill out. I'd never do anything to hurt your business. All I'll do is look to help you. But you married me to protect you, and I will."

She takes a deep breath.

I peck her on the lips, then lower my voice, ordering, "Eat."

She hesitates.

Squeezing her thigh, I challenge, "Would you prefer I do indecent things to you here?"

Her lips twitch. She removes my hand. "No."

I sit back, satisfied we're past our little incident. I hand her a fork, restating, "Eat before it gets cold."

She takes the silverware and then a bite. I do the same, and we eat in silence for a few moments.

"Oh no," she mutters.

I glance at her, finish chewing, swallow and ask, "What's wrong?"

Her eyes widen. "I missed Bridget's engagement party, didn't I?"

Guilt floods me. "Yep. We both did."

She cringes. "I'm sorry. How upset are her and Dante?"

I grunt, trying to act like it isn't a big deal. "They'll get over it. Dante's angrier that I won't tell him where we are."

"Why didn't you tell him?"

"Why do you think?" I take another bite of the omelet, waiting for her to answer my question.

Confusion appears in her expression. "Since when do you hide anything from Dante? And can't he just read your mind?"

I chuckle, admitting, "Sometimes he can. Not right now."

"Okay. So why don't you tell him?"

I slide my arm around her shoulder and lean into her ear, swiping my tongue over her lobe before declaring, "It's our honeymoon. No one knows where we are, and I'm keeping it like that. Do you know why?"

She turns her face toward mine, biting on her bottom lip.

I resist leaving breakfast early, pulling her out of the chair, and taking her back to the room. "I think you keep forgetting it's our honeymoon. The last thing I'm doing is having anyone interrupt our time."

She stays silent, and I can see the wheels turning in her head, fighting to either give in to our reality or continue to claim we aren't real.

I give her a chaste kiss, then return to focusing on my food, not wanting to hear her dismiss our marriage again. I motion to her plate, and she takes another forkful of her skillet.

We don't speak for the rest of our meal. When we finish, I sign the bill and lead her out of the restaurant. She stiffens as we pass the hostess. I make a note to talk to the manager and insist that woman isn't anywhere in sight for the rest of our stay. I don't care what I'll have to pay to make it happen. She's a nuisance to repairing my relationship with my wife.

I tug Cara tighter to my side. "You're going to love the amenities here."

She tilts her head. "Are you really spending the entire day at the spa with me?"

I grin. "Yep."

"Will you be taking calls during your treatments?"

"No."

"What about in the rest area?"

"Nope," I sing, understanding her disbelief. I always work when she's at the spa. She always told me to take a day off, yet I never did. It's something I regret. Looking back, nothing I had to deal with couldn't have waited. And my brothers are always able to step in if I can't do something. I should have cherished every moment I had with her. Nothing will stop me from focusing solely on her during this trip.

An expression I can't decipher fills her. I want to believe she's happy about my determination to take our honeymoon seriously, but I can't be sure. Years ago, it would have thrilled her. Now, she's so torn about whether to forget the past or not, her look might be disappointment.

I shake the thought out of my mind and push the elevator button. I kiss the top of her head, more resolved than ever to leave Canada with Cara back on my side and in love with me again.

12

Cara

ANY SAUNA YOU CAN IMAGINE IS IN THIS SPA. I GLANCE AROUND IN awe, shocked at all the options. A young blonde woman named Mindy gives Gianni and me a tour. Fragrant rose steam fills the air in one room. Another mimicks a pure salt cave. Mint flares in my nostrils the moment I step into the crystal steam room that boasts Swarovski elements. Sounds of crackling ice, scents of peppermint, and cold air hit my skin in an igloo. Hand-painted art inspired by Michelangelo covers the ceiling in the Finnish Classic Spa. Breathtaking panoramic views of green forested hills plunging into Okanagan Lake fill the glass in another.

"And this is the room you'll want to start or end in," Mindy states, opening the door to the Aqua Meditation steam room. The entire length of both walls has oversized white cushioned seating. Invigorating orange scents fill the air. Water drips into a Swarovski crystal basin creating a soothing, rhythmic sound.

Gianni tightens his hold on my waist. He kisses the top of my head, which he's done in every room. He asks, "We have an hour before our first treatment. Want to start here?"

"Sure," I reply.

Gianni pulls the belt on my robe and helps me out of it. He takes his off as well.

Mindy holds her hand out. "Let me hang those outside for you."

He gives her the robes, and we sit on the plush cushions. The only other couple gets up and leaves. Gianni pulls me on his lap and traces the bikini string around my neck. He states, "I knew you'd look amazing in this."

"How did you get all the clothes in our suite? If you didn't know Uberto's plans to kidnap me, then how did you do all this?" I blurt out.

Gianni's eyes darken. Hurt fills his expression. "You think I would have let that monster drug you then hold you captive to prance naked on stage in front of all those disgusting Abruzzos?"

My mouth turns dry. Hearing him say it that way makes me instantly think it's impossible. Yet, I don't acknowledge my gut feeling. I repeat, "How did you get all these things for me?"

"I'm a man who makes things happen. You know this, my Tesora."

"How long did you know the Abruzzos had me?"

He sniffs hard, and rage passes in his eyes. Disgust fills his voice. "Too long. Every moment that passed was a test of my patience. You don't know what went through my mind and how I had to restrain myself from acting on my thoughts."

One thing I've always known is Gianni isn't a patient man. He has a temper and tends to do things how he sees fit. If anyone gets in his way, he removes them from the situation.

I question, "What did you want to do?"

He takes a deep breath and moments pass while he counts in his head. I don't know how I always know when he is doing it, but I get to twenty before he states, "Rush in there and blow up the place. But you could have gotten killed if I did that, so I forced myself to be patient."

"Who is the man who bought me?"

He leans closer, hesitates, then says, "If I tell you who he is, you can't ever repeat it."

Curiosity fills me. I'm surprised Gianni is telling me since it relates to his business. He always keeps those details away from me. I reply, "Who is he?"

"Tell me you won't disclose what I'm about to tell you, Cara."

"I won't. I promise."

We're still the only people in the room, but Gianni glances at the door. He turns back to me. "His name is Luca. He's my cousin but no one besides my brothers and Papà know his relation."

"Why don't people know he's related to you?"

Gianni stares at me for several moments.

I shift on his lap. "What? Did I ask the wrong question?"

He arches his eyebrows. "You know who I am, my Tesora. While you aren't from a family like mine, you've been around my world a long time. There are advantages one has to having men in your pocket who are able to slide into certain situations and get the job done."

I ponder his revelation. "So...that's how he was able to get into the auction?"

Gianni nods. "I would never have gotten in there. And if the Abruzzos found out who Luca is, he, nor I, would have made it out of that parking lot."

My chest tightens. I put my hand on his cheek. No matter how much I don't trust Gianni in certain areas of our relationship, I know he risked a lot to save me. But I also need to be assured he didn't know ahead of time what Uberto planned. I want to believe all of this wasn't a calculated move on Gianni's part to force me to marry him. But I admit, "I need to know this wasn't part of your plan."

His eyes turn to slits. "Part of my plan?"

I tilt my head and soften my tone. "Can we not pretend I don't know you? For decades, I've watched you get whatever you want, even when in order to get it, you had to cross ethical boundaries. I want the truth. I need to know how long you knew about Uberto's plan and how it was possible for you to fill our room with designer clothes and toiletries."

Gianni's face hardens. His nostrils flare, and his chest balloons with air. I count to fifty before he replies, "I have told you the truth. I would never let that thug do what he did to you. And money can make anything happen. You're a smart woman, Cara. Is this not the first time I've had material possessions appear from nowhere?"

Years of memories flash in my mind. Gianni surprised me with last-minute trips and hotel closets full of designer clothes similar to this trip, too many times to count. Yet, instead of giving me comfort, it pains me to think about those times. I was always naive and happy. I would trust in his new promises.

During all those moments, I believed it was going to be us forever.

He sighs and mutters, "Jesus, Tesora. Are you ever going to trust me again?"

I open my mouth to speak but the door opening stops me. Two dark-haired men who speak Italian step inside. They both are wearing robes. One has abstract tattoos on his hands and shin. The other man has a claw curling around his neck. They pin their eyes on me, and I shudder as a chill runs down my spine.

Gianni's body stiffens. He moves me off his lap and stares at them, then barks, "You want to remove your eyes from my wife?"

The man with the abstract tattoos continues to assess me. The one with the claw tattoo locks eyes with Gianni. His thick accent fills the air. "Quite the body on that one."

"What did you say?" Gianni seethes.

A sinister smile curls on the man's lips. "I think you heard me."

"You better watch your mouth and move your eyes elsewhere," Gianni warns, tugging me closer.

"Last time I looked, Canada was a free country," the man still staring at me states, then licks his lips.

Gianni jumps up, pulls me with him, and before I know it, I'm outside of the room.

"Gianni! What—"

He puts his hand over my mouth, glances around the space, then grabs my robe. He drapes it over my shoulders. "We're leaving."

"What?"

He doesn't bother with his robe and maneuvers me quickly through the spa. When we step inside the elevator, the doors shut just as the two men turn the corner, speaking in Italian.

Panic fills me. "Are they following us?"

Gianni briefly shuts his eyes before hatred erupts in them. "I'm sorry, Cara. We're going home."

More anxiety expands in my belly. "Do you know them?"

He clenches his jaw. "I've never seen them before."

"But you know them?" I repeat.

He stares at the metal door as heat creeps into his cheeks.

"Gianni!" I demand.

He meets my eye. "They spoke Venetian dialect."

I throw my hands in the air. "What does that mean?"

His jaw twitches. He angrily states, "The Abruzzos speak Venetian. You should know this from your time with that pig."

My gut drops as the elevator doors open. The thought crosses my mind that Gianni might never forgive me for choosing Uberto over him. It shouldn't bother me based on our past, but an ache in my heart expands.

He glances in both directions then guides me down the hall to our suite. When we step inside, he pushes me behind him and does a quick sweep of the room. "Get dressed," he orders, then goes back to the door and secures the deadbolt.

I freeze, watching him.

He pulls yoga pants and a sweatshirt out of the dresser and tosses them to me. "I need you to do what I say right now."

"Wh-why are the Abruzzos here?" I ask but already know the answer.

Gianni holds my cheeks. "I should have known better than to go anywhere without security. I'm sorry, my Tesora. I promise you, I'll make up for this. But we need to get out of here now."

My mouth turns dry. I open it, but nothing comes out.

"Cara, it's time to get dressed," Gianni sternly orders. Then he picks up his phone, swipes at the screen, and starts speaking aggressively in Italian.

I snap out of it and throw on my clothes. Gianni slides a pair of joggers and a T-shirt on. He grabs his Glock and checks the chamber. Then he put the silencer on it.

I've seen him a thousand times with his gun, but I've never felt scared before. Not once did I ever feel anything but safe around him. Something about Gianni always made me feel infallible. Yet, I'm suddenly frightened about what might happen. I blurt out, "How did they know we were here?"

He sniffs hard. "I don't know."

The sound of the metal unlocking hits my ears. Someone turns the knob, but the deadbolt stops the door from opening.

Gianni pushes me into the bathroom, quietly ordering, "Don't leave this room."

"What are you going to do?" I cry out.

He puts his fingers over my lips. "This isn't the time for questions. Stay in here while I take care of this."

A loud bang erupts. Whoever is on the other side of the door wants to get in. They continue trying to open it again. My heart beats so hard I'm sure Gianni can hear it.

"Lock the door and step to the back of the shower," he instructs, then shuts it.

My hands shake as I obey him. I go to the back of the shower and attempt to calm my nerves.

Almost instantly, muffled sounds, then two sharp bullwhip-cracking noises hit my ears. I tremble harder and cover my mouth, praying Gianni is the one who pulled the trigger.

Barely any time passes before he's banging on the door. "Cara! Come out. We need to go!"

I race over and unlock the bolt, then whip it open. I throw my arms over Gianni, belting out, "Are you okay?"

He holds me tight for a brief moment. "Everything is fine. We need to go." He retreats from our embrace. Cold darkness looms from his eyes. He holds out a pair of tennis shoes. "Put these on."

I glance behind him. The two men from the spa lie on the floor. A pool of blood surrounds their heads and expands on the wood tile. I've never seen a dead body, much less two. I put my hand over my stomach, trying to keep the bile down, and turn away.

Gianni steps behind me, so his hard frame is against my back. He glides his hand over my waist and lowers his voice. His lips hit my ear as he states, "I need you to keep it together right now. We're leaving, and we don't have time to waste. Can you put your shoes on for me?"

I tilt my head, locking eyes with him.

He pecks me on the lips. His voice grows even calmer. "Everything is fine. I need you to stay with me, Tesora."

Snap out of it, I scold myself. I nod, then take a deep breath.

"Good girl." He kisses me again, then releases me.

I put the shoes on, and we step out of the bathroom. Gianni reaches into the closet and pulls out a coat. He holds it open, and I slide my arms into it.

He picks me up and carefully steps over the two bodies, avoiding the blood. He sets me down once we're in the hallway then steers me through the hotel and out into the cold.

The same driver that took us to the resort is waiting. He opens the door, we get in the backseat. Gianni immediately makes another phone call.

He gives orders in Italian, and the car takes off. He slides his arm around me and kisses my head between speaking. The conversation seems to go on for a long time before he finally hangs up. He tugs me on his lap. Concern fills his expression. "Tesora, are you okay?"

I nod. "Yes. Are you?"

He cups my cheek, faintly smiling. "All in one piece. I'm sorry you had to see that. Are you sure you're okay?"

"Yes."

He takes a deep breath, and I count to ten before he asks, "You haven't seen a dead body before, have you?"

My stomach somersaults with the vision of the bloody scene popping up. I push it to the back of my mind. I admit, "No."

He closes his eyes briefly. More anger fills his expression. "I'm sorry."

"It's okay. I'm okay," I assure him.

Silence fills the air. Neither of us breaks our gaze on the other. Gianni's face darkens further. Several moments pass, and he grinds his molars. In a cold voice, he states, "This is my fault."

"No. It's not. You—"

"Shouldn't have been so arrogant to believe we could get away without any security watching over us. You could have gotten killed. And the Abruzzos just showed that there's no boundary they won't cross, including crime family rules."

My heart beats harder. A new fear grows, expanding quickly in my chest.

Gianni slides a hand through my hair, cradling the back of my head. A look I've never seen appears on his face. I can only describe it as a deeper crazy than the past.

I've seen many sides of Gianni over the years, but this look sends chills down my spine. I'm unsure why. I always knew Gianni would kill to protect me, even before today. His cold expression isn't directed at me. Yet, I can't stop the bad feeling racing through my nerves.

He drags his finger over my cheekbone, then jaw. "I promise you, my Tesora. I won't ever make this mistake again."

"It's okay," I try to assure him.

His nostrils flare. When he speaks again, my blood turns cold. His controlled voice is emotionless. He speaks with such confidence, there's no way anyone would ever doubt that what he states is a fact. And I've never heard his tone carry so much hatred.

"My Tesora, I won't lie to you. There's a war and it's officially started. And I promise you on my life that when it's over, there won't be any Abruzzos left."

13

Gianni

"Make yourself at home, Tesora. You know your way to our wing. I'll be up shortly," I instruct, give her a chaste kiss, then nod toward the staircase.

She hesitates, glances nervously at Papà and my brothers, then gives me a tiny smile. "Okay."

I watch her climb the stairs and disappear down the hall. As soon as she's out of sight, Papà seethes in Italian, "My office. Now."

For the past few months, I've not been in good graces with my father. I grind my molars, bracing myself for the lecture I'm about to receive. Dante shakes his head at me. I don't need to ask him why he's pissed. He's still unhappy I kept my location from him. It's the only time in my life my brother didn't know my whereabouts. Looking back, I should have told him, but there's nothing I can do about it now. So I mutter under my breath, "Get over it," then follow my family into the other room.

Papà motions for Massimo to shut the door. His dark flames pin mine. I should be used to them by now, but they still make me uneasy. I don't like upsetting him, but nothing was going to stop me from trying to give Cara the honeymoon she deserves.

God. I fucked that up.

I curse myself again for not making a better choice. I don't know how the Abruzzos figured out where we were, but it was stupid of me not to assume we should have protection.

I'm going to kill every one of them or die trying, I silently vow.

"When are you going to learn?" Papà seethes.

I sniff hard, cross my arms, and don't respond.

Papà steps closer, shaking his head. "Don't you dare give me the silent treatment."

All the rage I've felt over the last few months and especially last week floods every inch of my blood. I spout, "Why? Do you even care that my wife was on the Abruzzo auction stage? Do you care that they drugged her, stripped her, and would have done the vilest of things to her?"

My father takes a deep breath. His nostrils flare so wide I can imagine steam coming out of them. He lowers his voice. More disgust spreads across his expression. "How did she end up your wife?"

Guilt mixes with my anger. I know how I got Cara to marry me isn't kosher, but I'm not admitting that to anyone. "My wife and my business is exactly that—our business."

"When you use Luca without my permission, go off the grid and abandon your responsibilities, then leave your brothers and me in a shit storm, I beg to differ," Papà scolds.

I turn to Dante, assuming he'll cover for me. "Didn't you agree to cover any work issues that popped up?"

Without flinching, he does what he's always done. I know I'm going to owe him and hear about it later, but he firmly states, "Yes."

"Was there anything you couldn't handle?"

His eyes narrow. "Of course not."

I spin back toward Papà. "You worry about things that aren't issues. And how did I leave you in a shit storm? Has something happened I'm not aware of?"

Papà belts out in Italian, "You let all the Abruzzos see Luca buy Cara. Then you end up with her. There's no way to utilize him with them anymore!"

"Not true. I bought her off him," I admit and try to contain the smile forming on my lips. I'm a bigger bastard than I knew. It's a mix of satisfaction for staying a step ahead of my father and the twisted happiness I feel about paying for my Tesora. Nothing has changed since I transferred the money to Luca. Something about technically owning her after all the ways she punished me over the last few years, including dating that Abruzzo pig when I told her who he was and to break it off, gives me great pleasure. It's as if it's a little bit of karma. She was always meant to be mine, and now there's no going back.

She's going to flip when she finds out.

Maybe I should never tell her.

Of course, I'm going to tell her.

When the time is right, I remind myself. I project that sometime soon, the reality of our situation will hit Cara again. She'll do something to try and push me away. And since I'm a total bastard, I'll use what I did to reinforce that she's mine.

"Damn, brother. I thought you knew what year it was," Massimo taunts.

"Buying women isn't in our business model," Tristano adds.

"Shut up, you dumbasses," I order.

"How much did you pay?" Massimo asks.

"None of your fucking business," I spit.

Papà growls, "Since when did all my sons become idiots?"

"Calm down, Papà," Dante states.

Papà points at him. "If you believe your brother is making good choices for our family, then you're not ready to lead."

"Once again, Dante is incapable," I mutter, over the constant opinion my father tosses out whenever things go wrong. Dante is nothing but capable of taking over. I believe in him, and Papà should too. And the constant assertion is getting old.

Papà waves his hands in the air. His cheeks turn redder. "You have no business speaking right now. You've jeopardized Luca!"

"I've done no such thing. Luca has always done whatever is needed to make a quick dime. This will look no different," I insist.

"Stupid fool. You've put him in a compromising position," Papà states.

The more Papà speaks, the more my wrath grows. I sniff hard, then belt out, "I don't believe I've put Luca in harm's way. If I have, then it had to be."

"It had to be?" Papà explodes.

"To make sure Cara wasn't sold to some Abruzzo? Yes! And I'll be damned if I apologize for doing what I had to do to rescue her."

"But how does she feel about it?" Massimo interjects.

"Shut up," Dante orders, slapping him on the head.

Papà motions to my youngest brothers. "You two. Out! Now!"

Tristano whines, "Again? It was just getting good."

Papà's cheeks turn purple. Daggers fly out of his orbs.

"Get out of here," Dante reiterates.

"Whatever. This conversation is getting stale anyway," Tristano claims.

"Agree. I have more important things to do with my time," Massimo adds.

"You better be referring to your business dealings," Papà warns.

Arrogance rolls off Massimo's expression. "My business is always in order."

"Sure it is," I mumble.

"What the fuck does that mean?" Massimo fumes.

I almost tell him it means he should stop fucking the librarian and open his eyes. She helped the Abruzzo thug Donato gain access to the library basement. He kidnapped my sister and held her hostage there. Massimo can claim all he wants she was an innocent pawn, but I don't believe a word she says. She's bad news, and he needs to stop thinking with his dick.

Instead of outing him to my father, I lock eyes with him. "You know what it means."

His eyes turn to slits. "Take care of your own house. I'll take care of mine."

"And what else do I need to know about?" Papà questions.

I refocus on him. "Nothing. Let's get back to Luca. He's not compromised. There is a paper trail to back up my purchase. The Abruzzos aren't any wiser."

"Jesus. My purchase. Listen to yourself," Tristano says.

"Get out!" Papà roars.

Massimo huffs. My two brothers leave the room. Tristano slams the door shut.

Papà goes over to the bar. He pours two fingers of Zambuca and drinks it, then spins toward Dante and me. In a quieter voice, he states, "We're already low on men. Luca has been invaluable over the years. If he is no longer able to infiltrate the Abruzzos, we have major issues."

"Except they'll all be dead soon," I vow.

Dante shifts on his feet next to me. I don't need to look at him to know he disproves of my statement. Not because of what I said, but because of the consequences of saying it to my father.

Anger resurfaces on Papà's face. He holds his tumbler out and points at me. "You don't make any moves without my approval. Do you understand me?"

Dante interjects, "He does. He was just—"

"The war has started. There is no question what needs to happen. It's us against them," I insist.

Papà slams his glass on his desk. "It's always been us against them. You will not—"

"Two thugs tried to kill my wife and me. *My wife.* I made it clear she was mine. They still attempted to take her out. There are no rules left. It's us against them, and we either strike first, or there won't be any Marinos left," I state.

Papà steps closer. "And who's fault would that be?"

Not willing to back down, I raise my chin higher. "This is not my fault. We've been on the edge of an all-out war for a long time. When they kidnapped Arianna, we should have attacked then. And that's on you."

The mix of emotions that always cross Papà's face whenever Arianna's abduction gets mentioned arise. He takes several long breaths, and I count to twelve. He finally says, "I am tired of continuing to explain why we needed to wait. And I do not owe you explanations. It's clear to me that no matter how much I try and set an example of how to lead this family, you don't have any intention of learning."

"That's not true. I've learned everything I know from you. But I will not sit back and let those goons destroy my wife or anyone else in this family. Enough is enough," I claim.

Papà exhales loudly. "And now, because of your actions, we have no choice but to be in a full-on war."

"It's overdue, and you know it."

Papà shakes his head. "Giuseppe is still training men to send here. We do not have the backup we need."

Giuseppe Berlusconi is the head of the Italian mafia. He lives in Italy. Over the years, he's been less and less of an asset to us. The amount of money my father pays him is insane for the services we receive. And it's not just me who sees this. None of my brothers thinks he's added any value to our situation in years. I blurt out, "He's been promising to send us reinforcements for months. They are never coming, and Giuseppe is stringing you along. We should sever from him as well."

Papà slams his hands on the wooden surface. "You are wrong. And do not speak ill of Giuseppe." Papà points in my face. "Your stupidity and lack of respect are going to get you killed one of these days."

There's no point in this conversation, much like most of the time my father is pissed off at me. I reply, "Did something happen with the Abruzzos other than them trying to kill my wife?"

Papà gives me another look of death but stays silent.

I nod. "When there's something to discuss, let me know. My bride is upstairs. Don't interrupt us unless needed." I spin, catching Dante's neutral expression. There's no doubt he's upset with me, but he does a good job hiding it from Papà.

I leave, going directly to my wing of the house and into the personal suite. I lock the door and go through the sitting room, bedroom, and then into the bathroom.

Steam fills the air, creating a beautiful silhouette of my Tesora behind the glass. Soft music plays. The outline of my Tesora's rinsing shampoo out of her hair is a vision of perfection.

Gratification expands in my belly. She's finally here, in my house, as my wife. Without hesitation, I undress and step in the shower behind her, sliding my hand around her waist.

She jumps. Tilting her head up, she says, "What—"

I cover my mouth on hers, sliding my tongue deep into her throat.

She turns into me, glides her hands up my chest, and locks them behind my head. Her tongue sweeps against mine with the same intensity raging through my blood.

Taking two steps forward, I move her to the tile wall, reach for her ass and pick her up, sinking my cock into her.

Her moan vibrates against the tile walls. She tightens her legs around my waist, then shimmies her hips. It's pure perfection, exactly how I like it, and another sign we're destined to be together.

I drag my teeth across her jaw and murmur into her ear, "No one is ever coming close to you again, Tesora. You're mine. Forever. It's you and me from here on out." I bite on her neck, then suck on the bruised skin.

"Gianni," she cries out, embracing me tighter. She rolls her hips fast while squeezing her walls against my shaft.

"That's it, gorgeous. Give your pussy what it craves," I order, fisting her hair and pushing my forehead against hers.

She opens and closes her eyes, breathing harder, as a pink flush overtakes her cheeks.

I press her closer against the tile until there's no room between it and me. I hold her hip, slowing her down and inching my body slower in and out of hers. "Tell your husband how much you missed him."

An expression I used to see all the time in her appears. It's honest and beautiful, but she doesn't speak. It's the same look she used to give me when she would proclaim her love for me.

It's the first time I've seen it in years. Her eyes water and I swallow the emotions creeping into my throat.

It hits me how badly I want her to love me again. I'd do anything to hear her confess she still does. I kick myself again for taking her affection for granted all those years. I slide my hand over her cheek. "I missed you. I love you—only you, Tesora. I'm going to prove it to you."

She blinks hard. Her voice cracks. "Stop talking." She tries to return to the pace she was riding me, but I have control of her.

I count to fifteen, decide I don't want to make her cry again, and focus on our current physical state. I sniff hard and declare, "I think your pussy needs a punishment."

She inhales sharply, then swallows hard. Her eyes light up, making my cock harder. "Yeah. That's what you need. Hours of punishment."

Her chest rises and falls faster. She opens her mouth, but nothing comes out.

I slow my thrusts down more. I lean into her ear, softly grunt, then taunt, "How long has it been since you were on my wall, Tesora? How many times over the years did you think about it? Hmm? Did you wish all those other men were me when they failed to give you what you need?" I slide my hand over her breast and tug on her nipple.

She whimpers, burying her face into my neck. Her nails dig into my shoulders, and pussy clenches my body tighter.

"Fuck," I mutter, then stop myself from finishing what we started. I had all new restraints put in my room the day after I learned she was back in town. No one's been in them. I reserved them for her and only her. And every devious thing I've been craving to do to her on the wall rushes in my mind like a movie reel.

"Please," she whispers, then shimmies her hips faster.

I step back and force her legs to the ground.

"Gianni?" she questions.

I push her back against the tile but don't pick her up. I grasp her chin and lean my face over hers. Sniffing hard, I count to twenty-five while staring into her blues. I finally state, "Time to get out of the shower, Tesora. Dry your hair and put on your collar. I'll have food brought up. You're going to need your energy."

14

Cara

"Dinner is in the sitting room. Put this on, Tesora," Gianni orders, holding out a gold silk robe.

"Where did you get that?" I question, setting down the top-of-the-line hair dryer that magically appeared when we got out of the shower.

His face hardens. "I had things delivered while we were gone. Do you not like it?"

"It's beautiful. You know I love it."

He shakes the robe. "Then slide in."

I glide my arms through the luxurious silk. It's a perfect cool temperature against my warm skin.

Gianni kisses my neck, and wraps his arm around my waist. He's in his boxers. His hard flesh against my body is like coming home. I've missed the feeling of him for so long. No matter who

I dated, no one ever made me feel like I fit with them. It was like a curse he bestowed upon me.

He ties the belt and then holds the collar in front of me, murmuring, "You have no idea how much I love looking at you in this."

My butterflies spread their wings. I still have a hard time understanding how I could be okay with the collar, yet the moment he told me I was to wear it, my entire body lit up further. Even worse, the determination I had to only submit to him last night seems to be gone. It's like he opened Pandora's box, showing me how much better we are together than in the past, and the need to have him focused on me the entire evening is so intense I can barely contain my inner cravings.

He secures the collar around my neck. I reach up and trace it. He traps my hand with his, sliding his fingers under the metal, so there's no room left.

The tension around my neck makes me borderline dizzy. My pussy throbs. I lean further into Gianni, fully relaxing, and close my eyes.

His lips hit my ear. "Time to eat, Tesora. It's going to be a long night for you. And anything you remember about being here in the past get out of your mind."

I open my eyes and tilt my head in question.

Smugness curls on his lips as he studies my face. I assume he's counting, and after a while he states, "Anything I've ever done with you is going to look like nothing compared to what will happen tonight."

I swallow hard against his knuckles, taking in a small amount of air which is all I can inhale due to my current physical state. Gianni and I have done everything. He's kept me for hours restrained, begging, and controlling my orgasms. I can't fathom how anything could be more intense.

Last night was, I remind myself. I shudder at the thought, wondering how it's even possible. A part of me still hates him. I'm unsure how to let it go and trust him again. But I can't deny a small part of me still loves him, even though I convinced myself I had gotten him out of my system.

The thought of unconditionally loving Gianni the way I used to scares me. I vowed to never be vulnerable to him again. Yet here I am, pining for his touch.

Or maybe it isn't love. Perhaps I'm confusing our chemistry with emotions I swore off.

Yes, that has to be it. This is only physical, and I only need to remember that Gianni Marino isn't capable of returning my love. So I'm never offering it to him again.

His cocky expression intensifies. I reprimand myself for how much I love his arrogance. It's what got me in trouble over the years. It's his signature look that he knows what I need, and he's the only one who can give it to me.

I wish I could deny his assumption and prove him wrong. But no other man ever scratched the itch I always felt whenever sex was over. No matter how much attention they gave me, or how good they were in bed, there was always something lacking. Now that Gianni's planted himself back into my life, I can't pretend that the urge I'm feeling isn't everything about him— and us—together.

He grips the collar tighter and kisses me, slowly sliding his tongue in my mouth, not deepening it, so I'm left wanting more. The cockiness only erupts further on his face. "Let's go eat."

I don't argue. I know better than to refuse food. If Gianni says I'm going to need my energy, then there's no questioning it. I would be a fool not to obey him.

He leads me to the sitting room. Several silver-covered platters, saran wrapped plates filled with salad, and a cloth-covered basket of bread is on the table. He pulls out my chair, and I sit. He takes the seat next to mine then pulls the covers off.

Calamari, a small olive tray, high-end cheeses, and Italian meats sit in the middle. Our plates boast fresh ravioli, salmon with a caper cream sauce, and artichokes.

I stare at the food and laugh.

Gianni arches his eyebrows. "What's so funny?"

I motion to the food. "I forgot how your house might as well be a five-star restaurant."

He shrugs. "We do have a Michelin chef. And now that means you do too, Mrs. Marino."

My stomach flips. It's strange to think about living in the Marino estate as Mrs. Gianni Marino. I dreamed of it for so long, then came to the conclusion it was never happening.

He leans closer and drags his knuckles over my thigh. Tingles race up my leg. I refrain from squirming in my seat. Gianni places his face next to mine. Pools of dark waves dance in his eyes from the candlelight. He says, "All of my luxuries are now yours. Whatever you want, I'll give you."

My chest tightens, contrasting with my butterflies. I blurt out, "I don't need anything. I have my own stuff."

Amusement crosses his expression. He tucks a lock of my hair behind my ear. "Yes. I'm aware. The movers will unpack your things tomorrow."

Another small laugh escapes me. "Of course they will."

That damn ego of his I've always been a fool for grows bigger. His voice matches it, as he confirms my statement, "Yes. Of course."

I elbow him in the ribs.

"Hey! What's that for?"

"For being cocky."

"You love my cockiness," he claims.

My face heats. It's just my luck that he's fully aware of how much I love it. Still, I deny it. "No, I don't."

He chuckles, sits back, then picks up a piece of Brie and holds it to my lips. "Sure. Whatever you say, Tesora."

There's no point arguing. Brie is my favorite cheese, and I'm hungry. So I allow him to feed me and take a bite of the creamy dairy. It melts on my tongue, and I groan. "So good."

Satisfaction appears in his expression. He nods then pops the remainder in his mouth. After he finishes chewing, he swallows, takes a sip of Barolo, then states, "If you want to discuss with the chef future menus, feel free."

Panic grips me. I drink a mouthful of wine, then shake my head. "I'm not going to be your little housewife, Gianni."

"What does that mean?"

"I'm not running this house. Besides, isn't that Bridget's job now that she's marrying Dante?" I may not know everything about the mafia world, but it's not a secret Dante is in line for the throne. That means Bridget is the queen. And I'm totally fine with that.

He holds an olive to my lips. I allow him to pop it in my mouth. He shrugs. "You still get what you want. We all live here."

I turn more toward him. "I'm not giving up my career."

"I never said I wanted you to. I thought I made it clear this morning when we discussed the fashion show how proud of you I am. Did I not?"

It's true. He did seem excited for me. Yet, I also know how the Marino men are. Arianna had to beg to work. It's only because of Killian's encouragement and insistence she was allowed to start her business. Gianni's mother was a successful model but retired when she got engaged to Angelo. Bridget fills her time with her children's school activities. I'm sure she'll easily fall into the role of running the Marino mansion. Something within me feels like I need to reiterate that I'm not quitting. "I mean it, Gianni. I'm never walking away from my business."

His eyes darken, turning to slits. "Did you not hear me?"

I acknowledge, "The Marino men make all their women stay home."

He closes his fist around my collar and gently positions me in front of his face. My heart races faster. His eyes roam my face, then he asserts, "I'm not like the other Marino men."

"Aren't you?" I challenge.

He sniffs hard. His voice becomes firmer. "No. Not regarding that viewpoint. And as long as you're safe, you'll work until you die if you want."

More alarms go off in my head. "Don't try to use safety as an underhanded way to force me to quit!"

Silence fills the air. I count to thirty, watching his chest rise and fall in calculated breaths, before he speaks. "Your safety will never be compromised. But I'll handle it. And you're going to have to work on believing me when I tell you something. My wife cannot question every statement I make."

"I don't—"

"Don't you?" he confronts.

I sigh, wishing I could wave a magic wand and forget about my trust issues with Gianni. Instead, I decide it's best to not answer him or fight anymore. I turn toward my plate and focus on my ravioli. We eat in silence, and a million different thoughts run through my head. When I'm at the point I'm almost full, I put my fork down. I lock eyes with him and admit, "I wish I could forget our past."

His face hardens. "Then do it."

"It's not that easy and you know it. But I do wish I could return to how it used to be between us."

He wipes his mouth with his napkin, puts it on his plate, and claims, "Guess we're making progress then."

My stomach flips. Is this progress? Am I falling under his spell again?

He rises before my anxiety has time to consume me. He holds his hand out. "Come on."

I don't question or fight him. I let him help me up, and he leads me over to the couch. He sits then pulls me on his lap, so I'm straddling him. His palm covers my ass, and his other hand cups my cheek. He asserts, "We can't go back, Tesora."

"No, we can't," I agree.

"How do I help you get past this?"

My pulse races. "I can't answer that question."

Gianni's slow, calculated breaths make me believe he's counting again. His thumb strokes my jaw, and an expression I've never seen before appears. It takes me a moment to realize its vulnerability, and that's something Gianni doesn't ever allow himself to be. He asks, "Do you know what it was like for me to see you with him?"

My stomach flips. I shift on his lap, saying nothing.

"You wanted to hurt me, didn't you, Tesora?"

My mouth turns dry. My insides quiver. Once I was back in New York and Gianni found out I was with Uberto, he warned me about him. When I wouldn't break it off, he accused me of staying with Uberto only to get back at him. As much as I denied it and tried to convince myself that wasn't the case, a small part of me relished the fact Gianni hated Uberto. It was like karma was finally catching up to him for all the misery he put me through.

Gianni takes a few deep breaths, not breaking our gaze. Pain enters his expression, which I've never seen before. He quietly confesses, "You did."

Those two words of admission should give me some satisfaction. At times, I assumed he didn't have a heart and was untouchable on an emotional level. Surprisingly, his statement doesn't make me happy how I thought it would. I blurt out, "I'm sorry."

He takes his index finger and drags it from my forehead down the side of my cheek. His next declaration throws me for another loop. It's not in Gianni's wheelhouse to ever admit fault. He states, "It's okay. I fully deserved it."

Speechless, I stare at him. My heart races faster. He doesn't move, and the vulnerable expression never leaves. I assumed hurting him would give me some gratification, but the exact opposite occurs. A wall crumbles within me. I slide my hands over his cheeks and reiterate, "I'm sorry," then kiss him, sliding my tongue against his the moment his lips part.

Everything disappears. It's like striking a match and burning everything around us. His hand slides in my hair behind my head. His other arm tugs me closer while his palm squeezes my bare ass cheek. My knees hit the back of the couch, and I do everything I can to get closer.

His erection grows, freeing itself from his boxers, and I sink on it, clutching him tighter. He allows me to ride him, slides his thumb between us then circles my clit.

Heat flushes my body, growing so hot sweat pops out on my skin. "Oh God," I whisper, grinding on him faster.

He slows his thumb, demanding, "Tell me you love me still."

I fight with my heart that wants to give in, and my brain that says not to admit anything. "Gianni, don't..." Emotions choke me. I'm unable to continue, too frightened of being honest and how Gianni will eventually use it to hurt me, even if he isn't planning on it.

He leans into my ear. His breath sends fresh tingles down my spine. "I know you still love me. Just give me this one thing, Cara. Tell me that the tiniest part of your heart still loves me."

I squeeze my arms around him as tight as possible, so I don't have to look at him. I shimmy my hips faster, wanting the release for both of us so I can avoid falling prey to him again.

But like always, I'm not in control.

Gianni is.

He asserts, "Admit it's barely there, but exists, my Tesora. And I'll make your pussy clench my cock so hard you won't think there's anything left to give me the rest of the night."

My butterflies flutter faster. More sweat breaks out. A haze fills my sight. My body doesn't only want what he offers. It's always craved it. When he has me like this, I can't reason. All it takes is one more prompt.

He thrusts up, teasing my g-spot, and growls, "I love you. Tell me you still love me."

"I still love you," I cry out.

Everything in my body turns into chaos. Adrenaline explodes from cell to cell like a minefield detonating. It's a drug you can't reproduce. The high is too potent. Once it starts, it's so powerful I become an addict lost in Gianni's body.

He's the perfect dealer, giving me hit after hit but not taking any himself, driving me to the point I'm a junkie owned by his touch. I faintly comprehend his words. "Fuck, Tesora. This is how it was always meant to be. You and me."

I whimper, collapsing against him, a ragdoll inside his strong embrace. The endorphins continue to rush through me until he grabs my hip and holds me still.

I bury my face into his neck, trying to catch my breath, not able to piece together all the words he murmurs in my ear.

Time slowly brings me back to reality. I stay in the cocoon of his warmth, trying to forget I admitted I still love him.

One thing I know about Gianni Marino is once he gets what he wants, he'll never let you forget it. Now that I gave him a taste of what he wanted, he'll use it to his advantage. It'll be at a moment when I'm least expecting it, powerless and unable to stop whatever it is he wants to happen.

And then he'll leave me empty, like a shell of a bullet with nothing of value inside.

When I lift my head away from his body, his intense gaze is one I've seen too many times. It swirls with satisfaction, reiterating every thought racing through my mind.

It's not a matter of if he'll destroy me again. It's a matter of when and I have no way of stopping it.

All I can wonder is how much worse it'll hurt this time. How will I survive? When the tears fill my eyes, I can't stop them from flowing down my cheeks.

Alarm explodes in his expression, but I can't answer him when he tries to get me to tell him what's wrong. I decide it's just better to feel other things and forget, even if it's only for tonight.

I close my eyes, pulling every ounce of strength I have within me to stop the river of tears. When I finally do it, I ask for the only thing that can give me a moment of stability. "Take me to the wall."

Gianni holds my cheeks in his hands, swiping my tears with his thumbs. "No. You aren't okay."

A broken laugh escapes me. "But I never will be, will I? Now that I'm your wife..."

His breath hitches. Dark pools lock into mine, widening. "Cara—"

"Take me to the wall, Gianni," I firmly restate.

He hesitates.

MAGGIE COLE

I close my eyes, whispering, "Please. The wall. I need it."

"You need it?" he questions as if he doesn't believe me.

Breathing slowly, I count to thirty then swallow hard. I square my shoulders and pin my orbs into his, reigning in every bit of confidence I can find before again ordering, "Take me to the wall."

15

Gianni

NOT ONCE IN MY LIFE HAVE I TRULY REGRETTED ANYTHING. NOW, it consumes me, and I don't know how to right my wrongs.

My wife's eyes are full of raw, deep pain. And while I'm not ignorant that my heart's mostly black, the small part of me capable of love bleeds.

She closes her blues and whispers again, "The wall. Please."

I've never once restrained any woman to the wall while they were in emotional distress. The last person I want to make any wrong moves with is Cara, especially in our bedroom. So I almost tell her no again, but she reaches for my cheeks and drills a desperate gaze on me while repeating, "Please. I need it. Give me what I need."

It convinces me not to deny her. I palm her head, kiss her on the forehead, then guide her to the new gold and platinum wall. To an outsider, it would look like an elaborate metal art piece.

Every part of it has a purpose, designed for all sorts of deviant sexual acts. Each restraint gets hidden in the ceiling until it's time for me to push the button and lower them, which I've already done for tonight.

The ornate structure used to be black, but I replaced that when I bought the new restraints. I figured if my Tesora was going to be on it, she deserved fine metal, not black steel. And now that I'm staring at her in front of it, I know I made the right decision. She's always beautiful, but right now, she's a breathtaking, glowing light surrounded by darkness.

I push the silk robe off her, so she's in nothing but her collar, then trace it. The longer I study her, the more her chest rises and falls faster. Flames dance in her eyes, growing hotter with every second. She swallows hard. Her voice breaks as she demands, "Make me submit to you."

Something in me shifts. It's as if she woke up the devil. I've ordered her to do all kinds of things in the past. Yet not once has she ever said that to me. Without hesitation, I order, "Kneel."

Surprise blinks in her expression, but she drops to her knees and looks up at me.

I count to fifty, not breaking her gaze, debating in my head what I want to do to her. Then I crouch down and hold her chin. Her hot breath merges into mine. A blush paints her cheeks. Her bottom lip quivers, so I swipe my thumb over it. I reach for her puckered nipple, rolling it between my fingers until it's a hard bud.

She inhales sharply, whimpering so quietly I question if I heard it.

My cock throbs, firing testosterone through my veins. I reprimand myself for getting worked up so early into this. If my

Tesora wants to be on the wall, I'm going to need to not get ahead of myself.

I sniff hard, counting to twelve, then starting over. I'm unsure how many sets of twelve I recite. It's the only way to gain control of my body. I eventually step back and command, "Legs spread, hands behind your back on your ankles, face toward the ceiling."

Cara's eyes widen. I half expect her to disobey, but she slowly inches her knees further apart until I order, "Stop."

She freezes, bites on her lip, then slowly slides her hands over her thighs and calves until she's able to grasp her ankles. She arches her back, pushing her nipples high in the air. Her long hair falls in waves toward the floor, and she gives it a shake while facing the ceiling.

"You fucking naughty girl," I mutter. Hot blood rushes through my veins. She's always been flexible, able to hold positions a long time, and colored every line outside the box I wanted. I lick my lips, studying every inch of her as if it's the first time.

Hell, maybe it is. Perhaps the fact that she's here, in front of the new wall I had created just for her, wearing a diamond collar signifying she's finally mine, means we're both different than in the past. And doesn't that mean we're a newer version of our old selves?

Satisfaction hits me like lightning. The wall is our fresh start. Tonight, I'll prove to her that I'm different...that I've changed. And all the demons we both carry, we can let go of and move forward.

I rise, lean over her face, and admit, "You thought you could escape our issues on this wall, but if anything, it only makes our problems appear brighter.

A puzzled expression appears. "What are you talking about?"

In a quick move, I grab the restraints and pull them. The chains slide over the metal, and a moment of panic fills Cara's face. Among the upgrades were other amenities. Instead of restraints only attaching to the wall, they now have the ability to create tension or slack.

I secure it around her wrist and ankle, ensuring the position is perfect and not going to dig into her, even though they are padded. The only marks on her body I'd ever allow on her would be from my mouth or slap of my hand on her ass.

"Gianni?" she questions.

My arrogance takes over. I fasten the other restraint. Any indecision I experienced is now gone. I peck her lips then boast, "You needed the wall, correct?"

She furrows her eyebrows then answers, "Yes."

"It takes you trusting me fully for you to be on the wall."

She stares at me.

"No? You don't have to trust me? You'd let anyone do this?" I challenge, and a brief moment of panic hits me that maybe she would let another man do this to her.

What if she has?

She blinks, then squashes my fear. "Of course, I wouldn't let anyone else do this to me."

The corners of my lips curl. I nod. "And you have to trust me."

"Yes," she admits.

I weave her hair around my fist, so there's no tension. She gasps, and I cup her pussy, teasing her slit with my index finger.

"You're different than when we were kids or even together years ago, my Tesora."

She scrunches her face. "Of course I am. I aged."

My lips curl. Her response couldn't be more perfect. I state, "You've gotten more beautiful, but I've aged too. And with age comes wisdom."

She stays quiet.

I slide my finger inside her, loving how she makes the slightest squirming movement, then stops when I bark, "I didn't give you permission to move."

The room turns silent except for my thumping heart and her breath. I rise, grab another restraint, and attach it to her collar, removing all tension, so her head barely rests against the wall. I add a second digit and pump into her at different speeds, rolling my thumb on her clit. Her face contorts, and deep pleasure fills me, knowing how badly she wants to circle her hips and ride my hand.

But she won't. She knows the one rule of the wall. Yet, I still make her state it. "What's the one thing you must abide by all night, Tesora?"

"You're in charge."

"Yes. And let me remind you of my rules. Are you allowed to do anything without my permission?"

She shuts her eyes and takes a deep breath, then opens them and answers, "No."

I step out of my boxers, cage my body over hers, and kiss her. She moans as I flick my tongue into her mouth, increasing the intensity, denying her and myself the deep kiss I know we both crave.

Utilizing the wall, I grip it, then slide my erection over her clit, watching every change in her expression.

Tiny whimpers fill the air. It's like an old song from childhood. One that no matter how many times you play, it only gets better with time. Her eyelids flutter, and I lean into her ear, reminding her, "I didn't give you permission to come."

"Gianni," she pleads. Her hot skin glistens, shimmering in the dim light.

It would be so easy to let her have what she wants, but I'm not an ordinary man. And I don't crave power.

I take it.

So I wait, and wait, and wait some more, continuing to play with her how I want, until her legs tremble and she's begging me in a hoarse voice. I allow several more minutes to pass, taking a few nibbles on her breasts and listening to her moan.

The air becomes air thick with the smell of her arousal. Her juices cover my hand and drip down her thighs. The tremors in her body grow more intense, and she shimmies her hips.

It's right where I want her. I smack her ass, and her clit slides along my shaft. She shrieks, "Oh God! Again!"

I growl, "Do not move. I didn't permit you!"

Her eyes glisten. "Baby...please."

I ask, "Do you know when I changed the wall?"

"I-I can't take anymore!" she cries out, then circles her clit against my cock faster.

I smack her again. This time, I pull my cock away from her. "Stop moving, Tesora. Answer me! Do you know when?" I demand.

She swallows hard, closes her eyes, then breathes, "No."

I lean closer, rubbing my dick on her again, then admit, "The day after, I saw you in the club. The first moment I knew you were back in New York."

Surprise erupts, mixing with her lust-filled desperation.

I keep everything slow, and she pleads, "Oh God! Gianni! Please don't...don't—"

I bark, "No one, Cara! There's been no other woman on this wall, nor will there ever be. Since I saw you that night, I've not touched anyone."

"Wh-what?" she asks, blinking harder.

"No one," I reiterate.

She stays quiet except for her labored breath.

It hits me that she might not trust in my word any longer. "Tell me you believe me, Cara."

She stays silent.

I speed up my thrusts against her clit. "Don't you dare come! Not until you tell me you believe me!"

"Gianni, please!"

"Tell me!"

"I believe you," she cries out.

The words aren't enough. I'm a bastard and need more. Instead of letting her release, I slow it back down.

"Gianni!"

Pinning my gaze on hers, I slide my hand through her hair, lowering my voice. My lips brush hers as I order, "Tell me again. I want to know that you really believe me."

There's only a slight hesitation, but one thing about Cara is she has honest eyes. She's not a liar like me. A tear slips down her cheek, and her voice cracks. "I believe you. I swear."

Relief floods me. I kiss her with everything I have, slide my erection faster against her and hold her tight against me as she loses all control. Our kisses muffle her moans until I move my lips to her ear, saying, "That's it, Tesora."

I do everything in my power to sustain her high, but when it's over, I do what I never do. Instead of repositioning her on the wall, I take off the restraints and pick her up.

She looks at me in question as I lie her on the bed.

I slide on the mattress next to her and pull her into my arms.

"Gianni? Why—"

"Shh." I stroke her hair and kiss her on the forehead. "Catch your breath."

"The wall—"

"Will be here the rest of our lives. Tonight, I just want to make love to you in our bed."

Her body stiffens.

My heart races faster, and I realize it's the first time I've said make love instead of fuck. I scoot down and turn to face her. Tucking a lock of her hair behind her ear, I confess, "My bed is new too. No other woman's been in it. No other woman will ever be."

A shock-filled expression lights up her face.

I cup her cheeks. "I've been a horrible man to you, Tesora. If I could do it all over again, I would. We'd have a dozen kids tearing this place up, and I'd have you knocked up again. But I can't go backward. We're married. I made a vow to you, and nothing—I mean nothing, is going to break it."

New tears form in her eyes. She tries to stop them from overflowing, but it's useless.

I swipe at them, firmly stating, "We need to move forward. You and me. This is our fresh start. And I need you to forgive me. *Really* forgive me."

Her eyes dart to the side, then back to me. "You always make promises, Gianni."

My gut spins so fast I swallow bile down. "Yeah. I know. This time, and going forward, I'm keeping them. I need you to give me one last chance."

Her lips tremble. She blinks hard, and so many tears fall it feels like a knife is shredding my heart. Not the black part, but the part that makes me human.

"Tesora. Please. Forgive me. Trust me again. Let me be the husband I always should have been for you," I plead.

I count to one hundred and ten, utilizing every ounce of patience I have, which has never been a lot. I finally can't stay quiet anymore. The realization that she might never give me another chance hits me hard. My throat thickens. I sniff hard, begging, "Please."

She shakes her head in tiny movements. My soul feels like it's dying. Her tears drip faster, and she states, "I shouldn't. You don't deserve it."

"I know. I—"

"This is it, Gianni. If you make me into your fool again, I will leave you. I will find a way to divorce you and disappear somewhere you'll never find me. Do you understand?"

Relief implodes inside me to the point I can barely breathe. I count to ten while nodding. "Yes."

Her voice grows stronger. She wipes her face. "Tell me again, Gianni. I want to hear you say it."

I kiss her on the lips and stroke my thumbs on her jawline. In my firmest tone, I vow, "It's you and me, Tesora. Forever. I will never do anything to dishonor you. I will never do anything to cause you to want to divorce me. I will spend the rest of our life doing one thing—loving you and making up for lost time."

She takes a deep inhale, and more time passes as she stares at me. I panic she might not be able to give me what I want. She finally states, "Give me some time, Gianni. But I'll work on figuring out how to forgive you and trust you again."

It's not the instant result I wanted, but it's better than where we were.

When I don't say anything, she slides her hand in my hair, adding, "I'll get there, okay?"

I smile and pull her closer. "Fair enough, Tesora. Now rest up. I plan on making you beg me some more."

She laughs, and everything in me lights up. I almost have her back and for the first time since she returned to New York, I can see progress.

We aren't perfect yet, but I'll take it.

16

Cara

GIANNI STRETCHES HIS ARMS AND YAWNS, THEN OPENS HIS EYES. A large grin forms as he slides closer to me.

I blurt out, "I need to return to work today."

His lips twitch. He drags his finger down my cheek. In a teasing tone, he replies, "Well good morning to you too, Tesora."

I sit up and criss-cross my legs. I've been up for hours thinking about my promise to Gianni, how I need to work harder to get over our past, and pushing down the fear that he'll hurt me again. One thing I believe in is keeping my word. Plus, I don't want to carry these ill feelings toward him. The reality is that we're now married, so it has to be best to try and move forward.

Not that it's easy to forget.

But I would give anything to return to Gianni being my every-thing and him making good on his word not to hurt me again.

So I'm committed to doing whatever it takes to hold up my end of our agreement.

He better not make me regret this, I think, then reprimand myself while pushing the thought out of my head. Those notions aren't going to help us get back to where we need to be in order to make this marriage work.

I state, "Morning. I'm serious, though. I've been gone too long. With fashion week right around the corner, I can't afford to waste any more time."

Gianni leans against the headboard and runs his hand through his hair. "Can you work from home today?"

My stomach tightens. "Why? What's wrong with my office?"

He holds his hands in the air. "Nothing is wrong, but I have to sort out your security."

A claw scrapes at my gut. Goosebumps break out on my arms, and the cold, damp feeling I had when I woke up in the cellar rushes through my body. For a brief moment, I forgot about the Abruzzos. Now, it all comes rushing back so fast it makes me dizzy. I put my hand on my stomach and breathe through it.

"What's wrong, Tesora?" he frets.

I've never had security before. I'm unsure how I feel about it, yet I also realize it's necessary. I quickly assess the tasks I need to do. I work through the nausea, shake my head, and then force a smile. "Can I go to the office and get my laptop and some other items?"

His face relaxes. "Sure. I'll take you after breakfast." He jumps up and holds his hand out toward me. "Come on, Tesora. Let's go face the music."

"Face the music?"

He nods. "Yep. All the questions we're going to get from my family."

I wrinkle my nose. "Can't we skip that part?"

He grunts. "Unfortunately not. Let's get it over with and move on with our lives." He reaches further for me, lacing his fingers between mine, then tugs me off the bed.

We go into the bathroom, brush our teeth, and I twist my hair before securing it with a claw clip. We step into the shower, and Gianni presses his lips to mine. Within seconds, he has me sandwiched between his warm body and the cold tile, as if we didn't spend hours wrapped around each other before falling asleep only a few hours prior.

When we finish devouring each other, we dry off, get dressed, and I add a thin layer of makeup on my face. Gianni leads me through the Marino mansion while the butterflies in my stomach wake up.

Since high school, I've been in this house too many times to count. Gianni and I have fucked in almost every room. Seeing the rich wood, bright colors, and ornate decor in the morning light sends a wave of deja vu rippling through me.

"Are you hungry?" He asks as we approach the dining room.

I nod. "Yeah. You?"

He palms my ass and leans into my ear. "I can eat, but I'd rather have you sit on the table and—"

"Cara!" Bridget's voice hits my ears.

My gut drops. I feel horrible I missed her and Dante's engagement party. A small amount of embarrassment also weaves through those emotions. She tried warning me about Uberto just as much as Dante did. But I was so angry with Gianni I wouldn't believe anyone. I take a deep breath, smile, and spin. "Hey, Bridget."

She embraces me tightly. "Thank God you're okay! I can't believe what that monster did to you!"

More shame fills me. Of course, the entire Marino family would know what Uberto did to me. Now that Bridget is marrying Dante and will take her role next to him to lead the family, it makes sense she would be in the loop.

Something about everyone knowing I was kidnapped and put up for auction makes my cheeks burn hot. I clear my throat. "I'm okay."

She retreats from the hug and studies me. I do my best not to cringe. Bridget and I were tied to the hip growing up. Then she moved to Chicago, I left for Europe, and life separated us. We recently got reacquainted, but my life is so different from hers. She's a dedicated mother and runs the PTA at her kid's school. I don't know anything about that type of life. My child has been my business.

More concern floods her expression. "I was so worried about you."

"I'm okay," I reiterate. Once upon a time, Bridget would be my confidant. Something about the fact she's going to be my sister-in-law as well as the head of the Marino family makes me a tad nervous around her. I'm unsure why.

"Bridget," Gianni states, then leans down and kisses her cheek. "I'm sorry we missed the party."

She turns her gaze toward him. In a cool voice, she replies, "Yes, well, someone had to make it interesting, right?"

"Then why do you sound irritated?" he asks.

"I'm not." Her lips form a tight smile.

Gianni arches his eyebrows. "Are you sure about that?"

"Why are you all standing in the hallway?" Dante booms.

I spin, and Gianni's arm sweeps behind me. He tugs me into his chest as if to protect me from his brother, claiming, "We were just going in." He slides me past Dante and pulls out my chair.

Relieved to not have to answer questions from Bridget or Dante, I offer Gianni a grateful smile.

He gives me a quick peck on the lips and winks. "Let's eat."

I take my seat. Massimo and Tristano's voices fill the air. I turn right as Angelo walks in. His piercing gaze locks into mine. He makes a beeline toward me and my stomach flips.

I rise. "Angelo. It's good to see you."

He embraces me, and some of my tension disappears. My nerves are uncalled for. Angelo has always treated me with kindness, just like the other Marinos. But now he's my father-in-law and the entire situation that got me here is screwing with my head.

Angelo pulls back and places his hands on my cheeks. In a fatherly tone, he questions, "Gianni assures me that you didn't get hurt?"

More fire burns my cheeks. I assure him, "No, I wasn't."

His dark orbs continue studying me.

I resist the urge to shift on my feet, lift my chin higher and insist, "Really, Angelo. I'm fine."

"Papà, let my wife eat," Gianni demands.

Angelo shoots darts at Gianni, then kisses me on the forehead. "Welcome to the family. If there is anything you need, you come to me."

"She can come to me. She's my wife," Gianni mutters.

Angelo ignores him, repeating, "Anything. Okay, Cara?"

I smile. "Yes. Thank you."

He releases me and takes his seat at the head of the table.

Dishes line the center of the table. The staff appears and lifts the silver lids, displaying a buffet of breakfast items any fine restaurant would die to present. Scrambled and poached eggs, bacon, sausage, salmon, pancakes, waffles, and fancy loaves of bread create a delicious aroma, making my stomach growl. Within minutes I'm sipping on coffee and filling my belly with a little of everything.

"Cara, the seamstress will be here later today. Since you missed the fitting, are you around so she can do your alterations?" Bridget asks.

Guilt gnaws at me. "I'm sorry I missed it."

"It's okay. It's not your fault you weren't here," she declares.

Her statement should give me some relief, but all I feel is more remorse. Bridget's been through a lot. I'm happy for her and Dante. Missing her engagement party and the dress fitting makes me feel like the worst maid of honor on Earth.

"Yeah, you didn't ask to get auctioned off," Massimo points out.

My stomach flips again. I put my fork down and shift in my seat.

Gianni must sense my discomfort. He slides his arm around my shoulder. "There won't be any more talk of Cara's abduction at this table."

I offer him a tiny smile.

"Why? It's not a secret," Tristano claims.

Gianni's head snaps toward him. He seethes, "Because I said so. Now change the subject."

Tension fills the air. I refocus on Bridget. "What time will the seamstress be here? Gianni and I are going to my office after breakfast to get my laptop and some other things so I can work from home. I don't have any other plans."

"Not until one. Will you be able to be back by then?" she asks.

"Yes. I can be here."

Her smile grows more prominent. "Great."

"Mom, tell Sean to give me my phone back!" Fiona demands, entering the room with her brother in tow.

"Jeez. When are you going to fight your own battles," he sneers.

"Sean, give your sister her phone back," Bridget orders.

He holds her cell above his head. "This one?"

She jumps to try and take it from him. "Sean! Stop being a jerk! Give me my phone!"

"It's right here. All you have to do is grab it," he taunts.

"Sean!" Bridget warns.

He looks at his mother. "Why don't you ask me why I have it?"

"Shut up!" Fiona cries out, jumping again but isn't able to reach the cell.

"What does that mean?" Bridget asks.

"Sean!" Fiona yells while glaring at him.

Bridget slides her chair back to stand, but Dante rises first. "Sean, give Fiona her phone back."

Sean shakes his head. "You're no fun anymore."

"Give her the phone," Dante repeats.

Sean huffs, handing the phone to Fiona. "Fine. Suit yourself. Don't come to me when you screw up."

"How's she going to screw up?" Bridget inquires.

"Nothing! Sean's being dramatic again," Fiona declares and pulls out her chair. "I'm starving. Mom, is the dress fitting still after school?"

Bridget hesitates, glancing between her two kids. Fiona avoids her and shoves a piece of toast in her mouth. Bridget's eyes narrow on Sean. "I want to know what's going on."

He crosses his arms and sits back, shooting Fiona a smug look. "I wouldn't want to start rumors."

Fiona's eyes turn to slits. She grits her teeth. "Shut up!"

"What rumor?" Bridget asks, pinning her eyebrows together. Wrinkles crease her forehead. She looks between them, and anger flares in her cheeks.

Dante slides his palm over her hand. "Sean, either spit it out or tell your mother you're just being a dick to your sister."

Sean and Fiona have another moment where they stare each other down before he sniffs hard, picks up his orange juice, and takes a mouthful.

"Well?" Dante demands.

He swallows his drink and puts two pancakes on his plate. "I'm just being a dick."

Relief floods Fiona's expression.

"I'm not buying it," Bridget states.

"All good," Sean claims, then pours syrup on his pancakes. "Do I have my tux fitting today as well?"

Bridget continues to assess him, then Fiona. Dante interjects, "Four o'clock. We'll get the third workout in after."

"Third?" Sean asks.

Massimo snorts, shoves a waffle in his mouth, then says while chewing, "What do you think Julio is doing? He's not going easy on his training."

Sean snorts. "Whatever. He can train ten times a day. I'm still going to kick his ass."

"Language!" Bridget reprimands.

"Sorry, Mom." Sean turns toward Gianni and me. "So you two really got married?"

"We sure did," Gianni answers. He kisses the back of my hand. Pride sweeps his face, and my butterflies spread their wings. It feels good being the center of his universe again. And it may only be his family he's showing his affection toward me to, but it's all I ever wanted—to be his and for everyone around us to know it.

Don't get too comfortable. You know his track record, races through my mind. I reprimand myself again.

"So you're going to be our aunt soon?" Fiona asks.

A smile plays on my lips. I nod. "I guess so."

"Cool. Aunt Cara, do you think you can get us fashion week tickets?" Sean asks.

"You want fashion week tickets?" Gianni asks in disbelief.

Sean grabs a waffle off the platter and holds it in the air. "I could care less about fashion week. However, Carly is super into it. And Cara is the only person I know who I assume can get me two tickets."

"Who's Carly?" I ask.

Fiona rolls her eyes. "His annoying, new girlfriend. She's a total user too."

"Shut up. She is not," Sean claims.

"Why do you think she's a user?" Bridget asks.

"She's not," Sean reiterates.

Fiona sits back in her seat and tilts her head. She smirks at Sean. "Do we need to go over this again?"

"Shut it!"

"No, you shut it!"

"Alright. Enough of the bickering. You two need to remember you're family," Angelo scolds, pointing at each of them. "You'll only have each other someday when we're all dead."

"Jesus. Not the death talk again," Massimo mutters.

"Bring out the coffin," Tristano adds.

Dante slaps the back of his head.

"Ow! What was that for?"

"Show some respect for Papà."

"Please." Massimo rises and tosses his napkin on his plate, then addresses Sean. "Are you ready to get in the gym?"

Sean turns toward me again. "So, can you help me get tickets?"

I nod. "Sure."

He grins. "Awesome. Thanks."

"And you should ask her why she can get those tickets," Gianni states.

Heat flashes my cheeks once more.

"She owns the fashion industry. Duh," Sean replies.

Gianni chuckles, then tugs me closer. "She sure does. But they chose her agency for fashion week."

Bridget jumps up. "Cara! That's amazing! Congratulations!"

Happiness fills me. "Thanks."

"Can you get me tickets too?" Fiona asks.

"Sure."

"Away from Sean's annoying girlfriend?"

"You're pushing it," Sean warns.

Fiona huffs. "Whatever."

"And we're back to the bickering," Angelo mutters.

Bridget moves around the table and hugs me. "I'm so excited for you. Well deserved!"

"Overdue too," Gianni adds.

"Agree! If you need help with anything, let me know," Bridget states.

"Thanks. I appreciate the offer."

Gianni rises. "We should get going. I have a meeting later today I need to attend."

"With Rubio?" Dante asks.

The twins lock eyes. Gianni nods. "Yeah."

"Did it arrive last night?"

"Five this morning."

"Five? But that's a lot later than what was on the schedule," Massimo blurts out.

The room turns quiet. Dante and Gianni both stare at Massimo. I count to ten before Gianni carefully questions, "What do you know about it being late? I don't recall informing you about the shipment time."

Tension thickens in the air. The hairs on the back of my neck rise, but I'm unsure why.

"Your schedule was laying out on your desk," Massimo claims.

"You were in my office?"

Massimo squares his shoulders. "Is that a problem?"

"What were you doing there?"

"Seriously?"

"Yeah. Why were you in my office?" Gianni interrogates.

Anger flares in Massimo's expression. "Why does it matter? I'm your brother. You think I'm out to screw you?"

"Didn't say that, did I?" Gianni replies.

Massimo scowls, shaking his head. "You disappear from planet Earth and want to question me?"

Gianni cracks his neck. His lips twitch. "Bro, all you had to say was that you missed me."

"Fuck off," Massimo hurls and storms out of the room.

"What's up his ass?" Gianni asks.

Dante shrugs and pours more coffee into his mug. "No clue. He's been acting all pissy lately. He'll work it out in the gym. Get moving." He motions for Sean to leave.

"Great. Lucky me," he says, gets up, and follows Massimo's footsteps.

Gianni turns to me. "Ready?"

"Sure." I spin toward Bridget. "I'll see you later for the fitting, okay?"

"Sure. Congrats again. I'm really proud of you."

"Thanks."

Dante gets up and hugs me. "Same here. Huge accomplishment."

Fiona, Tristano, and Angelo all give me their congratulations.

Gianni sweeps me out of the dinning room and through the mansion. Massimo is on the phone when we turn a corner. He's speaking in Italian and pauses when he sees us.

"We're going to Cara's office for a few things. When I get back you're coming to see Rubio with me," Gianni states.

Massimo shakes his head. "I have plans."

"So what. Cancel them," Gianni orders and moves me past Massimo. We get to the hall closet and he helps me into a coat, then leads me down the front steps. A black SUV is waiting. A man gets out of the passenger seat and opens the back door. I get in, and Gianni follows.

"It might be a few days before I can give you the green light to go back to your office," he admits.

Uberto's face pops into my mind. Nausea reappears. I take a deep breath as the car moves forward, managing an, "Okay."

Gianni slides his palm over my cheek. Light flickers in his eyes. "I really am proud of you."

My heart soars at his words and how genuine he appears. I lean into his chest, and we ride in silence for a while. We're almost to the expressway when the driver rolls the divider window down.

"Boss, I think someone is following us."

My chest tightens. "What?"

Gianni glances out the back window. I do too. Another black SUV, exactly like ours, is closer than it should be.

"Get down, Cara," Gianni orders and gently pushes my head to my knees.

"Who is it?" I ask. The pit in my stomach expands. I assume the only person following us would be an Abruzzo.

Gianni yanks a gun out from under his coat and cocks it. "Stay down," he sternly repeats, then orders, "Try to lose him."

The SUV speeds up, swerving around traffic. Several minutes pass when the driver yells, "Son of a bitch!" The SUV cuts hard to the right. Tires screech, and gunshots ring in the air.

"Mother fuckers!" Gianni barks. He rolls down the window, and cold air blasts the inside of the car.

My heart races faster. I turn my head, still keeping it down. He leans out the window and aims the gun.

More shots ring in the air. I scream as Gianni ducks back in the car. He drops the magazine and reaches below his seat, pulling out a fresh one. The sound of metal sliding hits my ears.

The bodyguard in the passenger seat climbs over the console and rolls the other window down. He orders, "Ambush on three."

"Stay down, Tesora, and cover your ears," Gianni demands.

"One. Two. Three!" the bodyguard counts.

I put my hand over my ears from the explosions going on all around me. The SUV moves to the left and right and seems to go faster. It feels like it lasts forever, and I'm too scared to lift my head.

Tires skid. A loud crash replaces the sound of the bullets.

"Great shot," I barely hear the bodyguard yell.

Gianni slides his hand around my shoulders. He leans into my ear. "Tesora, are you all right?"

I swallow hard and slowly look at him. My entire body shakes. The beating of my heart doesn't seem to slow.

He puts his palms on my cheeks. "It's okay. We're safe now."

"I'm-I'm sorry. I-this is my fault!"

"Shh." He pulls my head to his chest. "This isn't your fault."

"Wasn't it the Abruzzos?" I cry out, still trembling.

He holds me tighter. "Take some deep breaths."

"I-I'm sorry," I repeat, suddenly feeling on the verge of hysteria.

In a stern voice, Gianni states, "This isn't your fault."

"Was...was that Uberto? Did you kill him?" I ask, swallowing the dry lump in my throat.

Gianni's eyes darken. "I don't know who was in their vehicle. But if Uberto wasn't, he better run. Because I'm coming after him, and I'm not stopping until he's dead."

17

Gianni

"WHERE'S HE AT?" I FUME IN ITALIAN. THE ABRUZZOS AMBUSHING us in broad daylight is a clear sign they got the memo.

The war is on.

Rules we all usually follow no longer exist.

No one is safe.

Luca relays, "We still haven't located him. My guess is he ran from New York. He'd be a bigger fool than we thought if he's still in the city."

My pulse continues pounding faster. I sniff hard, watching Cara pack the few items she needs to take. "I want him brought to me immediately. You don't stop looking until he's in my custody, got it?"

"On it," Luca assures me.

I hang up and step into Cara's personal office. "We shouldn't hang around here very long. What else do you need?"

She shakes her head. "This is it."

I kiss her head and try to appear calm. The last thing I want is for her to be scared. She's already been through enough. And while she's always been a strong woman, I worry about how the past week's events could have mental consequences for her.

She gives me a brave smile. "Ready?"

I kiss her head again then grab the laptop bag off her desk. "Yeah. Let's go. The same rules apply as when we came in here. You don't step outside until I give you the all-clear."

Worry floods her blue orbs, but I don't stop to acknowledge it. After what happened earlier, being in public with her isn't helping me calm down.

I lead her through the building, then wait to get the all clear signal from my driver Manny. Once he gives it, I step in front of Cara. My bodyguard Sandro goes behind her, and we quickly get into the SUV. More anger erupts when I catch a glimpse of the bullet hole in the corner fender.

The ride home is quiet. No one speaks. I keep my arm tight around my Tesora, counting so many times to one hundred that I lose track.

They tried to kill my Tesora.

Again.

Manny pulls up to the front of the house. I guide Cara inside the house to find Papà waiting for us in the foyer. We lock eyes for a brief moment before he pins his gaze on my Tesora. He puts his hands on her shoulders. "Cara, do you need anything?"

She forces a smile and shakes her head. "No, Angelo. I'm okay." She nervously glances at me. "I'm going to your office to work if that's all right?"

"Of course. I'll check on you when I return."

She arches her eyebrows. "Return?"

"I need to meet Rubio at the docks."

"Oh. Ummm... Is it safe right now?"

The truth is, I don't know what's safe or not. We're at war. Nothing with allow me to drop my guard until every Abruzzo is dead. Still, I don't want Cara worrying about this. And our house is the safest place she could be right now. I kiss her on the lips then claim, "Everything is fine. You don't need to worry about me. Go do your work, and I'll find you when I'm back."

She hesitates for a moment, then puts her hand on my cheek. "Be careful."

"I will. Go on," I order, motioning for her to go to our wing of the house.

She obeys. Papà and I watch her until she gets to the top of the staircase and disappears down the hall. He turns, and we go into his office.

My brothers are all waiting. Massimo crosses his arms, sniffs hard, and snarls, "It's time we go to Jacopo's house and end this once and for all."

"I'm ready," Tristano agrees.

Papà flies across the room. He points at my younger brothers. "Have I taught you nothing?"

"You didn't teach us to be a bunch of pussy's," Massimo states.

"Shut your mouth and sit down," Dante orders.

Surprise fills Massimo's expression. "You want to sit back and let them shoot at us in broad daylight? What if Bridget or the kids were in the car?"

Dante clenches his jaw.

I interject, "Of course, he doesn't. But we can't attack Jacopo's. We're short on men right now. He's got just as many guards as we do, maybe more."

"I told you to hire the last recruits I brought in," Massimo states.

"Jesus. Are we back to this again? Those four wouldn't have lasted ten minutes in the line of fire," Dante claims.

"Bullshit," Massimo barks.

"Enough! I don't want to hear about those four again. They aren't our caliber. And no one is going to Jacopo's house unless I give the order. Get it through your head. Are the four of you crystal clear?" Papà asks.

Tension fills the air.

"I asked a question!" Papà exclaims.

"We're all clear. Aren't we?" Dante seethes, pinning his cold gaze on Massimo.

He shifts on his feet and grinds his molars.

"I'm good," Tristano states and plops down in an armchair.

I step forward and pat Massimo on the back. "Everyone is good. Sit down, brother."

He stares Dante down for another few seconds, then takes his place on the couch next to me. Once everyone is seated, I say,

"What I want to know is how they knew where we were going to be."

"When did Manny first notice them?" Papà asks.

"About fifteen minutes in," I reply.

"Besides the family, who else knew you were going to Cara's office?" he questions.

I shake my head. "No one. There wasn't any reason to tell anyone."

"No one? Not Rubio or anyone else you need to deal with today?"

"Rubio? What are you getting at, Papà? Rubio would never be part of the Abruzzos," Dante claims.

"I didn't say he was, but if you told him, who knows if he told someone."

"I didn't. I spoke to no one. Other than Manny and Sandro, the only people who knew were in this house," I point out.

"Maybe one of Bridget's kids said something to someone?" Tristano suggests.

"No way! They know better than to disclose any of our business to anyone. I don't even think they were in the room when you mentioned going," Dante defensively states.

Tristano continues, "It could have been by accident. Sean could have been talking to his girlfriend or—"

"There's no way Sean or Fiona said anything to anyone. You better watch your mouth," Dante warns.

"Okay. If it wasn't them, who else would have tipped someone off? If no one in that room told anyone, then how did the Abruzzo's know where to find Gianni and Cara?"

Massimo rises and paces the room. "What about Manny and Sandro?"

"Fuck off! Don't make my guys dirty. Besides, they wouldn't have been in the car if they had tipped them off. No one wants to get shot at," I point out.

"Someone tipped the Abruzzo's off. Sean and Fiona weren't even in the room when Cara mentioned it to Bridget. That leaves the five of us, Bridget and Cara. If the seven of us didn't have any conversations about where Gianni was going, then—"

"Massimo! Who were you talking to?" I demand.

He scowls. "You think I called the Abruzzos?"

I rise. "Who were you talking to when Cara and I passed you in the hallway. You were talking in Italian."

"So. Everyone in this house speaks Italian."

My heart pounds faster. "I mentioned we were going to Cara's office. Maybe the person on the other line heard me. Who were you speaking with?"

Massimo clenches his jaw. He crosses his arms, walks to the window, and stares out of it.

The more time that passes without him answering, the more my rage grows. I glance at Dante, and our twin senses kick in. His eyes widen as we both realize who Massimo was probably speaking to. I count to ten before I grab him by the back of his shirt, spin him, and explode, "Who the fuck was on the other line? My wife could have died!"

Massimo sniffs hard and glances at the ceiling.

"Jesus," Dante mutters.

"It was her, wasn't it?" I bark.

His silence is all I need to know that I'm right. He was talking to the librarian he's been banging who helped that Abruzzo thug Donato kidnap my sister.

When he still doesn't answer, Papà's voice sends a chill down my spine. "You have five seconds to tell me who your brothers are referring to."

Massimo's eyes turn to slits. "They're talking about Katiya."

"Who's Ka—" Papà's color drains from his face. "Tell me it's not that librarian."

Massimo steps closer. "She's a good person. It's not her fault Donato made her give him access to the cellar. She didn't know what he was going to use it for, and she wasn't there when he brought Arianna there."

More tension thickens. My father, brothers, and I all study Massimo. He doesn't flinch or back away, locking eyes with Papà.

"Is your dick more important than your sister?" Papà asks with a disappointed look on his face.

Insulted, Massimo questions, "Are you seriously asking me this right now?"

"Damn right I am! How could you ever think getting involved with her would be a smart idea?"

"She doesn't have anything to do with the Abruzzos," Massimo insists.

"Bull shit! It's too coincidental. The only person outside of our trusted circle who knew we were going there is her," I accuse.

"You don't know that no one else knew. And Katiya isn't working for the Abruzzos. She hates them as much as we do."

Papà pins his eyebrows together. "Why is that? Hmm?"

Massimo shifts on his feet. He grinds his molar but doesn't answer.

"I asked a question," my father seethes.

"Katiya's business is just that—hers. But I can vouch for her. She's—"

"For crying out loud," Papà shouts, slamming his hand on the desk. "Open your eyes. I didn't raise you to make stupid decisions."

"I'm done here," Massimo declares and brushes past my father.

I grab the back of his shirt again. This time, he spins and pushes back. "Get off me!"

"My wife could have died! You bring Katiya here. Tonight!"

He jerks his head back. "Absolutely not."

"That Abruzzo is responsible—"

"Do not call her an Abruzzo. She's no such thing," Massimo insists.

"Everyone, calm down. This isn't helping us figure out who tipped the Abruzzos off," Tristano voices.

"Tell me you aren't as ignorant as your brother," Papà roars.

Tristano holds up his hands. "Hear me out."

Disgust fills me. "It's clear who tipped them off."

"You don't know that. It could be someone inside our circle," he suggests.

I scrub my face then tug on my hair. I meet Dante's eyes. "Are they really this gullible?"

"Looks that way to me," he seethes.

"Watch your mouth," Massimo threatens.

"Or what? Are you going to tell your piece of ass where we station all our security guards?" I taunt.

Massimo's hand curls into a fist. He pulls his arm back. "You mother—"

Tristano grabs his bicep. "Everyone chill out."

"Chill out? They aren't accusing your woman of being an Abruzzo."

"If the shoe fits," I hurl.

"What do you think Arianna is going to say when she finds out?" Dante asks.

"She won't act like this, that's for damn sure," Massimo claims.

I snort. "Want to bet?"

"While you bastards fight, I'm going to try and figure out who could be a traitor in our house," Tristano declares.

"Everyone be quiet," Papà orders.

Silence fills the air. My brothers and I all glare at one another. Papà assesses all of us. He finally says, "Massimo, you bring Katiya to see me. Tonight."

"What? No."

Black flames burn in Papà's eyes. "You dare disobey me?"

Massimo's head bobs side to side. He adamantly states, "She isn't an Abruzzo."

Papà steps forward and puts his hands on Massimo's cheeks. "If she isn't, then you have nothing to worry about."

Five seconds pass. Massimo replies, "The Abruzzos put her through enough. I won't subject her to your scrutiny."

"Then tell me what they did to her."

Massimo sniffs hard. "No. It's no one's business but hers."

"Everyone out. Massimo, you stay," Papà directs.

"My wife almost died. I have a right to stay and hear whatever it is he's hiding from us," I proclaim.

"I'm not hiding anything. And that's rich coming from you," Massimo hurls.

"Excuse me?"

"You heard me."

"What the fuck does that mean?" I bellow.

Massimo sarcastically laughs. "God, you're such a hypocrite."

"I'm a hypocrite?" I ask in shock.

"Yeah. You take off to buy Cara at an auction. You use Luca to do your dirty work and tell none of us what's going on. Then you disappear to the middle of nowhere in Canada without telling any of us your location or when you're even coming home."

I cross my arms over my chest. "This isn't the same thing."

"Isn't it?"

"No, it's not," I maintain.

"You're delusional."

"You better watch your mouth," I warn again.

"Enough! Everyone but Massimo out!" Papà orders again.

I don't tear my eyes off Massimo until Dante puts his hand on my shoulder. "Gianni, let's go."

I point in Massimo's face. "If I find out she tipped off the Abruzzos and almost killed my wife, I'm going after her."

"Don't throw your threats around."

"Oh, it's not a threat, little brother. It's a God damn promise, and you'll be next on my list."

"Out!" Papà shouts louder.

I toss Massimo another dirty look and stomp out of the office. When the door shuts, Tristano and Dante huddle around me. Tristano states, "Can we just assume it wasn't Katiya for a moment?"

More anger seers through me. "You're asking for a punch in the face."

"Cool it. Tristano is right. We need to look at all angles," Dante says.

I close my eyes and count to thirty, attempting to stop my insides from shaking. When I open my lids, I catch Cara out of the corner of my eye. I tilt my head toward the top of the landing. "Tesora, are you okay?"

"Yeah. My stomach is growling. I thought I'd go to the kitchen and grab a snack."

I glance at my brothers and reply, "Good idea. I'll go with you. I'm over this conversation." I meet Cara at the bottom of the stairs and maneuver her through the hallway toward the kitchen.

She pauses and tilts her head when we get inside the kitchen. "You alright?"

I count to forty, staring into her blue eyes.

"Gianni, tell me what's wrong."

I slide my palm over her ass and tug her closer. Her floral perfume flares in my nostrils. Against my initial thoughts to not bring up any incident from this past week, I can't help myself and admit, "You could have died."

"I didn't. And you could have too."

"If I lost you—"

"Shh." She puts her fingers over my lips. "It's okay. I'm okay."

"Nothing that's happened to you over the last week is okay," I blurt out.

She turns her head and closes her eyes.

Anxiety fills my chest. I move her chin so she can't avoid me. "You've been through a lot. Do you want to talk to someone? Dante found Bridget a great therapist. Maybe you should see her?"

Cara opens her mouth then shuts it. She shakes her head. "I'm fine, Gianni. Just sort out my security so I can run my business. I'm not missing fashion week after working so hard all these years."

I wrap my arms around her and slide my fingers through her hair. "I will."

"Promise me."

I nod. "You have my word."

She takes a deep breath then smiles. "Thank you. Now, what can we eat? I don't know why but I'm famished."

I chuckle. "The chef can make you whatever you want."

She rolls her eyes, but her smile grows. She teases, "Of course he can. And he would be the Michelin chef, correct?"

Arrogance fills me. "Only the best for you, Mrs. Marino."

She laughs. "Well, if I'm Mrs. Marino now, I guess I should get the perks."

I lean into her ear, swiping my tongue on her lobe. "After your snack, why don't I show you the real perks?"

18

Cara

Two Weeks Later

ARIANNA BEAMS. "I THOUGHT A FRESH JUICE AND SMOOTHIE BAR would be a nice touch."

I agree, "Yes! That's perfect."

"Great. There's a new company I already spoke with, and they're so excited to be part of fashion week they agreed to discount their fee."

"Wow! That's even better."

"All that role-playing has come in handy," Killian boasts, wiggling his eyebrows and walking into Gianni's office.

Amused, I ask, "Role-play?"

Red creeps into Arianna's cheeks. "Killian thought my negotiation skills needed work."

"I think we're due for some more lessons," Killian declares, his eyes traveling down her body, which only makes her blush deepen.

She ignores his comment, asking, "What are you doing here? I thought you were going into town with Massimo."

"He got a call and needed to take care of something. I thought I'd see if you ladies wanted to leave the compound."

My heart races faster. I've stayed inside the Marino mansion for the last few weeks. The only place I've gone is outside for some fresh air. Gianni said he's working on my security, but the men he trusts are coming over from Italy. He assured me they'll be in place and ready to go for fashion week. And after the last incident, I'm not fighting him about staying here where it's safe. I blurt out, "Gianni won't let me leave."

Killian's eyes light up. "Ah, but that's where you're wrong."

"I am?"

"Yep."

"How?"

"We're going to take Arianna's bodyguards and mine. Plus, Killian can help me shoot out of the car if needed," Gianni states, entering the room and bending down to kiss me.

"Are we going to get shot at again?" I fret.

Gianni's face falls. "No. Sorry. It was a joke."

"Not a funny one."

"Yeah, well, I'm normally not funny. That's Killian's job."

I tilt my head and put my hand on his cheek. "Aww. Sometimes you're funny."

"Keep telling him that," Killian taunts.

"Funny! So I really get to go out?" I ask Gianni.

He nods. "Yep. And you're going to love where we're going."

I arch my eyebrow. "Where?"

Pride sweeps Gianni's face. "To your meetings."

Excitement fills me. I was supposed to check out the different venues today. Gianni had me cancel, stating it wasn't safe. I question, "I thought you said it was too dangerous?"

"I convinced him we have enough backup," Killian claims.

I stare at Gianni.

"It's true. You can thank him." He points to Killian.

I turn toward him. "Thank you."

"No problem. How long until you ladies are ready to go?"

"I'm ready now," I proclaim.

"Me too," Arianna adds.

We make our way through Gianni's wing and go out to the garage. Three black SUVs are waiting. Manny gets out of the middle one and opens the door.

"Wow. We have our own entourage," I tease.

"Nothing but the best for my wife," Gianni replies.

I slide into the seat, and everyone follows. Arianna and Killian sit across from Gianni and me. The vehicle pulls out of the garage and through the gate. As soon as we turn on the main road, Arianna puts her hand on her stomach and winces.

"Lass, what's wrong?" Killian frets.

She shakes her head. "Nothing. The baby is kicking again. Nothing major."

Killian doesn't look convinced.

"Honestly. I'm fine."

"Maybe we should have Silvio examine you. You've been having that happen a lot," he worries.

She laughs. "Yeah. I have a child with legs growing inside me. I don't need Silvio to give me an exam. Everything is fine."

"It won't hurt."

More amusement fills her expression. "If it were up to you, I'd have an exam every day of the week."

"It wouldn't hurt," he says in a serious tone.

She rolls her eyes and turns toward Gianni and me. "Please tell me we're going to lunch later. I'm starving."

My stomach growls so loud everyone hears it. "I guess I am too."

Gianni wrinkles his forehead. "I don't remember you eating so much before."

I smirk, "Are you judging me?"

"Only when you make me get out of bed in the middle of the night to get you gelato."

"Hey! You ate more than I did!"

He chuckles, then shrugs. "It was good."

"What kind was it?" Arianna asks.

"Mint chocolate chip," Gianni answers.

"Ugh! That isn't supposed to be in the house. You know Papà can't stay away from it," she whines.

"He's fine. He just had a complete physical, and Silvio said all his numbers improved," Gianni claims.

"Mint chocolate chip gelato isn't going to help keep his numbers good," she insists.

"Arianna, let the man have his gelato," Killian mutters.

She snaps her head toward him and jabs his chest. "Don't think I didn't see you spread extra butter on your toast today."

He groans. "Once again, my numbers are all in line, too."

"For now. How long can you eat butter and stay that way?"

"Do we have to get into this again? I'm Irish. We're meant to eat butter."

"We have a child on the way. You should be more conscious."

He picks up her hand and kisses the back of it. "Lass, you said you'd stop stressing about my health if my numbers stayed good."

More worry lines form on her forehead.

He rolls his head until it's next to hers and whispers something in her ear.

She turns bright red and elbows him in the chest.

"Ow!" he cries out.

"Did you decide on a name for the baby?" I ask.

Her face lights up. "Nicoletta."

Gianni freezes. "After mamma?"

Her eyes glisten. "Yes. That's okay, right?"

His voice softens. "Of course. Have you told Papà?"

"We were going to tell him tonight. Do you think he'll be happy about it?"

"Of course he will," Gianni asserts.

She takes a deep breath and smiles. "Are you still planning on coming to Chicago when the baby arrives?"

Gianni puts his arm around my shoulders, tugging me into his chest. "We wouldn't miss it."

"Did you finish the baby's room?" I ask.

"The crib hasn't arrived yet, but everything else is complete," Killian replies.

The divider window rolls down. Manny says, "Boss, Sandro said the back entrance is clear, but we can't stay parked there. We'll need to leave then return to pick you up."

Gianni's face darkens. He glances out the window then locks eyes with Killian. "Maybe we should go back home."

Killian shakes his head. "No. We've got plenty of backup."

"I really need to see the space we're working with," Arianna asserts.

Gianni stares out the window again, and I can tell he's counting in his head. My stomach flips, but I also want to do the best job possible. I put my hand on his fist. "I need to as well."

"We'll be fine," Killian assures him.

Gianni pauses but finally tells Manny, "Pull in the back. Stay as close as possible and keep watch for anything out of the ordinary."

"Got it, boss." He stops in front of the back door.

We get out, and bodyguards appear. They circle us, and Gianni guides me inside. When we get to the main area, a dozen professionals I've worked with in the past are here.

"Cara, darling," the stage manager Carmine Duplane exclaims while pulling me into an embrace. He kisses me on both cheeks, then steps back and furrows his brows in disapproval. His voice seethes with disgust. "Gianni Marino. What are you doing here?"

I cringe. Carmine worked in Italy with me the last time Gianni left me. After weeks of avoiding everyone, Carmine came to my apartment. He let me cry on his shoulder, and then he made me get back to work. I vowed to him I would never again let Gianni back in my life.

Gianni sniffs hard and stands straighter. He holds out his hand. "Carmine. Good to see you again."

Carmine's eyes turn to brown slits. He ignores Gianni and pins them on me. "What are you doing with him, Cara?"

My stomach flips. Killian scoffs in the background, but I ignore it. I blurt out, "We're married."

Carmine gasps.

"Let's not be all dramatic," Killian voices.

"Killian," Arianna mutters.

"What have you done?" Carmine asks me.

I wince. "Ummm..."

What do I even say? I can't exactly tell him about my abduction or wedding.

A smug expression grows on Gianni. "She vowed to love me for the rest of her life."

I shoot him some daggers. I don't need him ruffling Carmine's feathers.

Carmine glances between Gianni and me while an uncomfortable silence pursues. He finally puts his hand on my shoulder. "We need to talk in private."

"Anything you say to her, she'll tell me," Gianni arrogantly claims.

Carmine's head jerks toward him. "Why is that? You think you don't have secrets?"

"We don't," Gianni declares.

Carmine snorts. "So you have nothing you're hiding from Cara?"

Gianni crosses his arms and firmly repeats, "As I said, we don't."

"Sure. And pigs fly with rainbows all around them."

"Is that a thing? Rainbows and piggies?" Killian asks.

Arianna groans and once again mumbles in warning, "Killian."

He holds his hands in the air. "What? The dude obviously has it out for your brother."

Carmine pivots. "Why don't you ask me why I don't want him anywhere near Cara."

I grab Carmine's bicep. "Let's go talk."

He smirks at Gianni and begins to lead me out of the room.

Gianni follows.

Carmine spins. "Do not follow us."

"Sorry, but wherever Cara goes, I go."

Carmine huffs. "I don't know what century you think it is, but—"

"It's for Cara's protection."

"Why? What have you gotten her involved in?"

Gianni's jaw clenches, and his nostrils flare.

I motion toward an office. "That room doesn't lead anywhere. We'll be fine there."

Gianni gives me a disapproving look.

"I can go in with her," Killian offers.

"What? No. You're staying out here," I tell him.

"But what if the rainbow appears and pigs start to fly all around you?"

"Oh my God. Killian!" Arianna moans.

"Sandro, go check the office," Gianni orders.

Carmine glances at Sandro, then pauses to check him out. When he disappears into the office, Carmine leans into my ear so only I can hear him. "Who's Mr. Steel Ass?"

A laugh flies out of me.

"You've been holding out on me," he adds.

"All clear," Sandro calls out.

Carmine smirks at Gianni and Killian, then tugs me into the office. He slams the door. "Please tell me this is a horrible joke, and you did not marry that two-timing snake."

"He's never cheated on me."

"That you know of!"

"He hasn't," I insist.

"Let me get my attorney on the line. We can figure out how to get you out of this mess." He pulls his phone out of his pocket and swipes at it.

I grab it from him. "No."

He inhales a sharp breath then puts his hand over my forehead. "Have you gone ill?"

I sigh and softly say, "Carmine, Gianni and I are married. It isn't going to change."

"What happened to swearing him off? Did you forget what he did to you in Italy?"

I close my eyes, then open them and look at the ceiling. I count to twenty, then almost laugh when I realize how much Gianni has worn off on me.

Carmine snaps, "What's so funny? I remember peeling you off the floor the last time he deserted you."

I stop smiling. "Yes. I remember. And I'll forever be grateful. But things are different."

"Do not tell me you believe he changed."

I count to five before confidently proclaiming, "He did."

More disapproval fills Carmine's expression. "Men like him don't change. They take and take until there's nothing left but scraps and then douse those in flames."

I stay quiet. I don't blame Carmine for feeling this way. Italy was the worst time in my life after Gianni left. If Carmine hadn't helped me get back into the swing of things, I would have lost my business.

Carmine lowers his voice. "I know you have feelings for him, but—"

"I love him. I always have. I always will. No matter how much time passes, it's never gone away. And he is different," I insist, but as I say it, a small part of me wonders if I'm truly a fool.

"Cara, it's not too late to get out of this."

I square my shoulders. The last few weeks, I've felt closer to Gianni than I ever have, even in Italy before he left. And he does seem different. Since we got married, there have been too many moments to count where Gianni has been vulnerable. It's like he took his wall down, and only I get to see the true him. He's been nothing but a doting husband, and every day I fall deeper in love with him. I admit what I never thought I'd say the night I married Gianni. "I don't want a divorce."

"You've gone mad," Carmine declares.

A hint of anger flares in my belly. I firmly assert, "Gianni and I are married. He's my husband. I *want* him to be my husband. This isn't going to change. While I understand your concern, I can assure you he isn't the same man. I would appreciate it if you try to take that into consideration and show him the same amount of respect you show me."

Carmine's eyes widen. "He's brainwashed you."

I close my eyes and plead, "Please. Let it go."

"I can't. You're my friend, and he doesn't deserve you."

I pin my gaze on Carmine, softly saying, "Please. I'm begging you."

He sighs, shaking his head. "Fine. But when he shows his true colors, you come to me. I'll make sure you take that bastard for everything he has."

I hold in my groan. Knowing Carmine the way I do, this is a good first step. And Gianni isn't innocent. I can't just expect Carmine to forget the past when I barely could. I rise on my tiptoes and kiss his cheek. "Thank you. Now can you show Arianna and me what they plan on doing?"

"Who's Arianna?"

"My sister-in-law. The beautiful brunette. She was standing next to Killian."

"The arrogant ass who wouldn't keep his comments to himself?"

I cringe. "Yep. That's him."

"Poor girl, having to deal with that."

"While he is arrogant, he actually is a nice guy. Funny, too," I declare.

"Jeez, you are brainwashed."

I swat the back of my hand on his shoulder.

"Ow!" he shrieks.

"Oh, please. Enough of the nasty talk. Can you please be nice for my sake?"

"Why? What's your husband going to do? Lock you up and toss the key?"

"Carmine, please be nice," I beg.

"Ugh. Fine. I'll do it for you. But if Gianni steps out of line, he's going to have me to deal with," Carmine threatens.

"Deal. Now show Arianna and me the floor plan."

"Okay, but I have a question," he says.

"What's that?"

"What does Arianna have to do with fashion week? Did you hire her as your assistant?"

I smile. "Nope. She has an amazing event planning business."

"Have I heard of it?"

"I'm unsure. She lives in Chicago, and most of her work is there. But she does a lot in New York too."

"And she's good?"

"She's the best! I wouldn't want anyone else working on this event. You'll see!" I exclaim.

He scratches his cheek. "Did you know Michelle sold her business?"

Michelle is one of the top event planners in New York. I reply, "No, I didn't. Who bought it?"

"Casey."

"Ew. She hated Casey, and he does horrible work," I claim.

Carmine nods. "Yep. So everyone is looking for a new company. If Arianna's as good as you say she is, she's got a huge opportunity."

"She is, but she's also pregnant. I'm not sure how much she wants to take on. You can discuss it with her."

He scans my face.

"What?"

"Is she anything like your husband?"

I swat him again. "Stop it. You promised."

He throws his hands in the air. "Fine. But can he stay back? I don't need his mafia ass breathing down my back."

I hold in my laugh. "Sure."

"And Killian. Have them go stuff themselves at the doughnut table."

"There's doughnuts here?" I ask.

Carmine wrinkles his nose. "Since when do you eat doughnuts?"

I shrug. "They sound good."

He scrunches his entire face. "Ugh. Suit yourself." He leans closer and whispers, "Now, did you hear the real reason Vivian isn't hosting her big bash this year?"

19

Gianni

One Week Later

"SOMEONE HAD TO HAVE SAID SOMETHING ABOUT HIM," I INSIST. Almost a month has passed since Uberto kidnapped Cara. There's no trace of him anywhere. It's like he magically disappeared into thin air.

Luca lights up a joint, takes a long drag, then holds it out to me. I shake my head as he blows it out. He answers, "No one has spoken about him. Whenever I bring him up, the subject quickly gets changed."

"I want him picked up," I reiterate.

"We're all working on it."

"Work harder. I'm losing my patience," I seethe.

Luca inhales another lungful of smoke. He holds it out again.

Fuck it.

I grab it, mimic his motions, and hold the smoke in my lungs for as long as I can. After I release it, I add, "Every day that bastard lives is another day my wife is in danger."

Luca's eyes darken. "I understand. You have my word that I'm fully committed to finding him. But we should discuss this security issue."

I walk over to the window and stare out at the lawn. Snow covers the grass. The cold air created ice chips around the glass, and long icicles dangle from the bare trees. I relay, "Fashion week starts in a few days. I've called in the Ivanov, O'Malley, and O'Connor security to assist. There'll be more men than needed. Plus, the families are all coming into town for the event. If any extra backup is needed, they'll step in without hesitation."

Surprise fills Luca's face. "The O'Connor boys are back from Ireland?"

"Yeah. They've been here for a few months." I don't add that when they arrived back in town, they helped Dante track down Bridget's rapists. Then they took part when we tortured and killed them.

Luca clenches his jaw.

"What's wrong?" I question.

"Nothing. Do me a favor and give me Brody's number."

"Why?"

Luca crosses his arms. "It's between him and me. Now send it to me."

I pull out my phone and share Brody's contact info. Luca's phone pings, and he asks, "When are our guys from Italy arriving?"

My anger flares again. I scowl. "Giuseppe promised my father the new crew would arrive in two weeks."

Luca snorts. "His word is growing old, isn't it?"

I glance behind my shoulder. We're in my office, and the door is closed, but I still need to be cautious. Papà doesn't tolerate anyone speaking ill of Giuseppe. But my irritation with him is to the point if Papà allowed us to sever ties, I would. It seems like it's been years since Giuseppe has done anything for us except take our money. I admit, "That's one way to put it."

Luca pins his cool gaze on mine. "At what point does it become apparent he isn't capable of helping us or isn't making us a priority? All he does is promise, and I can't remember the last time he came through. Meanwhile, our strength is dwindling. If we didn't have our alliances, we'd be screwed."

I can't disagree with anything he said. It's a truth my father doesn't want to acknowledge. His loyalty toward Giuseppe is so strong he has blinders on.

Luca takes the final puff of the joint and stubs it out in the ashtray. He rises. "Let me know if they ever arrive."

"Don't hold your breath," I mutter, then open the door.

Luca pats me on the back and leaves.

As soon as he steps out, my cell rings. I glance at the screen then answer, "Rubio. Tell me this one is better."

"Ettore's back in town. He appraised it higher than we expected. He said to tell you that if you don't approve this one, then nothing will be good enough," Rubio states.

"I'm not looking for good enough. This is for my wife. I'm looking for exceptional...one of a kind," I remind him.

The same day the Abruzzos attacked our SUV, I met with Rubio. The diamond I ordered for my Tesora arrived, but it wasn't the caliber I wanted. So I've had Rubio searching for the perfect diamond. He's sent me over a dozen options, and the one I chose last week the supplier assured him was a caliber he'd never seen before.

"Ettore insists it's perfection," Rubio declares.

Excitement flies through me. Every time I look at Cara's bare hand, panic crawls through my chest. Her collar gives me some sense of peace, but no one knows it's more than a necklace. I want the world to know that she's taken and off the market.

Ettore has been our family jeweler forever. He's my Papà's generation and does everything old school. But no one knows gems the way he does. If he thinks it's perfect, I don't doubt it's flawlessness. I reply, "I'm on my way."

"Later," Rubio says and hangs up.

I leave the office, go to the garage, and hop in my silver McLaren 720S Coupe. I slide my hand under the seat and double-check I have several magazines for my Glock, then turn on the car. Within minutes, I'm flying down the road, taking the curves faster than I should with the snowy conditions.

Another driver blares their horn when I pass a truck and only get back on my side of the road within seconds of hitting them.

Adrenaline surges through my veins. It's been months since I drove. The winters in New York can be intense, so I usually don't risk it. But driving has always been something that calms me. And the last few weeks, I can't seem to release the anxiety over Uberto constantly plaguing me.

I cut a sharp right, and more horns blare. I hit my Bluetooth and direct, "Call Pina."

She answers, "Well, well, well! If it isn't my favorite twin."

"Tell Dante that next time he calls you."

"Oh, I will," she sings. "Now, why are you calling me? I know your assistant quit again...although I have to say, she lasted two months longer than your last one, so bravo to you. But Dante has me on overtime right now, so I don't have time to do her work," she proclaims.

I groan inside. Pina's been Dante's assistant forever. She's amazing, and no matter how much I try to steal her from him, she won't take me up on my offers. It's for the best since he'd want to kill me, but I go through three or four assistants a year. No one is like Pina. Plus, she doesn't get intimidated and back down from us. I answer, "I only need one tiny thing."

She laughs. "Sure. And the Pope isn't Catholic."

"What does that mean?"

"Since when do you ask me for only a tiny thing?"

"This time, it's true. Plus, you know I always take care of you. I don't remember you complaining when I expressed my thanks and threw you some cash last time you helped me." I claim.

She grumbles. "Fine. If it's not tiny, you owe me double."

I veer left and accelerate past several cars. "I need you to get me a reservation at Marcos for tonight."

A laugh fills the line.

"What's so funny?" I ask.

"You do realize it's Friday night, and Marco's has a nine-month waiting list."

I speed up and enter the expressway. "So? What's the big deal. Work your magic."

"Ugh! You're so out of reality."

"Five grand if you can make it happen."

The line turns silent.

I glance at the dashboard screen. Her name is displayed. "Pina, are you still there?"

Her voice is full of disbelief. "You're going to pay me five grand to get you a dinner reservation?"

"Tonight. Seven o'clock."

"Jeez, why don't you get a little more specific."

My grin widens. "Make sure I have a good table. The more private, the better."

"Good Lord! You're seriously pushing it," she claims.

"It's five grand. You don't want a handout, right?" I ask, knowing how much Pina hates not earning her money. She grew up on the wrong side of the Bronx. Maybe it's why she can deal with Dante and the rest of us when we need something. Perhaps it's what made her turn her eye to all the shady shit we do. But she pulled herself up out of poverty, and she didn't do it with anyone's help. She earned everything she has, and whenever she's seen others try to take advantage of us, she's the first to call them out.

She sighs. "You're such a bastard."

"Yep. I know. Shouldn't you get off the phone and get me my table? Time's ticking," I taunt.

"Another a-hole comment. Do you think about how to be a jerk, or does it come naturally?" she fires, but I can hear her smile through the phone.

"It's totally natural. One of my true talents," I reply.

"Ha! I bet!"

I swerve across three lanes and cut someone off to exit the expressway. "Gotta go. Text me when it's taken care of." I hit the button to disconnect the call and turn up the music. My go-to 80's station blares out Starship's We Built This City. I tap my fingers on the steering wheel and turn into the shipping docks.

My chest tightens when I pass the road I'd turn to get to the Abruzzos territory. It takes everything I have not to turn and start shooting anyone I come across.

I count to thirty before I get to our area and park next to the door. Rubio is waiting when I step inside.

"Gianni. Wait until you see this," he says, his eyes twinkling with excitement.

It makes me antsier to see the diamond. I ask, "Where is it?"

Rubio pulls a jewelry bag out of his pocket. He reaches inside, informing me, "Ettore already set it on the band." He removes it and hands it to me.

My breath hitches. It's the third time I've held an internally flawless diamond. In the past, I sold them. Thankfully, this one is larger than what I could have given Cara. Also, at first glance, I can appreciate Ettore's precision when he set it.

Several moments pass, and then Rubio questions, "Are you going to say anything?"

I spin the ring in the light again, straining to find some flaw, but there's nothing the naked eye can see. I don't take my eyes off the round, brilliant-cut and answer, "It's beyond perfect."

Rubio chuckles. "Cara's going to flip when she sees it."

I inspect the band. Per my instructions, Ettore engraved part of what I had put on the collar—*Forever means forever.* I put it in the pouch, stick it in my pocket, then pat Rubio on the back. "You did good. It's incredible."

He puffs his chest. "Told you I'd come through for you."

"That you did. Now, how's the rest of the African shipment? Did we get it out of the port?"

"Still working on it. Our suppliers said they're laying low because their customs are still ransacking shipments. They plan on setting off tonight."

My chest tightens. More money is in that shipment than anything I've ever procured before. My buyers are throwing a fit that it isn't here yet. And I'm getting worried I'll lose them if it doesn't arrive soon. I glance around the warehouse then step closer to Rubio, lowering my voice. "As soon as it comes in, I need it rushed through processing. We can't afford to have our buyers put their cash into something else."

He nods. "Don't worry. I'm on it. But we also have the new set of buyers in our pocket if needed."

I furrow my eyebrows. "New set of buyers?"

Surprise fills Rubio's expression. "Didn't Massimo tell you?"

A bad feeling fills my gut. I count to ten, then ask, "Tell me what?"

"About the new buyers he found."

Not wanting to look incompetent or like we aren't on the same page, I respond, "Yeah, he did. Sorry, I forgot. I've been a bit preoccupied lately with everything else going on. I'll talk to Massimo and make sure he still has them ready to buy in case we need them."

"Alright. I've got shit to take care of, but I'll let you know when the shipment arrives," Rubio states, holding out his fist.

I bump it and leave. I get in the car, start the engine, and call Massimo.

"What's up?" he answers.

"I just spoke with Rubio. Is there anything you want to tell me?" I fume, pissed he set up a buyer without discussing them with me.

His voice matches how I'm feeling. "What would that be?"

"Don't play with me," I spout.

"This conversation is getting old."

I blurt out, "Since when do you find buyers without discussing it with me?"

"That's what this is about?"

"Damn straight," I fire back and gun it out of the loading docks.

Massimo huffs, "You called to yell at me about expanding our ability to offload?"

I hit the accelerator until the speedometer reads 130 miles per hour, but even that doesn't give me any stress relief. I bark, "We have a protocol for a reason. I'm in charge of approving the suppliers. Not you."

"Here we go," Massimo snarls.

"You have something you want to say to me?" I provoke.

He hesitates then questions, "Is there a point of this call?"

"Don't play dumb, little brother," I warn.

"Get off your high horse."

I take a sharp turn, and my tires squeal. "I'm on my way home. Meet me in my office in fifteen."

"Sorry. Not home."

"You better get your ass home," I threaten.

He snorts. "Don't tell me what to do."

"This isn't a game, Massimo. I want answers about who these suppliers are, and I want them now," I shout.

"They're fine. I vetted them. End of story," he claims.

"No. It's the end of the story when I say it is. I want all the details, and don't keep me waiting."

"Sorry. I'm across town and have other responsibilities today. If there's something you want to know, ask."

Rage fills me. "Massimo, I'm warning you. If you don't come home so we can discuss this, I'm going to Papà with this information."

"Seriously?"

"Yes. You've overstepped. Now get your ass in my office," I order.

"As I said, if you have questions, ask. I have too much to do to deal with your temper tantrum. Talk to you later," he states and hangs up before I can respond.

"Mother fucker!" I scream and hit the wheel. I try calling him back, but he sends me to voicemail.

I text him.

Me: *How did you even meet them?*

I get all the way home before he replies.

Massimo: *I know people.*

I take another deep anger-filled breath. My brother's new attitude is going to get him in trouble. I start to wonder why he's acting like this. Then it hits me.

A claw scrapes in my gut. I close my eyes, count to thirty, then text him.

Me: *She introduced you. Didn't she?*

He doesn't respond, and the horrible feeling I have expands exponentially.

Me: *Answer me!*

But I never get an answer. When I walk inside, the first person I see is my Tesora.

"Baby, you okay?" she asks.

I straighten my shoulders and nod. "All good. Hold on a second."

I text Pina.

Me: *Did you get it done?*

Pina: *I was just about to text you that you're all set.*

Me: *Good.*

Pina: *You're welcome.*

Me: *Thank you.*

I look at my Tesora. "Go put on your nicest dress."

She tilts her head. Her lips twitch. "Why is that?"

I step forward and tug her into me. I brush my lips against her ear. "Because I'm taking my sexy wife out to dinner. Now get going, or I won't chain you to the wall tonight."

Heat bursts in her cheeks. Her blue eyes meet mine, and her chest rises faster.

I chuckle. "Don't make me make good on my threat."

She gives me a little salute. "Message received." She glances around her then murmurs, "Should I wear panties or not?"

My lips curve. "Surprise me."

20

Cara

GARLIC, FRESH BASIL, AND ROASTED ONION BURST ON MY TONGUE. "Mmm. This is so good," I chirp, then take another bite of the four cheese manicotti.

A humorous expression fills Gianni's face.

"What's so funny?" I ask.

His lips twitch. "Nothing."

I finish chewing, swallow, then insist, "Something appears to be entertaining you."

His grin widens. "I'm just happy you're enjoying dinner."

I take a sip of my Barolo then pat the napkin over my lips. "I can't believe you got us in here. I couldn't get a reservation until June."

His smile turns into a smirk. He sits back in the booth and shrugs. "Nothing to it."

I laugh. "So you just snapped your fingers, and we got in?"

"Something like that. Anyway..." He picks up my hand and kisses the back. "I have something for you."

I set my fork down. "What is it?"

His face turns serious. "Something I wish I were able to give you a month ago. And it's been driving me nuts you don't have it."

Gianni's always lavished surprise gifts on me, so it's not out of his character, but I'm unsure what he's going to give me. I tilt my head. "Okay. But I have everything I need."

He grunts. "No, you don't."

"I don't?"

He slides closer to me and traces the edge of my collar. Over the last few weeks, I've worn it daily. It's a stunning piece, and I put it on no matter what I wear. Plus, something about the way Gianni's eyes spark when he sees me in it gives me an extra incentive.

Tingles erupt under his fingers and race down my spine. I inhale sharply, shifting in my seat. I still don't understand why the collar turns me on so much, but it's only intensified since he gave it to me in Canada.

His hot breath hits my ear. He slides his fingers under the collar, drags his other hand over my thigh until he's cupping my pussy, and murmurs, "It's time to be clear who you belong to."

My butterflies spread their wings. I turn my head so our breath merges. "I'm yours. You know this."

The corner of his mouth curves up in an arrogant manner. He claims, "Everyone needs to know you're mine."

A tiny laugh flies out of my mouth. "I'm pretty sure anyone who looks at us knows I belong to you."

"But do they know I'm your husband? Hmm?" he asks. His face returns to a determined expression.

"You tell anyone who doesn't already know we're married," I point out.

He picks up my hand and kisses it. Then he reaches into his coat pocket and pulls out the most impressive diamond ring I've ever seen. He raises it, so it's eye-level to me.

My mouth turns dry, and my pulse increases. It sparkles from the flickering candlelight, which only seems to magnify its brilliance. All I can do is gape.

Gianni palms my cheek and says, "A flawless diamond for my perfect woman. Now everyone will know you're mine." He takes my hand again and slides the ring over my finger.

It's all I ever wanted—not the caliber of the diamond because I would have been happy if he had given me a gummy ring and asked me to marry him—but to be his.

And this ring is totally Gianni. It's over the top, makes a statement, and I can't even imagine what it costs. He wants everyone to know I'm not on the market. This ring not only screams that but makes it clear my husband is a man of wealth and power.

I study my hand, trying not to cry, but a few tears fall. All I can manage is, "It's beautiful. Thank you."

He swipes at my tears and lowers his voice. "If you weren't married to me and I asked you to, what would you say?"

I swallow the lump in my throat then lick my lips. My answer is honest. I reply, "I'd say yes."

Arrogance lights up his face mixed with happiness. "You're happy with how things are between us then?"

More waterworks run down my cheeks. I take a moment to analyze his question. There isn't anything I'd change about our marriage. Gianni's been the perfect husband. He's kind, attentive, and can't keep his hands off me. Since we said our vows, he's put me first.

Worry fills his eyes when I don't respond right away. He asks, "Is there something you aren't pleased with?"

I shake my head. "No, baby. I love how things are between us."

Relief floods his expression. He gives me a chaste kiss. "Good, Tesora. I've never been this happy. More than anything, I want you to be happy."

"I am," I assure him without taking any time to ponder my answer. It's true. Things have been a bit chaotic between Fashion Week, figuring out the new normal, and the Abruzzo issues, but I've never felt so alive. I go to sleep with Gianni's arms wrapped protectively around me. I wake up to the same embrace, and everything feels perfect.

Yet it isn't only about our physical connection. In the past, he didn't display any vulnerability. Now, it's as if he's on a mission to show me his inner self, and I enjoy every minute of it. My love for him has only grown deeper.

He doesn't look convinced I'm telling the truth. He asks, "You are?"

"Yes," I assure him.

"Good. I want you to be happy, my Tesora," he restates.

"I am," I repeat, then kiss him, putting every part of my soul into it. When I retreat, I examine my ring again. "Thank you. This is stunning. Honestly. I've never seen anything so beautiful."

Pride sweeps his face. He tucks a lock of hair behind my ear, then dips his fingers to my collar. "Nothing is as beautiful as you. And I love you in this, too. Every time I see you wear it, my dick turns hard."

I bite on my lip, sliding my hand over his thigh and stroking it. I admit, "When I put it on, it makes me feel like I'm yours."

He laces his fingers through mine then closes our hands into a fist. He nods toward the diamond. "And this? Does this make you feel any more mine?"

I put my free hand on the back of his neck, moving my thumb under his ear. It's strange how something material can give you a sense of belonging to someone else, but that's exactly what the collar and ring do. I answer, "Yes. I feel completely yours."

Satisfaction fills his expression. His eyes gleam brighter. He presses his lips on mine, deepening his kiss until it's all-consuming, and I forget everything around me but him.

"Boss, time to go," Sandro barks.

Gianni's body stiffens. He breaks our kiss, turns his head, and looks up at Sandro. Concern laces his voice, but he keeps it calm. "What's going on?"

Sandro's forehead wrinkles. He has his hand near his gun, which he keeps under his sport coat. "Manny called and said we need to leave now. There are visitors in the building."

"Let's go, Tesora." Gianni jumps up, helps me out of the booth, and tosses cash on the table. He glances around the room then circles his arm around my waist.

Goosebumps break out on my arms. The damp cold from the cellar the Abruzzos held me captive in hits me, digging into my bones. I shudder, then try to push the memory out of my mind.

Sandro steps behind me. Gianni whisks me through the bustling restaurant, keeping me close to his side. He pulls his phone out, swipes at the screen, then says, "Is it clear outside?"

There's a pause then Gianni nods to Sandro. We step out of the building, and the cold wind whips into us so fiercely it would push me backward if Gianni weren't holding me so tightly.

Manny is waiting at the curb with the SUV. We all get in, and he pulls out into traffic the moment the door closes.

Gianni rolls the divider window down. "Who was inside?"

"Jacopo, his top three men, and their families," Manny replies.

"I didn't see any of them," Gianni comments.

Sandro turns in his seat. "They had the private room. From what I gathered, it was Jacopo's daughter's birthday."

Gianni releases a deep breath and tugs me tight into his chest. "Keep a close eye and make sure no one is following us."

"Got it, boss," Manny replies.

Gianni puts the divider window up. He kisses the top of my head. "Are you okay?"

I tilt my head up. "Yes."

"I'm sorry, Cara."

"It's okay. It's not your fault," I try to assure him.

His fingers caress my biceps. "My job is to protect you. Putting you in a room with a bunch of Abruzzos isn't going to keep you safe."

"You didn't know."

"I should have."

"How would you do that? You can't get the reservation list for every restaurant in the city. Nor can you control if we're out and they show up," I point out.

His eyes darken. He studies me for a moment, then sniffs hard. He turns and stares out the window.

I count to twenty. He still doesn't take his eyes off the glass. I straddle him, turn his face toward mine, and place both hands on his cheeks. "Let's not let the Abruzzos ruin our night."

Hatred swirls in Gianni's orbs. "You didn't even get to finish your dinner."

I shrug. "Isn't that why we have a five-star Michelin chef?"

"I wanted tonight to be special for you," he admits.

"It was and still can be."

He sighs. "You didn't get to finish your manicotti or have dessert."

I sit back on his lap, then pull his phone out of his pocket. I hold it in front of him and say, "You're a man who makes things happen. Call the chef and have him recreate our dinner. We'll eat in our suite."

He slides his hand through my hair, pulling me closer to him and resting his palm on my skull. His lips are inches from mine, and he questions, "How did I get so lucky to marry you?"

My heart soars. It always happens every time Gianni compliments me, but I feel the shift in him. He's not holding back as he used to. It's as if the wall came down, and he's able to wear his heart on his sleeve where I'm concerned. I tease, "You saved me and hijacked me to Vegas, remember?"

Something passes in his expression. I'm unsure if it's regret or anger. Maybe it's a mix of both. He closes his eyes briefly then seethes, "I *will* kill all of them for what they did to you."

As much as I want them dead so we can be safe and move on with our lives, I also don't want to let them steal anything else from us. I move my knees another inch, so they touch the back of the seat. I caress the side of his head then reply, "Let's forget they exist for the rest of the night. Now call the chef."

His lips twitch. "I kind of like this bossy side of you."

"Ha ha! Start dialing!"

He grabs the phone, swipes at his phone, then holds it to his ear. He says, "Cara and my dinner got cut short. We're on our way home. Can you whip up some manicotti and the new dessert you were telling me about the other day?"

He listens and pecks me on the lips. His hand slides up my thigh and under my dress until it reaches my ass. He squeezes my cheek and gives me another kiss.

He retreats and says into the phone, "Great. We'll eat in our suite. Thanks. Ciao." He tosses his phone on the seat, then puts his lips back on mine, rolling his tongue inside my mouth.

I wrap my arms around him, kissing him back with the same intensity and grinding my lower body against his growing erection.

He mumbles between kisses, "You didn't wear panties."

I move my mouth to his ear, nibble on his lobe, and reach for his zipper, freeing his cock. He groans when I lightly drag my nails over his shaft. I sink over it, taking all of him at once while letting out a shaky breath.

"Fuuuck Tesora," he murmurs, gripping my ass cheek tighter and pulling on my hair until I'm facing the ceiling. He scrapes his teeth down my neck, then bites my collarbone.

A sensual mix of pleasure and pain shoots through me. Lately, everything Gianni does to me feels more intense. I moan, "Oh God."

"Who do you belong to?" he growls.

"You baby. Only you," I reply, trying to ride him faster, but he moves his hand to my hip and keeps me at the same speed.

"When we get home, I'm licking and sucking every inch of your pussy. And when you come, I'm going to do it all over again until you have no voice left," he declares.

My insides clench his shaft. The nerves on my walls awake in delight. My breath hitches more, and I try to move faster again, but he keeps me at the same slow pace. I plead, "Please."

He replies with a kiss, then releases his grip on my hip, moving it back to my ass. "You're greedy tonight. Tell me how much you love me again."

"So much, baby. I love you so so much," I whisper, pressing my forehead to his and riding him faster.

"Tell me you love being my wife," he demands, his eyes piercing into mine.

"It's all I ever wanted," I confess.

"And you love it?" he repeats.

Heat sweeps through my veins so hot pellets of sweat break out on my skin. Tiny sensations grow, causing spasms against his erection. I cry out, "Yes. I love being your wife. I love you."

His breath picks up. He keeps his hand firm on my ass and his other arm around me, caging me as close to him as possible. He moves his mouth to my ear. "All night, Tesora. I'm going to make you orgasm so many times tonight, you'll be too sore to walk in the morning. When you can't take anymore, you'll beg me to stop. But I'm not going to. I'm going to give you more and more until you have nothing left to give me. Do you understand?"

A burst of tingles erupts in my spine. I shudder, then adrenaline rolls through my body, bringing me to the edge.

Gianni holds my face in front of his. "You're beautiful. Now ride me like this is the only chance you have to have me tonight." He brings his hand to my hip, slams me down on him, moves me back up, then does it all over again.

All hell breaks loose in my body. An orgasm hits me like a lightning rod. It feels like it comes out of nowhere and electrifies every cell in my body. I cry out, "Baby! Oh, God! Baby!" Then my eyes roll back.

He holds me tight, stroking my spine, and guiding my hips to extend my orgasm. In a firm voice he proclaims, "From now on, you tell me when you're coming. I want to hear it all night long. Understand?"

All I can reply is, "Baby, I'm still coming!"

21

Gianni

Several Days Later

"We located Uberto then lost him," Luca informs me.

"How did you let that happen?" I bark in a low voice, then glance back at my Tesora.

She only fell asleep a few hours ago. Since I gave her a ring, we've not had a lot of sleep. And I don't know who's more insatiable, her or me. Any chance we get, we're wrapped around each other.

It's barely four in the morning. She needs to wake up at four-thirty. I want her to get the extra half-hour of rest.

Fashion Week starts today, and it's taking everything I have not to make any stupid moves. I assumed we would have found Uberto by now. The thought of Cara running around backstage and at all the events doesn't sit easily with me. I may have assigned more security on her than I'd typically issue, but I'm not taking any chances. Yet the extra precautions still don't ease my worries.

Luca coughs and clears his throat. "The bastard is sneaky."

I move into the bathroom and shut the door. "He's getting help from someone. Find out who and bring them here."

Luca goes into another coughing fit. It lasts for about a minute. When he catches his breath, I ask, "Are you coming down with something?"

"Think I caught a bug upstate."

"Would only be worth it if you had brought him back," I mutter.

Luca lowers his voice. "Listen, Gianni. I think we need to pull the O'Connors into this."

My body stiffens. If Bridget's brothers or their men help us, her father Tully will want something in return. We have an alliance, and our families are close. However, Tully can hold favors over men's heads, and he always uses it to his advantage. He doesn't play that game with my Papà, but the few times my brothers and I needed his son's help, he always got us to return the favor with something more complicated. He'll claim it won't be, but it will always be a task we'd prefer not to do. I reply, "You know how Tully gets."

"Yeah. There'll be a price to pay for sure. But we need some more trackers. I spoke with Brody. He's in if you're good with it," Luca says.

I run my hand through my hair and stare at myself in the mirror, counting to fifty, debating if I want to owe Tully.

Luca interrupts my thoughts, confessing, "Until Giuseppe makes good on his promise to send over experienced trackers, we don't have the proper manpower for this caliber of a hunt. We would have gotten Uberto a few nights ago if I had more men. You have to give me some more resources. Brody's assured me he and his guys can focus on this with me."

Luca's right. He's needed more manpower for a while now. I curse Giuseppe in my head for continuing to not come through for us.

Luca adds, "If I don't show my face to the Abruzzos soon, they're going to suspect something. I can't be in two places at once. Your Papà will go mad if anything happens to my cover. And you know we don't have anyone on the team who can run this while I'm away. We need Brody."

I release a breath, and it comes out in a groan. I'm going to owe Tully. I hate being in that position, yet I need my Tesora to be safe. "Fine. Pull Brody and his men in on this. But I want Uberto found now, Luca. You capture him and bring him to me."

"On it. Later." Luca starts coughing again, and then the line turns dead.

I pace the bathroom, then open the door and step into the bedroom. I'm lost in thought facing the window when Cara slides her arms around my waist from behind. She presses her warm skin against my back, saying, "Penny for your thoughts?"

I close my eyes, reach behind me and slide my palms over her ass. "You should try to get a few more minutes of sleep."

She laughs.

I spin and cup her cheeks, tilting her head up. "What's funny?"

Her eyes gleam with excitement. "There's no way I can go back to sleep. It's Fashion Week!"

As much as I'm concerned about her security, I'm so proud of her for this accomplishment. She's earned it, and I want her to enjoy every minute. Still, I tease, "No way! Is it?"

She rolls her eyes. "Funny."

I give her a quick kiss. "Go get ready. I'll have some breakfast brought up."

She beams, "Good. I'm starving after the workout you gave me last night. I'm sure I burned more calories than I ate."

I pat her ass. "You might want to eat all day. I'll be looking to do the same tonight."

"Ohhh, don't tease me, Mr. Marino," she chirps, then struts into the bathroom, dramatically swaying her hips and long brown hair.

I chuckle, then text the chef what I want his staff to prepare. I stick my head past the bathroom door and tell Cara, "Breakfast will be up soon. I'm going to get a quick workout in."

"Okay, baby. Thanks," she replies, then steps into the shower.

I toss on shorts, a T-shirt, and socks. Then I lace up my sneakers. When I get to the gym, Massimo is already there. His hand is in his hair, and his shoulders are tense. He's facing the wall and on the phone. He seethes, "I told you not to go."

I stay quiet, cross my arms, and lean against the wall.

He states, "No. I told you how I felt about you seeing those people. You promised me you wouldn't go."

Pissed, I shake my head. I have no doubt he's talking to the librarian and didn't cut it off like I told him to.

He scolds, "I don't want to hear your excuses. This conversation is over. I have shit to do." He hangs up and spins. When he sees me, his scowl deepens. He accuses, "Are you spying on me now?"

I push myself off the wall. "That was the librarian, wasn't it?"

"Not your business," he hurls, then steps in front of the squat machine. He picks up a fifty-pound weight and adds it to the bar.

I grab another one and put it on the other side. We both keep adding more until I ask, "Why are you playing with fire? Her past relationship with Donato is too coincidental. She's working for the Abruzzos. You're smart. Use your head on this one."

He throws his hands in the air. His face turns red with rage. "Jesus, you're arrogant. You don't know anything about her. And for the last time, she has nothing to do with the Abruzzos."

I snicker. "Really? Who did she go see last night?"

Massimo's eyes turn to slits. "None of your business."

"Was it an Abruzzo?"

"Are you kidding me? You think I would put up with that?" Massimo angrily shakes his head. "Not only are you severely misinformed, you apparently think I'm a traitor too."

"No, brother. I think you're making decisions with your wrong head."

"Fuck off, Gianni," he curses, then sits down on the machine.

"You're both up early," Finn O'Malley calls out, walking into the gym with Maksim Ivanov. Both families are staying here with their wives for Fashion Week.

"I'm trying to explain to my little brother which head he should think with," I reply, walking toward Finn and Maksim.

"Enough, unless you want to take it out in the ring. And I'm warning you. I won't hold back," Massimo threatens.

Maksim arches his eyebrows. In his Russian accent, he states, "Boris will be here in a few minutes. He's due for a good ass-kicking."

"Why? What did he do?" I ask.

"I said to drop it," Boris barks, stepping toward us with Killian in tow.

"Don't you think you should put some more weight on there?" Killian jests at Massimo.

He grunts and continues his squats.

I glance at Finn and Maksim so they can tell me what the deal is between him and Boris, but Maksim is too busy glaring at Boris.

Finn pats me on the back, muttering, "You don't want to know."

I take the hint to drop it and move toward the treadmill to warm up. The rest of the Ivanovs and O'Malleys trickle in, as well as my other two brothers and Bridget's son Sean. The gym becomes a crowded room of sweat, loud music, and taunting jokes.

When I finish my workout, I return to the suite. Cara is putting her makeup on. Breakfast is sitting on the table, and she has a plate with a half-eaten piece of toast and some scrambled eggs on her vanity.

I lean down. She looks up, and I peck her on the lips, inhaling her fresh floral scent. "Is that the new perfume I left on your vanity?"

"Yes. Thank you. I love it," she chirps.

I kiss her again. "Anything for you, Tesora. Let me refill your coffee." I pick up her mug and go to the table.

"Thanks, Baby."

"Like I said, anything for you." I wink at her, then add cream and sugar. I set it back on her vanity. "I'm going to shower and get ready."

"Okay. I'll be here," she sings.

I kiss the top of her head and get in the shower. I don't take long and am soon drying off. I step out of the bathroom and ask, "What are you wearing?"

"The new black dress you bought me last week. It's hanging on the door hook."

I bought her several black dresses when I went on a little shopping spree, so I'm unsure which one she chose to wear.

I open her walk-in closet and glance at the dress, nodding in approval. It's classy and chic. I bought it because it's perfect for the occasion but also not so flashy it'll make it seem like Cara is trying to compete with the models. It's a genuine concern Cara voiced when she was looking in her closet and picking out her and my outfits for this week.

I reach for the hanger and look at the gold cocktail dress behind it. "I assume you're wearing this one tonight?" I ask, holding it so Cara can see.

She peeks at it and returns to putting her mascara on. "Yep."

"Will you have time to come home and change?"

"Probably not. We'll have to change there."

"Okay." I go into her closet, find a garment bag, then put the gold dress inside it. Then I find my outfits and add the tuxedo. I slip into my black dress shirt, slacks, and sport coat.

Cara comes into the closet. Her black lace bra and matching thong set is see-through.

My dick starts to harden, and I tug her against me, palming her ass. "I think you're trying to make yourself late, Mrs. Marino."

She softly laughs. Her blue eyes sparkle with happiness, and that makes me elated. She flattens both hands against my chest. "Sorry, my Italian Stallion. You're going to have to save it for later tonight."

I exaggerate my groan and tighten my palms on her cheeks, pulling her, so her stomach is against my erection.

She laughs again, pushes my chest, and announces, "I need to get dressed."

I don't budge. "I could bend you over the dresser, and we could have a quickie."

She pushes harder, laughing. "Nooo! Not this morning!"

I chuckle, kiss her until she's breathless, then murmur, "You sure you want to skip the quickie?"

She wiggles out of my grasp and high-tails it to her closet. "Sorry! Maybe tomorrow!"

"You're killing me, Tesora," I shout after her, then pick out my shoes.

"You'll live, loverboy!"

I grab black loafers and my Rolex. I take everything to the couch. My phone vibrates, and I read the text message.

Killian: *Arianna's trying to get ahold of Cara, but she isn't answering her phone.*

Me: *Everything okay?*

Killian: *Yeah, just something about later today. Can you have Cara check her phone?*

Me: *Done. See you in a few.*

"Cara, check your phone," I shout, then slide into my shoes. I secure my watch to my wrist, then go to the table. I take a few mouthfuls of scrambled eggs, toast, and the bacon I don't think Cara even touched.

She walks out, and I do a double-take. The dress fits her like a glove, hugging her curves in all the right places and giving her the perfect amount of cleavage. She has on a pair of blood-red ankle boots and the red ruby bracelet I gave her years ago.

"Wow! You look amazing," I tell her.

Her smile is so bright it lights up the room. She holds out her necklace. "Thanks. Can you help me with this? I can't seem to clasp it."

"Sure. You want this?" I ask, handing her the bacon.

She wrinkles her nose and shakes her head. "No."

"What's wrong? Since when don't you like bacon?"

"Don't you think it smells funny?"

I glance back at the tray of bacon, sniff hard, then look at my Tesora. "No. It's delicious too."

She steps back. "No bacon today."

"Okay then." I put the bacon down, wipe my hands, then move her hair over her shoulder. I take the matching necklace and secure it, then kiss the back of her neck. "How old were we when I gave you these?"

She spins into me and shrugs. "I think you were in your twenties, and I was barely legal."

"Sounds about right. I'm glad you kept them."

She touches the gem hanging below her neck. "They're timeless."

I lean down and kiss her. "They sure are. Everything okay with Arianna?"

"Yes. One of the vendors never got their order delivered. Arianna just wanted me to okay the substitution. Thankfully it isn't any of the model requirements. No biggie."

"Well, that's good. God forbid they should drink the wrong type of water or something," I jest.

Cara smirks. "Yep. God forbid. Are you ready?"

"Let me brush my teeth," I reply, then go into the bathroom. I quickly brush then swish with mouthwash. I spit it out, wipe my mouth, then join Cara. "Let's go." I grab her hand and lace my fingers between hers. We go through my wing and down the stairs.

Killian and Arianna are sitting on the bench waiting for us. Arianna's pale. Her belly looks a lot larger than a few weeks ago. Killian hands her a bottle of water.

"You okay?" I fret.

"She just has a little morning sickness, that's all," Killian relays while she takes a sip.

More concern fills me. "Isn't she past that stage?"

Killian shakes his head. "The doctor said it's fine for it to come back in the last trimester. He said it happens to a small portion of his patients." He pushes a lock of her hair behind her ear.

"Do you need anything else? Ginger or something?" Cara asks.

Arianna shakes her head. The color slowly returns to her cheeks. "I'm okay. I have some ginger suckers in my bag if I need them."

"Ginger suckers?" I question.

"They help with nausea," Arianna replies.

I frown. "Are you going to toss your cookies?"

She rises and hands the bottle to Killian. "Nope. All good." She smiles at Cara. "Let's go to Fashion Week!"

We leave the house and get into the SUV. A second one leads while a third one is behind us. It's dark, but the morning light is trying to peek through the clouds. Snow covers the ground. Ice hangs off trees. Dense fog blocks my vision past ten feet.

"Cara, make sure Arianna takes some breaks today," Killian orders.

"Of course."

Arianna groans. "Killian!"

"What?"

"I'm capable of figuring out when I need a quick rest."

Killian pins his orbs on Cara. "I'm serious. She never stops unless you make her."

"Can't help it if I'm younger than you and have more energy," Arianna teases.

Killian smirks. "More energy? Is that a challenge?"

Arianna's cheeks heat. "Sure. Bring it on."

I turn my head toward Cara, not wanting to think about what their challenge entails. I'm glad my sister is happy, but she's still my little sister. I say, "You'll have four guards watching you at all times."

She scrunches her forehead. "They're going to blend in, correct? So no one thinks they're mine?"

"That's right. And I'm not going anywhere today. If you need me and can't find me, just call," I add.

She tilts her head and strokes my cheek. "I'm sure I'll be fine. No one will get to me with four guards. Why don't you and the guys go do something fun?"

I grunt. "No way. We've already discussed this."

"Okay then. Thought I'd give you one more out," she claims.

I lean closer to her, pinning my eyes on hers. In a firm voice, I state, "I don't want an out."

She smiles, and her blues glisten. I wasn't talking about the event, and she understood what I meant. It's a sign of how far we've come. She kisses the back of my hand as we pull up to the building and admits, "Me either."

My heart soars. It's two words that never meant anything in the past but mean everything to me now.

The door opens, and cold air tears my gaze off hers. I get out, then hold out my hand to help my Tesora out of the car. "Let's see you in action." I guide her into the building. Killian, Arianna, and all the guards we assigned both of them follow.

Within seconds of getting through the show's security, Cara and Arianna go into work mode. As much as I planned on keeping her within eyesight, it's impossible. There are too many people who need her. She gets pulled into different areas, including dressing rooms I'm not allowed to enter.

When she completely disappears, my stomach flips. Panic grows, so I try to follow her into the room she's in, but the show's security guard stops me. "No one beyond this point unless you have clearance."

"My wife is Cara Marino," I seethe.

He puffs up his chest and steps closer to me, firmly restating, "Like I said, no one beyond this point unless you have clearance."

I square my shoulders. "Do you think you intimidate me?"

"Are you looking to get banned for the week?"

"Is that a threat?" I hurl.

"Whoa. Easy there." Killian grabs my arm and pulls me back.

I spin on him. "My wife—"

"Needs to do her job. And you don't need to get banned. Just chill."

"Don't tell me—"

"Gianni? Oh my God! Gianni Marino!" a woman shrieks. I spin and cringe. A model, Veronica Galanis, who I dated a few years ago throws her arms around me. I lose my balance so I grab her waist to steady myself and not fall backward.

She grabs my cheeks, then plants a lipstick-filled kiss on my lips. "I've missed you! Did you come to see me?"

Before I can respond and tell her how ridiculous that notion is, my gut drops. Standing in the doorway next to the guard, my wife is glaring at me with a hurt expression.

I try to push Veronica away, but Cara shakes her head, spins, and rushes back into the room. As soon as she gets through the door, the guard steps in front of it, smirking at me.

All the rage I've been feeling exponentially expands. Killian tries to step between us, but it's too late. I reach back and land a fist in the guard's nose.

Blood bursts everywhere. Veronica screams, and chaos begins to bloom all around me.

22

Cara

MY INSIDES QUIVER, AND NAUSEA HITS ME. I RUSH TO THE bathroom, hovering over the toilet. Beads of sweat pop out on my skin. I force the bile rising up my throat back down.

Pull it together. I have work to do, I reprimand myself.

Not Veronica Galanis.

Anyone but her.

I close my eyes and lean against the stall door, breathing through my anger. Veronica Galanis is one of my top clients. She's the epitome of a beautiful Greek woman, has the body men fantasize about, and gets top dollar for her work.

She's also a self-conscious, nasty bitch who needs constant attention and someone to pump up her ego. Every time I get a request to book her, I have to reassure her she's one of the most gorgeous women on the planet. At shows like this, I spend too much time telling her to breathe and get on the stage.

"Ugh." I groan, then think, *he could have slept with anyone but had to do it with her.*

Now I get to imagine them together for the rest of my life.

I'm going to kill him for allowing her to kiss him.

I knew he'd only be faithful for so long before he couldn't help himself.

Arianna's voice interrupts my thoughts. "Cara. Are you okay?"

I manage to drag myself off the ground. I take a deep breath, step out of the stall, then point to Arianna. "Don't you dare come in here and stick up for your brother."

Her eyes widen. "I'm not. I wouldn't."

"No?" I question in surprise.

She shakes her head. "Of course not. I'm not naive. I know he's no saint."

I sarcastically laugh then splash water on my face. I pat my cheeks dry and state, "That's calling the kettle black. But glad we're on the same page."

Arianna steps closer. She pins her eyebrows together. "What did he do?"

"You didn't see it?"

"No. I just saw you run in here looking green."

I take several breaths, count to eight, then curse Gianni further for putting his habit in my head. "He just kissed Veronica Galanis."

She wrinkles her nose. "Ewe. Yuck."

Another emotion-filled laugh comes out of me. It's the perfect response but doesn't reduce the hurt. "You aren't a fan?"

Arianna scrunches her face further. "Of Veronica? No way! She's a self-absorbed, psychotic leech. Gianni couldn't tolerate her for very long either."

A tiny part of me calms. "No?"

Arianna shakes her head. "No. She came to one of my Papà's parties years ago. Something happened that night, and Gianni told her to leave. For several weeks she showed up at our house. The guards stopped letting her in after the first encounter because Gianni banned her from entering the premises."

More relief fills me, but I'm not going to roll over and act like nothing just happened. I blurt out, "If that's the case, then why did he just kiss her?"

Arriana bites her lip, deep in thought. I count to five, and she cautiously asks, "Did he kiss her, or did she throw herself on him?"

"What makes you ask that? See, I knew you'd stick up for him," I snap.

She throws her hands in the air. "I'm not! I just know what happened with Killian and his ex and—"

"What are you talking about? Did he cheat on you? I'll kill him!" I hurl.

She shifts on her feet, takes a deep breath, then looks at the ceiling. She meets my eyes and states, "No. He didn't. But his ex came into the pub and threw herself on him."

"And he let her?" I bark, disgusted with him as much as Gianni.

"No! She was drunk. He tried to push her off him. It... it's a long story."

"So you have to worry about this woman all the time?"

Arriana huffs. "No. I wouldn't put up with that. He banned her and her friends from the pub. Plus, I taught Killian a lesson."

"How?"

A blush crawls through her cheeks. "I don't want to get into it. The point is that he didn't want her. Sometimes these women are so forceful throwing themselves on men it puts the guys into a situation they don't want to be in."

I snort. "I'm sure that's what your brother will claim."

She puts her hand on her hip. "Maybe you should talk to him and find out what happened. He's crazy about you. You're the only one he's always gone back to. I'm not sticking up for him, but I know him. He's always been into you."

The past comes back to haunt me, and it hurts. I huff, "Interesting you think so because he sure as hell didn't show me that all these years."

She nods. "Yeah. I know. I love all my brothers, and like I said, none of them are saints. He's a moron, but he finally got smart and married you, didn't he? And Gianni's changed since marrying you. I see it. My brothers and Killian see it. Even Papà notices."

I cross my arms, biting my tongue from any further revelations of my fears. No matter what Arianna claims, she's his sister. Blood will always be thicker than water. And right now, I don't want to hear anyone stick up for Gianni. When Veronica finds out I'm married to him, there'll be hell to pay. This is the biggest event I've ever gotten to be a part of, and now isn't the time for her to have a hissy fit. I take a deep breath and order, "Don't tell Veronica I'm married to Gianni."

Confusion fills Arianna's expression. "Why? She needs to know not to touch him again."

I release an anxious breath. "I can't afford for her to not be on her game. She's bad enough normally. If she's still into your brother and finds out about us, she's going to be a major thorn in our side for the entire week."

Arianna rolls her eyes. "She's such a drama queen."

"You have no idea."

"Okay, but I think you should go talk to Gianni."

I stay silent and count to twenty, then shake my head. "No. I don't want to hear his excuses. I have a job to do, and so do you. Are you ready to do it?"

Hurt fills Arianna's face. "Yes. Of course. I'm not trying to get out of my duties."

I sigh. "I'm sorry. I didn't mean it like that."

She pauses, giving me the Marino staredown I know too well.

I add, "I mean it. My intention wasn't to offend you or insinuate anything about your work ethic."

"Okay. Apology accepted." She steps forward and hugs me. "Just promise me you'll talk to Gianni about this and keep an open mind. I honestly can't see him wanting anything from Veronica except for her to stay far, far away. She annoys him to no end. Plus, I've never seen him so happy since you got married. He's always loved you, and you've always been the one."

I want to believe her words but all my past fears are like a hammer pounding into me. And Arianna has always been a romantic at heart. Regardless, I don't want to keep talking about this. I force a smile and put my arm around her shoulders. "Let's get out there before people start to look for us."

We leave the bathroom. Organized chaos is everywhere. Seamstresses are sewing final adjustments made on wardrobe pieces. Makeup artists and hairstylists are everywhere. The scent of hair products flares in my nostrils. My stomach flips from the smell, but I put my hand on a table and steady myself.

Arianna and I part. I study the scene. A line seems to divide the room. My veteran clients are on one side and my more inexperienced ones on the other. It doesn't surprise me, yet it's not what I'm trying to achieve. Veronica sits on a couch with her legs crossed while two nail techs, one on each side, adhere her acrylics. I manage to avoid her for a mere two seconds before she seems to sense me. She pins her steel gaze on mine, making my stomach pitch.

I know her expression all too well because I've seen her in action too many times. She knows I'm Gianni's wife, yet instead of backing down, her eyes are challenging me.

Great.

Better to get this over with now rather than later.

Calm down first. She has the most time in the show. Plus, she's the grand finale.

Screw her. He's my husband. I need to make it clear what's appropriate behavior around Gianni and what isn't.

Narrowing my eyes, I square my shoulders and walk over to her. Neither of us flinches. I state, "When you're done with your nails, we need to talk in private."

A sinister smile grows on her lips. Her voice oozes fake sweetness. "Whatever about?"

"Gianni."

"Oh? What about him?"

All ability to keep my cool flies out the window. "Let's not play dumb, Veronica. We're married. I'm not sure what that spectacle was out there, but I can assure you, I won't put up with it."

She feigns a yawn. I want to smack her. I crumble my hand into a fist at my side. She bats her eyelashes and smiles bigger. "If you have an issue with Gianni, you can take it up with him."

I demand, "Stay away, Veronica. This is your only warning."

She turns to the nail tech on her right. "Did you hear her threaten me?"

The nail tech glances nervously between us.

I remind myself I'm here for work. I quickly order, "Don't answer her." I turn back to Veronica.

She smirks, "You know what I find amusing about Gianni?"

Don't fall into her trap. Tell her to stay away and walk away.

My willpower is too weak. I can't help myself. I fall into her tap, asking, "What's that?"

Her eyes brighten. Arrogance expands in her expression. "He gets bored so easily."

Her statement hits my last nerve. I blink hard to avoid showing her the effect her statement has on me. I lean down near her ear and murmur, "You know what I find interesting about you?"

She turns her head, facing me, taking the bait quicker than I took hers. "What's that?"

"You're running out of time. Your career will one day be over. The only thing left will be memories and your has-been status. When that happens, you're going to think of me. Do you know why?"

All the insecurities I am too aware of flood her eyes. She swallows hard and chokes out, "Why would I think of you?"

I harden my voice. "Because I'm through with you. After this week, I'll no longer represent you. The phone call I'm making as soon as we finish this conversation is going to be to my attorney. He's going to sever our contract. And you're going to learn just how much bull shit of yours I've put up with that all the other agencies won't."

A nervous laugh flies out of her mouth. "You wouldn't. I make you too much money."

I stand straighter. "Is that what you think?"

She huffs. "Of course it is."

I pat her shoulder. "Thanks for letting me know your thoughts." All the rationale I normally have to keep things professional disappears. The crap I'm tired of putting up with takes its toll. I pledge to no longer be any model's doormat. Maybe it's career suicide, but if it is, so be it. I step back and shout, "Can everyone give me your attention?"

The room turns to silence. I glance around it, making eye contact with all the models. I pause a few seconds longer on those who have grown an ego lately and become prime Madonnas.

"Well, go on and get on with it," Veronica snarls.

I ignore her. "A lot of you have been with me for a long time. At one point, you were over there." I point to the side of the room where my newer models are getting ready, then continue, "At every point of your career, I've been there for you. I've taken care of scandals, so they don't hurt your career. I've convinced companies to hire you when they weren't entirely sure if you were the right fit. And I've bent over backward to fulfill your silly whims."

Some of my veteran models shift on their feet. Other's eyes dart around the room.

I continue, "I want to be very clear. I'll continue to fight for you to get the work you do, but I'll no longer put up with your abuse. It includes any nasty behavior toward your colleagues." I point between the veterans and newbies. "Starting next week, I'll be evaluating who I want to work with and who doesn't fit into my agency's culture. What you do during our Fashion Week time together will go into my decision. But I should mention I've already made one decision. The first person I'm parting ways with is Veronica Galanis."

Loud gasps fill the room. Thick tension fills the air as different reactions fill my client's expression. Some seem horrified. Others lips twitch. These are the ones who Veronica has made a point to make uncomfortable over the years.

Her voice shakes as she claims, "I was going to fire you anyway."

I smile at her. "Good to know." I turn back to the others. "If my agency represents you, then you represent me. I expect you to act with decency toward everyone. That includes the professionals who make you look amazing, other models, and me. If you can't do that, let me know right now."

If a pin dropped, you'd hear it. No one moves.

Studying the room again, I state, "Since you'll all eventually find out, I recently got married to Gianni Marino." I pause, assessing expressions to give me an idea about who's dated him.

Shakira Knightly, another veteran model, has guilt in her eyes.

I focus on her. In as friendly of a voice as I can muster, I declare, "I'm not naive. I realize many of you in this room have dated him. Hell, let's be honest. You've slept with him. Let me be very clear. The past is the past. I hold no bad feelings toward any of you, but as I stated, the past is the past. If you try to disrespect my marriage, I will drop you."

"Right on," shouts Katrina Cabrera, the first client I ever signed. Unlike many of my clients, she's never gotten the ego and always stayed down to Earth. No one knows, but this is her last show. She wants to retire and told me she prefers to go out with a bang. She claimed there's no better place to do it than Fashion Week. I couldn't argue her rationale.

I take a deep breath, smiling as big as I can. "With that said, I want you all to know how proud of you I am. You've worked hard to get here. Going forward, I want us to continue the amazing work we do. This is your moment. Let's have a great week together."

I spin to walk out of the room and get some fresh air. One of the hairstylists, who is the only one who seems to be able to deal with Veronica, steps in front of me. "Hold on."

I arch my eyebrows.

She puts her arm on my shoulder and spins me. "I think Cara deserves some appreciation. I've worked with her from the start. All I can say is many of you have never thanked her. And the truth is most of you wouldn't be where you are without her."

Someone begins to applaud. Soon, the entire room is clapping. It all overwhelms me. A tear escapes, and I wipe it away, nodding, "Thank you." Several people hug me, which only makes me more emotional. When I can finally leave the room I scurry out.

"Ma'am," the security guard nods. His eyes are black and blue. One is swelling so much his eye is a mere slit.

I don't remember it from earlier, and I wonder what happened, but I don't ask about it, attempting to not focus on it. I smile at him, spin away, and reach for my phone. My gut drops when I realize it's in my purse.

I walk around the area searching for Gianni. Arianna has a point. I don't know what happened with Veronica. And he has changed. I truly believe that in my heart. So, I need to find out. I'm not going to wait all day and let this stew.

Men's shoes clicking on the floor follow me. My chest tightens. The air in my lungs turns stale. I glance behind me. All four of the guards Gianni assigned to me are in the vicinity, and one is directly behind me.

I sigh in relief and keep looking for Gianni. I run into several people I know. We exchange quick conversations before I excuse myself to keep trying to find him.

I finally return to the entrance of the room the models are occupying. I ask the guard, "Do you know where my husband went?"

He sniffs hard. His nostrils flare wider than any man's I've seen before. If I were in a dark alley by myself, I'd be scared. He scowls deeper, questioning, "The dark-haired man who Veronica Galanis kissed?"

She kissed him! So much relief floods me I could hug the guard. Still, I blurt out, "She kissed him? He didn't kiss her?"

He shakes his head. "No ma'am. Not from what I witnessed."

My heart pounds faster. "Have you seen him?"

The guard's face hardens further. In a firm but emotionless voice, he informs me, "I assume he's getting processed."

"Processed?" I inquire in confusion.

"Yeah. He and the other guy he was with got arrested."

"Arrested?" I shriek, imagining Gianni in handcuffs. My chest tightens until I feel like I can't breathe.

The guard crosses his arms. "When men punch me, there are consequences."

My mouth almost drops to the floor. I gape at him, speechless for a brief moment, before pointing at his face and questioning, "He did that?"

"Yes, ma'am."

"Why?"

The guard cracks his neck. I wince, and he replies, "He tried to follow you inside. He doesn't have clearance. The other guy got involved as well. It took four of us to diffuse the situation."

I freeze, imagining Gianni and Killian fighting the guard. A large lump forms in my throat. I swallow it and spin, running toward the door.

"Ms. Marino!" A man calls out, but I don't stop.

I get outside, and a woman steps out of a cab.

"Ms. Marino!" the man yells again.

I don't stop. I jump inside and slam the door. "Take me to the nearest precinct and step on it!"

23

Gianni

"TURN TO THE SIDE," THE OFFICER INSTRUCTS.

Pissed, I grind my molars. I follow his orders and stand with my shoulder against the wall that has height markings on it. For all the crazy stuff I've done, not once have I ever gotten arrested. My plan was to not take my eyes off Cara the entire week. Now I'm stuck here, doing my best to stay calm. And there's no doubt Papà is going to be upset. He's probably already planning another stern lecture for me.

"Now the other way," the officer demands.

I sniff hard, do what he asks, and he snaps another photo. I keep my hands balled into a fist, still feeling the ink on them from when he took my fingerprints.

"Let's go," he states and leads me down a hallway.

I assume I'm going to a cell with Killian, but instead, he takes me to an interrogation room.

I stop outside the doorway and question, "Why are you putting me in here for a fist fight?"

"Do what you're told," a man barks.

I glance to the side of me. Two detectives step forward. One has a neutral expression. Another has hatred all over his face.

A bad feeling races through me. I stay frozen, not moving. I've never gotten interrogated before. Papà has several times. It's always been out of the blue when they picked him up. Each of my brothers has strict instructions on what to do if this happens, but it still makes me uneasy. "What's this about?"

"Inside," seethes the man. Hatred fills his expression. He motions toward the room.

Assessing the situation, I assume it's best to obey. I sit on the metal chair and start counting. The officer who booked me removes my handcuffs and leaves.

The two other men take seats. The one with the neutral expression says, "I'm detective Anderson. This is detective Contray."

Not flinching, I stare at the mirrored glass and begin counting. They both study me, but I keep my gaze between them. Anderson rises, then paces the tiny room. He says, "Gianni Marino. It looks like the apple doesn't fall far from the tree."

The piece of shit has a lot of balls insulting my Papà. Not flinching, I remind myself of everything he's instructed me to do in this situation. I count through my anger.

"It seems you've been busy," Contray declares.

I cross my arms, sit back in my chair, and scowl at him. I continue counting, resisting the urge to give him a piece of my mind yet also wondering what he's referencing.

Contray violently taps the table. "The club. The docks. It seems wherever you go, bloodshed follows."

My pulse pounds faster. Upon Dante's instructions, Finn and Killian O'Malley, along with my brothers, shot multiple high-ranking Abruzzos to rescue Brenna. Dante and I also took out more Abruzzos at the docks a few months back. I doubt these fuckers have any hard evidence I'm involved, but it's still nerve-wracking. I'd be in prison for life if they attached me to anything.

Still, I maintain my cool, not changing my demeanor. In an emotionless voice, I state, "I don't know what you're referring to."

Anderson chuckles. He turns to Contray. "I assumed he was a lot of things, but stupid wasn't one of them."

I wiggle my toes in my shoes, keeping my expression the same but wanting to show Anderson just how 'stupid' I am with my fists. I sniff hard, then lean forward. Lowering my voice, I claim, "Want to know what I think?"

Contray arches his eyebrows. "What's that?"

I study each man's face until they shift in their seats, then reply, "I think you don't know shit about anything. If you did, you wouldn't have me in here since I have no clue what you're refer-encing. But what I do know is that I have a right to an attorney if you want to have me in this room. So let me make my phone call."

"Lawyering up already, huh? It sounds like you've got lots to hide," Anderson accuses.

Ignoring him, I look at the mirrored glass. "Did you hear me say I'm utilizing my right to my attorney?"

Ten seconds of silence passes. I glance up at the camera in the corner of the room. "Are you recording this? I'm now stating for the third time I want my attorney."

Three seconds pass, and there's a knock on the glass. The door opens, and Contray scoots his chair back so fast it scrapes across the floor, making a loud shrill sound. He mutters under his breath, "Didn't think you were a pussy." He stomps out of the room, and Anderson follows.

The door slams and I stay in the same seated position for several minutes. An officer I haven't seen before steps inside. "Time to go. Rise and put your hands in front of you."

I assume the position, and he cuffs me. He leads me down the hallway and through another door. Cells line each side, and men begin to shout. He opens one and uncuffs me, then pushes me inside.

Relieved to be out of the room, I glance around my new surroundings. A homeless man sleeps on the bench. Another man with skull and dagger tattoos is wearing a white tank top and dirty, ripped jeans. He scowls, and I give him a similar look, so he knows not to attempt to mess with me. A third man smells like a brewery. I assume he's still drunk, high, and possibly has some mental issues. He's babbling to himself.

"Does he ever shut up?" I ask the man wearing the tank top.

He moves his jaw from side to side as if contemplating whether to answer my question or not. He finally responds, "He'll shut up in about two minutes before starting again."

I hold in a groan and nod. I pace the cell, wondering how long I'll be in here. They haven't allowed me to make my phone call. I decide I'll kick up a fuss when the next guard comes through.

After a few hours of listening to the drunk guy on and off, I get antsy. I turn to the tank top man. "Does a guard ever come down here?"

He shrugs. "Not unless they're adding someone else to a cell."

"Great. How long have you been in here?"

"Three days."

My gut drops at the thought. In disbelief, I question, "Three?"

He glowers. "Yep. That's what happens when you can't afford an attorney. The court-appointed ones don't do shit for you."

"But you got your phone call?"

"I was offered one but told them I didn't have an attorney, and they needed to find me one."

I cringe at the thought but also feel some relief that he got offered a call. "How long was it before they let you call someone?"

He shrugs. "Few minutes after booking."

Shit, shit, shit. They're going to keep me in here forever.

Where is Killian?

Maybe they let him go. He'll get my attorney to get me out of here.

"What did they pick you up for?" I ask the man.

He shifts on his feet. His lips curve slightly as his face hardens. It's a look I know too well. This is a man who'll dance with the devil and not think twice. He drills his gaze into mine. "Nothing."

I nod. "Of course you didn't." I step closer. "Now why don't you tell me what they are keeping you here on?"

He glances around. The homeless guy is sleeping, and the junkie is staring at the corner singing. He steps closer and lowers his voice. "Murder."

I don't blink. "Yeah? How many men?"

"How do you know it's more than one?" he asks.

"Isn't it?"

His grin widens. "They're trying to pin two on me. But they have the wrong guy."

Sure they do.

I study him for ten seconds, then hold out my hand. "Gianni Marino."

He arches his eyebrows. "As in the Marino crime family."

I stiffen. "What if it is?"

He takes my hand and grasps it firmly, shaking it. "Then I'd say you're a man I'd want to know."

"Yeah? Why is that?" I ask.

His eyes darken, and I have no doubt he killed those two men. One thing I can quickly pick up on is a man who doesn't think twice about killing another. He shifts on his feet. "A man like you doesn't let anyone push him around."

I grunt. That's normally the truth. Except these bastards have me in a cell, and I can't do anything about it right now. I reply, "You didn't give me your name."

"Garrett Steelworth."

"Steelworth. What's your nationality?"

He shrugs. "Not sure. I'm a mutt."

I stifle a laugh, assessing him further. "Which culture do you resonate the—"

"I want my phone call," Killian's voice interjects.

I spin, glancing past the bars. His face is bright red with anger, and I've never been so happy to see my brother-in-law. But it's short-lived when I realize he's in here still and hasn't gotten his call either.

"Shut up and get in the cell," the officer orders and opens the door. He uncuffs Killian and slams the metal shut. It echoes throughout the chamber, and I refrain from holding my hands over my ears.

Killian spouts, "Bastards wouldn't let me have my phone call. Did you get yours?"

"No," I admit.

He motions for me to go over to the corner. I follow, and he says in a low voice, "What did they say you were in here for?"

"No details. Just the club and docks. You?"

"Club."

We stare at each other for a while.

He glances behind him and steps even closer. "Angelo has cops on the payroll, correct?"

"Yeah."

He takes a deep breath and releases it, then pats my back. "Good. We'll be out soon."

"Have you been booked before?" I ask.

Killian snorts. "Yeah. Of course."

I stay silent.

He arches his eyebrows and jerks his head backward. "You haven't gotten arrested before?"

"No."

"Never?"

"No," I repeat.

"Damn. Lucky you," he mumbles. He spins and focuses on Garrett. "Who's your friend?"

Garrett scowls, but it isn't as big as when I came into the cell. "What's it to you?"

"Easy," I order. "Garrett, this is my brother-in-law, Killian."

Garrett peers closer at Killian. "Smart move marrying into the Marino family."

"Excuse me?" Killian asks as if insulted.

"You know."

"No, I don't. Why don't you fill me in," Killian sneers.

Garrett itches his nose, then replies, "Protection. The backing of a legitimate family. And hey man. No offense, but I can see why a man like you would want that."

Killian's face turns maroon. "A man like me?"

Garrett nods. "Yeah."

Killian glares at him then steps forward. He points in his face. "You have no idea who I am. You should watch your mouth."

Garrett cockily asks, "Yeah? Who are you without the Marinos?"

Amused, I lean against the wall.

Killian's green eyes glow wild. He threatens, "I'm the mother-fucker who might just become your worst nightmare."

Garrett raises his chin, flaring his nostrils. "Is that so?"

"Jesus, you're ignorant." Killian turns to me. "How long do your brothers normally stay in here when they get arrested?"

My chest tightens. I say nothing.

Killian's eyes widen. "None of you have been arrested before?"

My silence is his answer.

Disbelief erupts on his face. He mumbles, "You're kidding me."

"Not everyone can be as well-rounded as the O'Malley's," I taunt.

"Fuck off. We're in here because you can't control yourself," Killian states.

All the rage I'm feeling over this situation comes to a boil. I briefly forgot about the scandal at the fashion show. I spout, "Seriously? Are we really going to have this conversation?"

"What's that?" Killian charges.

"Fuck you. Don't act like you're Mother Teresa," I seethe.

"Man, I don't know how many more ex-girlfriends you have on your wife's client list, but you might want to know that going forward. And thanks to you, my wife is pregnant, without me there to protect her," Killian fumes.

I turn away and walk to the bars. I wrap my fists around them to steady myself. Killian's right. Cara and Arianna are both in a situation without us now. While I have faith in their security, the additional backup of Killian and me wasn't for show. The Abruzzos are sneaky and know how to hurt someone. They'll stop at nothing to get what they want. Now, the two women I love the most are in additional danger.

"Marino! O'Malley!" a guard calls out.

We put our argument aside for the moment, and Killian stands next to me. We wait for the guard to unlock the doors. I nod to Garrett as I walk out. "Good luck, man."

"Yeah. See you on the outside," he states.

Killian and I go through the additional protocol and they release us. When we step outside, Papà sits in one of our black SUVs.

We get in. Silence fills the vehicle. The driver pulls out of the parking lot. Papà sits, pushing the pads of his fingers together, his dark eyes moving between us. I brace myself for another lecture. We drive a block before he says, "I want to know exactly what you both told the cops."

"Nothing. You think I'd tell those bastards anything?" Killian blurts out.

"Yeah. It's not his first rodeo," I add.

"Shut up," Papà scolds, and Killian glares at me. "What did they say?"

"They said they knew I was involved with the club shootout," Killian states.

Papà takes a deep breath, clenching his jaw. He's still angry about how things went down that night. Dante defied a direct order from him, which meant we all did too. But there was no other way to safely remove Brenna and make sure the Abruzzo thug who had bought her didn't come after her. Papà asks, "I want to know the exact way you responded."

"I told them I had no idea what they were talking about, and I wanted my attorney," Killian replies.

"What else?" Papà presses.

"That's it. I'm not an idiot," he claims.

Papà refocuses on me. "And you?"

"They said I had something to do with the club and docks."

Papà closes his eyes and shakes his head. He opens them and pins his cold gaze on mine. "The docks. What part of the docks?"

My stomach drops further. It was another fight Dante, and I had with him. I admit, "I don't know. They said bloodshed seems to follow me."

"What do they have on you?" Papà inquires.

"Nothing, or he wouldn't be in this SUV," Killian points out.

"I'm not talking to you," Papà scolds again, then turns back to me. "What do they have?"

"Nothing. Killian's right," I state, but the uncomfortable feeling grows larger.

"What did your guys on your payroll say?" Killian asks.

"If I have to tell you to shut up one more time," Papà warns.

Killian groans. "Jesus, Angelo. What are you going to do? Kill the father of your daughter's unborn baby? Come on. We've got a problem. Stop playing boss, and let's have a conversation to figure this out."

It's rare for Papà to back down, but he glances out the window, tapping his fingers on his knee.

I glance at Killian, who shakes his head in frustration at me. Nothing gets said for miles until we stop in a busy parking lot next to another SUV with blacked-out windows.

"Send our attorney to represent Garrett Steelworth. He needs to get released immediately," I instruct.

Papà arches his eyebrows. "Why would I do that?"

"Because he's a man who doesn't flinch. And he's going to owe us," I state.

"You serious?" Killian spouts.

"Shut up," I order.

Papà assesses me.

"Do it," I demand.

Papà crosses his arms. "Okay. If I end up regretting this, it's on your head."

"Fine. What's going on?" I motion toward the other SUV next to our vehicle.

Papà points to both of us. "You two have a debt to repay."

"What debt?" I ask.

The window of the SUV rolls down. Bridget's father, Tully, curls his fingers, his lips turning up at the corners.

"Oh fuck no! I owe nothing to Tully," Killian mouths off.

"Is this a joke?" I ask.

Papà takes several deep breaths, then scrubs his hands over his face. He gives me a look I've not seen before. I don't know what to make of it, but something tells me things are worse than I'm aware of in our family. He states, "Tully owns the police. The guys on my payroll are all dead."

My insides flip. The blood drains down my cheeks making me almost dizzy. I question, "What are you talking about? When did this happen? And why didn't you tell us?"

Papà's expression turns angrier. "If you and your brothers weren't always doing whatever the hell you wanted, then I would be able to trust you."

"Trust us? You seriously think you can't trust us?" I ask in disbelief.

Disappointment fills Papà's expression. For the first time ever, I see the stress on his face. He looks like he's aged twenty years. Cold fills me, and a new worry takes root.

He sighs and points to Tully's vehicle. "Go pay off your debt. When you come home, we're having a family meeting."

Tension fills the car, and no one moves.

Killian finally speaks. "Well, I guess Tully can't make me marry anyone."

"Is that supposed to be funny?" Papà snaps.

Killian holds his hands in the air. "Yeah. Chill out, Angelo." He opens the door and slides out of the car.

I say, "Papà—"

"Go! I don't want to hear it. Pay off your debt and get back to the house. We have issues to deal with and quickly," he declares.

I open my mouth but decide to shut it. I follow in Killian's footsteps and get out. Once the door shuts, Tully chirps, "Boys. Get in."

"Fuck sakes," Killian mutters but opens the door and slides over the seat.

I once again follow, wondering what Tully has up his sleeve. I cringe further when I realize Aidan is in the car, too. There's no doubt he'll enjoy every moment of Tully's payback chore.

Tully rolls up the window, the driver pulls out, and he gives us his grin. It's an expression I hate to be on the receiving end of, especially right now. He seems extra excited, which only makes the pit in my stomach grow. Knowing him, it's going to be something Killian and I detest.

Tully looks at Killian, taunting, "You didn't think you'd be back in this seat after a stint in the slammer, did you?"

"Get it over with, Tully. Whatever it is, spit it out," Killian hurls at him.

"Watch how you talk to my father," Aidan warns.

Killian snorts. "Or what? Don't make threats you can't make good on, Aidan."

Aidan scoffs. "What is it about you O'Malleys?"

"Excuse me?" Killian demands.

"All right. Enough," Tully orders.

Killian and Aidan stare each other down. Tully rubs his hands together and focuses on me.

"Tully, I don't have time to spare. I need to get back to my wife. Whatever this is, can we get on with it?" I question.

He chuckles, then his grin grows.

My pulse races faster. I've known Tully my entire life. He's way too happy. Whatever it is he has up his sleeve isn't something I'm going to not want to do.

He chuckles louder, sits back in his seat, and states, "Relax, boys. We're going for a little ride. When we get there, I'll make it clear what you're going to do for me."

Cara

"YOU NEED TO WAIT YOUR TURN, MA'AM," THE OFFICER SCOWLS.

The anger and worry I'm feeling are growing bigger with each second. No one will tell me where Gianni is or when he'll get out. I assume there's a law against withholding information about a spouse's whereabouts when you have them in custody. Yet these officers act as if it's not real. Or if it is, it doesn't matter to anyone in this precinct. I tap my finger on the counter. "I've been waiting for hours. I want to know where my husband is and why no one will give me any information!"

She points to the back of the line. Her eyes turn to slits. She seethes, "Don't make me tell you again."

"Tell me where my husband is!" I repeat.

"Ah, Mrs. Gianni Marino," a man's voice chirps behind me.

I spin, then assess him. Unlike the uniform officers, he's wearing a dark brown, cheap suit. A potbelly protrudes past his belt about six inches. His slicked-back hair is so oily it makes me cringe. I ask, "Who are you?"

His lips form a tight smile. He keeps his gaze pinned on mine as if to intimidate me.

This game, whatever it is they're playing, is getting old. I don't disrespect the law, but I know my husband and his family aren't saints. The lack of information they're giving me makes me wonder if they have something on Gianni. My pulse beats faster. I stand straighter. In a firm voice, I question, "Do I need to call my attorney and have them file a lawsuit?"

He grunts, giving me the impression I somehow am entertaining him.

"You find my question amusing?" I seethe.

He grins. "A bit."

"Why is that?" I snap.

He shifts on his feet. "Come with me, Mrs. Marino."

I freeze, then count to ten.

He steps closer. "We should talk."

"I'm not going anywhere with you. Now I've asked your name and want to know where my husband is, and I better get some answers," I threaten, wishing I had my phone with me. I don't know how to get a hold of anyone without it. I make a mental note to memorize all the Marino's numbers, not that I'm sure who in this hellhole would even be kind enough to allow me to make a call.

He holds his hands in the air and smiles as if we're friends. "Please calm down. I'm Detective Contray. If you follow me, I can fill you in on all the details about your husband."

I hesitate, not wanting to go anywhere with this man, but unsure what other option I have to find out anything about Gianni.

He motions for me to go ahead of him down the hallway. Seeing no other choice, I walk a few hundred feet, and he orders, "Turn right into room seven, please."

I obey and freeze when I step inside. It looks exactly like an interrogation room.

"Have a seat, Mrs. Marino," he states.

I spin as the door bangs shut, blurting out, "Why are we in this room?"

"I thought you would want some privacy to discuss what we're charging your husband with," he proclaims.

"Charging him? With what?" I inquire, attempting to stay calm but not doing a very good job.

He points to the table. "If you sit, we can discuss this."

I swallow the lump in my throat then take a seat on the cold metal chair. Mirrored glass faces me. It makes me feel as if I'm somehow in trouble. I wonder if others are behind it watching me.

Detective Contray sits across from me, taps his index finger on the table, and studies me.

I do everything in my power not to shift in my seat, even though the cold metal hurts my ass. After what feels like forever, I lose the little patience I have remaining. "Where is my husband?"

Contray gives me a pitiful smile and softens his voice. "You're husbands in a lot of trouble, Mrs. Marino. He's looking at life-time in prison."

My stomach flips so fast I put my hand over it. My throat turns dry, and my voice sounds scratchy. "For what?"

"We have significant evidence that involves you as well," he states.

I jerk my head backward. "Excuse me?"

He nods. "Your DNA is all over the place."

My heart thumps so hard against my chest I'm sure he can hear it. "What are you talking about?"

Thirty seconds pass, making me feel so hot I'm on the verge of sweating. He finally replies, "You have two choices, Cara. Do you mind if I call you Cara?" He shoots me a friendly smile, and I want to throw up.

I glare at him. "Yes. I do mind."

He scoffs in amusement. "Fair enough. Mrs. Marino, here are your choices. Are you listening closely?"

I've had enough of his condescending bull shit, but I also am freaking out about Gianni going to jail and Contray's DNA comment. I cross my arms over my chest, wishing Gianni was here to protect me while trying to decipher whatever is happening in this room.

He takes my silence as a yes. He leans closer. "Choice one. You go to jail for life."

My insides quiver. I've never committed a crime in my life. I have no idea what my DNA has to do with anything or why it would be on any crime scene. I keep my gaze on Contray and tell myself to pretend I'm Gianni. I attempt to harden my expression, so I don't appear to be scared. "I'm unsure why you believe a judge would ever sentence me to prison. I've been a law-abiding citizen my entire life."

He tilts his head while a new wave of pity washes over his expression. I become more emotional, and I blink hard, willing myself not to tear up. He glances behind him then tugs his chair closer to the table. "Mrs. Marino, you have a second option."

"An option to avoid prison when I've not done anything?" I angrily spout, sitting up taller and finding my strength.

"Ah, but you have, haven't you?" he replies.

"What are you talking about?" I question again, slightly louder.

He sits back in his seat. His tone turns to no-nonsense. "Option two. You help us, and you get to keep your record clean and your freedom."

The room seems to get smaller. My chest tightens, making it harder to breathe in the stale air. Everything about this detective makes me feel sick. The thought of helping him do anything makes me want to gag. Losing my cool, I spout, "Help you do what?"

"I think you know the answer to that," he arrogantly states.

He wants me to take down Gianni.

More nausea hits me. I start to count, glancing at Contray's oily hair, greasy skin, and potbelly hitting the table. He's the opposite of everything my husband represents. And Gianni may not be a saint, but this guy isn't either. The difference is Gianni doesn't hide who he is or his faults. He recognizes them. I bet Detective Contray goes to sleep at night thinking he's righteous. But my gut says there's no way he's never bent the law in his favor.

He runs his fat paws through his locks. Then he picks up a thick folder and drops it on the table in front of me. "Go ahead, Mrs. Marino. Take a look."

I curl my toes in my heels, so I don't fidget. My insides tremble harder, and after a short stare down, I cautiously open the folder then immediately shut it. I turn my head, trying to erase what I just saw.

"No. I want you to really look at these photos," Contray orders, grabbing a photo and holding it in front of me.

As soon as I see the man with no life left in him and a bullet hole in his head, I squeeze my eyes shut, willing my nausea to disappear.

Contray's voice hardens. "There are twenty more men in this folder. Each one, your husband, murdered or played a role in."

The sound of metal scraping on the floor hits my ears. I open my eyes to find Contray sitting at the end of the table, less than a foot from me, putting all the photos on the table in view. Each one represents another display of gore and death.

Contray's musk cologne flares in my nostrils, adding to my qualms. I muster all the strength I have, scoot my chair back, and rise. "I want to see my husband right now," I repeat, but it sounds weak. Dizziness slams into me. I place my hand on the desk then quickly sit back down.

"Ah, yes. I see you're affected by these photos," he cockily states.

I avoid looking at the dead men. "I don't know anything about this. My husband doesn't either, I can assure you."

Contray begins to chuckle as the door flies open. A skinny man wearing a similar cheap suit in navy steps inside and shuts the door. He drills his eyes on me and pulls the other chair back. "I'm Detective Anderson. I just spoke with the District Attorney. He's willing to make a deal with you for your cooperation."

The hairs on my arms rise. I grit my teeth, breathing several breaths and counting. I finally reply, "I've committed no crimes. I want to see my husband now."

He shakes his head as if I'm a stupid child who just isn't under-standing what he wants me to. "I'm sorry, Mrs. Marino. Your husband is in custody and won't be leaving anytime soon, if ever, unless you cooperate."

My lips tremble. The tears I've tried to keep in check flow down my cheeks. My voice breaks as I cry out, "I want to see my husband!"

Contray turns to Anderson, speaking like I'm not in the room. "She doesn't seem to be scared of prison."

The walls feel like they're caving in on me. I screech, no longer able to maintain any composure, "I've not done anything!"

Anderson angrily barks while pointing at me, "Your DNA states otherwise."

I glance back and forth between the two men, not believing what's happening. Then I mutter, "Fuck you." I walk past them and try to open the door, but it's locked.

I stare at it, my heart racing and fear exploding all around me.

Are they going to keep me here forever?

Is this what they're doing to Gianni?

Does anyone know we're here?

I spin and straighten my shoulders. "I want my attorney."

"Who would that be?" Anderson smirks.

I don't have a criminal attorney, but I'm a Marino. The family has to have them.

I need to call Angelo.

I don't know his number.

Oh, God! I don't know anyone's number!

I seethe, "Am I under arrest?"

Both men exchange a look.

I scoff. "I'm not, am I?"

"What happens when you're next? Hmm?" Anderson asks, arching his eyebrows.

I push all responses out of the way, stating, "If I'm not under arrest, then I demand you let me go right this minute!"

"I give her under six months before she disappears off the face of the Earth," Contray declares.

I spin and bang my hands on the mirror, shouting, "Are you hearing me? Let me go, or I'm suing all of you personally and the department!"

The door swings open. Another man steps inside. He holds out a badge with identification attached to it. "Mrs. Marino. I'm Agent Bordeaux with the FBI. I'd like to speak with you in private."

I blurt out, "I clearly stated I wanted to leave."

He holds up his hands and nods. "Yes. I understand. Please. Give me a few minutes."

I put my hand on my hip. I ask again, "Am I under arrest?"

"No."

"So I'm free to go?"

"Yes. However, I think it's in your best interest to wait a few minutes. I promise you, as soon as we finish speaking, I'll show you the way out if you still want," he states.

I don't move, feeling paralyzed.

Bordeaux nods to the detectives, and they leave. As soon as the door shuts, he motions to the table. "Please sit back down."

I sigh and begrudgingly sit, unsure why I'm still here and didn't leave.

He takes the seat across from me. "Mrs. Marino, the FBI is willing to go to great lengths to reward you for your efforts."

"Excuse me?" I ask, confused.

He pauses, then states, "Your husband's a bad man. I don't believe you're naive or that you don't know what crimes he's capable of committing."

I rise. "I'm ready to leave now."

He stands too, belting out, "Mrs. Marino! We can protect you."

I sarcastically laugh. "Protect me from what?"

"Your husband. His family. Anyone else who's working for them who scares you."

I step closer to him and cross my arms. Tilting my head to meet his eyes, I snarl, "My husband and his family, *my family*, would never hurt me. No one who works for them would dare lay a hand on me."

"Do you realize what happens to women like you?" he asks.

"Women like me?"

"Yeah. One of two things happen. You either end up in prison or dead."

"I'm out of here," I claim, moving toward the door. I reach for the handle, and he presses his palm against the door.

"I can help you prevent all those things. All you need to do is help us out, and I'll give you full witness protection," he states.

I release the doorknob and gape at him.

His eyes widen. His voice turns fatherly. "Stop thinking it won't happen to you. All I need is for you to cooperate—"

"Listen to me closely. I will never—never—do whatever it is you want me to do. Whatever you're trying to pin on my husband, stop," I demand.

"Don't be stupid—"

"I'm ready to leave. Let me out," I order.

He clenches his jaw and doesn't move.

"Now," I seethe.

"Last chance," he states.

"No."

He shakes his head but removes his hand from the door and steps back.

I yank it open and practically race through the hallway and out into the main area. I don't stop until I step out into the fresh air. Five times I breathe deep, then glance around.

I need to get home and talk to Angelo.

The cold air quickly seeps through my clothes and into my bones. I don't have a coat since I ran outside of my work event without thinking. All I want to do is get away from this police station and figure out how to get Gianni out of there.

Oh, God. He's still in there, I fret while walking down the street. Several taxis sit on the corner, so I move faster. I open the door and slide into the back of it. I give the driver the address to the Marino estate.

The taxi takes off, weaving in and out of traffic. I stare out the window, trying to calm myself from everything that just occurred, but I can't.

The gruesomeness of the photos stick in my mind. I don't know if Gianni did it, but if he did, I assume the men deserved it. Regardless, I wonder if they actually have anything on him or if it was all a lie.

Angelo will take care of this. I just need to get home.

Based on where we're at in the city, it'll be at least another forty-five minutes with traffic. I lean my head back against the seat, closing my eyes and trying to quiet my mind. I almost fall asleep, but the car veers sharply, and the driver yells, "What the hell!"

My body tenses. Panicking, I open my eyes and sit up. "What's wrong?"

Several black SUVs surround us. One pulls near the left side of the car. The window rolls down, and a man sticks out a gun. He shoots, and a loud bang explodes in my ears.

Glass shatters, blood spurts everywhere, and the taxi driver's body slumps in the seat. I scream, and more shots ring in the air. The car drops as if the tires are shot out and scrapes on the pavement.

The SUVs stick with the taxi while it rolls forward until it slows to a stop. I lock the door, unsure what else I can do to escape whoever these men are, but it's pointless.

My chest tightens, and my lungs feel as if they can't take in any more air. I put my head between my legs, closing my eyes, wanting all of this to go away, yet knowing it's not my reality. Sharp pains shoot through my heart.

Everything becomes loud. More shots ring in the air. Men's gruff voices float all around me. Someone grabs me and pulls me toward the door.

"Let me go!" I choke, reaching for the seat belt and gripping it as tightly as possible.

The man yanks me so hard I release the belt. I struggle, attempting to get free, but it's pointless.

I get shoved into a black SUV. The first breath of air I take makes me feel ill. Before I see any face, I know it's him.

A new fear overpowers me as I raise my head, locking eyes with the devil. My stomach curls, spinning over and over.

Uberto's dark glare swirls with both excitement and hatred. The last time I saw that look, he drugged me and put me up for auction. The ironic thought that I used to be in his arms, and now I'm his enemy crashes into me. A renewed sense of needing to escape him fills every cell in my body.

I turn to try and run for it, but his huge goon stops me. My legs and arms flail in the air until Uberto puts his hand on my throat, barking, "Stop, or I'll squeeze until there's no life in you."

I freeze except for my trembling insides and lips.

Uberto drags his finger down my cheek, and I shudder, wincing with tears. He squeezes my cheeks, forcing me to face him and states, "It's time to show you what I do to traitors."

25

Gianni

TULLY PUFFS ON HIS CIGAR, TAKING HIS TIME TO BLOW IT OUT AND extending his response to my question.

"Jesus Christ, Tully. What the fuck are we doing here?" Killian asks, his face red with fury. The abandoned office building looks like the perfect location for a crack deal. Busted windows, a door that is barely on the hinges, and a roof that looks like it's going to cave in doesn't make any sense as to why Tully brought us here.

"Don't disrespect my father," Aidan warns.

Killian scowls. "Don't give me that bull shit. Your father's playing games with us, and you know it."

The more time that passes, the more irritated I become. Both Killian's and my phone batteries are dead. It's probably from trying to find a signal in the concrete building of the police station. And not having the ability to talk to Cara after everything that happened is killing me. I bark, "Tully, I don't have time to waste. Both Cara and Arianna are at the Fashion Show without us. We need to get back there."

He inhales again, and in his smoke-laden, Irish accent, replies, "You have security on them. Stop worrying."

"Tully, I'm warning you," I threaten, then look at Aidan, who I've always seen eye to eye with. "Help me out here."

He shifts on his feet. "Okay, Dad. Let's get on with this. I've got a date."

Tully raises his eyebrows. "Fiona's friend's mom?"

"Yeah."

Tully whistles. "She's a milf if I've ever seen one."

"You should see what she picked up to wear tonight." Aidan's grin grows wider.

Killian groans. "Keep your dick in your pants, and let's do whatever it is you want us to do."

Tully puffs out his chest then points to the door. "I just bought this. Go inside."

"Why?" I ask.

"Because I said so," Tully responds.

"Looks like you bought a gem. Maybe you should get a new real estate agent," Killian muttered, then shoots me an annoyed look and stomps toward the door.

Tully grunts, as if all of this is amusing him.

I suppose it is. I sigh, then follow Killian.

There's a small padlock on the door. He doesn't bother to ask for the key. He takes his hand and yanks on it, detaching the metal from the wood. He holds the lock out to Tully. "You should also fix your security issues."

Instead of getting angry, Tully chuckles. "You're too predictable. Now stop wasting time and follow me."

Killian glares at him and we follow him through the doorway and into an empty, open space. Dirt covers the floor, including the only item in the room, which is a filthy rug. The wooden walls have holes in them in several spots. Air from outside flows freely, creating a damp atmosphere.

"I think Killian is right. You need to take some lessons from a real estate developer," I state, glancing around at the emptiness and wondering why Tully would ever buy this place.

"Ah, but there's where you're wrong," he replies, then motions to the rug. "Roll it up, boys."

"Roll it up?" I repeat.

"You need to hire a decorator if you think this is a piece worth keeping," Killian mutters.

"Who's wasting time now?" Aidan asks.

"I'm going to slap you," Killian threatens.

"Shut up. Both of you," I demand, then go to the corner of the rug.

Killian begrudgingly goes to the other side, and we begin rolling the rug.

"Tight. I want it nice and tight, boys. Start over. Don't do it half-assed," Tully instructs.

Killian and I scowl at each other but unroll it and do as he says.

We get half the rug rolled up when Tully calls out, "Stop."

We both look at him.

He takes another drag of his cigar then nods to the center floor. "That's why I bought this place."

Aidan walks over and opens a trap door. He grins, stating, "After you."

"Tully, what's this all about?" I question again. I'm not a person who enjoys surprises. These sketchy situations only make me anxious.

"You'll see. Down you go, boys," Tully answers.

I glance at my designer suit and groan. Then I turn and step down the metal ladder. The air becomes so damp I shudder from the cold. Darkness surrounds me, and I shout, "Do I get a light?"

"String is above you. Pull it," Aidan replies.

Killian's footsteps bang on the metal. I struggle to find the light, but just as he steps on the dirt near me, I find it and turn it on.

Aidan and Tully join us, and my eyes adjust to the surroundings.

"Holy... Christ," Killian mumbles.

Four men hang naked upside down, with contraptions stretching their limbs as far as possible. Each one has a rusty metal ball in their mouth. It's connected to an inverse collar. When they move their neck, spikes dig into their skin so deep a mix of dried and fresh blood coats their faces. Eight fear-filled eyes stare at us. I ask, "Who are they?"

Aidan steps forward and puts his arm around my shoulder. "Our gift to you."

"Your gift?" I repeat, clueless as to what it means. I've never seen any of these men before.

Tully finishes his last puff then tosses it near my feet. He squishes it in a circular motion and clears his throat. "Consider my get out of jail card a freebie. You want to know how to end the hunt for Uberto? Now's your chance."

Confused, I study the men, then claim, "I don't understand. Who are they?"

"They're O'Leary's," Aidan says with disgust then spits at their feet.

"Never heard of them," Killian states.

"Me either," I agree.

Tully steps closer to the men. The one in the middle pisses himself. The urine runs down his torso, neck, and face, then puddles under his head. Tully scowls. "The O'Leary's seem to think they can come onto our turf without consequences." Tully crouches, releases the ball gag, and grabs the jaw of one of the men. The man coughs, but Tully squeezes his chin until the guy turns purple.

When Tully releases him, he tries to catch his breath. A thick Irish accent, one that only a foreigner would have, fills the room. "Fuck you, Tully."

Tully steps back, takes his boot, and kicks his torso. The sound of his ribs cracking hits my ears.

The man screams, choking some more.

"You've got a new family from Ireland coming after you?" Killian asks in surprise. He shouldn't be. New families come in all the time, but in fairness, it's rare they come straight from the mother country.

"Yeah. These bastards thought they could waltz in, and we wouldn't notice their business in our territory or their alliance with the Abruzzos," Aidan states.

"Abruzzos?" I blurt out. The hairs on my neck rise. The last thing either of our families need is a new enemy on our turfs.

"Does Liam know about this?" Killian questions.

Tully nods. "Yeah. He's aware."

Aidan leans down next to his father, grabbing one of the man's head of hair. His eyes narrow with hatred. He tugs hard, so the man whimpers in pain. "This motherfucker seemed to underestimate me when we met in Ireland. You won't do that again, will you?"

Blood drips down the man's neck. He gives Aidan a hateful look.

Aidan's hand flies to his cheekbone, and a crack echoes through the air. Another muffled scream erupts. Aidan laughs, then releases the man and spins in front of me. "Guess who's been in contact with Uberto?"

Visions of my Tesora naked and on stage fill me. My chest tightens. Breathing becomes harder. I'm so tired of not knowing where Uberto is and wondering what next threat faces my wife. I seethe, "Where is he?"

Aidan points to the four men. "Don't ask me. Ask them."

Three of the men stay still, not making eye contact with any of us. The man Aidan hit flinches. It's quick, but I don't miss it.

I remove his gag, take out my gun, press it against his skull, and demand, "Where is Uberto?"

He doesn't answer, grinding his molars, but his body begins to shake.

I cock the trigger. He spits at me and taunts, "Go ahead, you Italian piece of shit."

I stand back and aim at his foot, shooting the middle of it.

He screams, and the man next to him throws up.

"Now we're talking. Let's see what kind of pussys we have in front of us," Aidan shouts, clapping, his eyes growing more crazed. It's the Aidan I've known since we were kids. Like my brothers and his, he's always ready to defend his family, always ready to take down any enemy he deems a threat with or without proof.

"Give me your lighter, Tully," I demand, holding my hand out.

"You should bring some gasoline down here the next time you use this place," Killian adds.

Tully shakes his head and chuckles. "You O'Malleys and your gasoline. I've told Liam to upgrade you."

"To what?"

Tully turns on a pocket flashlight. He points it to the corner. Dozens of red plastic cans sit on the floor. He arrogantly states, "Kerosene."

Killian scrunches his face. "Why is that better?"

Tully steps in front of the man he kicked and pushes on his rib that's sticking out. The man screams, his body barely flailing against the restraints due to the lack of tension, but it's enough to hurt him further. His agonizing sounds turn louder, and tears roll down his face. Tully sniffs hard, his lips twitching, stating, "Kerosene burns slower. It's also harder to put out."

"Which can make people die quicker before you get information from them," Killian points out.

Aidan picks up a can and sets it next to me. "That's why you need discipline and precision. It makes it more painful. Isn't that right, Dad?"

Tully pats him on the back. "That's correct."

"Huh. I'll talk to Liam then," Killian declares.

Aidan hands me a fire poker. The gleam in his eye sparks brighter. "Remember how we strung our first Abruzzos up on that tree?"

I smile at Aidan. "No way I'd ever forget that. It's been a long time." I hold my fist out to him. That kill was Aidan and my first one. We were only seventeen, out at the sex club, and two thugs were slipping drugs into women's drinks. Aidan and I heard them bragging about it in the bathroom.

We already had a bad taste in our mouths for Abruzzos. We knew that eventually, we'd have to take people out. Something within Aidan snapped, and I could see there was no way to stop him. Before I knew it, we kidnapped those thugs when they stepped outside the club.

When I called Papà, I assumed he'd want us to bring them back to the dungeon. I got an earful for disobeying club rules, as did Aidan. Then Papà redirected our driver to a field in Jersey. He told us to wait until he and Tully arrived. They made us string them up in the tree then they spent hours teaching us torture techniques. Part of that lesson was how much damage you can do to a man with a hot poker stick, anything flammable, and patience. To this day, I can still see those men's faces, cocky in the club, yet a complete fearful mess outside of it.

Aidan opens the kerosene can, and I dip the poker stick in it. Tully flicks his zippo, touching the end of the metal pole.

Flames burst on the end, intensifying from the kerosene until the metal is bright red and glowing. I rotate the pole in my hand, watching the flames spin, smelling the unique odor. Then I ask Aidan, "You remember how the vultures came once we put the fire out?"

The corners of his lips turn up. "The best part was hearing them scream as the vultures tore them apart." He steps up to the man I held my gun to and crouches down. He places both hands on his cheeks then slowly moves his head, so the spikes in the collar dig into his neck, sending a fresh stream of blood rolling over Aidan's hands.

The man begs for him to stop, yet Aidan only laughs, continuing to do it, then screams, "Where is Uberto?"

He still doesn't answer.

Aidan turns his head. "Ready?"

I sniff hard, feeling a slight high from the kerosene and what I'm about to do. I step forward, demanding, "Last chance. Tell me where Uberto is!" I hold the poker in front of his eye.

"Please! Don't!" he begs.

"Where is he!" I yell so loud spit flies out of my mouth.

"I don't know!"

"Liar!" I scream and poke his eye. It singes, and his cries turn more desperate. The anger and distress I've felt over this situation make it hard to maintain my control. I step back, count to fifteen, then order Killian, "Turn this motherfucker upright."

Killian and Aidan flip him. Tully lights up another cigar. The stench of body fluids mixes with the smoke and kerosene. It would make most people vomit. But I've gotten used to it over the years. It's become a smell I look forward to since it means an enemy is dying, even though it'll take weeks for me to no longer smell it.

The man screams some more. The others around him tremble. Killian grabs three pokers and tosses one to Aidan and Tully. He dips his in kerosene and says, "Well, don't keep me from the fun."

Tully flicks his lighter again. Killian's stick erupts in flames. Aidan follows his lead, then Tully lights his.

For the next thirty minutes, we burn them, forcing information out of them piece by piece until they're pleading for us to kill them.

Two men pass out, but we don't let them stay out of it for long. I start to worry that we'll kill them before we get any information out of them. The man I interrogate finally mumbles, "Brownstone."

I freeze. "What did you say?"

The room turns silent except for the moans and sobs of the men.

The guy in front of me spits blood. His eyes roll, and his head lobs forward.

I hold his head and slap him, fearful he's dying, and I'm not going to get anymore. "Wake up, you piece of shit!"

His eyes fly open.

"What about the brownstone?" I question.

His mouth hangs open.

I tug on his head. "Tell me now!"

"He...he..." He chokes, and more blood flies out of his mouth.

"He what?"

"Jacopo's new building," he chokes out, then his eyes turn solid with death.

"Wake up!" I scream again, slapping him harder and harder, but no life comes back in him.

"Where is it?" Aidan screams.

The man Killian's torturing mutters something.

"What did he say?" I ask.

Killian furrows his eyebrows. "He said Queens."

"Where in Queens? Tell me now, or I'm shoving this up your asshole," I bark.

His voice gets louder. "No! Please!"

I stand behind him, put the poker as close to his ass as I can without touching him but so he feels the heat, and lean into his ear. I growl, "Tell me!"

"B-Bow Street," he whispers.

"Where on Bow?" I question, grabbing his hair and yanking his neck so it rests on my shoulder.

"Cl-cl-closest t-to Q-Q-Queens B-Boulevard," he stutters.

I take a deep breath, then take my poker and stab him in his back, pushing through his heart. In a few seconds, he's dead.

Aidan yells, "How many men are guarding the brownstone?"

I step behind his thug and drag the tip of my stick down his spine. He tries to scream, but his voice is hoarse, and you can barely hear it. Blood oozes past his singed skin.

"Kill me," he sobs.

Aidan's voice turns soft. He tosses his poker stick and holds his face in both his hands. "You want us to kill you now?"

"Yes," the man sobs.

"I will. I'll kill you fast, and all this will be over. Is that what you really want?"

"Please!"

Aidan nods. "Tell me how many men and what rooms they're in."

The man struggles to take a breath, and the only other thug whispers, "I'll tell you if you'll kill me."

Tully grunts. "Pleasure will be mine. How many guards on the door?"

"Three."

"And what about after the main entrance?"

"None."

"Bullshit," I yell.

"It's true! Now kill me!" he screams with renewed energy and desperation.

"You think you can lie to me?" Tully asks in a calm voice.

"Three is all," the man Aidan is torturing states.

I exchange a look with Aidan. Neither of us believes only three men would be guarding a property where Uberto is hiding out.

Aidan shrugs then leans into the man. "See, here's the thing. You play with Abruzzos. That makes you an Abruzzo. So I'm going to pull every ounce of pain out of you," he points to the other man, "and you. When I finish, the sun will be coming up. Do you know how many more hours have to pass before that happens?"

A burst of energy appears out of nowhere. He tries to free himself, yanking on the restraints and sobbing like a crazed man, "Kill me, you O'Connor piece of shit."

Aidan laughs. It's a long, borderline psychotic, taunting one.

Tears drip off the man's face. He loses the energy he displayed less than a minute ago and recites, "Hail Mary, full of grace, the Lord is with thee; blessed art thou among women and blessed is the fruit of thy womb, Jesus. Holy Mary, Mother of God, pray for us sinners, now and at the hour of our death. Amen. Hail Mary, full of grace, the Lord—"

Killian interjects. "Tsk, tsk, tsk. Do you think Mother Mary will save you? You can't do penance for this. Both Jesus and God don't give two flying fucks about your pathetic Irish ass."

"Our Father, who art in heaven, hallowed be thy name; thy kingdom come; thy will be done on earth as it is in heaven. Give us this —"

"Let's speed it up, shall we. Deliver us from evil," Aidan screams, throwing his arms in the air.

"Kill me," one man cries out while the other keeps praying.

Every second I stay here is another chance Uberto has to disappear again. I toss my poker stick. "I'm over this scene. Let's go."

"They aren't dead yet," Aidan states, the wild expression on his face darker than I've seen it before.

"We need to go," I state, motioning between Killian and me.

Tully studies Aidan then hands his poker to him. "I think we got enough information. I assume you want to stay and finish this?"

Aidan nods, his eyes darting between the two men. "Send Devin and Tynan to help me on disposal."

Tully assesses Aidan again then pats his back. "Have fun, son."

The three of us climb up the ladder and get into Tully's SUV. Kerosene and death continue to flare in my nostrils, keeping my desire to be violent at the forefront. Tully turns on his phone and mutters, "Shit."

"What's wrong?" I ask.

He swallows hard, pins his steel gaze on mine, and my stomach drops. "Angelo text. Arianna is home freaking out. No one can find Cara."

26

Cara

THE RIDE THROUGH THE CITY SEEMS TO LAST FOREVER UNTIL WE stop outside of a brownstone in Queens. At that point, I wish we were still driving. The entire way, Uberto and his thug sat on both sides of me, saying nothing.

Uberto grabs a coat and orders, "Put this on with the hood over you, so no hair is showing."

"No," I blurt out, deciding it's safer outside in the car than going into the brownstone.

He fists my hair and tugs my head back so hard pain shoots through my neck.

"Owe!" I cry out.

His stale breath merges into mine. He seethes, "You will not disobey me. Now put it on." He studies me for a few moments, challenging me to defy him, and pulling my neck further.

I want to, but the pain is too intense. A tear falls down my cheek. "Let go! You're hurting me!"

He moves his face even closer to mine. "If you think this hurts, go ahead and try to argue with me again."

My lips shake harder. I squeeze my lids shut, wishing all of this was a nightmare. The fighter in me backs down. The sharp ache in my neck is too much. I choke out, "I'll put it on."

He tugs even further, holding me firm so I can't move.

"Please," I beg through tears.

He finally releases me, and I slowly move my neck back to a normal position. It's still throbbing when he holds the jacket in front of me again.

I take it, slip my arms through the sleeves, and put the hood up.

Uberto tucks some hairs that escaped under the fabric and sneers at me. "We're going inside. I'll slice you into a million pieces if you attempt to run. Do you understand?"

My stomach lurches. I sniffle, nod, and try to get it to stop somersaulting.

"I want to hear words," he demands.

A lump feels lodged in my throat. I whisper, "Yes."

He knocks on the window, and the man in the front seat opens the door. A cold blast of air hits me, but the fresh oxygen fills my lungs. It's a relief but doesn't last long. Uberto guides me up the steps and leads me into the building.

Two scary-looking men stand at the bottom of the steps near the door. They're huge, and I get the impression they spend a lot of time in the gym. There's no doubt they'd crush me in an instant if I attempted to run. One checks me out, scanning every inch of my body. He licks his lips as Uberto warns, "Don't even think about it."

The guard's eyes dart from my body to Uberto's scowl. "Sorry, boss."

Uberto slaps my ass and points up the staircase. "Go."

I open my mouth to protest, but his eyes darken. I snap it shut and do as told. Anxiety expands in my chest, giving me heart palpitations. Every step I take feels like I'm walking toward my death.

At the top of the stairs is a door. My mind screams not to open it. I freeze, and Uberto pushes into me, towering over my petite frame. He barks, "Did I tell you to stop?"

I tilt my head up, attempting another pointless plea, "Please. Let me go."

A tight smile forms on his lips, making the sharp pain in my chest increase. "You know, it's quite entertaining watching you beg me for your life." His smile falls, and he yanks my hair again.

"Stop!" I cry out.

Disdain overpowers his expression. In a low voice, he spouts, "It's time I show you what we do with Marinos..." He studies me for ten seconds, then spit flies out of his mouth as he snarls, "Mrs. Marino."

A deep chill runs down my spine. I shudder, and more tears fall while I curse myself for not thinking before I ran out of the fashion week building. If I had, my bodyguards would have offered me some protection. I wouldn't have been in that taxi. I would have my phone, and Gianni could at least track me if this happened.

Right now, I have no way for him to find me.

My dread intensifies when I think about how Uberto seemed to slide off the radar the last month. I try not to think about the low odds of Gianni finding me or wonder if he even knows I'm gone.

Then it hits me that he might still be locked up in the precinct. If that's the case, I'm doomed.

A wave of nausea washes over me again. I put my hand on my stomach and the other over my mouth. Sweat breaks out on my forehead.

"Well, don't get weak on me now. That won't be any fun," Uberto sarcastically states, knocks on the door, then turns the knob. He shoves me inside.

I almost trip but grab the arm of the man positioned next to the entryway.

"Tsk, tsk, tsk," Uberto taunts. "Once a whore, always a whore."

"It's not her fault. I'm irresistible to women, slut or not," the arrogant goon states, locking eyes on mine.

I try to jump away from him, but he has a tight grip on my shoulder.

Uberto snorts. "Did your mamma tell you that, Adamo?"

He keeps his orbs on mine. "My mamma, all the women I've ever screwed, should I continue?"

"Whatever. Get your hands off her and your ass downstairs with the others," Uberto orders, motioning to the door.

Adamo pauses, then releases me. He continues to stare me down, then calmly announces, "Sure. I don't want to hear her scream all night."

Another wave of fear annihilates me. I turn away, staring at the wall while tears fall. The sound of his footsteps, the door shutting, and a deadbolt clicking hit my ears. It all makes me feel like the room is closing in on me.

Uberto grabs my elbow and drags me through another doorway. It's a living space, complete with luxury furniture, professionally decorated, and large windows covered in expensive window treatments.

It's dark outside, but I assume the drapes aren't going to get pulled back anytime soon. The faint sound of the city traffic seeps through the glass. It's another reminder of how cruel this situation is. Gianni is so close to me, but how will he ever find me?

I swallow the lump in my throat, wishing I had a glass of water. My entire mouth is as dry as the Sahara desert. It hurts to swallow as if my throat might bleed.

Uberto turns on the gas fireplace. He moves toward me, and I retreat until I'm against the wall.

His lips twitch. I study him and realize he looks like he's aged ten years. Deep wrinkles extend around his mouth and eyes. When he pins his eyebrows together, his forehead erupts in more lines than in the past. Dark circles hang in bags under his orbs. "This is going to be a lot more fun for you if you tone it down a bit."

"Tone it down?" I ask, confused.

He nods, then drags his knuckles over my cheek. The sensation makes bile move up my throat, but I swallow, managing to keep it down. "If you let the fear rule you, it's going to hurt worse. Not for me, but you."

My insides quiver harder. I make the mistake of asking, "What will hurt?"

A full-blown smile erupts on his face. He leans closer, tucking my hair behind my ear. A combination of his sweat and musk cologne flares in my nostrils, and I can no longer stop the nausea.

Vomit flies out of my mouth, covering his chest. I bend over, continuing to empty the few contents in my stomach from this morning along with acid.

"What the fuck, Cara!" he shouts.

My head spins. I crouch to the ground, trying to make it stop. It doesn't help. Dry heaves overwhelm me.

Uberto orders, "Stop it! Now!"

But I can't. The smell of him, my puke, and the hammer-like feeling beating into my brain make me unable to regain my balance.

He grabs me from under my armpits then drags me across the room and into a bathroom. I hug the porcelain toilet for what seems like forever as sweat coats my skin. When my stomach settles, chills take over.

"Get out there and clean up your mess," Uberto's harsh voice states from behind me. I glance at him, wondering how this cruel man could ever have meant anything to me. He spins and leaves the room.

I take a few breaths, pry myself off the ground, then step out of the bathroom.

Uberto rips off his shirt, tossing it in the sink. He rummages in a kitchen cabinet under the sink. Then he slams cleaning products on the counter along with a towel. "Take off your clothes and get to work."

I gape at him in horror.

He smirks. "Ah. You thought I wasn't going to treat you like the slutty slave you so clearly are?"

My teeth chatter. "Wh-what are you talking about?"

He points to the vomit. "Get your clothes off and clean up this mess, or I'll make you lick it off the floor."

The thought makes my stomach pitch again. I put my hand on my gut, close my eyes, then take deep breaths.

Uberto counts, "Three. Two—"

My eyes fly open. "Okay! I'll do it," I cry out, holding my hands in the air.

He crosses his arms. "Well, get to it."

Seeing no other option, I strip down to my bra and underwear. I grab a bottle of cleaning solution, and Uberto laughs.

Heart pains shoot through my chest again.

He questions, "You didn't think you would get to keep your undergarments on, did you?"

I cringe. "Please. I'm freezing. I need a hot shower."

He grunts and points to the floor. "Take them off and clean up your mess."

My hands shake. I turn away, barely able to release the hooks on my bra. More tears drip down my cheeks, rolling off my jaw and onto the floor.

"Panties, too," he orders.

I squeeze my eyes tighter, wishing all this would go away. I just want to be back in Gianni's arms, far from this sadistic man. The thought only makes me cry harder. I slide my panties off, then crouch to the floor, trying to hide, but it's impossible.

Uberto sits on the black leather chair, lights up a joint, then takes a long drag.

The scent of weed makes me nauseous again, but there's nothing left in my stomach. I dry heave some more.

"Jesus. When did you become so weak?" Uberto accuses, then takes another hit of his joint.

I don't answer him, try to block out the odor of the smoke, and concentrate on cleaning up my mess. The towel isn't enough to get even half of it. I glance up, "I need more rags."

He gives me a look. It makes me feel like I'm pathetic. Then he nods to the kitchen. "Then get up and go get them."

I wince, not wanting to stand up or parade around in front of him nude. I hesitate, then ask, "Could you please get it? I'm still not feeling well."

Hatred resonates in his voice and face. "Bitch, if you puke anymore, you're going to be cleaning that up as well. I don't care either way. But get your ass off the floor and do whatever you need to make that tile spotless again."

I shake my head, blurting out, "Why are you doing this to me? Did our time together mean nothing to you?"

They're both dumb questions. I shouldn't have wasted my breath asking them. I already know the answer, so maybe it's a stall tactic.

He jumps up so fast the chair scoots back. He lunges toward me and tugs my hair until I'm on my feet.

"Stop it!" I scream.

"You want to know what you meant to me?"

"Let me go," I sob, pushing against his chest.

He grips my chin and yanks it upward. His bloodshot eyes have the same crazed look I saw in them the night he drugged and kidnapped me. Spit flies into my face as he seethes, "Do you think I didn't know your history with Gianni? Or that anything I said to you was true?"

The blood drains from my face to my toes.

Uberto laughs. "You thought we met by chance? That it had nothing to do with your bastard husband?"

"Wh-why would you..what...oh God." I shake harder, and he becomes blurry from my tears.

He leans into my ear. "Every word, every act, every moment, I planned."

"But-but why?" I choke out.

He positions his face in front of mine. "Are you stupider than I thought?"

Silence fills the air. Arrogance fills his expression, then disgust. "Yep. You are."

I scrunch my face, so confused.

He states, "Wake up, Cara. You married a Marino. Even before you said your vows, you were his obsession. Everyone could see it. And anyone associated with them is fair game."

"Fair game? I...I don't understand."

He sighs, then steps back. "It's not your business to understand. Now clean up this mess." He slides his hand through his greasy hair and paces in front of the window.

I use the distraction to find more towels in the kitchen. When I'm walking back, I can feel his eyes on me, piercing onto my bare skin. I crouch down and continue to clean the floor, not stopping until his loafers are inches from me.

Slowly, I glance up, my anxiety shooting higher. A new expression sends fresh terror throughout me. His cocky look is one I've seen in the past. It's what drove me to be attracted to him, but now it only repulses me. He grins, "At least while we're passing the time, we can have some fun."

My hands tremble harder. I shake my head, but it only makes him laugh.

"Ahh, dear Cara. So stupid. Do you know what it's like to be on the run?"

"N-no," I stutter.

He licks his lips, then puts his hands in his pants, stroking himself. "It gets lonely. You didn't think I'd make you take your clothes off and not service me, did you?"

I close my eyes. "Please. I'm married. Just...just let me go. I won't tell Gianni about this. I promise."

"Gianni!" He laughs louder than before then crouches in front of me. His fingers dig into my neck, and he lowers his voice. "Are you under the illusion I'm scared of your husband?"

I stay quiet, willing myself to stop crying, but I can't. I try to look away, but he doesn't allow me.

"Besides, he'll never find you. I've been under his nose this entire time, and he's not even come close. He'll never see you again until I'm ready for him to do so," Uberto claims.

All my trepidation grows.

He sits on the couch then pats his leg. "When you finish cleaning up your mess, get your ass over here and ride me."

Gianni

MY SKIN SUDDENLY FEELS TOO TIGHT. THE THOUGHTS RUNNING through my head aren't anything a man should ever think about regarding his wife.

It was my job to protect her.

I failed.

Maybe when I get home, it'll all be a misunderstanding, and she'll be there.

Fat chance. He has her.

Inhaling new oxygen seems impossible. My heart could be in a vice having all the blood squeezed out of it right now. I roll down the divider window. "Drive faster."

"I'd doing 110 mph," the driver states.

"I don't fucking care! Step on it," I demand, then hold out my hand to Tully. "Give me your phone."

He tosses it to me. I call Papà, and he picks up. "Tully. How far away are you?"

"It's me. Tell me she's there," I ask, knowing she isn't and feeling like my entire world is collapsing around me.

Papà clears his throat. "She's not. How far are you?"

I glance at the expressway sign. "Getting off the exit now."

"See you soon." He hangs up, and I grind my molars while opening and closing my fists.

I'm going to find him and slice him to pieces.

He better not touch her.

The notion makes me break out in a sweat. I wipe my forehead and try to keep it together, but I'm a bull in a china shop, ready to destroy everything in front of me.

I dial Luca.

It rings once, and he answers, "Tully."

"No. It's me."

"Why are you on his phone?"

"No time. Listen, I need you to scour Bow Street, closest to Queens Boulevard. He's in one of the brownstones, and he's got my wife," I snarl.

Silence fills the air.

"Did you hear me?" I spout.

Luca clears his throat. "Yeah, man. On it."

"We're out of time, Luca," I warn, feeling sicker.

"On it. Keep your cool," he orders, then hangs up.

I hand Tully his phone back. More tension fills the inside of the SUV. He cracks the window and lights up a cigar.

Killian rolls his down, too. "Christ. That shit is going to choke me."

"Shut up," Tully barks, blowing his smoke out the open inch of the glass.

Killian turns to me. "Gianni. How did our guards not prevent this?"

More rage explodes all around me. "I don't know. But there's going to be hell to pay when I get my hands on them."

"You got a traitor in your house?" Tully asks.

My stomach sinks deeper. If I had any doubts about any of the men I assigned to protect Cara or Arianna, I wouldn't have given them this job. Yet it wouldn't be the first time I was wrong about someone.

"We don't know what's happened. Let's not assume things," Killian warns.

"My wife is missing," I bark.

"You need to stay calm," Tully states, and the gates to the house open.

I ignore him, jumping out of the SUV before it even stops. As soon as I step into the house, I yell, "Papà!" running toward his office.

He steps out as I get there. His hardened face matches his eyes. The one thing I can always count on my Papà to do is stay focused and lead during a crisis. He orders, "Come inside."

I follow, not knowing what else to do, but blurting out, "Uberto's been hiding out in Queens. Luca's looking for the brownstone now. We need to go."

Massimo adds bullets to his Glock. "I'm ready."

"Where's Dante?"

"He and Bridget aren't back from Fashion Week yet. He's stuck in traffic," Tristano replies.

I count to ten. Dante and I know each other's moves before we make them. I always feel better when he's with me, but Massimo and Tristano will have to do.

"Do you know how many men are with him?" Papà asks.

"They told us three, but it could be a lie," Killian answers, stepping into the room with Tully.

"Is anyone else back?"

Papà shakes his head. "Everyone is in traffic. Arianna only got back because she left early."

"Where is she?" Killian asks.

"In her room."

He rushes out of the room.

"So there are no Ivanovs, no O'Malleys besides Killian, and only the three of us?" I ask.

"I'll go," Tully volunteers.

"No. You stay. I need you to interview all the guards. You've never met them. We need to know if there's even a slight possibility someone could be playing us. You're the best person to do it right now since you're not biased," Papà insists.

He laces his fingers together, then stretches them outward, cracking his knuckles. He moves his neck to both sides, cracking it too. "Done."

"Let's go," Papà orders.

They leave. My brothers and I follow them out. Papà gets into the SUV with us.

I pin my eyebrows together. "What are you doing?"

His nostrils flare. He's possibly as angry as I am. He grits his teeth. "He took a Marino woman."

It's all he has to say. It's another rule the Abruzzos can't seem to respect. But it's not just a rule to Papà, my brothers, or me. It's an oath that no one should ever disregard. Most women in crime families don't participate in anything illegal. They don't hurt others or know most business details or secrets. Stepping over this line opens the door, so no one's families are safe, and the Abruzzos are the only ones to have done it in several decades.

Tristano leans over the seat and retrieves more weapons. He hands all of us an extra Glock and pocket knives with easy releases. If we need to use them, they'll open in a second with little effort.

The SUV races toward Queens. A few blocks from Bow Street, Papà's phone rings. He answers, "Yeah."

The hairs on my neck rise as I watch his facial expression, not that it ever changes.

He sniffs hard. "Are any of his guards visible?"

Our driver turns the corner. I glance out the window, wondering which building it could be.

Massimo shifts and scrunches his face.

"What's wrong?" I ask.

He blinks a few times, then shakes his head. "Nothing. Ready to kill some Abruzzos."

"So they're all inside. Anyone on the roof?" Papà declares then nods. "Good. Which building can we utilize?"

The car slows, and my pulse beats hard in my neck. I put my hand on the door.

Massimo puts his hand over mine. "Wait. Don't go blowing through there. She could get hurt."

I scowl but know he's right.

"Three more buildings then stop," Papà instructs the driver and returns to the call. "We're coming in. Give us an all-clear."

A front door opens. I catch the brief outline of Aidan's brother Brody. He makes a quick motion with his hand then steps back out of view.

My brothers and I get out of the car, quickly moving into the brownstone. Brody and Luca both step forward. Luca claims, "We need to go up to the roof. There's access to all the units. It's the next building, and the jump is about a foot."

"A foot?" Massimo questions.

"Don't puss out," Tristano taunts.

"Shut up. I'm just verifying."

"You should have brought your knee brace."

"Seriously, shut up," I order, pissed that Tristano is taunting Massimo while my wife is inside, having God knows what done to her.

Luca shakes his head in irritation. Brody slaps Tristano on the head.

"What the fuck!" Tristano cries out.

Brody points in his face. "Grow up."

"Follow me," Luca directs, taking two stairs at a time.

I do the same. My brothers and Brody trail us. We quickly get to the roof. Luca opens a door, and the cold air slaps my face.

I continue following him over several units then jump onto the other building. I don't even stop to see if the others make it. There's a lock on the door. Luca says, "Step back."

I obey, and he shoots the lock. The gunshot rings in the air.

"Time's ticking. Let's go," I yell at the others, cock my gun, and go first into the small staircase, hoping an Abruzzo pops up so I can take him out.

Blood pounds between my ears with every step I take. I get past the third level, take four steps down then hear voices. I hold my hand up for the others to stop, and I freeze on the staircase.

"I don't know what it was, boss," one of the thugs claim.

Uberto's voice fills my ears. "Find out!"

I creep further, doing my best to stay quiet, and my heart almost leaps out of my chest. The soft sobs from my Tesora are faint, but I hear them.

At the bottom of the landing, I turn the corner to assess the situation.

The first person I see is her. She's naked, surrounded by cleaning products and what looks like vomit.

Cara also sees me. Her glistening eyes widen, releasing even more tears. I quickly glance around, then point my gun at Uberto's thug and shoot.

He falls, and Uberto spins. As much as I want to torture him for years, there's only one option. I put a bullet right between his eyes. He drops on top of the thug, and blood pools everywhere.

In two seconds, I cross the room and pick up Cara. She sobs in my chest, and I run toward the staircase.

Massimo passes me, and two shots fire, ringing in my ears.

Cara screams, but my chest muffles it. I get to the second floor then go into a bedroom. She sobs and shakes harder. "Shh. It's okay, Tesora. I've got you. We're getting out of here."

I tug a blanket off the bed, wrap it around her shaking body. I kiss her quickly then continue up the staircases. At the top, I pause. "It's going to be cold. I need you to hold onto me, Cara. No matter what, don't let go. Keep your head pressed against my chest."

"Oh-okay," she chokes out.

I kiss her on the lips and refrain from telling her how sorry I am for fucking up. I push the thoughts about what might have already happened away for the time being and focus on the roof.

It feels like it takes forever. The others are hot on my heels. I jump over the building and land safely on the other rooftop.

Cara keeps her arms wrapped tightly around me. I run over the other units and get to the one we came in from.

"Three more buildings," Luca calls out.

"What?" I ask in surprise.

"Go," he says, running in front of me.

I follow him, and we jump over several more buildings. We finally get to the third building, and the door is open. Papà stands on the roof, glances at Cara then meets my eyes with a worried expression.

I nod and blink hard, overcome with emotion. He kisses the top of her head then motions for me to go. I run down the flights of stairs and pause at the door.

"All clear," Papà informs me.

I rush outside, get to the SUV as quickly as possible, and slide into the back seat with Cara on my lap. The others join me, slam the doors, and the SUV takes off.

Sirens scream, getting louder, then softer the further away we drive. I avoid everyone's stares, trying to calm Cara and holding her tighter.

She sobs harder, her body convulsing in my arms. No matter what I do, I can't seem to help her. I want to know what he did to her, but part of me doesn't. I've never been so terrified, including when she was on the stage. That seemed like a situation I had control over. It was something routine, and I knew no one would lay a hand on her before she got auctioned off. This was an entirely new ballgame of Abruzzo despicableness.

"It's okay, Tesora. You're safe," I confidently tell her in her ear.

My shirt becomes soaked with her tears. She trembles so violently I get scared she might be in shock. I bark at the driver, "Go faster." Then I say to Papà, "Make sure Silvio gets to the house."

"He's already on his way," Papà replies.

A small amount of relief hits me, but it's short-lived. The longer Cara's distressed, the antsier I get. I bark to the driver, "I said drive faster."

He steps on the gas, and the next few minutes seem to stretch forever. The gate's already open when we pull up to it. As soon as the SUV parks, I open the door and carry Cara inside, going straight to our bedroom suite.

Arianna and Killian stand at the top of the staircase.

"Is she okay?" my sister frets.

"Yeah. I think," I add, suddenly fearful again of all the things I don't know that occurred. I brush past them and hustle to my wing.

I go straight to the bathroom and turn on the shower. Cara retreats from my chest and puts her hand on my cheek. "Gianni," she whispers, then she sobs further.

"Shhh. It's okay, Tesora," I claim, but I can't shut up the voice in my head telling me I don't know if she's okay. I kiss her on the lips. "You're shaking badly. Let's get in the shower."

She nods through her tears. I drop the blanket. "I'm going to set you down. Can you stand?"

"Y-y-yeah," she replies.

I cautiously set her on the floor. When I'm confident she has her balance, I tear off my shirt and drop my pants. I don't even take my socks off. I step into the shower with her, hoping my body heat and the water will help her convulsions stop.

We don't speak. I take my time washing her hair and body, then hold her while the water runs over us. Her sobs quiet, and her shaking is almost gone when the water turns cold.

I turn off the shower, wrap a towel around her hair, then dry her off. I reach for her robe and take it off the hook, putting it on her and tying the waist.

Her blue eyes meet mine. She swallows hard then puts her palms over my cheeks. Her eyes well up again. She sniffles, then cries out, "I didn't think you'd find me."

I pull her back into my arms. "Shhh. I'll always find you, Tesora. Always. You're my heart and soul. But no one, and I mean no one, will ever take you away from me again."

"Promise," she chokes out, her chest heaving.

I blink away my tears. "Yeah. I promise. Come lay down. You need some rest." I lead her to the bed, pull back the blankets, then take her robe off her. She slides into bed, and I pull the covers up. "Let me get you a nightgown."

"Why? Just come into bed with me. Please."

I wipe her tears away with my thumb. "I will, but Silvio needs to examine you first."

She shakes her head. "No. I'm fine."

"Tesora, I need him to make sure that's the case," I admit. I open my mouth to ask her what he did to her but snap it shut.

She tilts her head. "What were you going to say?"

"Nothing."

"Don't lie to me," she states.

I deeply exhale and count to fifty while staring at her. I finally get the courage to ask, "What did that bastard do to you?"

She closes her eyes and shakes her head. "Nothing. I... I threw up. He made me get naked to clean it up. If you... oh God." She takes a deep breath and opens her eyes.

I hesitate but ask, "If I what?"

She looks away and scrunches her face. "If you hadn't gotten there..." she breaks down sobbing again.

I sigh, partly from relief, partly from worry. I lay down and pull her as close to me as possible. "I'm so sorry."

"It's not your fault," she states.

I have so many questions I need answers to, but they all will have to wait. Right now, there's only one important thing.

For several minutes she cries. When she calms down, I kiss her on the forehead and force her to look at me. "Tesora, I need Silvio to examine you."

"I'm okay. Really. I am," she insists.

I sit up and bring her with me. I push her locks behind her ear. "Humor me. Please. I won't stop worrying until I know you're okay."

"Gianni—"

I put my finger over her lips. "You're the most precious thing on Earth to me. I need you to give me this."

More tears fall, but she nods. "Okay, then."

Relieved, I kiss her then get up. "Let me tell Silvio to come in."

28

Cara

GIANNI RETURNS TO THE BEDROOM, SHOOTING ME ANOTHER ONE of his worried looks. He sits on the mattress and drags his knuckles over my cheek. "Silvio is speaking with Papà. He'll be up shortly."

The feeling of Uberto's knuckles on my skin overpowers me. I close my eyes and turn my head. More tears well in my orbs, and I curse myself. I just stopped crying, and here I am, starting all over again.

Why am I an emotional basket case?

"Tesora! What's wrong?" Gianni frets, his body stiffening.

I shake my head but don't look at him, claiming, "Nothing. I'm fine."

In a firm voice, he declares, "Something just spooked you. What was it?"

I sniffle and sit straighter, forcing myself to meet his gaze. "I'm fine. Can you ask Arianna to come here?"

He pins his eyebrows together. His face hardens, and he asks, "What did he do to you?"

"I told you."

"No. Something I did just freaked you out. I want to know what caused your reaction."

I close my eyes, breathing through the vision of Uberto touching me. I'm lucky. I know I am. It could have been so much worse. And I hate how I'm acting weak right now. The auction stage represented just as much danger, yet I didn't react like this. I whisper, "He dragged his knuckles on my cheek. It's not a big deal. I just panicked for a moment. I'm sorry."

Silence fills the air, and I avoid Gianni, adding to the tension. I count to thirty before he states in a lower voice, "I'm sorry. I won't do it again. Is there anything else he did?"

I jerk my head toward him. "No. Don't say that. I don't want you to stop touching me how you do."

Apprehension fills his expression.

It pains me to see him not his usual, confident self. I decide it's better to get off this topic. I request again, "Can you have Arianna come here?"

"Why?"

"I need to talk to her about what happened at the fashion show today. I can't believe I left how I did."

He shifts on the bed. "What happened? I still don't know all the details."

"I'm sorry. I-I shouldn't have run out. The guard told me you got arrested, and I just freaked out," I admit. My stomach flips at the memory of Veronica in his arms.

He squeezes his eyes shut, and I count to ten. Then he opens them and says, "I'm sorry. I was trying to talk to you. I swear to you, I've not seen Veronica in years. And I can't stand her. She threw herself on me before I knew what was happening."

I don't speak. For years I've worked with Veronica and witnessed her antics. She believes she's the most important person in the world. Everyone kisses her ass, but she acts bizarrely around the few people who don't. It's like she can't handle them not falling over backward to compliment her twenty-four-seven.

Gianni takes my silence as doubt. He blurts out, "Tesora, you have to believe me. You're the only one for me. Nothing has changed. I'm devoted to you and only you."

More tears fall, but they aren't from pain or sorrow. I reach for his cheek, telling him, "I believe you."

"You do?"

"Yes. I know Veronica better than anyone. I fired her after the incident. And I'm sorry I reacted how I did. I know you've changed. There's not an ounce of doubt in my body regarding your love for me," I confess.

He places his palm on my cheek, and I lean into it. "That's right. So you understand there's no other woman I want now or ever will?"

My heart swells. For the first time in years, I believe him again. Only now, I feel it differently than before. He's a different man than when we were kids. He's done nothing but show me the new side of him. What we have isn't something you can find easily. My entire being believes he knows this as much as I do. I reply, "Yes, baby. I understand."

Relief mixes with happiness in his face. His expression softens. He questions, "You really fired Veronica?"

"Yes. And I made an announcement and told everyone else what the new rules are going forward."

He arches his eyebrows. "What are the rules?"

"I'll tell you a different time. But it basically has to do with respect."

His grin widens. "It's about time. I'm proud of you, my Tesora." He leans down and kisses me.

I slide my arms around his shoulders, holding him as tight as possible, kissing him with everything I have.

He retreats, his eyes narrowing. He inquires, "How did you end up without your security?"

I wince. "When the guard told me you got arrested, I freaked. I ran out and hopped into a taxi. But what happened at the police station? They scared me."

His eyes darken. "Who scared you?"

"Those two detectives and the FBI agent. I threatened them with an attorney and wanted to call your father, but they wouldn't let me. They showed me these pictures, claiming you killed all the men. I tried to leave the room, but they stopped me. Then they kept pressuring me to help them in exchange for witness protection," I relay.

The blood drains from Gianni's cheeks, causing the hairs on my arms to rise. Forty-two seconds pass before he states in a tone that makes me think he's doing everything possible to stay in control, "They showed you photos?"

I nod. "Yes. A huge stack."

Anger radiates from Gianni. He seethes, "They put you in an interrogation room?"

"Yes."

"And they didn't let you leave?"

I shake my head. "Not for a long time."

"What were the photos of?"

I hesitate but then say, "Dead men. A lot of dead men."

Gianni's face hardens.

"Did..." I swallow the lump in my throat. "Did you kill those men?"

He slowly inhales, squaring his shoulders. "I don't know what pictures you saw, but it's possible I did." He stares at me for a moment then asks, "What if I did? What would you think of me?"

There's no hesitation on my part. I grab his hand and reply, "Then I would say you had your reasons, and they got what they deserve."

He kisses my hand then studies me. He asks, "Were the detectives Anderson and Contray?"

"Yes."

"And who was the FBI agent?"

"He said his name was Agent Bordeaux. Have you met him before?"

Gianni sniffs hard. "No. I need to talk to Papà and see if he knows anything about him." Gianni opens his mouth then snaps it shut. He glances at the ceiling.

"Baby, what is it?"

He calmly questions, "What did you tell them?"

A tiny laugh escapes me. "What do you think?"

"I hope you told them to fuck off."

I laugh again. "I'm unsure if I used that exact phrase, but that's about right."

He gives me another kiss. "That's my girl. Thank you."

I hold his face. "Don't thank me. You're my husband. My entire world is you. My heart is you. Do you understand me?"

He nods. "Yeah. I do because everything you feel, I feel."

I smile. "Good. Go talk to your Papà. Please have Arianna come in. I need to know what happened when I left."

He strokes the side of my head. "Okay. I'll send Arianna then have her call for Silvio."

I peck him on the lips. "Thank you, baby. For everything, including killing him."

He grinds his molars, inhales deeply, then responds, "I'm sorry I couldn't locate him to do it sooner."

"No more sorries. Now go get your sister, please."

He rises. "Okay, bossy."

"Ha ha!"

He kisses my forehead then leaves the room. A few moments later, Arianna knocks, sticking her head past the doorway. "Hey."

I smile. "Come in."

She walks over and sits in the same spot Gianni did. Her expression is full of worry. "How are you feeling?"

It hits me how much she's a Marino, even if she doesn't seem to have the brutal traits her brothers and father do. I force a smile bigger than I'm feeling. "I'm good. There's no need to worry."

She tilts her head, then opens her mouth before closing it shut and biting her lip.

"Go ahead. Say whatever it is you want," I encourage.

She shifts on the bed. "Are you okay? Really okay? I... I know what it's like to..." She swallows hard.

I grab her hand. Dante told me how an Abruzzo kidnapped and tried to rape her. "I'm okay. Promise."

She bites her lip, studying me. "If you ever need to talk, even if it's months from now, I'm here."

"Thanks. I appreciate that." I clear my throat then cringe. "I almost don't want to ask, but how did the rest of the day go once I left?"

She smiles. "It was fine. Excellent really. Your assistants stepped up and handled everything. Everyone thought you were attending to other issues. And after your speech, there was a big shift in the model's attitudes."

My chest tightens, wondering if my antics made things worse. "What do you mean?"

"They were great. Nice to everyone, including each other. I think they took what you said to heart," she claims.

"Really?"

"Yes."

"Wow. I wish I would have done that years ago then. But honestly, you'd tell me if there were any issues, right?" I ask.

Her eyes widen. "Of course! I promise you. Everything went off without a hitch! It was a great show. I wish you could have seen it."

A tiny amount of disappointment fills me. My entire life fashion week was the unattainable I was trying to attain. I hate I missed a moment of it.

"Don't worry! You have the rest of the week to attend!" she assures.

I force a smile. "That's true."

"You'll just have to get past Gianni," she adds.

My gut sinks. "Ugh. He's going to try and keep me home, isn't he?"

She winces. "They're all down there discussing security."

"It wasn't their fault. Honestly, I just ran outside when I heard Gianni got arrested. I wasn't thinking clearly," I admit, reprimanding myself again for my stupidity.

She rolls her eyes. "I told Killian there are plenty of guards to cover. I mean, all the Ivanovs and O'Malleys are here. How many guards are needed when all their husbands are also here?"

I shrug. "No idea. I leave those details up to Gianni. But please, do whatever you can to try and convince him to let me go tomorrow."

My stomach growls, and she laughs, then rises. "I'll go get Silvio so you can get your exam over with and eat."

"Thanks. And thank you for doing everything you did for the show today," I add.

"Not a problem. It's an honor." Her face drops, and she lowers her voice. "If... If you want to talk, let me know. I..." She looks at the floor, then back at me, sighing. "Sometimes I have flash-backs. It can hit you when you don't expect it. Killian made me see a counselor for a while."

Surprise fills me. I had no idea about any of that. "Did the counseling help?"

"Not the first one. But then I went to the one Gemma went to, and it did help," she confesses.

"I'm glad. The counselor helped Gemma too?" Gianni also told me what Nolan's wife Gemma went through before they got married. It sounded like it was straight out of a horror movie.

"It did. She's the one who told me to switch. The counselor had a waiting list but made an exception for me since I was related to Gemma."

"That's good."

Arianna hesitates. I wait for her to speak. She chirps, "Okay. I'll let Silvio know you're ready, work on Gianni for tomorrow's show, and what do you want me to tell the chef to prepare for you?"

I laugh. "I can see why you're so good at what you do. I'm good with whatever the chef is preparing for the house."

"Should I instruct him to have it brought up here?"

I shake my head. "No. I want to eat with the family."

"Are you sure?"

"Yes."

She nods and walks to the door, then turns. "Bridget is freaking out and wants to see you. Should I send her in?"

I consider it, then shake my head. "Tell her I want to get past Silvio. I'll come down after."

"Okay." Arianna leaves.

Within minutes, Silvio knocks on the door.

"Come in," I instruct him.

He moves slower than I remember, but he's probably in his 70's. Wrinkles cover his face and hands. The glimmer I always noticed about him is still in his eyes. He pulls the desk chair next to the bed. "Cara, it's been a long time."

"Yes. How are you?"

He searches my face. I assume it's to see how I am. He replies, "I'm good. Old, but good."

I laugh. "Are you retiring anytime soon?"

"Already have. My sons run the practice now. The only thing I still do is take care of the Marinos. I told Angelo my sons will need to replace me soon, but you know how stubborn he is when new people are involved with his family," Silvio states.

"Ah. Yes. I can imagine Angelo's insistence you stay on," I admit.

He leans closer. "I'll tell you a secret."

"What's that?"

356

His lips twitch. "I'm glad. It gives an old man like me something to look forward to."

I swipe my hand in the air. "Come on now. You can't be over fifty, right?"

He chuckles, pointing at me. "And you just became my favorite Marino." His face turns serious. "Does any part of your body hurt?"

I almost say no, but then stop. "He yanked my neck hard. It's still throbbing a little."

"Can I examine you?"

I agree. "Yes."

He touches my neck, and I wince. Silvio pulls his hand away. "I want to get X-rays and an MRI. It's better to find out if anything is pulled now versus later. You have a bruise forming."

I don't disagree. "All right."

Silvio glances at the door. "Whatever I ask you is between us, okay? If you want to tell Gianni or the others, I'll leave that up to you."

"You will?" I ask, doubtful.

"Yes. They may be the Marinos, but I still value patient-doctor confidentiality."

"Thank you," I reply, not sure what I wouldn't want Gianni or the others to know, but grateful I have the option.

Silvio's eyes turn softer. He asks, "Did he force himself on you?"

My gut flips. I twist my hands in my lap. "No. It didn't get to that. I did throw up all over him."

Silvio's eyes widen. "What made you throw up?"

"I'm unsure. I got nauseous and dizzy."

"Has it happened before?"

I think then meet his eye. "Yes. It's been going on for a few weeks, maybe."

"You've thrown up previously?"

"No. Just today."

He puts on his stethoscope and takes out his light. He gives me a thorough exam, and when he finishes, he pulls a urine cup out of his bag. "Do me a favor and go pee in this."

"Why?"

"Just routine. Make an old man happy and do as you're told," he orders.

I laugh. "Okay. You're the boss."

"Just leave it on the counter when you finish," he instructs.

I get out of bed, take the cup, then go into the bathroom. I can't pee, so I turn on the water and finally fill the cup. I place it on the counter then leave. I announce, "All done."

"Good girl. You get an A-plus on your patient record," he teases.

I snort. "Well, now I can die a happy woman."

"No. No death," Silvio states and takes his bag into the bathroom.

I step into my closet, put a sweatshirt and yoga pants on, then sit on the couch waiting for Silvio.

A few minutes pass. He sits on the couch next to me, his eyes gleaming.

My butterflies spread their wings. "What's going on? Why are you looking at me like that?"

He takes my hand. "Were you and Gianni trying to have a baby?"

My mouth turns dry. I gape at him.

He chuckles. "I'll take that as a no. Were you using any protection?"

"I forgot about my birth control pill since we got married," I blurt out.

"How long were you on it?" he asks.

I cringe. "My entire life..."

His face gets brighter. "Well, it's sometimes hard for women to conceive when they've taken birth control for so long. We'll want to get you scheduled for an ultrasound as soon as possible. There's a mobile unit that Angelo likes to use, so you don't have to go into the office."

"Are you saying I'm pregnant?" I gape at him.

His grin widens. "According to the pee stick, yes."

Panic hits me. If Gianni finds out I'm pregnant, there's no way he'll let me out of the house to finish fashion week. I reach for Silvio's bicep. "Don't tell Gianni or anyone else. Not-not yet. Please!"

He keeps his gaze locked on me. "I told you my policy. This will stay between us, but you have to promise me you won't let this go on too long. I need you to get that ultrasound."

Relief fills me. "I won't. I just need a week."

Amusement pops into his expression. "Fashion week?"

I grimace. "Is it that obvious?"

He grunts. "Maybe a bit predictable, but I know the Marino men. A week won't hurt. I'll send over some prenatal vitamins so you can at least start those."

"All right. Thank you."

He pats me on the shoulder then rises. "I'll set up the different tests. The MRI and X-rays I'd prefer you get now."

I groan. "Gianni will probably have a fit about that too. Can't we wait?"

"I'm afraid not. Let's get the tests done and see what the results are. I don't think anything serious is going on, but it's not prudent to wait," he asserts.

I sigh. "Fine. But can you try to make Gianni think it's not a big deal?"

"Sure. And congratulations! Gianni and Angelo are going to be ecstatic," he claims.

I ask, "Can you tell the others I'll be down in a few minutes? I just need a moment by myself."

He pats me on the shoulder. "Consider it done. If you need anything, let me know."

"Thanks, Silvio."

He leaves.

I get up and stand in front of the mirror, looking at myself and my stomach.

Pregnant.

I'm forty-one.

How is this possible?

Several minutes pass. I take a deep breath. I just need to get past this week.

How's Gianni going to react?

Was he serious when he talked about having kids?

I stare at my stomach a few more minutes then rub it. I whisper, "Hey baby. I'm going to be your mommy."

29

Gianni

"PICK HIM UP," I ORDER, HANGING UP.

Dante glances behind him, then asks in a hushed voice. "Did Luca find that FBI pig?"

I step closer, keeping my voice low. "Yeah. Did Massimo or Tristano call yet?"

"No."

"I want all of them picked up tonight," I say for the tenth time.

"Agree. You talk to Aidan yet?"

I pause, waiting for a nurse to pass us. Silvio arranged for Cara to get an MRI and X-rays at an imaging center he owns. I've been beyond livid since she told me how the detectives and that FBI agent interrogated her, ignored her request for a phone call or attorney, and tried to turn her against us. All the rage I've felt about what happened to her with Uberto only multiplied. I'm not worried she'll turn. She would never cross me, and I know this in the deepest part of my soul.

Those fuckers made a bad decision. They disrespected her by taking her into an interrogation room, showing her gruesome photos, and scaring her. The frustration and irritation I experienced when they held me captive was bad enough. Learning what they did to my wife leaves me no option but to act.

No one ever again will put Cara in any situation that isn't good for her. I don't care if it's the law or not. I'll make damn sure of it. So the first thing I'm doing is going right to the elimination process, even though Papà refused to give us the go-ahead, insisting if they show up dead, it's going to put more heat on our family.

At this moment, I don't care. My head spins so fast with outrage and visions of my wife getting threatened by the authorities that all I can focus on is revenge.

And when I'm through, it'll send a message to any agent who wants to attempt to talk to any Marino woman ever again.

It's time the Feds learn a lesson. Our women are off-limits. Mess with them, and you're going to have hell to pay.

As soon as we left Papà's office, my brothers huddled together. Relief filled me when Dante didn't fight me. All I had to do was ask him how he would react if the authorities had done the same to Bridget, and he didn't argue. Instead, we gave Massimo and Tristano the job of picking up Anderson and Contray. Their first stop was meeting with Luca and telling him to pick up this Agent Bordeaux.

Dante came to the imaging center with me. While I checked the X-ray and MRI rooms to ensure they were safe, Dante called Aidan. Since Papà ordered us not to touch any authority figure without his permission, we need another place to take these bastards. Tully's new purchase seems like the perfect place.

Dante's phone rings. He glances at the screen, then locks eyes with me, answering, "Is it done?"

My pulse increases. I close my fists at my sides, still fuming they had the guts to disrespect my wife.

"All done! I have a clean bill of health," Cara beams, stepping into the hallway. Her bodyguards step behind her. Right now, we took Bridget's since she's safe at the house. I suspended the bodyguards who didn't follow Cara when she left the fashion show. They're lucky I found out about the situation with my Tesora at the police station. I couldn't take my focus off it, so they only lost their pay and not their lives. As soon as I deal with this situation, I'll be doing a full investigation on what happened earlier today.

More relief fills me that she's okay. I slide my arm around her shoulders. "No issues?"

"Nope! They gave me instructions to ice my neck and said an adjustment might help with the pain, but everything is in good order," she chirps, then yawns.

I kiss her forehead. "Good to hear. Let's get you home and in bed."

She doesn't argue and falls asleep on my chest the way home. Our driver pulls up to the steps of the house, and I carry her up the stairs. I try to undress her, but she opens her eyes. "Hey. Did I fall asleep?"

"Yeah. Let me get your clothes off, and I'll tuck you in."

A soft laugh fills the air. "Tuck me in, huh?"

I give her a chaste kiss on the lips. "Yep."

"Hmm." She kicks off her shoes.

I tug her yoga pants off her, and she's soon naked. I hold the blankets up, ordering, "In."

"Now who's bossy," she teases while sliding into the bed.

I tuck the blankets around her then kiss her again. "I have some work I need to do. I'll be back later."

She tilts her head. "What kind of work?"

"Since when do you ask me that question?" I ask.

She crosses her arms and arches her eyebrows.

I freeze. "What?"

"I know you, Gianni. What are you going to do?" she states.

My heart pounds into my chest. I stay quiet, afraid if I open my mouth, it's all going to come out.

"Gianni—"

"Cara, you know I'd die for you, right?"

She blinks hard. "Yes."

"Okay. Good." I tug her into my arms, murmuring in her ear, "No one, and I mean no one, will ever attempt to harm you in any way again. I don't care who they are. You have my word."

She pulls back. "You can't promise that. It's not something you should put on your shoulders either. Things happen out of your control, Gianni."

Rage builds inside me. I hold her face, firmly restating, "I'm your husband. You are a Marino. Never again, Cara," I vow.

She sighs. "Baby, I love you, but that's a lot to put on yourself."

I kiss her lips and order, "Go to sleep and let me handle what I need to."

She hesitates, studying my face. In a lower voice, she demands, "Tell me what you're going to do."

I look at the ceiling, count to twenty, then take a deep breath.

"Gianni!"

I pin my gaze on hers. "All I'll say is I'm eliminating a threat."

Her eyes widen. "Is that smart?"

"Tesora, don't worry about this. It's all under control," I assure her. "Stay in bed. I'll be back as soon as possible."

"Back? They aren't in the basement?" she inquires.

I freeze. "What do you know about the basement?"

She bites her lip then cringes. "When Arianna was in her early twenties, I found her crying in her room. She had drunk quite a lot. It was your mamma's birthday, and she was having a hard time. She missed her and was struggling. None of you would let her work, so she complained about that and told me about the dungeon. She didn't mean to, but it came out."

Annoyance floods me. "Great. Who else did she tell?"

"No one. It was only her and me. But it was a long time ago, so don't go yelling at her," Cara insists.

I sigh. "Fine."

"Why aren't they downstairs? Why do you have to leave?" she asks.

I debate but finally tell the truth. "Papà didn't give the order. We have them somewhere else."

Cara gapes.

I ask, "So you see why I need you to stay in the bedroom and go to sleep?"

She swallows hard. "Will you be somewhere safe?"

"Yes. You don't need to worry about anything. Now go to sleep, okay?" I kiss her on the lips.

She reaches for the side of my head and caresses it. "I'll go to sleep if you give me something."

I chuckle. "What do you want? Name it."

"I'm returning to Fashion Week tomorrow and finishing it."

Her statement hits me like a wrecking ball. I firmly assert, "Absolutely not."

She sits up in bed. "I'll get you access to the back area. You can add whatever guards you want, but you can be by my side the entire time. But don't take this from me."

I close my eyes, count to fifty, then open them.

"Gianni, I need this. Please," she whispers.

I take a deep breath, then nod. "Okay. But you don't go anywhere without me attached to your hip."

She beams, and it tugs at my heart. "Thank you, baby. Promise me you'll be careful."

I give her another kiss. "I promise. Now sleep, Tesora."

She scoots down under the covers and holds her arms out. "I need another kiss but a good one this time."

I laugh, then kiss her until she's breathless. I tear myself away from her and leave, meeting Dante at the end of my wing.

We go into the garage and get in the SUV. During the ride, we both check our Glocks and sharpen our knives. For the second time today, I go into the building Tully bought.

"How the fuck did Tully find this place?" Dante mumbles, looking around.

I shrug. "Who knows." I open the door to the basement, and we climb down into the damp cellar.

Aidan, Massimo, and Tristano are waiting. The two detectives and FBI agent lie on tables, naked, gagged, and with their limbs stretched.

I glance at Aidan. "When did the tables arrive?"

His lips move into a sinister smile. He shoots the authority figures a look as if they're his prey, and he can't wait to tear them to shreds. He answers, "I thought it was only fitting if we use their own tactics on them. I had my guys bring them over an hour ago."

Massimo interjects, "We're in luck. Tully installed the water system yesterday." He points to the wall where multiple hose lines are connected to faucets.

"How did I not notice that earlier?" I ask.

Aidan's eyes gleam. "We were having too much fun."

Massimo grabs a hose and turns on the water. He sniffs hard. "You don't mind if I take Anderson, do you?"

"No. I get Bordeaux. Why do you want Anderson?" I ask.

"No reason. Just a feeling I have," He states, but something passes in his eyes. It's the first time I've ever caught him in a lie.

I glance at Dante. He saw it too. If something has gone on with Massimo and Anderson, Massimo should have told us. Neither

Dante nor I speak, but I decide to deal with Massimo later. I permit, "Go ahead."

"Don't leave me out of the fun," Tristano adds, then picks up another hose.

"Take Contray," I order. I grab another hose and say to the others, "Sorry. You'll have to sit back for the time being."

Aidan's mouth contorts. He motions toward the table. "Have at it. I'm going to wait until halftime."

"Halftime?" I question.

He walks to the corner and grabs one of a dozen Mason jars off it. "I'll be biding my time."

"What is that?"

"Pigs need to be fed. It's their dinner," he asserts.

I step closer. The jars have body parts—eyeballs, tongues, fingers, and more.

"Jesus, you're twisted," I claim, slapping him on the back.

"It's a gift," he brags.

I turn on my hose and hold it over Agent Bordeaux, so the water hits his stomach. "You crossed a line when you threatened my wife. You won't make that mistake again." I release the ball gag from his mouth. "Now, open wide."

Cara

A Week Later

GIANNI MOVES MY HAIR TO ONE SIDE. HIS LIPS TEASE THE BACK OF my neck. He murmurs, "Stay still."

I freeze.

He drapes soft fabric over my shoulder. "I know you loved this, so I made Pietro sell it to me."

I gape in the mirror. The fushia cashmere wrap by Pietro Dominico was added at the last minute to today's final show. He's an up-and-coming designer, and the stylish piece was a huge hit. Numerous buyers wanted it, but Pietro refused to sell it.

"How did you get him to agree?" I ask, still stunned it's hanging on my body.

Gianni's arrogant expression lights me up. He kisses the back of my ear. "I have my ways, Tesora."

I softly laugh. "You offered him an exuberant amount of money, didn't you?"

Gianni chuckles. "Possibly. You ready?"

I spin into him. "Yes. Thank you for the wrap. I love it."

He grins. "I'm glad. I've been dying to have my wife to myself all week."

I tease, "You were such a good boy sharing me all those days."

He grunts. "I don't share, Tesora."

I slide my arms around his neck. "Neither do I."

He kisses me and takes my hand. "Let's go." He leads me out of our room and down the hall. We turn the corner and run into Dante.

He claims, "I need a few minutes, Gianni."

He groans. "Nope. I'm taking my wife out."

"Two minutes," Dante insists.

"It's okay. I'll wait downstairs," I say.

Gianni shakes his head in annoyance and palms my ass. "I won't be long."

I get on my tiptoes, peck him, and then stroll through the house and down the stairs. When I get to the lobby, Massimo is on his phone.

His hand is in his hair. He's staring out the window. The muscles in his shoulders flex with tension. He snarls, "It's too much of a coincidence. I'm not letting you play me anymore, Katiya."

My instinct is to make sure he's okay. I've never heard of Katiya before. I don't know the situation, but he sounds so upset. I fight the urge to stay and figure out what's going on. Instead of eavesdropping, I step into the den so I don't hear any more of his conversation. Then I sit on the couch and wait for Gianni. A few minutes pass. He sticks his head through the doorway. "Ready?"

"All set," I reply, standing.

He puts his hand on the small of my back and guides me outside to the SUV. We get in, and the driver shuts the door.

Gianni rolls the divider window up. Once it's completely shut, he tugs me on his lap. "I want to tell you something."

I raise my eyebrows. "What?"

He strokes my cheek. "Every moment of this week was amazing. Watching you in action, all I could keep thinking was, that's my wife. I'm so proud of you."

My heart soars. I've always loved Gianni, but this past week it's only deepened. I adjust myself so I'm straddling him and lace my fingers around his neck. "I love you, baby."

"I love you too, Tesora."

My smile grows so big it hurts my cheeks. "I have something to tell you."

"Oh? What's that?" he asks.

My butterflies flutter fast in my stomach. I've thought about how to tell him all week, but I don't know the best way or when. Silvio scheduled my ultrasound for tomorrow, so I'm out of time. "Do you remember when you said you were ready to give me kids?"

He smirks, "We can start trying tonight if you want."

I lean closer. "We don't need to try."

He opens his mouth then closes it. He peers closer at me. "Are you..." His eyes grow bigger. "Are you pregnant?"

My emotions take over again. Tears well in my eyes. I nod. "Yes."

"You are?" he asks as if I'm not telling the truth.

I affirm, "According to Silvio."

Silence fills the car. Gianni's eyes never leave mine. Ten seconds pass, and he puts both palms on my cheeks. "We're having a baby?"

I suddenly worry that maybe I misunderstood things. Perhaps he isn't ready for one. My smile falls, and I reply, "Yes. Are you not happy?"

He jerks his head backward. His voice goes up several octaves. "Are you kidding? Cara, we're having a baby!"

I cautiously question, "So...you're happy?"

He pulls me to his lips. "Tesora, you just made me the happiest man on Earth."

"Really?"

"Yes!" He kisses me then retreats. "Wait! Silvio knew about this?"

"Yes. He gave me a test a week ago."

"A week ago!" he exclaims.

I bite my lip then wince. "Sorry. I asked him not to tell you."

Dark pools swirl in Gianni's eyes. "Why?"

"I figured you wouldn't have let me finish the show," I admit.

He drags his finger over my jawbone. I shudder from the tingles running down my spine. "You've been naughty, my Tesora. What should I do to punish you?"

"You aren't mad at me?" I question.

He sighs. "No. You're right. I wouldn't have let you do the show. But I'm glad you did. Stopping you would have been a horrible mistake on my part. You deserved to be there. Every minute of it, I watched you and thought you were glowing from the excitement. But now..." he leans into my ear. "You're glowing because I knocked you up."

I laugh then swat him. "Don't get cocky!"

His hands slide up my thighs. Zings fly straight to my core. He glides his fingers under the string of my thong, taunting, "You don't like it when I'm cocky? I thought you did." He moves his hand to my pussy, stroking the slit.

I squirm on his lap then declare, "I'm not feeling like going out anymore. Take me home."

He arches his eyebrows. "You need to eat. Especially now that you're carrying our baby."

I lean into his ear. "Call the Michelin chef. Order whatever. I don't care. All I want is you and the wall."

He fists my hair and tugs it.

My breath hitches, and my chest rises faster.

His lips curl. "If I put you on the wall, you're not going to have any energy."

"I can sleep tomorrow."

He studies me then shakes his head. "No. I can't keep you up all night."

"Please," I plead, then hit the button for the divider window. "Manny, take us home."

Gianni smirks. "Is it the mother instinct in you that's making you bossier?"

I press the button again, and the window rolls up. Then I unbuckle his belt and unzip his pants. "You know what, I don't think we should wait."

"Tsk, tsk, tsk. Such a greedy..." he gently bites the curve of my neck, slides a finger in my pussy, and circles his thumb on my clit, "...wet..."

I moan and grind on his palm.

His tongue swipes my ear. My insides clutch his finger. "...sexy wife." He works my body until I'm on the verge of coming and stops.

My voice cracks, "Please, baby. Please don't stop."

He lifts his hips, drops his pants, and holds my hips, so his cock hits the head of my entrance. His deep voice only turns me on further. He tugs my hair again and moves his face over mine. "You want me, Tesora?"

"Yes!"

"Right now?"

"Please!"

He presses his lips to mine, gliding his tongue in my mouth and setting the pace. I let him lead, returning his affection. He deepens the kiss and circles his tongue faster, then thrusts his hips up while pushing me over him.

"Oh, God!" I cry out.

He doesn't show me mercy, not pausing, continuing to thrust before I'm used to him.

"Baby," I whisper, clutching my arms tight around him.

He moves his hand back to my clit, taking me back to the edge of a high, but this time, he doesn't stop.

Adrenaline explodes in all my cells. I match his thrusts, whimpering, dizzy, seeing white light.

Gianni grows harder inside me. His shaft teases my walls, adding to my chaos of endorphins. He thrusts deeper, groans, then mumbles, "Mine, Tesora. Your pussy. Your heart. Your goddamn soul. It's all mine."

"Yes, baby. I'm yours," I choke out, right as my eyes roll back and an earthquake rips through my body.

"That's it, Tesora. Fuuuck, that's it. Squeeze your tight pussy on my cock," he growls, changing the speed of his thumb on my clit, which only extends my orgasm.

"Oh! Baby!" I cry out, shaking harder.

"I need to taste you," he states, then pushes me off him and on the seat.

"No! Oh, God! I need you back in me," I beg.

He drops to his knees, widens my legs, and asserts, "You need my mouth on you." His tongue fills my body, and I moan. He slides it up until it's on my clit, teasing me with a slow flick.

"Oh shit! Baby, please!" I plead again, wanting another high like a junkie.

Two fingers slide in me. He scissors then curls them.

"Oh," I breathe.

His lips lightly suck on my clit, then he creates a pattern of flicking and sucking while taunting my g-spot.

Everything intensifies, igniting a heat I've never felt before. My skin glistens, blushing from the fire burning inside me. And then the world doesn't exist anymore. It's Gianni and me and an orgasm train that he's the conductor of, controlling my body like he owns it.

But I guess he does.

He always has.

He's Gianni Marino, and I'm Mrs. Gianni Marino. We belong together no matter what happened in the past. My heart is his forever, and I finally have no doubt I'll always have his.

When my voice becomes hoarse and my cries barely audible, he retreats. He wipes his mouth on his forearm, then moves his lips an inch from mine. His hand slides through my hair, and he asks, "Will you marry me?"

I panic and freeze. Was everything on the plane not real? Am I not married to him? Did he somehow just make it all seem legal? I fret, "We aren't married?"

He nods. "We are. But I want new vows."

"What do you mean? I actually loved your vows," I confess.

He arches his eyebrows. "Not mine. I want new ones from you. I want to re-marry you in front of our families, friends, everyone who means anything to us. I want us to have the wedding we should have had years ago."

I gape at him, taking it all in.

His face falls. "You don't want to?"

I smile and blink back tears, then hold his head. I kiss him. "Yes, I'll marry you. And I want to give you new vows."

"You do?" he asks.

"Yes. And I promise I'll love, cherish, and honor you until the day you die," I pledge, and I mean it. No other sentence has ever been so important to me. Until the day I die, I'll relish the fact that no one will ever love me harder than Gianni Marino.

Somehow, I got everything in life I've ever wanted.

I got him.

EPILOGUE

Gianni

A Month Later

"WHAT DO YOU THINK?" I ASK CARA, PUTTING A FORKFUL OF wedding cake in her mouth.

"Mmm," she groans, licking some excess white chocolate off her lips.

I chuckle then stick a bite in my mouth. I mimic her groan.

She backhands my chest while laughing. "I think we should get this one."

I swallow and take a sip of water. "If that's what you want, that's what you shall get," I declare, buzzing from happiness. Not a second goes by that I don't think about how lucky I am. I not only got my dream woman, but she also is carrying my baby. I have the world at my fingertips, and nothing can bring me down.

She beams at the cake maker. "That one for sure!"

"I thought you'd love it. Now I have some ideas I think you'll go crazy over. If we do a dessert table, I thought we could—

"Gianni!" Dante's voice roars.

The cake maker jumps. Cara furrows her eyebrows.

I internally groan and spin. "What's going on?"

"Now," Dante seethes and points toward the hallway where Tristano paces.

My stomach drops. It's been a tad too quiet since Fashion Week came to an end. I've rather enjoyed the lack of drama. Every moment I've spent wrapped up in Cara and wedding planning. I always assumed it would be boring, but everything I do with my Tesora ends up being fun. Yet I should have known the calm wouldn't last long. Dante's tone and seeing Tristano pace means I'm not going to be happy with whatever is occurring.

I kiss Cara on the forehead. "I'll be a minute. Please excuse me."

She offers a big smile. "It's okay. I'll just eat your samples."

I chuckle. "Don't you dare!"

"Gianni!" Dante barks.

I exhale deeply and count while I walk. As soon as the door shuts, the happiness I feel disappears. "What's so important you had to interrupt me?"

"Tell him," Dante orders Tristano.

A mix of guilt and anger swirls on Tristano's expression. He nervously glances at Dante, then pins his cold, Marino gaze on mine. He fumes, "I found out some things about Massimo's girlfriend."

My chest tightens. "Katiya? I thought he broke up with her?"

Tristano shrugs. "I don't think so."

"Why?" I demand.

"It seems like our dear brother is confused," Dante seethes.

The hairs on the back of my neck rise. "Meaning?"

My brothers exchange another look. Tristano closes his eyes and shakes his head.

"What the fuck is going on?" I bark, fed up with the drop in my stomach I can't escape.

Tristano sniffs hard. "She lives in that brownstone."

Goosebumps pop out on my skin. I already know the answer but hope I'm somehow wrong. Through gritted teeth, I ask, "Which brownstone."

Dante's voice grows deadly. "The one we rescued Cara in. The Abruzzo one. And Massimo knows it. He goes there often."

The world seems to stop. "How do you know that?"

Dante and Tristano once again lock eyes.

The bad feeling only grows, digging into my bones. I ask, "What have you done?"

Dante crosses his arms. "I wanted to know for myself. I put Luca on him. It's true. I have photos with time and date stamps on them."

"You had Massimo followed? And you didn't tell me?" I accuse.

"You had a lot going on," Dante claims. "But that isn't the point. Let's not lose focus."

"We need to talk to him," I claim.

Dante shakes his head. "No. None of us are going to say anything. If Massimo has flipped to the Abruzzos, we need to know."

I gape at him. "Are you crazy? He would never—"

"He's dating an Abruzzo! He knows it and is still going to see her!" Dante foams.

One. Two. Three. Four. Five—

"From now on, Massimo gets tracked. I'm tapping into his phone and laptop too." Dante glances behind him. "No one tells Papà about this. Until we have all our facts straight, we keep this between us."

"Massimo is *not* a traitor," I claim.

My brother's expressions make me ill.

Tristano replies, "We hope to God he isn't."

Printed in the USA
CPSIA information can be obtained
at www.ICGtesting.com
CBHW021533010624
9373CB00072B/658